Sweet Surrender

"Whoa," she cried, pulling back desperately on the reins. "Stop, dammit!"

O'Malley stopped very suddenly. His powerful hindquarters slid beneath him and his front hooves pawed the air. Rachel bounced free of the stirrups and canted to the left, headed for the ground—until a strong arm caught her around the waist and pulled her free.

"Oh, Mr. Tyler! Thank you."

"How many times have I asked you to call me J.C.?"

Her toes dangled a foot above the earth. Her breasts were flattened against his collarbone. Blue eyes burned into hers, and she forgot to demand that he put her down.

He did put her down, though. Slowly, so that she slid over the hard length of him. One of his arms circled her waist. The other hand slid down to cup her behind. A numbness stilled her spirit, while every fiber of her body drowned in a host of forgotten sensations. When he lowered his mouth to hers, she could no more object than she could fly to the moon.

His lips were dry and cool, soft and firm at the same time. They moved on hers with hungry fervor that woke an answering need in her. Of its own accord, her mouth opened beneath his. He tasted of whiskey and dust and desire. . . .

Also by Emily Bradshaw

CACTUS BLOSSOM
HEART'S JOURNEY
HALFWAY TO PARADISE
MIDNIGHT DANCER
SWEET SORCERY

EMILY BRADSHAW

BOUNTY BRIDE

A Dell Book

Published by
Dell Publishing
a division of
Bantam Doubleday Dell Publishing Group, Inc.
1540 Broadway
New York, New York 10036

The trademark Dell® is registered in the U.S. Patent and Trademark Office.

ISBN: 0-440-22135-8

Printed in the United States of America

Published simultaneously in Canada

December 1996

10 9 8 7 6 5 4 3 2 1

RAD

Prologue

The Willows,
Savannah, Georgia, 1867

This house, the home of her childhood, was a poor refuge, but it was the only one she had. Beyond these confining walls lay the unbearable. Within were walls that had sheltered three generations of Manchesters. Walls that had withstood hurricanes and pillaging Yankees. Walls that she had gladly escaped seven years ago on the arm of the man she loved. Then she had been a sixteen-year-old bride with worshipful adoration in her eyes and bright expectations in her heart. Now the adoration had fled and the expectations had tarnished. Would these cold walls receive her now that she had come crawling back? She would find out soon enough.

Rachel Manchester Dorset twisted a damp handkerchief in her fingers as she tried to summon her last reserve of courage and dignity to see out the night. She wasn't sure that any courage remained. This day—no, not just this day, but all of the last three years—had sapped her dry of anything save despair. Yet she had to be strong for just a little while longer. Not for herself, but for Peter.

The chill of the room seeped into her bones, undermining her resolve not to shiver and tremble like a cornered mouse. The lack of warmth was not so much of temperature, for the February night was mild, and a fire crackled in the big fireplace. It was a coldness of spirit, a lack of welcome in the frigid formality of the drawing room. That Saul, the family butler since before she was born, had escorted her to this room instead of to the family parlor was perhaps a foretaste of her welcome here.

"Ma, can we go home now? I'm tired!" Six-year-old Peter looked up at her from the pillow of her lap, his mouth downturned in the threat of a tantrum.

"I'm tired too," Rachel admitted. "Soon we can both go to bed."

"My own bed!" Peter demanded. "I want to go home!"

How did she explain to her son that home was no longer a place of safety and comfort? Home was not a place where they could go ever again. She brushed her fingers through his bright red curls. "Everything will be all right, Peter. Really it will."

Everything would be all right, she repeated silently to herself, a litany against doubt.

The double oak doors opened. From the dim hallway Saul regarded her bleakly. "Yo' father'll see ya now, Miss Rachel. I'll take Massa Peter to the kitchen."

"I'll keep him with me."

"The Massa said you was to come alone, Miss."

Saul firmly took Peter by the shoulder and steered him toward the back of the house. The ebony-skinned butler had always regarded children as an inconvenience, Rachel remembered. Her brother, Steven, and she had been nuisances that littered his ordered existence and stood in his regard several notches below unhousebroken puppies. Even now, as a matron of three and twenty, she still couldn't stand up to him.

"The door to the left of the stairs," the butler reminded her, as if Rachel had not grown up in this house and known very well where the master's study was, though she had not often been allowed into her father's private retreat.

The room was as imposing as she remembered. The light of the a half-dozen lamps did little to brighten the dark paneled walls or the heavily draped windows. Shadows hugged the corners and lurked in the recessed windowseat that overlooked the garden. The bookshelves that climbed one wall were dusted daily by no less a personage than Saul himself, Rachel knew, but the books that crouched therein had always looked moldy. To her knowledge none had been removed from the shelves since her mother had died three years ago.

Rachel's father awaited her behind the massive oak desk that, when she had been a child, had seemed as formidable as a mountain. Portly and graying, her father was almost as daunting as the huge desk. Before the War he had looked younger than his age. Now he looked much older.

"Rachel."

"Father."

He peered at her over the top of steel-rimmed spectacles. "This hour of the night is an odd time to be calling, Daughter. I perceive this isn't a social call."

"No, Father." No point in beating about the bush, Rachel told herself. "I've . . . I'm leaving Cabell."

Silence thickened the air until Rachel could scarcely breathe. Her father's gaze never left her. She searched his face for a glimmer of sympathy, of horror, even of anger, but found only disappointment.

"You're leaving your husband," he said softly. "Leaving for good?"

"Yes."

"I'd have hoped that a Manchester might have more courage, more sense of social responsibility, more honor than to mock such serious vows as those taken in marriage."

Rachel had no answer for that. She fought the urge to hang her head.

His eyes shifted slightly. "Did Cabell do that?"

She touched the bruise on her cheek. She had uglier ones hiding beneath her clothes. "Yes."

"What did you do to provoke him?"

"He'd had too much to drink."

"And . . . ?"

"And nothing! I did nothing!"

"A wife is supposed to bend with her husband's moods. If he is surly or taken with drink, it is your responsibility to stay out of his way and not upset him."

"I'm a good wife! He has no reason to hit me! Tonight . . . tonight he came home at dinnertime, staggering like a sotted derelict. I'd promised Peter he could dine with us instead of in the nursery, but I didn't want him to see his father in such a state. When Peter objected to returning to the nursery, Cabell got angry and shoved him. When I stepped in, he hit me."

"A wife should not interfere with a man disciplining his son. The father-son bond is sacred."

Rachel's mouth tightened. "Cabell has beaten me before, Father. The dislocated shoulder last year was not from a fall down the stairs, as I put about, but was from my husband flinging me about in a drunken tantrum. This is the first time he's laid a hand on Peter, though, and it will be the last. I will not stay in a house where I must fear for Peter's as well as my own safety."

"Nonsense!" her father scoffed. "Cabell would not truly injure either one of you. You're indulging in womanly hysteria."

The swollen, angry bruise beneath Rachel's eye throbbed as if denying the old man's words.

"Decent women do not leave their husbands, dammit!" He rose, shoving his chair back hard enough that it almost toppled, and paced to the windowseat and back. "I warned you not to marry Cabell Dorset, girl! But would you listen to me? No! A sixteen-year-old chit knows better than her father. You and your mother were both charmed by a handsome face and pretty manners, and I never should have let the two of you talk me into it! Well, you made your bed, Daughter. You should have the backbone to lie in it. Don't come crawling to me!"

Rachel tasted bitter bile in the back of her throat. Her fists tightened until her fingernails bit into her palms. "Father, you are the only one I have to crawl to. For Peter's sake. I want to come home."

"A woman's home is with her husband! Do you know how many grieving widows there are in the South, women whose husbands marched off to war and never returned? Like your brother's widow, Carrie. Any one of them would trade places with you, grateful to have a husband alive and whole. They wouldn't whimper about a man taking a drink too many and getting a bit surly."

Rachel forced herself not to back down from her father's contemptuous gaze, though she cringed inside. Only her fears for Peter kept her from bolting out the door.

"Have you really thought this through, Rachel? Have you thought of what this will do to me? I'll be disgraced, a laughingstock! A woman who would desert her own husband is a slut! It'll be the scandal of the year! All our old friends already look dirt at me because I've managed to keep house and fortune intact by doing business with the carpetbaggers. They'll pounce on this as an excuse to ruin what's left of my reputation. Probably ruin my business as well. That damned Northern scum are always anxious to find reasons to look down their noses at us Southerners."

"Father . . . Surely no one beyond ourselves will pay more than passing heed. Everyone has their own troubles to occupy them."

"You know better than that! Creating trouble for others has always been society's way of making their own loads seem lighter."

He had a point, Rachel admitted. She had thought that her spirits could sink no lower than the nadir they'd reached when she'd packed a valise for herself and Peter and stolen out of the house to the accompaniment of Cabell's drunken snores. She had been wrong. Now she felt more wretched than ever.

"Father, I can't go back. Peter—"

"Don't whine to me about Peter. A beating never did a boy any harm."

"He's only six years old!"

"You always did have a damned stubborn streak in you, Rachel. Your mother used to say that once you set your feet on a course, God himself couldn't make you swerve. Who am I to try?" He sighed wearily, then speared her with a look suddenly sharp. "Does Cabell know you're here?"

"No. He fell asleep over his dinner. A cannon attack wouldn't have awakened him."

Her father dropped once again into his chair and gazed at the door, heavy gray brows drawn together in thought. "Perhaps something can be salvaged, then."

"No." Rachel heard the shakiness of her own voice.

Tears were perilously close to flooding her eyes. When she thought of the months it had taken her to work up the nerve to leave, she knew that she couldn't falter now. "I won't go back."

Her father's black scowl beat upon her resolve, but she merely clenched her jaw and sent it back upon him full force. She had never in her life disputed the right of men to rule her life. Now, in one anguished evening, she was forced to defy both husband and father. The effort of such defiance set her stomach churning.

"You can't stay here," her father said. His eyes dropped, then caught hers again in a gaze that encompassed both anger and shame. "You are my daughter, and I will not abandon you, but I will not ruin what's left of my reputation by harboring a runaway wife and being seen as approving your behavior. I have a cousin in Texas. A widow who lost both sons in the war. You can go to her. I'll give you enough money to get you and Peter there. Then . . . well, then you must live with the choice you've made."

"Go west?" Rachel choked.

"As far from me, and as far from Cabell, as possible. Your husband is not going to take this insult lying down, you know. If Cabell finds you and exacts retribution for deserting him and stealing his son, don't come crying to me for help."

Rachel stood in stunned silence after her father left the room to instruct Saul to see that beds were prepared for her and Peter—beds for only one night. The next day he would send her out of his life—to the savage, uncivilized West. She had expected his anger and disappointment. She hadn't really expected expulsion. All her life she had been taught that women must depend on the men of their family for guidance and protection, but she had been betrayed and abandoned by the very men who by rights should protect her. She had never learned how to protect herself.

Weary and deflated past standing, she sank into her father's chair. A map pinned to the paneling of one wall caught her eye, a depiction of the United States and its territories as they existed at the end of the War. She raised one hand, as if she could reach out and touch the vast, forbidding area west of the Mississippi. Recalling an ancient description of the unknown, she whispered bitterly, "Here there be dragons."

1

El Paso, Texas
1870

Drinking rotgut whiskey in a dark cantina was one hell of a way to spend a bright April morning, J. C. Tyler mused. Still, it beat what he'd been doing the morning before, which was getting the stuffing beaten out of him by "Two-Hand" Joe Torrance. Torrance had gotten his name from his deadly two-handed handling of pistols. The gunfighter, stage robber, and murder-for-hire outlaw was just as quick with his fists, which talent he had enthusiastically demonstrated yesterday on the trail to El Paso. The skunk had beaned J.C. with a half-full coffeepot, stolen the key to his handcuffs, freed himself, and tried to send the nearly unconscious J.C. the rest of the way into oblivion. The outlaw hadn't counted on how much J.C. wanted that two-thousand-dollar reward riding on his head. Nor had he known how stubborn J.C. could be when he was riled, and someone knocking him over the head with his own coffeepot had gotten him good and riled. Torrance had been in worse shape than J.C. when they'd finally arrived in El Paso, and the outlaw didn't get to ease his bruises and bumps with good rotgut. If the law had its way, Torrance would soon be in a place where whiskey wouldn't be of any comfort—six feet under the dusty Texas sod.

J.C. tilted his chair back against the wall behind him and downed the last swallow of amber liquid in his glass. He had a yen to order another but thought better of it. He hadn't sunk quite low enough to get tight before noon. Not yet, at least. Bad enough he was having rotgut for breakfast.

The door to the cantina swung open, admitting daylight along with a tall, barrel-shaped figure that was all too familiar. J.C. sighed. The morning wasn't getting any better.

"John Charles Tyler!" came a rusty-sounding greeting. "Thought I saw you come in here."

"Howdy, Chester." J.C. sat up. The front legs of his chair hit the floor with a heavy thump.

"Heard you brought Torrance in." Chester Williams pulled a chair over to J.C.'s table, swung it deftly under his rear end, and sat. "That's one mean sonofabitch."

"Yeah. Well, if old Judge McCready has his way about it, he won't be around to bother the world much longer."

"Won't nobody cry tears over that one." Williams motioned the saloonkeeper to bring a bottle. "Hear you took some licks bringing 'im in. That why your head looks bigger on one side than t'other?"

"I've got a bump or two."

"Guess it won't keep you down," Williams commented.

J.C. lifted a brow. "Mighty concerned, are you?"

"Just bein' friendly."

The barkeep set a bottle and glass on the table. Williams pulled the cork from the bottle, offered to pour some into J.C.'s glass, and when J.C. shook his head, served himself a generous amount. "Just bein' friendly," he repeated with a grin. "After all, birds of a feather have to flock together, now, don't we?"

J.C. watched with mild distaste as the other man downed his drink. He certainly hoped he wasn't the same kind of bird as Chester Williams—a vulture. Maybe he was, though. When people looked at him, perhaps they saw the same hard eyes looking out from a hollow soul, the same cynical twist of mouth, the same lines of casual cruelty etched into his face. If they didn't now, they would before long. That was the price a man paid for making a living hunting down other men.

Undeterred by J.C.'s silence, Williams kept up his side of the conversation. "To tell the truth, John Charles, I was a tad surprised to hear you'd dragged ol' Torrance all the way to El Paso. Seems like you could'a easier turned him over to the law in Amarillo. Closer to where he was operatin', wasn't it?"

"Could be," J.C. admitted.

"So I says to myself, young John Charles—he's no green stupido. If he hauled Two-Hand Joe to El Paso instead of turning east and takin' him to Amarillo, then there's some good reason he wants to go to El Paso. Could be my good friend John Charles has been fol-lowin' the same trail I have for the last two months and is huntin' down bigger game than Two-Hand Joe. Bigger game with a five-thousand-dollar price on their heads." Williams poured himself another glass and downed it in one gulp. The look he sent J.C. was wary but still amia-ble. "Bigger game like Emilio Gonzales and Ramon Morales."

"They in this neck of the woods?" J.C. asked, smiling innocently.

Williams wiped his mouth with his sleeve, leaving a sneer behind. "You know damned well they are! And it's no goddamned coincidence that you're here, too."

He poured himself another glass, drank it down, and slowly his face settled back into its amiable mask. "I tell you what, compadre. We'd do well to take after them together. What do you say? You and me, we bring down Emilio and Ramon—the nastiest scum in all of Texas, New Mexico, and Arizona. And Old Mexico too."

J.C. shook his head. "I work alone."

"So do I, but there's two of them, and both of them regular badgers in a fight. Five thousand dollars is enough to split between us and still be worth our while." His voice took on a slightly mocking note. "Still paying on that piece of land over by Santa Fe?"

J.C. grimaced, regretting confidences spilled in times past when he and Williams had gotten drunk together.

Williams laughed at his expression. "Still wantin' to settle down to the dull life, eh? Still huntin' the moon. Well, twenty-five hundred dollars might not go as far as five thousand to get you what you want, my friend, but it'll go a hell of a lot farther than a pine box six feet under, and that's what you're likely to get goin' after those two alone."

"Not this time, Chester. I don't fancy changing my style this late in the game."

Williams's smile turned predatory. "Well, then, John Charles, seein' as you won't join me, I'll just have to get those boys first."

"Be my guest," J.C. said mildly.

Williams growled out a rusty, humorless imitation of a laugh. "I do love a good race. Can't say I didn't offer to share."

"Can't say you didn't."

The older man wiped his mouth on his sleeve and got up. His eyes flicked to the wall behind J.C. "Some advice, friend. Leave the bad boys to me. Here's a hunt that's more your style." He reached behind J.C. to tear a poster off the wall. "Four-thousand-dollar reward," he read. "Peter Dorset. Nine years old." Williams chuckled contemptuously. "Do you suppose the kid is armed and dangerous? Oops! Nope! Says right here the poor little lad was snatched from the loving bosom of his crippled father by one Rachel Dorset. The ungrateful woman deserted her lawful husband and made away with their only child. The lady stands five foot two, weighs a hundred pounds, and has red hair and green eyes. Tsk, tsk. Sounds like a dangerous criminal to me. Maybe I'll go after her myself if I get time. Sounds real excitin'." He folded the poster and stuck it into J.C.'s shirt pocket. "Thanks for the whiskey, John Charles."

J.C. grinned. "I'll say hello to Emilio and Ramon for you, Chester."

"You want to say hello to those boys? I'll be sure to bring them into town so you can talk at 'em. And watch out for that redhead with the nine-year-old."

Williams left J.C. with the empty whiskey bottle and the bill.

The moon that night was just short of full. Hanging over the badlands west of El Paso in a slightly lopsided ball, it turned the hills and arroyos into a treacherous black-and-white crazy quilt of impenetrable shadow and light. J.C.'s normally surefooted mount stumbled for the third time into a hole disguised as a shadow.

"Steady there, O'Malley."

The stallion's ears swiveled back toward the sound of J.C.'s voice. The animal's nervous prancing settled back into a walk.

"Damn fool idea, eh, fella? Wandering around this godforsaken land in the middle of the night?"

It had seemed a good idea while sitting in the cantina after his conversation with Chester Williams. Williams had guessed that J.C. knew where Gonzales and Morales were hiding. Otherwise he never would have tried to bring him in on his own chase. Bounty hunters were lone wolves. They didn't hunt in packs.

Williams was right about one thing, though. J.C. did know where to find the renegades, thanks to an encounter a month ago with a man who once ran with them and served five years in prison for doing so. Hector Ramirez had been happy to rat on his former comrades for the price of a couple of drinks. His story had started J.C. on the path to a cave hidden in the trackless, broken desert of west Texas, and to five thousand dollars.

But only if he found his prey before Williams, who wouldn't have been above following him had he seen J.C. leave town. Williams also wasn't above making sure that J.C. was somehow put out of the picture once he'd led him to the outlaw den. Men who made their living hunting other men weren't often troubled by scruples in dealing with rival hunters.

So leaving under cover of night had seemed a smart idea at the time. After four hours of stumbling over hidden rocks and holes and straining to recognize landmarks in the deceptive light of the moon, however, J.C. wasn't so sure.

"This'll be the last one, O'Malley, old boy," he told the horse. "Two thousand for Torrance and five for this pair. We'll hand over the last payment on those three hundred acres at Glorieta and settle down with some mares for you and a lot of peaceful days for me. We've been in this business long enough."

He'd told Chester Williams about his plans to give up bounty hunting one time when they'd gotten drunk together in Denver. "Never do it," Williams had slurred at him. "Once the hunt's in your blood, can't give it up. Might as well hunt the moon as try to settle down."

The lopsided moon sailed serenely through the night sky. So close. So visible. But a man could ride forever and not get any closer.

J.C. tethered O'Malley at the mouth of the canyon that Ramirez had told him about. The cave should be about half a mile farther up. He made his way carefully through the darkness on foot, finally finding a niche in the canyon wall that should give him a clear view of the cave once the sun came up. With an hour left before dawn he settled down to wait, cradling his rifle in his arms and feeling the rush of adrenaline that was the precursor to every encounter. The tail end of the night dragged by, punctuated by an occasional coyote serenade, the hoot of an owl, a rustling of the night wind through the dry brush. No hint at all that the outlaws were holed up like weasels in a cave on the opposite canyon wall. But they were there. They'd better be there, or J. C. Tyler had just wasted a good night's sleep, not to mention five bucks' worth of good whiskey on Hector Ramirez.

Slowly the sky paled, then grew pink. Light slowly diluted the blackness. The cave was there all right, J.C. was relieved to see, and it showed every sign of habitation. This far out into the broken country, the fugitives didn't bother to disguise their den. The still morning air carried the sounds of conversation and the smell of coffee. The cookfire at the mouth of the cave winked red in the pale dawn light.

"Time to go to work," J.C. told himself. For the fourth time he checked the loading of his weapons. Then he took careful aim with the rifle and let a shot fly that sent the outlaws' coffeepot into the cookfire. "Good morning, boys," he called out in greeting.

Some colorful curses echoed from the cave's mouth. A man's bearded face appeared briefly, then disappeared when J.C. sent a bullet close enough to singe the beard.

"I've got that whole cave in my sights, boys. You can't get out without getting some lead pumped into you. Why don't you just surrender and make this easy on all of us?"

The answer came in a hail of bullets. Chips flew from the rock in front of him.

"Shit!" J.C. clapped his hand to where one of the rock shards had cut his face. It came away smeared with blood. "Now I'm mad," he muttered.

"One more chance, boys! Come on out and throw down your guns."

The canyon rang with the outlaws' laughter. "Sí, señor!" came a heavily accented voice. "Me and Ramon, we tie ourselves up for you, too! Save you the trouble, sí?" More laughter.

"I'm getting madder," J.C. rumbled as he cocked the rifle. Holding very steady, not breathing, he aimed carefully. His shot went true, hitting the roof of the cavern and ricocheting off to wreak havoc inside. Another hail of lead assaulted the rock that he crouched behind.

"Okay. Now you asked for it." J.C. ignored the spray of bullets and sent a deadly series of ricocheted shots into the cave, as quickly as he could fire and reload. The answering barrage ended at the same time a cry of pain echoed around the canyon walls. Suddenly the canyon was filled with a heavy silence. The restless whinny of a horse echoed eerily. Not O'Malley, J.C. noted. One of the outlaws' horses. No other sign of life stirred.

"Well, shit!" The familiar sick feeling rushed through his body. He didn't like killing. He hadn't liked it in the War, and he didn't like it now. Shooting an outlaw wasn't any less gut-wrenching than shooting a damned Yankee. Unfortunately it was about the only thing in this world he had much talent at, and a man had to make a living somehow.

He waited a full ten minutes before leaving cover to make his way across the ravine to the opposite wall. The path to the cave was well worn and wide enough for a horse. There was no sound from the cave as he cautiously approached.

"Gonzales? Morales?"

No answer. No sound at all. Pistol ready, J.C. stepped through the entrance. Remnants from a pan of biscuits lay scattered over the dusty floor. The coffeepot lay in the fire, which steamed from its dousing with coffee. One man lay dead about ten feet into the cave, his chest covered with blood. From the sketches on the wanted posters, J.C. guessed the dead man was Ramon Morales. A rawboned bay gelding twitched its ears at him from the back of the cave. Of Emilio Gonzales there was no sign—until a bullet smashed into the cliff wall just below the cave entrance. The second shot ricocheted off the ceiling, bounced off the floor, the wall, and the opposite wall before smashing into the cave floor six inches from J.C.'s foot. The gelding reared up and jerked against the rope that tethered it to an iron ring in the wall of the cave.

"You see, señor!" came a taunt from the ravine. "Two can play that game, eh?"

J.C. dove for the back of the cave. The back wall was not the end. It slanted gradually toward a wide tunnel. A dusty ray of light revealed a path—steep but passable by both man and horse—that led toward the surface. Another way out. Good old Hector Ramirez hadn't mentioned that little detail. J.C. got to his feet and started toward the opening when a barrage of whining lead forced him to crouch behind a fallen section of the cave ceiling. The ricocheting of the bullets magnified the sound and deadliness of the attack tenfold. The noise thundered around him, pounding his ears. The whole cave seemed to vibrate with the cacophony—until a hornet with a stinger of fire slammed into his head. Everything faded abruptly into dark silence.

The light outside the cave was dying in shades of sunset red when J.C. came back to his senses. His head pounded unmercifully, and a furrow above his temple was crusted and sticky with blood. The bay gelding was still tethered to the ring in the wall and gazed at him in resigned patience. Ramon still lay dead near the cave mouth, his body thick with droning flies. Apparently Emilio had thought better of returning to the cave to bury his partner and take the horse. A good thing for J.C.

"J.C.," he groaned to himself, "you're a jackass." His voice cut through his head like a whipsaw. Nausea assaulted him as he stumbled to his feet. He was getting too old for this sort of thing, and if he wasn't more careful, he wasn't going to get much older. He glanced at Ramon and grimaced. If he was lucky, he might get half the offered reward for bringing in half of the bad guys. Better than a kick in the shins, but not enough for what he needed.

A wave of vertigo washed over him along with a surge of sickness. He bent over, groaning. A folded square of paper fell from his shirt pocket.

He almost had to laugh remembering Williams's taunts and how close the man was to being right, but laughing right now was out of the question. A gust of wind swirled into the cave and caught the paper, turning it about and unfolding it. *Four-thousand-dollar reward for the return of Peter Dorset,* it read. *Nine years old.*

Stolen from the care of a loving father by Rachel Dorset.
Four thousand dollars.

Arizona Territory
July 1870

Rachel wiped the sweat from her brow with a ragged
kerchief. The mesquite smoke from the cookfire burned
her eyes, as did the caustic tang of the hot chili peppers
that were frying alongside the steaks. She shooed a couple of hens from beneath her feet. "I don't see how
those men can stand this stuff!" she complained to the
chickens. "Their stomachs must be lined with iron."

"How is it coming?" Aldona Perez called into the
yard from the back door of the little adobe roadhouse.

"Done soon." Rachel choked on a lungful of smoke.

"We got some hungry hombres in here."

"Just tell them to hold their danged horses. It'll be
done when it's done."

"Hokay!"

Rachel turned the beefsteaks again, then piled them
high with the sizzling chilis. With the deftness of much
practice, she flipped the tortillas that cooked on the iron
plate to the left of the grill. They would be good and
brown about the time the steaks were done.

Men around here didn't like to wait for their food.
That was one of the things Rachel had learned in her
year of running the tiny roadhouse in Tubac with Aldona Perez. She'd also learned to cook on the adobe
brick hearth that stood behind the roadhouse, using the
open-fire grill on one end and, on the other end, a
horseshoe arrangement of half-bricks that supported a
round iron cookplate on top of charcoal. On this she
prepared three meals a day for the boarders in the two

rooms upstairs, any travelers who happened by, and the local ranchers and town citizens who dropped in.

Cooking wasn't the only talent Rachel had acquired. She'd learned to cut firewood, bake adobe, make soap, milk a cow, skin a rabbit, butcher a pig, and deal with snakebite, blisters, festering thorns, gunshot wounds, and other hazards that came with living in a country ruled by scorpions, thornbushes, and wild Apaches. All these talents would have been entirely unnecessary to the genteel and meek Georgia flower she had been three years before, but they were essential to the less-than-genteel woman she had become.

Rachel took a step back from the fire to grab a breath of fresh air and survey her surroundings—an exercise that never failed to remind her how grateful she was to be here. The dusty adobe town of Tubac was less than charming, but all around the little settlement nature provided a backdrop that was both breathtaking and soul-stirring. To the east, south, and west, mountains swept upward in stark, rugged splendor, purple ranges that bore Spanish names—Santa Rita, San Cayetano, Tumacacori, Sierrita—and Spanish legends of gold and silver. They stood guard over a high desert valley of mesquite, cactus, and scrub grass. The grass grew lush and green on the fertile alluvium where the Santa Cruz River flowed northward on its journey to meet the Gila. Everywhere Rachel looked, colors collided and blended with a brilliance that was almost painful. Purple, red, lilac, amber, and green. The sky was a sweep of purest blue. The shadows that raced across the mountains were so deep they were almost black. Life flourished every-where. Hardy, brawling life. Grasses whose roots could shatter rock, cactus that could survive a year or more without water, birds that made their homes among vicious thorns. Even the blossoms were not as delicate as they seemed. Everything that lived here was a survivor.

As Rachel had become a survivor. She looked at this land and felt a kinship with the elemental struggle that existed everywhere around her.

The sizzling of the steaks told her they were done. She reluctantly pulled her attention back to the mundane. Just when she had piled the beef and chilis onto a platter and topped them with well-browned tortillas, the wind whipped up a dust devil that seasoned the food with grit and blew streamers of dark red hair across Rachel's face. She shook the hair out of her eyes and brushed ineffectively at the dusty tortillas. Not that it mattered much. People in Tubac were accustomed to their food being liberally spiced with dirt.

The little dining room of the roadhouse was hotter than it was outside. The place was unusually crowded tonight, and the smell of cigar smoke and unwashed bodies greeted Rachel when she brought in the platter of steaks.

"'Bout time!" called Bull Larsen. "What'dya do? Kill the cow and butcher it before ya cooked the steaks?"

"No complaints, hombre," Rachel replied. "Or I feed yours to the dog."

"Better damned not, missy! I'm hungry enough to eat the whole goddamned cow."

Bull was almost as big as his namesake, and ornerier to boot. Usually he minded his manners in the vicinity of "good women," which he deemed both Aldona and Rachel to be, but on this night every breath was a hundred-proof alcohol and every other word an obscenity.

"Watch your language," the foreman from the nearby Alvarez ranch warned. "There's ladies here."

Bull merely snorted.

Aldona helped Rachel dish the steaks onto tin plates.

Within minutes the only sounds in the room were the clatter of knives and forks and the satisfied sound of chewing.

"Just in time," Aldona said with a smile.

"I'll say. I'll be out back getting in the wash. The wind's kicking up a load of dust. Have you seen Peter?"

"He was off on some adventure with Manuel a few hours ago."

"He's supposed to be here doing his chores. If he comes in, snag him, please. I vow that boy's gotten wilder than a jackrabbit."

The laundry flapped wildly on a line strung between a mesquite tree and the little shed shared by a cow and a host of chickens. The wind had cooled even in the short time Rachel had been in the dining room, and the air was fragrant with the promise of rain from the thunderheads marching west from the Santa Ritas.

"I don't know why we bother to wash these." Rachel shook out the sheet she had taken down and grimaced at the dust that flew. "In Savannah it was mildew. Here it's dust."

Only half the sheets and towels were off the line when an angry commotion from inside the roadhouse made her drop the laundry basket and run for the door. The sight that met her eyes, though neither uncommon nor unexpected, made her curse under her breath. Not that anyone could have heard her unladylike lapse had she shouted at the top of her voice, for the dining room was abroil with flying fists and careening bodies. Three tables were overturned. Tin cups, plates, pottery, and tableware were being smashed beneath heedless boots. And in the middle of it all, wading through the knuckle-flying, shin-kicking, skull-smashing crowd, Aldona did her best to save the furniture, dishes, and a customer or two.

Rachel elbowed her way into the crowd, more concerned with rescuing Aldona than saving the tinware and pottery. In the center of the fight, as she had suspected, was Bull Larsen and a few of his friends, who were going at it tooth, fist, and nail with the Alvarez foreman, the man who'd had the audacity to chide Bull for his language. The other brawlers had simply used Larsen as a fuse to set off an explosion of manly entertainment. There was no better fun for most of these rough riders than breaking a few heads and tossing about the furniture.

Ducking fists and dodging around bodies, Rachel pushed her way toward Aldona. Will Horner, the storekeeper, noticed her and paused a moment to tip his hat. "Evenin', Widow Manchester." The next moment the hat went flying as someone decked him with a chair. Rachel pushed on. A tin mug flew past her head. Joe Garcia, the stablehand, careened helplessly her way after bouncing off several sets of knuckles. Her elbow in his ribs encouraged him to career back the way he'd come.

"Stop it, you ruffians! Right now! Sit down! Stop that!" She grabbed the arm of a man who was about to bash his opponent over the head with her best water pitcher. He swung around and sent her crashing to the floor with a mighty shove.

"Omigod!" he cried, instantly contrite when he saw whom he'd toppled. "Sorry, missus!" He helped her up and made an uncertain attempt to dust her off until her glare made him retreat.

Against the far wall Bull Larsen had knocked the foreman cold and was pressing a different kind of attack upon Aldona, who was trying to extricate herself from his grip.

"That's enough!" Rachel muttered. Shoving bodies

aside, she marched into the kitchen and returned to the fight armed with a heavy cast-iron skillet. Swinging at anyone who dared get in her way, she cut a swath through the crowd to Bull, who had pushed the hapless Aldona up against the rough plaster wall.

"Take this, you lout!"

The skillet rang with the tone of a fine church bell as it made connection with his skull. He dropped with a thud. The room grew gradually quiet.

"Anyone else need a lesson in manners?" Rachel asked as she swung the skillet gently back and forth.

"No, ma'am!"

"No."

"Hell, no!"

"Uh-uh!"

"Not me!"

The negatives sounded in an anxious chorus.

"Then get this lump of no-good chicken shit out of here. And you and you!" She pointed to his cronies. "If you boys want to brawl, go back to the saloon. Don't show up here with more rotgut in your brain than sense!"

Bull's friends hastened to drag him out the door, all the while casting a nervous eye toward Rachel and her skillet. Satisfied that the fight was over, Rachel turned toward Aldona, but bumped abruptly into a hard and definitely masculine body. Out of reflex she raised her skillet. Her eyes flashed across bronzed features and shaggy black hair, but what held her attention were the eyes—eyes like windows to the burning blue desert sky. Momentarily mesmerized, Rachel hesitated just long enough for the stranger to reach for her.

2

The woman's eyes went wide as J.C. grabbed the arm that wielded the lethal skillet. Those eyes were set like deep green emeralds in a face dotted with soot and freckles. Red hair escaped a single long braid and curled about her face in undisciplined wisps and curls. In the drab dust-colored room, she was a bright splash of color, color formed into smooth-looking skin, brilliant eyes, and firm, rounded breasts . . . oh, yes, breasts. . . .

She jerked her arm out of his hold and glared, ending his perusal. Before she could take aim with the skillet, he threw up his hands in hasty surrender.

"I give up! You win!"

For a moment she stood frozen, unabashedly returning his stare. Then slowly she lowered the skillet. A smile softened her mouth. That mouth, J.C. thought with sudden distraction, was made to smile, among other things.

"I'm sorry. I guess the brawl made me edgy." Her voice was soft and melodious, but it lacked the Southern drawl he'd expected.

"My fault, ma'am. Shouldn't have gotten in your way. I came in on the last of it. Thought you might need some help."

"Oh, our little Rachel doesn't need any help to send a few sorry cowboys running with their tails between their legs," Aldona said as she straightened her mussed clothing. "Does she, hombres?"

A ragged chorus of chargrined agreement came from the customers who remained.

"And she still has her skillet in her hand," Aldona pointed out. "So why don't you boys get to work cleaning up the mess you made before she decides to teach you a lesson, eh?"

Within five minutes the room was set to right and the erstwhile brawlers were docilely drinking coffee and ordering slices of Aldona's dried-apricot pie.

"I really am sorry," Rachel apologized as she poured J.C. a mug of coffee. "Usually the place is very quiet."

"Really? You looked as though you've had quite a bit of experience bashing heads."

"Only when necessary."

When she blushed, J.C. noted, her freckles got brighter. One wouldn't think that freckles could be appealing, but these definitely were.

"Can I get you some pie?"

"Sure, to start with. Those steaks that were flying around the room looked mighty good. Any left?"

"The fire's still burning out back. I can put one on the grill for you, but it will take a few minutes to cook."

"That'd be fine. I'm in no hurry."

He watched her as she served pie and poured coffee around the room. Several more customers came in and sat down. One had heard about the fight and teased her about her deadly skillet. She was friendly to all, smiled often, and parried an occasional flirtatious remark with an absolute lack of interest. All in all she was certainly not what he had pictured as a woman who would desert her husband and callously steal a crippled man's only son. He supposed he had expected a bona fide Southern belle, hoop skirts and all, her face and manner reflecting the flawed character of an inconstant woman.

The dried-apricot pie was good. J.C. pondered as he ate it. This trip to Tubac might have been a wasted effort. This green-eyed redhead might not be the one he was looking for. The West was a big place. It might hold more than one young white woman who answered to the same description and had a son the right age. Whose name was Rachel. Whose recent history—or so it appeared from the towns where he had found trace of her—included the frequent moving from place to place of someone who was running. It might, but the odds were unlikely. There weren't that many white women in this part of the country to choose from.

She walked toward him. Her stride was that of a woman used to the desert distances, not of a belle mincing beneath swaying hoops. "More pie, Mr. . . ."

"Tyler, ma'am. John Charles. My friends call me J.C."

"Mr. Tyler."

Her eyes, J.C. noted, had to be the deepest, clearest green he'd ever seen. They were damned distracting.

"There's plenty more, if you'd like another piece."

"Yes, ma'am. Thank you kindly. It's mighty good."

"Señora Perez made it. She makes the pies, I cook the beefsteaks. Yours should be done in a minute or two."

She cut him a fat slice of pie and gave him a quick grin that made his heart jump. It had definitely been too long since he'd seen a white woman, J.C. reflected.

"Don't eat so much pie that you spoil your supper."

"No, ma'am. I can smell those beefsteaks from here,

and they smell mighty good. Your husband's a lucky man to have a cook like you."

"I'm a widow, Mr. Tyler. My husband was killed by Comanches in Texas."

"Sorry to hear that," J.C. said as she refilled his coffee.

Her answer had flowed smoothly from her lips, with just the right amount of regret. Well practiced, J.C. thought cynically. What had he expected? That she would saunter up to him and admit she was a selfish, faithless bitch who left her poor crippled husband to seek greener pastures?

Yet, if she had sought greener pastures, what was she doing in a dusty piece of nowhere in the middle of Apache country? If she was a runaway wife from the Deep South, where was her Southern drawl?

By the time Rachel brought him a steak topped with sizzling chilis and accompanied by hot tortillas, J.C. had changed his mind at least five times about the likelihood that the woman he'd tracked here was the woman he sought. He preferred hunting down murderers and holdup men. When he ran them to ground, they generally started shooting, leaving no doubt at all he was on the right track.

J.C. took his time eating. It wasn't often he got a meal that he didn't cook himself—usually beans boiled over a campfire—and this Rachel was a damned good cook. Most of the customers had cleared out by the time he was finished. He was just about ready to investigate the possibility of a third piece of pie when a small whirlwind blew into the place.

"Ma! I'm hungry!"

There was no doubt about who was his mother. The kid's hair was as red as Rachel's and his face considerably more freckled.

"Where have you been?" Rachel's tone was the same one all mothers everywhere employ for that question. "You were supposed to be back in time to split wood for the fire."

"Me and Manuel were helping Señor Ortega at the stable."

"Getting in the way is more likely."

"No, we weren't! He likes us to help."

"Aldona and I would like your help also."

"Sí," Aldona chimed in as she came in from the kitchen. "Your mother had to split the wood, and I had to carry the water."

The boy looked sullen rather than sorry. He might be nine or thereabouts, J.C. guessed. He didn't have enough experience with children to say.

"Next time do your chores before you run off with Manuel. And Manuel should be home helping his mother and sisters instead of helping you bother poor Señor Ortega."

"Manuel's mother doesn't care if he spends all day away," the boy complained.

"So he says," Rachel replied.

"I never get ta do anything but work!"

"That's why God made children," Rachel teased gently. "To be slaves. Now, go down to the creek and bring up some more water to heat for washing dishes."

The boy stumped to the kitchen door, then took a wrinkled envelope from his pocket and tossed it to his mother. "Post rider made it in for a change. You got this."

"Thank you, Peter."

The boy snorted and disappeared through the kitchen door.

Peter was the kid's name, J.C. noted. *Peter Dorset,*

nine years old, the poster read. There couldn't be two red-headed Rachels with a son named Peter.

This was the bitch who had left a crippled man in loneliness. This was the runaway wife who had not only deserted her lawful husband but had dragged his only son along with her.

As he watched Rachel look after Peter, hands on hips in an exasperation that contrasted with the fond smile on her lips, J.C. felt a twinge of regret.

Rachel was regretting as well—regretting that she hadn't had the patience to deal with Peter in private instead of scolding him in front of the customers—even though there were only two left. She was harried and tired, her nerves on edge from the fight, so she had taken it out on her son. Still, Peter could try the patience of a saint. Where had her sweet little boy-child gone? The one who wouldn't go outside without her holding his hand. The one whose favorite playmate was his mother.

A quick glance around the room revealed that only one of the remaining customers had paid attention to the family squabble. Mr. John Charles Tyler had his startling blue eyes fastened on her for the better part of the time he'd been in the roadhouse, and just now he was giving her a look of undisguised speculation. He didn't even have the grace to hide his interest when she caught him at it, but kept that level-eyed, unnerving gaze upon her as if he had every right to be staring.

Rachel had gotten accustomed to being stared at since coming west. Everyplace she'd been—from Amarillo to Santa Fe to Albuquerque to Prescott to Tubac—a white woman was often the target of stares and comments, usually chivalrous. She'd done a bit of looking herself where Mr. Tyler was concerned. He had a smile that any woman would notice, a sensuously curved mouth, and thick black hair that framed his face in windblown disarray. Fine lines etched his face with character, and blue eyes burned a startling contrast against bronze skin.

A woman noticed such things, even if she wasn't remotely interested in a man as a man. But J. C. Tyler's smile wasn't as nice now as it had been. Combined with a disturbing glitter in his eyes, it gave Rachel a chill.

She was imagining things, Rachel told herself. Bashing Bull Larsen over the head had made her jumpy.

"More coffee, Mr. Tyler?"

He held out his mug. "Nice-looking kid. What is he, around nine or so?"

"Yes." She sighed. "He's a good boy. I think sometimes the fairies or elves or whatever pulled a switch on me and substituted a changling. I never know from day to day whether he's going to be sweetness and light or doom and gloom."

"I guess it's—"

The door crashed open, cutting off whatever comment J.C. was about to make. Bull Larsen filled the doorway, breathing heavily, surveying the little dining room through reddened eyes. He looked like a bull about to charge. Even across the room Rachel could smell the fumes of rotgut alcohol he exhaled. He was much, much drunker than he'd been earlier.

"Where's the bitch that bashed me head?" he roared.

Aldona came through the kitchen door, a rolling pin in one hand. "Get out of here, you tanked-up bullyboy, or you'll bet another bash on the *cabeza*. Vamoose!"

Bull ignored Aldona altogether. "Where is she? I'll show her a thin' or two!" His bovine gaze focused with difficulty on his prey. "There y'are!"

Bull lurched forward, through the tables rather than around them. Chairs toppled. Tables tipped and overturned. The man who'd sat at one with a piece of pie and coffee abandoned his food and jumped to safety.

Rachel backed away, arm outstretched to fend him off. "Bull Larsen, just get hold of yourself! You go dunk that hard head of yours in the water trough and sober up!"

Aldona advanced, rolling pin raised ominously. "You're going to have two lumps on your head instead of one!"

Bull hesitated, scowling blearily at the two women. He might have backed down had Peter not chosen that moment to play hero. He burst through the door from the kitchen and tackled the troublemaker, head down and hell-bent for retribution.

"You get away from my mother, you piece of mule shit!"

Rachel gasped. "Peter, no!"

Bull grunted when the boy plowed into him, but didn't move. He looked down at the furiously flailing fists and kicking feet, his features darkening from drunken determination to real anger. He drew back his arm, fist clenched into a ham-sized lethal weapon.

Rachel screamed and lunged for him, but J.C. got there first. His hand closed around Bull's arm. Bull snorted in irritation and tried to wrestle free. He couldn't. J.C. didn't have the bigger man's cumbersome bulk, but Bull couldn't remove his grip.

"It's not real gentlemanly to punch out kids, friend. Women, either. So why don't you just apologize and then take a walk out of here?"

Rachel dragged Peter away and knelt with her arms wrapped around his bony shoulders. She held her breath as Bull gathered himself, preparing to knock J. C. Tyler across the room and no doubt smash the poor man's skull in the process.

Bull's fist met only air, however. J.C. dodged and shook his head at the man's clumsiness. His return punch met with the solid bone of Bull's jaw. Bull staggered backward.

"Now, Bull," J.C. advised, "apologize to the lady."

Bull launched himself for J.C.'s throat. Again his target wasn't there. J.C.'s second punch sent blood spurting from Bull's nose.

"Come on, man. This is getting boring. Apologize and go stick your head in the horse trough. Things will look brighter tomorrow."

Bull came out swinging. For his efforts he got a series of bone-cracking blows to his jaw and a knee in his belly. He doubled over and staggered against the wall, which was the only thing that kept him from falling.

"Well?" J.C. prompted.

"Sor . . . sorry!" he garbled.

"Good enough?" J.C. turned icy-blue eyes on Rachel. Wide-eyed, she nodded.

"All right, Bull. Let's just help you out of here."

He had no trouble half dragging Bull's bulk to the door and hefting him out. "The water trough!" he called after him. "Over there. That's a good boy."

Rachel clung to Peter, somewhat stunned by the rapid flow of events. In the sudden quiet she reevaluated her first assessment of J. C. Tyler as a pleasant, rough-cut sort of gentleman. When need be, he was neither pleasant nor gentle. Poor Bull hadn't even landed one punch.

"¡Olé!" Aldona cheered. "Thank you, Mr. Tyler."

"Don't mention it."

"Poor Bull," Aldona said. "He's gentle as a kitten when he's sober, but when he's liquored up . . . whoooee!" She threw up her hands. "We were lucky you were here, señor. The men around these parts . . ." she looked pointedly at the one other customer, who was just now emerging from the corner where he'd taken cover. "Not a one of them will take on Bull when he's acting loco."

"I took him on!" Peter squirmed out of Rachel's grip. "I could'a taken care of fat ol' Bull. Didn't need *him* to butt in!"

"Peter!" Rachel collared her son, but the shamed look in his eyes made her bite back her reprimand. "Thank you for coming to my rescue, son. That was very brave. But I think you should thank Mr. Tyler for stepping in to help."

Peter's lower lip came out. "Didn't need his help!" The boy stalked out and slammed the door behind him.

Rachel sighed helplessly, embarrassed. "I'm sorry. That was dreadfully rude of him."

"Don't worry about it," their rescuer said. "Before our friend there blew in, I was about to ask for another piece of pie."

Aldona laughed, breaking the awkward tension. "You do like my pie, don't you, señor? After what you just did, I'll bake you one of your own. Until then, help yourself." She handed him a pie tin with a good half of a pie remaining, righted an overturned chair, and gestured for him to sit. "Rachel, *amiga,* get the gentleman some more coffee."

"I wish there were a better way we could thank you," Rachel said.

"Well, actually, the fellow at the stable said you rent rooms here."

"We have two rooms," Aldona said. "One is empty. If you need a room, it's yours for as long as you want."

"Won't be here long," J.C. told her.

"You have business in town?" Rachel asked.

"You might say that."

He flashed her a quick glance, then concentrated on

his pie. Something in that look made Rachel want to question further, but Aldona nudged her.

"Coffee, *amiga*. The poor hombre cannot do justice to my pie without coffee."

Rachel felt his eyes on her as she hurried to the kitchen. She couldn't decide if his interest was flattering or frightening.

Two hours later the kitchen and dining room were clean, their new guest had been settled into his room, Peter had finally fallen asleep in the upstairs room that he shared with Rachel, and Rachel finally got a chance to sit down with a cup of coffee and look at the envelope that had been delivered by the post rider. Mail was a precious commodity in Tubac. Two post riders had been killed by Apaches in the last year, and several more had made narrow escapes. Understandably the mail riders weren't anxious to take on the run between Tucson and Tubac.

"It's a letter from my friend Nell in Savannah," Rachel told Aldona.

Aldona sat down opposite her with a piece of pie and a cup of milk.

"My goodness!" Rachel said. "This was written back in March!"

"With what those Apache devils have been doing around here, you're lucky you got it at all. This is the same lady who sent you the little book of poems at Christmastime?"

"Yes. Sweet Nell. We've been friends forever—or at least as long as I can remember. She's the only one who knows where I am. I think she's the only person in the world I trust." She glanced at Aldona and smiled. "Except you, of course."

"Of course, *amiga*. Read, read! What does your friend say?"

Rachel scanned the first few lines. Nell's precise, flowing script carried her back to Georgia, to the time when she and Nell were girls together and had laughingly read each other's diaries. Both of them the only daughters of neighbors, they had been as close as sisters. Many a time they had sat together behind the upstairs balustrade at the Willows and watched during one of Rachel's mother's grand parties. In those bright years numerous plots had been hatched between them to sneak away from the dull pursuits expected of young ladies. Together they planned gambols in the park, afternoons fishing at the pond, or—even worse!—swimming in nothing but underdrawers and shifts.

Those had been good times, days of laughing mischief, days of innocence. Before interest in balls and courtship had completely replaced mischief and mayhem, the War had started. Not yet a woman, Rachel found herself a wife, then a mother. Childhood had ended abruptly for Nell also, when her father was killed during the first year of the War and her mother faded away to die six months later.

Rachel passed her finger fondly over Nell's graceful script. "She says my cousin Richard married Ann Ballantyne. Who would have thought? Annie was still playing with dolls last time I saw her. Nell's brother, David, now has two little boys, both of them scamps of the highest order. My father . . . oh, goodness! . . . my father bought the Barton plantation north of town. Stephen Barton had to sell it to pay what he'd borrowed against the cotton crop. Nell says there's some resentment against my father for buying up land that the old families are losing to Yankee taxes and Yankee profiteers." Rachel shook her head. "Father always did have a way of ending up on the winning side, one way or another."

Aldona chuckled. "I'd challenge your father to end up on the winning side with Cochise and his cutthroats."

"If there was a way," Rachel said, "Father would find it."

She read on aloud for several lines, then stumbled to silence as her eyes caught the shocking words. Anxiously she scanned the next two paragraphs, then put the letter carefully on the table and leaned forward on her elbows, suddenly feeling sick and weak. "What is it, Rachel?"

"Cabell has divorced me," she said softly. "Nell says the final notice was published in the newspaper the morning she wrote this letter."

In the silence that followed her words the faint scrape of Aldona's fork on her plate seemed a veritable rasp. Rachel could hear her own heart beating, thudding a solemn cadence as Nell's message sank irrevocably into her mind. The stretch of silent moments seemed to divide one part of her life from another, the known from the unknown, the uncertain.

Finally Aldona's lips curved in a slight smile. "This should be good news. Now you are a free woman."

"Free," Rachel said softly, testing the feel of the word. She didn't feel free. Sighing, she let her head drop wearily into her hands. "Free. Divorced."

"Rachel, *mi amiga,* what did you expect?"

She looked up from the refuge of her hands. "I don't know. I suppose I didn't think about it. I didn't expect . . . well, divorce! Scarlet women get divorced. Good families don't. Decent people don't."

"Rachel, you left him. Deserted him. Ran away."

"Yes." She sighed. "From time to time he's sent men looking for me. That's why I've moved from one end-of-the-earth town to another. I thought maybe he wanted me back. Cabell was never good at giving up something he thought belonged to him." She laughed weakly and shook her head. "There's some romance and mystery to being a runaway wife, but none whatsoever in being divorced. Once that's known, no decent woman will walk on the same side of the street with me."

"*Amiga,* I will not only walk on the same side of the street, I will walk with you arm in arm. Besides, why should anyone know of this? Here in Tubac, everyone knows you are Rachel Manchester, a respectable widow woman. And that is so in other places where you have lived, is it not?"

"Yes," Rachel admitted. "I will exchange one lie for another."

Aldona reached out and patted her hand. "If you had it to do over again, my friend, would you stay with your husband?"

"No," Rachel said quickly.

"Well, then, what is the purpose of regret?" She poured them both another cup of coffee. "Who is so perfect that they can walk far on the road of life without gathering some regrets? If you let them weigh you down, the burden simply makes the rest of the road harder to walk."

"You're right." Rachel smiled sadly. "By the time you're wise enough to avoid life's pitfalls, you've already fallen into most of them."

"You must have been very young when you married your husband."

"Sixteen. Father thought I was much too young, and he didn't like Cabell. Thought he was spoiled and impetuous." Rachel sighed. "I thought impetuous was romantic. Lord above! I think I was infatuated with Cabell from the time I could walk. He was a friend of my cousin Richard and my brother, Steven. He and Nell and I practically grew up together. Mama liked him. Together she and I convinced Father to let us marry before Cabell went off to the War. By the time he left, I was pregnant."

"And when he came back?"

Rachel rose and wandered around the kitchen, adjusting a stack of bowls on a shelf, straightening a towel. She scarcely registered anything she saw or did, but the movement satisfied a sudden restlessness. She'd never talked about this to anyone, not even Aldona, and the reliving of it in her memory was painful.

"Cabell came back just before the War ended. He'd been shot, and his leg had healed stiff. He couldn't ride or walk well. He spent hours just staring into space, it seemed. He'd become very quiet, except when he drank. That's when he shouted and ranted and ended up hitting something. Often it was me he hit. A wiser woman might have found a way to help him. I couldn't. I was too afraid of him. Afraid for myself. Afraid for Peter."

"Men and their wars!" Aldona grumbled. "Take a boy, put a rifle in his hands, and teach him to kill. He'll grow up fast, but not into the man he should grow into."

Suddenly bereft of energy, Rachel dropped back into her chair. "Aldona, the court awarded custody of Peter to Cabell. I guess they think leaving my husband makes me unfit to raise a child."

"These magistrates are men," Aldona scoffed. "What do they know about children? How much time does it take for a man to become a father?" She huffed indignantly. "A few short moments of grunting, eh? And then they think they have done the great deed. Ah! What do men know?"

Both of them sat in gloomy silence for a moment, then Aldona shrugged.

"Cheer up, *amiga*. Tubac is a long, long way from your Savannah. And as you say, you have been like a jackrabbit jumping from place to place since you left.

Perhaps by the time your husband finds you, little Peter will be grown big enough to defend not only himself but you too."

"Cabell will never find us," Rachel declared, as if taking a solemn oath. "He will never find us."

"Sí. He will never find you here. So go to bed, *niña*, and get some sleep."

Rachel reached for Aldona's hand and squeezed it. "Sometimes you remind me of my mother. She used to tell me to leave the evil of the day behind when I went to sleep."

"A good idea," Aldona agreed. "Leave the evil of this day behind. Because for certain some devil is busy plotting enough evil to fill the days ahead."

3

Savannah, Georgia
1870

July in Georgia was soft and steamy, best fit for drowsing and drifting. Even the birds in the Blanchard garden seemed to nap, for as Nell Blanchard swung lazily in the big swing, looking up into the lush greenery of the magnolia branches, scarcely a twitter or chirp scolded her from above. It was tempting to take a little snooze herself, with her brother, David, tending to business in town, his wife, Elizabeth, paying a call on a friend, and their two little boys napping peacefully in their room. The book she had been reading—a romance of derring-do and noble passion—lay open beside her on the seat of the swing. A tall lemonade sat beside it, the glass beaded with condensation from the humid air.

Nell sighed, drowsy, relaxed, and utterly bored.

She could have worked in the garden—heaven knew it needed a good weeding and trimming. The once-beautiful roses and hydrangeas looked like a jungle now that there were no slaves to tend the grounds. But the day was far too hot for such work. She might read or sew. But Nell was sick and tired of stitchery, and the exploits of the virtuous hero in the book that lay beside her were as dry and lifeless as the pages the story was written upon.

She closed her eyes and let herself drift with the gentle movement of the swing. When the boys awoke, she would have plenty to keep her busy. Elizabeth had all but turned their care over to her. Having a spinster sister-in-law as a permanent houseguest had its advantages, Nell thought. She didn't mind, though. The boys were darling little imps, and she loved them dearly. Prospects of having children of her own were dim, so she was grateful to have her brother's children to adore.

"Miss Nell."

Samuel's soft summons brought Nell from her drowsy state. The houseman stood in the shade of the back veranda, his ebony skin glowing with the heat, his hair as white as the snowy cravat Elizabeth insisted he wear. The old butler was one of the few Negroes who'd not left the household to revel in their new freedom after the War. "I'se too old to change my ways now," he'd told Nell. "Here I got good food and a soft bed. Massa and Missy, they's my family. I'se too old to be free."

Nell had been glad he'd stayed. Sometimes it seemed old Samuel was her only true friend.

"Miss Nell. Massa Cabell's here."

"Oh, my," Nell said with a sigh. "I suppose he's here to see David."

"He say he want to see you."

Nell's brows lifted in surprise. "He does, does he? All right, Samuel. Bring him out here. Ask him if he wants a cool lemonade, and if he tells you to put rum in it, don't."

"Yas'm." The old man's smile wreathed his face in wrinkles. "I won't give 'im no rum. Thas for sure."

A few minutes later Cabell strode onto the veranda, limping slightly, his hand holding a lemonade, his face wearing a slight smile. He was as handsome as ever, broad-shouldered and tall, blond and bronzed and easy smiling. Gentle brown eyes twinkled as he approached her. "You're looking very fetching today, Nell."

Nell chuckled. "Compared with what?"

"Compared with almost anything," Cabell answered. "You fit right in with the garden."

Overgrown and weedy, Nell thought dryly, but she didn't decline the compliment. Cabell was a true Southern gentleman. He could go on for hours with the chivalry nonsense if he had to.

"David isn't in, Cabell. I'm not sure when he'll be back."

"I didn't come to see David."

"Really!" Nell lifted one brow. She didn't have any illusions about Cabell Dorset coming to call with romantic intentions. She had been a spinster too long and knew Cabell too well for such a fantasy to tease her.

"In fact," Cabell continued, "I was counting on David and Elizabeth being away at this hour. I wish to speak to you privately."

"Indeed. Well, I must say, Cabell, you've piqued my curiosity."

He merely smiled. "May I sit?" He gestured to the space beside her, occupied by the book and lemonade.

"Of course." She hastened to move the obstacles.

If she had been a young belle of sixteen or seventeen, sitting in the garden alone with a man, especially in the intimacy of the old swing, which was big enough for two, but none too big, the situation would have been scandalous. But Nell was not a young belle. She was a plain-faced spinster with no grace to speak of, and long past being coy or flustered in a man's presence. Still, the way Cabell sat beside her in silence, studying her, brought a flush of heat to her cheeks. Men usually didn't pay much attention to her, and when they did, the results were often humiliating.

Nell still remembered a time years ago when her family had attended a summer picnic at the Dorset family plantation. Cabell had teased her unmercifully, calling her horse face and spindle shanks. And yet later that afternoon he had allowed her to go fishing with his circle of friends and had shown her how to take a fish from the hook, not laughing at all when she squealed at the wriggling, slimy thing. Such a contradictory boy Cabell had been, and as a man he was no less confusing.

"We've been friends for a long time, Nell," Cabell said finally.

"Yes, we have."

"I remember when you, Rachel, Steven, Richard, and I were nearly inseparable."

Inseparable was too strong a word, Nell thought. She and Rachel had been inseparable. But they had been close to the boys in sort of a love-hate relationship.

"Sometimes I think it's a shame we couldn't have stayed children forever," Cabell said softly.

"Those were good days."

"They were." Cabell sighed. "Have you heard from Rachel?"

Nell smiled. He had come about Rachel. She should have guessed. "Yes, Cabell. I have. Rachel is doing just fine. And so is Peter."

His mouth twitched in irritation, then thinned to a determined line. "I divorced her, you know."

"I know," she said, not bothering to keep the disapproval from her voice.

"What did you expect me to do? Pine away my entire life hoping she would come back? It's been three years. The law in Georgia allows divorce for desertion after three years. It was a clear-cut case of Rachel breaking both her sacred vows and her legal contract. She behaved in an irresponsible and unforgivable manner, so the court awarded custody of Peter to me."

"So I read," Nell said.

An awkward silence stretched between them. Nell thought sadly that Cabell was right. They should have remained children, she and Rachel and Cabell. Of the five of them who had run together as children, only Richard, Rachel's quiet cousin, seemed to be making a success out of being an adult.

"I expect you know where she is," Cabell said quietly.

Nell got up from the swing and dropped into the grass to lean back against the trunk of the magnolia.

"I know Rachel well enough to be certain she can't do something without talking about it, and she always talked to you about everything, didn't she? Not me." His mouth scribed a bitter line across his face. "She seldom talked to me. But she'd bare her very soul to you."

Nell sighed. "Do you expect me to tell you where she is, Cabell? Rachel is my best friend, my sister in everything but birth. Do you think so little of my loyalty?"

"What about your sense of right and wrong?" Cabell demanded. He stood, sending the swing rocking violently with the abruptness of his movement. "She ran away from me, goddammit!"

"Cabell!"

He dragged a hand down his face and sighed. "Sorry. You don't deserve to be subjected to such language. But it hurts, Nell. It hurts a lot. All during the hell of the War I dreamed of coming back to Rachel and our baby. Then when I got back, she was different. I suppose," he said bitterly, "she didn't like being married to a cripple. Every time I looked at her, I could see the pity in her eyes."

"You know better than that," Nell said mercilessly. "Your leg didn't have anything to do with her leaving. Cabell, I saw her face the day she left. And before that, there were times she hid from me, broke an engagement with some flimsy excuse. I knew why. She was ashamed to be seen in public with a face that was black and blue."

Cabell closed his eyes and pinched the bridge of his nose with shaking fingers. He didn't answer, and the silence grew.

"What kind of a man raises his hand to a woman half his size?" Nell asked softly. "God save me, Cabell, but if a man ever did to me what you did to Rachel, I'd give him back as good as he gave."

"Don't be ridiculous!" Cabell scoffed. "You talk as though I'd done something heinous! All I did was cuff her a few times. A man has a right to discipline his wife when the need arises."

"Discipline? You call what you did discipline?"

"Yes! I was angry. A back-talking, sassy wife should expect a husband's anger."

"Back-talking and sassy? Whom do you think you're fooling, Cabell? You've always been an expert at pulling the wool over people's eyes, and maybe this time you're pulling the wool over your own. Rachel never back-talked anyone in her life. She's so meek, she wouldn't club a snake if it were about to bite her." Nell got to her feet and advanced on Cabell, her finger stabbing toward him in accusation. If Cabell wanted to see back-talking and sassy, she'd give him an example he wouldn't forget. "Likely you were too drunk to know what Rachel said to you, or why you hit her. I'm surprised you even remember doing it!"

He flinched, and she knew she'd made her point.

"The truth is, Cabell, that you drove Rachel away.

She was the best thing that ever happened to you, and you let her slip right through your fingers because it was easier to feel sorry for yourself and take comfort from liquor than act like a man and pull yourself together after the War."

He backed away a step, his face set in rigid anger.

"Instead of divorcing her, you should have chased her down and begged her forgiveness."

He raised his hand, and for a fearful moment Nell thought he was going to hit her, but he merely stabbed with his finger in an imitation of her own gesture of reproach.

"What do you know of it?" he jeered. "What do you know of marriage? You're a dried-up spinster who lives with her brother. You know nothing about what goes on between a man and a woman."

"I know right from wrong!" She refused to let him intimidate her. For a moment they stood finger to accusing finger, like duelists waiting to fire the first shot. Then Cabell growled an imprecation, folded his hand into a fist, and straightened his spine in wounded dignity.

"I'll chase her down, all right. But it won't be to beg her forgiveness. She should be the one apologizing to me, and the court sees it that way as well. I have a right to have Peter with me. He's my son. My heir. My pride and joy."

"He's her son as well," Nell reminded him.

"She gave up legal rights to him when she ran away."

Nell returned his glare with one of her own. His expressive brown eyes were no longer gentle. They were angry. And hurt. And beneath the anger and hurt, Nell guessed, Cabell was desperately trying to believe his own version of right and wrong.

"Next time you write to Rachel," he said with quiet

intensity, "you tell her for me that she'll have not a moment's peace until she returns my son to me. I know she's somewhere in the West. That much I learned from her father's cook. I'll find her. She can depend upon it."

"You're a fool, Cabell Dorset."

"I'm a man, and a man's immortality is in his son. Rachel won't take him from me. You tell her that."

He stalked away, visibly making an effort not to limp. Nell returned to the swing. She felt like trembling, but wouldn't allow herself that weakness. In a way her heart went out to Cabell, but she wouldn't allow herself to feel pity for the man. If he wanted to find his immortality, he would have to crawl out of the bottle first. She remembered the teasing, sometimes cruel, but often kind boy; the charming, debonair young man with too much money and too much arrogance for his own good; and then the man who'd come home from the fighting, wounded in much more than his leg. Her heart ached for him, just as it ached for Rachel in her exile.

Nell had always had a soft spot for helpless fools.

The sky was scarcely light with the first hints of the new day, and already the air was too hot to sleep. J.C. pushed back the bedsheets and yawned. Another morning waking in a strange bed, a strange room. He wondered what it was like to live in a house that you returned to night after night, to sleep in a room filled with memories of the days, the years that had gone before.

He took the pistol from beneath his pillow and shoved it into the holster that hung from the bedpost. Then he looked around the room. Where was he this morning? Tubac, he recalled. Tubac, Arizona Territory. A nameless roadhouse in a festering boil of a town.

Engaged in hot, dangerous pursuit of a helpless woman and a sullen kid. What an exciting life.

Nameless roadhouse or not, the room had a homier feel than most places where he'd slept. The window curtains were a flower print with a silly little ruffle around the bottom, a bit threadbare, but clean and freshly ironed. A rag rug on the floor partially hid floor planks that were well scrubbed and waxed. The bed's counterpane matched the window curtains, ruffle and all. The final touch almost made him laugh. On the dresser sat a small pottery vase of wildflowers. In this dusty and harsh land peopled by wild Apaches, wilder outlaws, and settlers too tough and too stubborn to be beaten—wildflowers, of all things!

He'd bet his last dollar that it was Rachel who decorated this room. It looked like her: threadbare but pretty.

She didn't seem like the sort of woman who could desert her husband. She seemed more like the type who would stand by a man through war, sickness, and poverty, who would fight at a man's side, if need be, to defend home and children.

Well, he'd been wrong before.

Still, taking a child from its mother was a serious thing. A serious thing indeed. It wouldn't hurt to stick around a few days, just to make sure that this redheaded Rachel was truly the woman he sought. And the time would give him a chance to get acquainted with the boy. Getting away with the kid would be easier if the boy knew him.

The day somehow seemed brighter once J.C. had delayed the deed he'd come to do. And the possibility that he might have been tracking the wrong woman for these past weeks was less annoying than it might have been.

The sky was brightening from pale gray to blue as J.C.

ducked his head in the rainwater barrel behind the roadhouse. There wasn't much water in the barrel, and what was there had a scum of dust and insects floating on the top, but it was cool and wet, and brought him fully awake.

"Good morning, Mr. Tyler."

J.C. pushed dripping hair out of his eyes to see Rachel trudging up from the creek bearing two brimming buckets. Despite the hard work of hauling water, she looked fresher and cooler than the morning itself. The first rays of the dawn struck fire off the deep, rich red of her hair and painted a shimmering halo around her slender form. The flyaway, undisciplined locks of the night before were tamed and neatly captured in a thick braid that hung to her waist.

J.C. thought with sudden distraction that her hair looked better flying around her face in unruly wisps and curls, and that he hadn't noticed the night before how direct and disconcerting those green eyes were. Suddenly conscious that he had nothing but bare skin above his belt, he reached for the shirt that hung over the side of the barrel.

"Mornin', Mrs. . . . uh . . ."

"Manchester," she supplied with an easy smile.

He hustled down the path to take the buckets from her. "Those look a bit heavy, ma'am. Your well dry?"

"No. But the pump handle's broken. We haven't had time to fix it. The haul isn't so bad. The creek's just over there." She nodded to a line of paloverde and acacia trees that ran along the bottom of the little hill. The line of trees stretched eastward to blend with the thicker vegetation along the Santa Cruz River. "At least we don't have to carry water all the way from the river."

That didn't sound like a pampered Georgia belle talking, J.C. noted.

"But it's very nice of you to help," she concluded.

She directed him to empty the water into a barrel in the kitchen. Then she grabbed another bucket and they went back to the creek for more. By the end of the third trip J.C.'s arms ached. He could imagine what hers felt like.

"I'll take a look at that pump handle after breakfast," he said.

"You don't have to do that, Mr. Tyler."

"No trouble. After all, you and Mrs. Perez aren't letting me pay for the room. The least I can do is lend a hand here and there. Besides," he told her with a grin, "if I fix the pump, I won't feel obligated to haul water again. My arms are already six inches longer than they were when I woke up."

She looked up at him and laughed, and the face that had been merely pretty seemed to glow with heart-aching beauty. J.C. suddenly had difficulty breathing.

The melodious laughter trailed off into a smile. "You're very kind, Mr. Tyler."

"Call me J.C., please."

"J.C., then. It would be nice to have someone around who can lend a hand," she admitted. "I'd like to pay you more than just board and room for as long as you're here, but . . . well, I'm afraid we're just making ends meet as it is. We don't get a lot of business. There's not many people left in Tubac, and with the Apaches always making trouble, not many travelers come through."

"Yeah, I can understand why. I've seen a bit of Apache handiwork a time or two."

Breakfast was hearty and good—corned beef hash topped with eggs, and a stack of bread slathered with butter and a sweet jelly that Aldona, who served J.C. and the boarder, said was made from the fruit of the prickly-pear cactus.

"Rachel made it," Aldona told him. "She's a very good cook for a gringa, eh?"

After stuffing himself with the ladies' excellent cooking, J.C. started working on the pump. The morning passed while he fashioned a new, strong handle and labored at fastening it onto the pump rod. The sun beat down on the baked earth, making the air shimmer with heat. Sweat rolled down his face and drenched his shirt.

Twenty feet away from where J.C. worked, the widow "Manchester" stirred a tubful of laundry that was boiling over an open fire set in a circle of soot-blackened stones. One by one she ladeled each piece of laundry from the cauldron, scrubbed it vigorously on a washboard, rinsed it in a second tub, and hung it on a line strung between a mesquite tree and the stock shed. The steam from the operation had made her hair go wild. Her face shone with dampness, and her blouse clung to her in a way that made J.C.'s breath stick in his throat.

The woman seemed unaware of her sensual appeal, however. She hummed a vague tune while she worked, seemingly ignorant that each breath molded her full breasts against the damp cotton of her blouse. Moisture beaded on her smooth, freckle-dusted skin and trickled languidly downward to disappear beneath the gaping scoop neckline, an invitation to enticement.

He had definitely been without the company of a woman too long. When his makeshift pump handle was secure, he went to the rain barrel to douse away heat from more than just the sun.

After he had dashed the water from his eyes, he caught her looking his way. In fact she was staring with what seemed to be rapt appreciation. When his gaze caught hers, her freckles joined together in a flaming blush.

"Sorry," he said, reaching for the sweat-drenched

shirt. He ought to remember that decent women got nervous at the sight of bare male skin.

"That's all right. Give me the shirt. I'll wash it. If you want to change out of those trousers, I'll wash them, too."

"You don't need to bother."

"It's no bother. And in this heat they'll be dry in an hour."

"That's mighty nice of you." He handed over his shirt.

By the time he'd changed into his one set of clean clothes and brought his trousers down to her, Rachel was scrubbing away at his shirt. The sight of her intimacy with his clothing sent a shot of desire through his veins. Long, slim fingers probed the seams and caressed the threadbare collar. The indecorous thought of her doing the same thing to the crotch of his trousers made sweat bead on his brow.

"You have a few ragged seams," she told him. "I'll mend them for you this afternoon."

She took the trousers he handed her and fulfilled his fantasy by running her seeking fingers over those seams as well. Heaven help him! He smiled weakly, unable to say a thing.

"These seem sturdy enough."

He had definitely been without a woman too long.

J.C.'s trousers—along with his imagination—were left to boil while they tried out the new handle on the well pump. Cool water spurted from the pump outlet.

"Wonderful!" she exlaimed. "Thank you!"

Was that a hint of the South he heard in her voice? If she were truly from Georgia, could she have trained herself to speak without an accent?

His speculation was interrupted by a small whirlwind of dust that blew around the corner of the building, practically careening into them. The dust settled to reveal a scuffed and grinning boy.

"Ma! Manuel and me are goin' fishin' down at the river. I need the shovel to dig worms."

"When are you going to split the firewood for tonight?" his mother asked.

"I'll cut it when we get back."

Rachel reached out and ruffled the boy's fiery hair. "Why don't you cut it before you go?"

"Ma! Manuel's waiting!"

"If he's so impatient to go fishing, then Manuel can help you."

"Ma!"

"I mean it, Peter. Yesterday I cut the firewood because you didn't get back here until long after it was needed. You have to start taking your chores more seriously."

"All I ever do is work! It's not fair!"

"You've spent the whole morning running about like a wild Indian. I think it won't hurt you to spend a couple of hours in fruitful labor."

"A couple of hours?" Peter cried in dismay. He wore the expression of an innocent man just sentenced to hard labor on a chain gang.

"Maybe if I help, it'll get done faster," J.C. offered.

His overture drew a look from the boy that could have frozen the steaming wash water. *So much for getting on the kid's good side,* J.C. mused.

"I'll do it when we get back," Peter declared. "And I'll dig the damned worms with my hands."

"Peter!" Rachel scolded. But the boy had already dashed away in a spurt of dust and hostility. Rachel sighed, her lips pressed tight, her eyes mingling sorrow and frustration. "What am I going to do with him? He used to be such a sweet boy." She shook her head. "Forgive the scene, Mr. Tyler. Peter lost his father three years ago, and sometimes he takes his anger out on the world around him."

"Yeah. I guess every boy needs a father."

A bitter smile escaped Rachel's guarded reserve. "That's true, I know. But some fathers are worse than no father at all."

Peter didn't return to the roadhouse in time to cut firewood for supper. He nursed his temper all through the afternoon. Fishing with Manuel wasn't much fun. When Peter bragged about his confrontation with authority, the little turncoat had the nerve to say that a son shouldn't use such language with his mother. Stupid Manuel even said he should have stayed to cut the wood. He would have helped, the traitor insisted.

They ended up wrassling in the dirt, pulling hair and ears, gouging with fingers and nails. Peter got the worst of it. Manuel was bigger than he was and a year older. Besides, he had a father and three brothers who'd taught him how to fight. Sisters too. Peter had no one.

Reluctant to return home and display his bruises to his mother, Peter took refuge in his favorite spot—the livery stable and corral. The warm smells of horse, leather, and hay always made him feel good.

"¡Hola, Señor Ortega!"

"¡Hola, Peter!" The wrinkled old man who ran the livery gave him a suspicious look. "You been fighting Apaches, boy?"

Peter shrugged nonchalantly and was grateful when the man didn't press the question. His mother, on the other hand, would have fussed over a few scrapes and bruises as if the world were coming to an end. He didn't really blame her, her being a woman and all. But a guy could only put up with so much.

"You got anything that needs doing, Señor Ortega?"

"After a bit of work, now, are you?"

Tasks around the stable didn't really seem like work to Peter. For one thing, no one ordered him to do it; it was his own idea. For another, working with the horses gave him a satisfaction that little else could.

"You could clean out the first two stalls if you've a mind to," Ortega told him. "And go up to the loft to bring down another couple of sacks of grain."

"Okay!" Peter grabbed the pitchfork and started down the center aisle of the stable, only to be brought up short by one of the loveliest visions he'd ever seen.

Who is that?"

His voice dropped to a reverent whisper as he gazed at the horse tethered at the far end of the aisle. Sunlight streamed through the open door behind the magnificent creature, backlighting it in a blaze of appropriate glory.

Ortega stuck his head out of the tack-room door and glanced down the aisle. "Nice, eh?" he commented. "Belongs to an hombre who rode in yesterday. He's cleaning the stall." The liveryman chuckled. "Picky about where his horse sleeps."

Peter propped the pitchfork against a wall and walked closer to the horse. On close inspection the animal proved to be a stallion—a leggy chestnut whose coat glowed red in the sunlight. Firm muscle flowed beneath the flashy coat as the horse shifted restlessly at Peter's approach. Beautifully formed ears pricked alertly in his direction, and intelligent eyes examined him as if to divine his intentions.

Then the owner stepped out of the stall. Peter froze in surprise.

"Hi there," J.C. greeted him.

"This is your horse?" Peter asked.

"Yeah. Like him?"

Peter didn't answer. He felt a stab of resentment that this man should have such a grand horse. This was the fellow who'd butted in and saved his mother the night before, as if Peter was a helpless baby who couldn't have done the job himself. And then today he'd pushed himself in again, trying to help his mother weasel Peter into cutting the stupid firewood. Who did he think he was, anyway? Besides, Peter didn't like the way the man looked at his mother. Mothers shouldn't be looked at that way.

"His name's O'Malley," J.C. told him. "Mine's J.C."

"That's a stupid name for a horse," Peter said. He couldn't resist getting a bit closer. He'd never seen a prettier head on a horse, or a stronger-looking chest and hindquarters.

"You can look him over if you want," J.C. offered. "He's a stallion, but he's gentle."

Peter ran a hand down the graceful arch of the stallion's neck. "How'd you come by him?" he asked. "You didn't steal him, did you?"

"What makes you think I stole him?"

"Fella like you doesn't look like a man who'd have a horse like this."

J.C. laughed. "Well, I guess you got that right. You might say I got him by plain good luck. Named him for the man I got him from."

"He's a winner," Peter admitted. "I'll bet he's faster than the wind."

"And he can go all day. Strongest horse I ever had. Would you like to brush him?"

Peter couldn't resist. He was oblivious to J.C. and everything else in the stable as he curried the shining red coat, combed the lustrous mane and tail, and lifted each hoof to pick dirt, grass, and pebbles from around the sensitive frog. The well-behaved stallion stood like a rock and patiently let him do the work. Peter decided the horse must like him. The thought made him feel good.

"Someday this big fella's going to sire a whole herd of foals that are just as good as he is," J.C. confided. "When I was a boy, I used to dream of finding a horse like him." His chuckle was friendly. "I can see you're just as crazy about horses as I was at your age."

Peter felt himself begin to thaw toward the stranger. "Yeah. I really like horses. They're special, ya know. But . . . well . . . I can't say as I ever learned how to ride one. I had a pony once, a long time ago, but I've never been on a real horse."

J.C. looked at him in surprise. "You don't know how to ride? And you're how old?"

"I'm nine."

"Well, it's past time you learned, wouldn't you say? I could give you a few pointers."

Peter's heart started to beat faster. "On him?"

"Sure. O'Malley's a real gentleman. He wouldn't toss you off."

Peter wrestled with temptation. It was a fiercer match than the one he'd had earlier with Manuel. "My ma wouldn't like it," he admitted finally. "She's right scared of horses. Got kicked once."

"Well, if you don't want to ride . . ." J.C. untied the lead rope as if he was going to put O'Malley in the stall.

"Wait! Uh . . . hell! I'm not the one who got kicked. There's no reason I should stay away from horses!"

J.C. grinned. "That's right. A man can't always let his mother do his thinking for him, can he?"

"Hell no!"

"Why don't you fetch my saddle from the tack room, son. It's on the first rack to the right of the door."

Peter ran down the aisle before J.C. changed his mind about letting him ride that magnificent stallion. Funny how first judgments could sometimes be wrong. He was beginning to really like the big stranger.

 4

"Just keep those arms and legs still and let O'Malley walk quiet like. Keep him settled." J.C. leaned on the railing of the corral behind the stable and watched Peter's face as the kid rode the stallion along the fence. The boy's eyes glowed. His smile was so wide, it stretched every freckle on his face. He swayed easily with the rhythm of the horse.

The kid was a natural horseman, but he wanted to fly before he could crawl. J.C. understood that. He'd been the same way as a youngster. His father had put him up on a horse when he was three years old, and he'd right away wanted to jump the nearest ravine and gallop into the wind. The horse—a twenty-year-old mare named Jess—had known better, fortunately for him. His father had been little more than a poor Kansas dirt farmer, but he'd always had good horses.

O'Malley knew better too. He knew the burden he carried was young, green, and fragile, and the stallion wasn't about to do anything to get the boy tossed off.

"Okay, Peter, move him into a trot. Easy now. Just

pick the reins up a bit and press with your knees. That's right."

O'Malley moved into a fluid, quiet trot. Peter chortled, bounced, then found the rhythm and settled in to move with the horse. His grin was pure bliss.

"Keep your feet still," J.C. warned. "Don't be bouncing those heels against his ribs."

Damn but O'Malley moved like a dream, J.C. thought proudly. Power in motion. Grace and strength and good temper rolled into one beautiful horse.

J.C. had gotten him on a fluke. His owner, Tom O'Malley, had been a rich fool from Virginia who'd come west and turned drunk and mean. He'd killed a whore in Denver, and J.C. had been the one who caught up with him. The fool had tried to shoot it out—a stupid idea, because J.C. was a man who lived by his gun, and he was good with it. J.C. hadn't got much of a reward when he brought back the body. Killing a whore was a hanging offense, but no one got worked up enough over it to offer much money for the killer. J.C. had gotten Tom O'Malley's horse, though, and that horse, dubbed for its unfortunate former owner, turned out to be the best reward he'd ever collected.

"I wanna gallop!" Peter called. "Can I?"

"Next time," J.C. promised. "Rein him down to a walk and bring him over here. You can do some backs and turns and other fancy stuff."

"Okay."

The kid on O'Malley was certainly different from the sullen little monster who'd run off from his mother earlier that same day, J.C. reflected. The boy's whole face glowed with enthusiasm and wonder.

"I'll come out and brush him every day if you let me, Mr. Tyler! I'd clean his stall, too, and I'd clean it real good! I think he likes me! Don't ya think so?"

"I think he probably does. And you can call me J.C."

He showed Peter how to signal the stallion to back, to whirl gracefully on his hind feet first to the right, then to the left. The kid looked like he was in heaven. It was hard not to like him.

J.C. wondered how he would feel if he had fathered a son like Peter and that son was whisked out of his life. It was hard to reconcile Rachel with a woman who would do such a heartless thing. How would Rachel react when Peter was taken away from her?

As if summoned by his thoughts, Peter's mother came around the corner of the stable. She stopped abruptly when she saw Peter atop O'Malley. Placing balled fists on her hips, she glared.

"Uh-oh!" Peter muttered under his breath, just loud enough for J.C. to hear.

"Hello there!" J.C. greeted her.

"Hello, Mr. Tyler." Then to Peter. "I thought I might find you here at the stable, but I admit I didn't expect to find you up on a horse, especially such . . ." Her face went a bit pale as she took in O'Malley's size and musculature. ". . . such a big horse."

J.C. halfway expected a maternal temper tantrum, but Rachel remained calm as Peter slid down from the saddle. "Are you going to tell me what's going on?" she gently prompted her son.

"Uh . . . J.C. . . . Mr. Tyler was teaching me how to ride." He gave her an uncertain smile. "This is O'Malley."

She gave the stallion a dubious look, but held her ground.

"I don't think you should be bothering Mr. Tyler, Peter."

"It's all right," J.C. assured her. "I offered to let him ride. O'Malley's very gentle."

Rachel shot him a look that told him he should definitely hold his tongue.

"Mr. Tyler is very generous to take the trouble," she said stiffly. "Thank him, Peter, then go home, please. We have a couple of things to discuss, you and I, and there's still firewood waiting to be cut."

"Yes'm." Peter's manner notably lacked the sullen rebellion of before, even though he'd been caught in the act. He crooked a finger at J.C. to urge him down to nine-year-old level. "I did warn you," he whispered as J.C. bent close. "Now we're both in for it."

"We'll both have to take it like men, then, won't we?" J.C. whispered back.

"Could you talk to her?" Peter pleaded, his eyes bright with hope.

"I'll try," J.C. promised.

Peter gave his mother a suitably humble look and scampered off toward home.

"Mr. Tyler. I appreciate your paying attention to a lonely boy, but I would have preferred that you ask me before encouraging him in such a dangerous activity." A touch of the expected temper frayed her usually melodious voice. "Now he'll be pestering you every day, as long as you're here, to get him up on that horse again."

"Thought you were going to call me J.C.," he said with what he hoped was a winning smile. "Unless 'Mr. Tyler' sounds better for a tongue lashing."

"I'd appreciate your not making light of this!"

J.C. collected O'Malley's reins and gave him a fond whack on the neck. The stallion slanted him a sympathetic look.

"It seems harmless enough for a boy who loves horses to learn how to ride," J.C. ventured.

"I think that should be my decision. He's my son, and I'm responsible for his safety."

"Well, yes, ma'am. But I'd hardly call riding a horse a dangerous activity."

"I happen to think differently." She folded her arms across her chest. At her movement O'Malley shook his head and stomped. Rachel jumped back, then tried vainly to gather the cloak of maternal dignity around herself once again.

"Horses are a big part of our world, Rachel. They're big and some of 'em are a bit boneheaded." He glanced an apology to the stallion. "But they're not really dangerous to someone who knows his way around them."

"That may be, but Peter's not old enough."

J.C. couldn't help but snort at that remark. "He's nine years old, right? And he's a sturdy kid. If you coddle him like that, he'll never grow up."

"Coddle him?" Rachel grated out.

He could see the temper flare in her eyes. He knew she had to have one. Redheads generally did.

"I do not coddle my son, Mr. Tyler. And I'll thank you to keep your nose out of the way I raise my child. You've been acquainted with Peter but two days, and you think you know better than his mother what he should learn and what he should do? It's hard enough to raise a child in this godforsaken savage land without . . ."

J.C. listened to the upbraiding with only half his mind. The other half focused on Rachel herself. Even when she was in the throes of a temper, he couldn't help but admire her, standing there raking him up one side and down the other, hands on hips, hair a fiery halo, eyes bright, cutting emeralds of indignation. Just as he'd guessed, the temper matched the color of her hair, running like a sizzling red streak across what first appeared to be a mellow personality. A touchy independence ran right along with it.

Most white women who ventured into this country wore themselves down to pathetic drones inside a year, their spirit eroded by heat, dust, endless distances, loneliness, and the constant threat of violent death, Apache style. Not this one. This one went into business in the heart of Cochise's domain and knocked mountainous drunken louts with her skillet when they got out of hand. This one read the riot act to possibly dangerous men who stepped over the line with her kid. A man had to have respect for that kind of spirit, even when it was flailing him like a rawhide quirt.

Finally Rachel paused for breath, and J.C. held up his hands in surrender. "Yes, ma'am. You're right. I should've asked you first."

"It's not that I don't appreciate—"

"Yes, ma'am. Any mother would be concerned. I understand."

"Well, I . . ." His abject retreat apparently defused her indignation. He could tell she was trying hard to keep a good scowl on her face, but she couldn't quite do it. Her eyes softened. A smile hesitated on her lips, then broadened. "I do have a short fuse when it comes to my son, don't I?"

"Yeah. Well, there's nothing wrong with a mother protecting her child. It's only natural."

"I am overprotective, though," she admitted with a sigh. "Aren't I?"

He laughed and held out his hands as if to fend her off. "I'm not treading on that ground again."

"Sorry." She shook her head. "My mother always did say I have the temper of a troll."

"Did she? Where was that?"

"Where was what?"

"Your mother. Where were you raised that it was so terrible to have a temper?"

Rachel's smile faded slowly. He sensed the shell of her reserve closing about her once again.

"Now, me," he said hastily, "I was raised in Kansas. Out there you've got to have a temper, just to do the twisters one better. My ma's temper could take the twist right out of a tornado's tail, but I'll bet you could give Ma a run for her money."

The corner of Rachel's mouth twitched upward. "Mr. Tyler, I think you're a spinner of tall tales."

"Now, why would you say that?"

The smile returned to full bloom. Peculiar, J.C. mused, how a woman's smile could light up her eyes and soften her whole face—at least this woman's smile. With an effort, he dragged his mind back on track.

"Seriously, though, Rachel—you don't mind if I call you Rachel, do you?"

"I suppose—"

"Good. As I was saying, Rachel, if you don't know your way around horses, you should learn. They're wonderful creatures."

She glanced dubiously at O'Malley. "I'm sure they are."

"It's hard to get along in this world without a good horse."

"It's not that I have anything against them—"

"Peter said you got kicked. How'd that happen?"

"I snuck up behind a horse—when I was a little girl. My cousin was on the horse and I wanted to surprise him."

"Surprised the horse instead of your cousin, eh?"

She laughed. "Oh, my cousin was surprised too."

"You can't blame the horse for that."

"Well, I don't blame the horse—"

"Good. Then come meet O'Malley. No one ever surprises him. He's too smart."

"No. Really. I don't—"

J.C. took her arm in spite of her protest. "Come on. O'Malley's a real gentleman. His feelings would be hurt if he thought you didn't like him."

She relented rather than make a scene. J.C. didn't know exactly why he was playing with her in this way. He could use the excuse that he needed to learn more about her, but it would have been a lie. As things stood, he was just about certain that she wasn't Rachel Manchester, but Rachel Dorset, and within the next few days he was going to take her son away from her and earn her everlasting enmity. But just now he didn't want to let her disappear around the corner of the stable as quickly as she'd appeared. Just now he wanted to enjoy that contagious smile, watch the light come and go in those jewel-green eyes, and see the sunlight play games with the red sheen of her hair. Most of the time his life stank. He had a right to enjoy something for a change, instead of just endure it.

O'Malley stretched out an inquisitive nose toward them as they came near. J.C. felt Rachel stiffen. "That's just a friendly hello," he said. "Don't worry. It's the other end that got you before, wasn't it?"

"This is ridiculous," she muttered.

Giving her a leg up to the saddle was like trying to push a limp rope up a hill. When she finally got a foot in each stirrup, she held on to the saddle horn for dear life, refusing to let go even to straighten her skirt into a more modest arrangement about her ankles—which were, J.C. noted, slender and about as well turned as a feminine ankle could be.

"I think I want to get down."

"No, you don't. Just let me lengthen the stirrups a bit. You'll be as comfortable as if you were in your rocking chair at home."

When he gently took her left foot from the stirrup, she clung even tighter.

"I don't think this is a good idea."

"It's a wonderful idea. Trust me."

"It's the horse I don't trust. I don't think he likes me."

She was probably right. O'Malley's ears were pinned back at an unhappy angle, and he was beginning a restive dance in place. Rachel's stiff posture and tense voice emanated fear, and horses everywhere, no matter how well behaved, regard fear as a license to take advantage of the situation. O'Malley was no exception.

"I told you he'd get hurt feelings if he thought you didn't like him," J.C. chided. Finished with the stirrups, he swung up behind her. "Why don't we just take a few circuits together to show you how easy this is?"

Rachel was almost startled out of her fear when J.C.'s arms closed around her from behind and his hands picked up the reins. The stallion danced as his master urged him forward, and Rachel uttered a little squeak. She was making a total fool of herself, but she couldn't help it. Why had she allowed this man, this total stranger, to drag her into such an absurd situation?

"Relax, now. Give up the death grip on the saddle and lean back a little," J.C. advised.

She could hear the laughter in his voice, the swine, but she tried to do as he said. When she leaned back, her shoulders came in contact with his chest. It was a bulwark, hard and broad. His arms curved around her in a cage of male muscle. Suddenly she felt uneasy about more than just the horse.

"See how easy it is?" he asked.

Rachel took a deep breath. This was absurd. She was no fainting virgin or green girl. There was no reason in the world for her to be tingling like some ninnyhammer debutante during her first waltz.

"That's better," he encouraged softly. "Let your spine go loose and supple. Grip with your legs and let your body move to the rhythm. Good."

O'Malley had settled into a sedate trot, but Rachel forgot all about the horse. She was too aware of the man who sat so closely behind her. His breath tickled her hair, his arms pressed along the sides of her breasts, his chest buttressed her back like a warm, solid tree. She felt the vibrations of his voice, smelled the dusty, horsy, salty scent of him—the very male scent of him. The sensations made her breath come faster and her heart pick up speed.

"See? You're doing fine."

Rachel imagined that a new huskiness permeated his voice. As he reined in the stallion, the large, bronzed hand that gripped the reins drew back against her breast. It jerked away as if she were hot as a burning coal. The stallion started.

"Whoa there," J.C. said.

Rachel wondered if he was soothing himself or the horse.

"See how well you did?" he said rather hoarsely, then swung down from behind her.

Without his support, disturbing as it had been, Rachel instantly stiffened.

"Take him around once yourself," he instructed. "Just keep to a walk and you'll be fine."

O'Malley took off without her signal, as if he'd heard his master's command. Rachel grabbed the saddle horn. "Oh, no!"

"You're fine. Just relax."

She was not fine! Without the distraction of J.C., her mind was jerked back to her height above the ground and the jolt of each heavy hoof hitting the ground. She was certain the stallion was walking stiff-legged because he didn't like her. Not that she blamed him, because she didn't like him at all!

"I'm going to get off!"

"No! Don't! Just turn him around and bring him back. I'll help you off."

Turn him around how? She lifted the reins higher. O'Malley twitched his ears and broke into a trot.

"Oh, noooo!"

"Oh shit!" J.C. said.

Rachel was going to get off this homicidal beast, and she was going to do it now! "Whoa!" she cried, pulling back desperately on the reins. "Stop, dammit!"

O'Malley stopped very suddenly. His powerful hindquarters slid beneath him and his front hooves pawed the air. Rachel bounced free of the stirrups and canted to the left, headed for the ground—until a strong arm caught her around the waist and pulled her free.

"Oh, Mr. Tyler! Thank you."

"How many times have I asked you to call me J.C.?"

Her toes dangled a foot above the earth. Her breasts were flattened against his collarbone. Blue eyes burned into hers, and she forgot to demand that he put her down.

He did put her down, though. Slowly, so that she slid over the hard length of him. One of his arms circled her waist. The other hand slid down to cup her behind. A numbness stilled her spirit, while every fiber of her body drowned in a host of forgotten sensations. When he lowered his mouth to hers, she could no more object than she could fly to the moon.

His lips were dry and cool, soft and firm at the same time. They moved on hers with hungry fervor that woke an answering need in her. Of its own accord, her mouth opened beneath his. He tasted of coffee and dust and desire.

"Damnation!" he muttered against her mouth, then his fingers wove into her hair, urging her head to tilt back. His mouth came down upon hers in a gentle assault, wet this time, stealing her breath and breathing desire into her at the same time. Sensations assailed her with dizzying ferocity—the scrape of his day's growth of beard, the hard, unyielding heat of his body, the tantalizing press of his hand on her buttocks, the scent of horse, soap, sweat, and her own rising desire.

The need for breath forced them to break apart. The world snapped back into focus, and the folly of what she was doing hit Rachel like a club.

"Oh my!" She twisted out of J.C.'s grasp. A flood of heat rose to her face. "Oh, my goodness!"

"Rachel . . ." He reached out as if to recapture her, but she backed away, her eyes wide. "Rachel, I'm sorry."

"It was my fault," she claimed, still backing away. "I should know better. I'm not . . . I'm not . . ." Her throat closed with embarrassment. He was still looking at her as though she were some sort of sweet confection he could devour. "Oh, damn!"

She turned and fled, but the blaze that had burned in his eyes still scalded her soul.

Business at the roadhouse was light that evening. A few customers wandered in for pie and coffee. Only one or two ordered dinner. Aldona chased Rachel out of the kitchen and insisted she take a nap.

"You look broke down and wore out," the Mexican widow declared. "What will I do around here if you let yourself get sick? Climb right up those stairs and sleep for an hour or two. I'll see that Peter eats his dinner, and he can help me clean up after the customers are gone."

Rachel had little choice but to obey, though she was reluctant to be alone with herself. What she'd done that afternoon floated close to the surface of her mind, and she didn't want to think about it. The realization that she had the capacity for such foolishness was alarming.

Aldona was right, however; Rachel was worn out, and sleep came quickly, even though the late afternoon sun blazed through the window of her little upstairs room and glowed incandescent gold in the dusty air. Perhaps it was this warm haze that invaded her dreams, for when she woke, her mind swirled with vague images of churning heat and feverish longings that uncomfortably resembled desire. What monster had she foolishly awakened within herself?

She jolted all the way awake to the faint sound of gunshots. Distant as the sounds were, they brought her leaping off the bed in fear of marauding Apaches. She grabbed the shotgun that always stood in the corner of the room, then paused. The gunshots came again—faint staccato cracks in measured cadence.

Brushing her hair away from her face, she sighed. That was not the sound of an attack. She put the shotgun back in its place, tied back her hair, and went downstairs. The dining room was empty. Aldona and Peter were in the kitchen washing dishes. Rachel heard her name bandied between them. No doubt Peter was complaining about his mother and Aldona was lending a sympathetic ear. This was not the time to intrude.

She walked onto the front porch to admire the quiet dusk. The mountains were deep purple shadows against the nearly colorless evening sky. The dusty wind had died, and the only sound was the rasping song of cicadas rising into the quiet air—until distant gunshots once again echoed through the valley.

Curious, Rachel followed the sound into the creekbed

and up the ravine. She walked for ten minutes, until finally she rounded a bend. There was J. C. Tyler shooting at a line of bottles and cans standing against the far bank of the wash.

For a moment Rachel stood and watched. J.C.'s back was to her, and he made no sign that he was aware of her presence. Rachel didn't think he could be aware of anything over the racket his rifle was making. She didn't really want him to see her, to speak to her, perhaps to wonder if she'd followed him here to seek out more of his attentions. She considered going back to the roadhouse with him none the wiser. If she'd known he was the one making all the noise, she never would have come.

That was a lie, Rachel admitted to herself. Something inside her had hoped it was J.C. that she followed. Something inside her was leading her down a very unwise path.

Another barrage of lead left one lonely survivor on the opposite bank. J.C. did not seem at all pleased with his marksmanship, and Rachel heard a muttered curse that she couldn't quite make out—only that it was something derogatory about women. He threw the rifle aside and drew a pistol so rapidly that Rachel thought she must have imagined it. The surviving bottle shattered, and fragments of others were destroyed along with it in an angry spray of bullets. From where Rachel stood, the targets were scarcely visible. She knew enough about weapons to realize that while the rifle shot had been difficult, the pistol shot had been well nigh impossible.

What a strange man this J. C. Tyler was, so proficient with fists and guns, yet patient with a pesky boy and gentle with her.

Yes, he had been gentle, Rachel admitted. She had

been subject to enough ungentle masculine attention to recognize restraint when she saw it. Not that her shameless behavior had merited his restraint. One touch of his mouth and the part of her long since dead—or so she had hoped—had surged to life and flooded her with an overwhelming tide of need.

No doubt J. C. Tyler thought her a loose woman. Rachel didn't want to care what he thought, but she did, and that alone was enough to frighten her. Piece by painful piece she had erected a shell of independence and self-sufficiency over the past three years. She didn't want her emotions escaping that shell.

The ravine seemed unnaturally silent as J.C. reloaded his weapons. Rachel took a step back, meaning to slip back around the bend, out of his sight. A pebble rattled beneath her foot.

J.C. whirled around, pistol in his hand and a cold, practiced menace in his eyes that made Rachel's heart stop. She froze.

"Damnation, woman! Don't you know better than to sneak up on a man with a gun in his hand?"

"I didn't sneak up on you. I've been here for some minutes. With all the noise you were making, a whole band of Cochise's warriors could have come around the bend and you wouldn't have known it."

"I'd've known it," he assured her. Then grinned suddenly. "When I was stuck full of arrows I'd've known it."

His grin was contagious. Rachel couldn't stop her mouth from twitching upward at the corner.

"I mean it, though, Rachel. Don't ever startle someone who has his finger on a trigger."

"I'll try to remember that."

He shoved his pistol into the holster that was tied to his leg. "Didn't mean to snap your head off."

"Better than blowing my head off. You have an admirable proficiency with weapons, J.C.. Are you a gunfighter?"

"Nah."

"Then what are you?"

He picked up the rifle, took a seat on a rock, and wiped down the barrel with an oily cloth that had been stuck in his belt. "I'm a horseman, in a manner of speaking."

"A horseman?"

"Yep." He sighted along the barrel, then wiped vigorously at an invisible piece of dirt that supposedly marred the gleaming gunmetal gray. "I've got property north of Santa Fe, near Glorieta, and I'm down here to earn some money to buy stock for my ranch."

"By hauling water and fixing pump handles?"

He laughed, but he didn't meet her eyes. "Not exactly. I'll tell you about it someday, probably."

Something in his voice made her not want to hear about it. "I'm sorry," she said, dropping her eyes. "I know out here one isn't supposed to ask too many questions. There are too many men trying to get away from a past they'd rather forget."

"Well, I'm not running from the law, or anything like that," he assured her. "And I've got nothing in my past that I need to escape."

She dared a look at him, and found that he had her pinned on a gaze that was sharp and gentle at the same time.

"Rachel, are these questions because of what happened this afternoon? I am sorry for that. I don't know what came over me."

Perhaps, Rachel thought silently, the same thing that had come over her. "No. I . . . really . . . there's no need for you to apologize. That was as much my fault as yours."

"Was it?" His level-eyed gaze seemed to probe effortlessly into her soul without revealing a thing about his own feelings.

"Yes," she said hastily. "It was. But, to tell the truth, I am concerned about Peter. Since this afternoon he's done nothing but sing your praises. When you put him up on that horse of yours, I'm afraid you became quite a hero to him."

He smiled suddenly. "Didn't have the same effect on you, I see."

Suddenly feeling very vulnerable, she refused to return his smile. "Are you someone a small boy should look upon as a hero, J.C.?"

He glanced down, sighed, and gave the rifle barrel a final wipe. "Probably not," he finally admitted. "But don't worry about Peter. He's a good kid underneath all that sass. If he thinks I'm a hero, then I'll try not to let him down."

Rachel wondered why she wasn't reassured, either for Peter's sake or for her own.

 5

Peter was in a helpful mood the next morning. He had the day's firewood split before breakfast, and after breakfast he helped Rachel clean the boarders' rooms. His mother suspected that his new attitude had something to do with J. C. Tyler's horse and the hope that she would give permission for him to ride it again. He talked incessantly of the stallion, of its tractability, easy gaits, clean, strong limbs, and superior intelligence. Peter also took pains to point out how diligent J.C. was about watching him to make sure he didn't get hurt.

Rachel had something more important than O'Malley to discuss with Peter that morning, however. She wished the subject were as simple as cautioning her son about J.C.'s horse, but it was a good deal more painful. She put it off for as long as she could. By midmorning, however, the roadhouse was swept, scrubbed, and dusted from top to bottom, the firewood cut, the cow milked, and the eggs collected. Rachel could find no more excuses to postpone what she had to say.

So when Peter ambled into the kitchen looking hungry, Rachel suggested that he pour them both a cup of milk. "We can sit at the table and relax a bit," she said. "You've been very busy this morning. It's time to take a break."

"Okay."

Rachel watched him as he poured from the big jar of this morning's milk into two tin mugs. He was a fine boy, she thought lovingly, despite the problems she'd had with him recently. Little wonder that he could be angry and resentful. She had dragged him from one place to another, never giving him time to make friends or get settled in a school. What kind of life was that for a child? Soon they would probably have to move from Tubac as well, for the Apache menace had gotten steadily worse since the year before, when the troops that had been stationed in Tubac were moved to Tucson. People were leaving in a steady stream. Tubac was a far cry from what it had been during its days as headquarters of Charles Poston's mining companies. Poston's store had closed after the troops had left, and everything else was closing down as well.

Rachel vowed she would find a safe place for them both, somewhere where they could settle for good and have a normal life, somewhere Cabell would never think to look for them.

"It's kinda warm," Peter said as he gave her one of the mugs of milk.

"That's okay. It's very fresh."

"Yeah, ol' Brownie gave a lot this morning. I showed J.C. how to milk a cow. He had a cow when he was a kid," Peter told her. "But he's lost the touch. That's what he said. Milking a cow takes a special touch, just like gentling a horse."

If Peter got onto the subject of horses—specifically J. C. Tyler's flashy red stallion—Rachel would never get him off of it. She couldn't delay any longer.

"Peter, I have something important to talk to you about."

The boy's face instantly assumed a look of pleading. "Ma, I should be able to ride a horse! O'Malley's real gentle. He'd never throw me off. J.C. will—"

"I don't want to talk about the horse right now."

"But—"

"We'll talk about J.C. and his horse later, and I promise to listen to what you have to say. Right now we need to talk about your father."

The eagerness fled from Peter's face, leaving his expression blank.

"I got a letter from my good friend Nell Blanchard. You remember Nell?"

"Sorta," Peter said cautiously.

"She wrote me that your father has gone to court and talked to a judge, and that the judge has granted him a divorce. That means that your father and I are no longer married."

"Not married? How can you not be married? You're my parents. Parents are always married."

"Sometimes people get unmarried. That's what's called divorce."

"Why did Father do that? That's stupid!" Peter's lower lip started to creep out. His brows puckered in confusion. "I don't understand."

Rachel sighed, wondering how to explain the half-truths she'd told her son to spare him the harshness of reality. "I once said we were taking a long vacation away from your father, Peter. Divorce means we won't be going back, ever."

"Not ever?"

"No. Not ever. I'm sorry."

Peter frowned into his cup of milk. Rachel could almost see the wheels turning in his mind. How much did he remember of their life with Cabell? she wondered. Had he nourished a hope that they would go home to Georgia and be a family again?

Perhaps she herself had nourished that hope, Rachel realized. In spite of everything, had she secretly, illogically expected that somehow her story would have a happy ending? Was that why she had been truly surprised that Cabell had divorced her?

"Did Father divorce me too?" Peter finally asked.

"Darling, no! Parents don't divorce their children. Your father will always be your father, even if you don't live with him. And he loves you. I know he does."

"He doesn't!" Peter declared vehemently. "And I don't love him either! He doesn't want us! He doesn't want me! He's not my father anymore!"

"Peter . . ." Rachel didn't want him to think of Cabell that way. Cabell might not be her husband any longer, but he would always be Peter's father. Throughout these difficult three years she had encouraged her son's memories of the good times and hoped he'd been too young to take much notice of the bad ones. "Peter, your father has some things that are making him . . ." Crazy? Angry? Pitiful? What word could she use that wouldn't paint a black image in a child's mind? ". . . that are making him sad. Right now it's better that you and I are away from him, but he'll always be your father, and when you're older, you'll want to visit him and make up your mind if you can be friends with him. Don't make up your mind now."

"I won't ever visit him!" Peter declared. "I don't ever want to see him again. He could die and I wouldn't care!"

"Peter! You don't mean that!"

"Yes, I do." He got up, overturning his chair in the

process. "Father doesn't love us. He doesn't love me. I wish I didn't have a father!"

He bolted into the dining room and was out the front door before Rachel could stop him. Helplessly she watched him run down the street.

A misty Georgia morning had given way to blue skies and a pleasant, cooling breeze in time for the church picnic. Today was a special celebration for the congregation, for their place of worship had been burned by Sherman's troops during the War. The Yankees had left only a scorched shell standing. Even the steeple had collapsed. It had taken the congregation six long years to gather the funds and accomplish the planning to have another church built. That just-dedicated edifice now stood proudly above the gardens and lawn and the little fenced cemetery. With its colonnaded portico and fine bell tower, it was much grander than the former church.

The congregation who gathered on the lawn had not recovered their glory quite as well as the church, however. The women's gowns showed evidence of mending and much wear. More than one man bore the scars of war—a limp, a missing limb, or simply a once-arrogant face soured by lingering bitterness and painfully earned humility. Plow horses and nags now stood in the harnesses of carriages once pulled by matched teams of high-stepping, highly bred carriage steeds.

"The South may rise again," Stephen Barton said, toasting Cabell Dorset with a glass of lemonade, "but I fear that I won't rise with it. I suppose I should be grateful that a neighbor and Southerner acquired Serenity instead of some grasping carpetbagger, but damned if it doesn't hurt. My great-grandfather built that house and first planted those acres. I always thought my great-grandchildren would live there long after I'm gone."

"Perhaps when things get better, you can buy the place back from Manchester," Cabell suggested.

"Not likely. He's planning to sell off a good deal of the acreage. To his enterprising Yankee friends, no doubt. Things are never going to be the way they were before."

"Don't I know it!"

The bitterness in Cabell's voice silenced Barton for a moment. He cleared his throat awkwardly. "You've had a rotten time of it, Cabell, with your wife leaving and all. I must say, man, that I admire the way you've borne up. I hear your business is doing well."

"Import-export is safer than planting in these times. My father would never have admitted it when he was alive, but it's only because of my business profits that the Dorset family has been able to hang on to River Oaks."

"You're fortunate in that way. I'm glad to see one of the old families, at least, able to stay on the land."

Bored, Cabell glanced around the gathering, looking for a reason to excuse himself from Barton. The man was an idiot and a whiner who secretly despised Cabell for having the acumen to keep his fortune and property intact after the War. Even though his words were cordial, his eyes glittered with contempt. He'd alluded to Rachel's leaving as a goad, not as an expression of sympathy.

Cabell smiled when he spotted the perfect excuse sitting in the shade of a tree across the churchyard. "Excuse me, Stephen. I see my lunch partner. Spent a whole two dollars buying her basket."

"Certainly. Go right ahead. Was thinking of going to eat, myself." He followed the direction of Cabell's gaze. "Nell Blanchard? You bought her basket?" he asked with a chuckle. "Good God, man! You're a wizard in business affairs, but you've certainly fallen behind where the ladies are concerned."

"I beg your pardon?"

"Nell Blanchard? I ask you, Cabell, can't you do better than that? If she ever had any life in her, it's dried up by now. Don't you remember the names we used to call her when we were boys?"

"We're not rude boys any longer, Stephen. Some of us, at least, have grown up to become men. Nell Blanchard may not be a charmer in either looks or simpering sweetness, but she's honest and courageous, and she has more wit in her little finger than you have in your whole head."

"Well, damned, Cabell! You don't need to be insulting. I didn't mean anything personal by it."

"Then you should keep better watch over your mouth when you're talking about a lady!"

Cabell stalked away, but he knew that his limp marred any dignity in his departure. He cursed the rifle ball that had ruined his leg. It had gone a long way toward ruining his life as well. It hadn't ruined his eyes, though, and as he looked at Nell, he admitted that Barton, on the surface of things at least, had hit the nail on the head. Nell did look spinsterish and prim, and she was certainly past the bloom of youth. Her face was too long and thin, her hair a plain mousy brown, and her body was so angular, it couldn't lay much claim to femininity.

So why the hell, Cabell wondered, had he gotten so hot with Barton? It wasn't as though he was courting the woman, or had any plans to do something so ridiculous. He sought her company because she knew where Rachel and Peter were hiding. That was all. Besides, Cabell told himself, there was no reason why he shouldn't pass a little time with Nell. They'd known each other since they were children. In some ways her lack of beauty and feminine wiles was refreshing. She was like a drink of cool, pure water after a lifetime of enduring sugary lemonade. One never had to pretend with her, because she saw through every subterfuge. Likewise there was never any doubt about where one stood in Nell's estimation.

Right now, Cabell feared, he didn't stand very high.

Nell didn't look his way as he walked toward her. Her attention was riveted on the children's game of tag, which chased this way and that over the lawn in front of her. Her nephews appeared to be the star players. She might have been their mother, she looked so proud as she watched them.

"Hello!" he said.

"Oh! Hello, Cabell."

He sat down beside her. "Lovely day, isn't it?"

"Yes, it is."

"I bought your lunch basket, you know."

Her brows lifted in surprise. "No. I didn't know."

"It's the one with the yellow checkered cloth and matching ribbons?"

"Yes."

"That's the one I bought." He grinned. "Paid a hefty price, too, in case you didn't hear the bidding. I think that means you're obligated to eat lunch with me."

She chuckled. "What I do for charity!"

He fetched the basket and returned before she could change her mind about being obliging. "Fried chicken," he noted aloud. "My favorite. Did you cook it yourself?"

"Maizie helped me."

"That's even better—no offense! But everyone knows that Maizie's fried chicken is the best in the South. I've been trying to hire her to cook for me, but she won't come."

"Before the War," Nell said, "you could have simply bought her."

"Your mother would never have sold her. Rumor had it that she kept her chained to the stove so that no one would steal her away."

"Mother never would have done such a thing."

"I was teasing."

"Were you really? Are you regaining a bit of your sense of humor, Cabell?"

"Only when I'm with you." Cabell realized that oddly enough, he was telling the truth. Only when he was with Nell did a smile come to his lips almost as easily as it had before the War.

Between them they demolished the lunch. Fried chicken, cucumbers in sour cream, biscuits, and cherry pie.

"Was that worth whatever exorbitant price you paid?" Nell asked when there was nothing left.

"Every penny. The company as well."

"You didn't buy the company, Cabell. Only the lunch. I'm not for sale."

"I didn't mean to imply that you were, Nell."

"I don't suppose I need to ask why you are showering me with this flattering attention."

He stretched out on his side in the cool grass, propping himself on one elbow. "Perhaps I simply want to retrieve my reputation by being seen with a woman of such sterling character as yourself."

She sent him a blistering look.

"It certainly doesn't do me any harm." He gave her his most charming smile. "Right now there isn't a mama here who would let her daughter be seen with me."

"No more than you deserve," Nell commented. "Did you think the stigma of divorce taints only female reputations?"

He was taken aback by the sharpness of her voice. His own bitterness, a familiar companion, rose to the surface. "Why not? After all, I'm the one who was deserted."

"For good reason, I remind you. Why do you still labor under the impression that I might have some sympathy for your plight, Cabell? We've had a similar discussion before, and I told you then what I think of your behavior toward Rachel."

Cabell forced himself to swallow the caustic reply that sprang automatically to his lips. Harsh comebacks had become a habit that was hard to break. "Yes, you did tell me. Quite clearly, I remember." He plucked absently at the grass. "Let's not fight, Nell. It's too nice an afternoon to argue."

She gave him a look as hard and bright as diamond. "If you don't want to argue, Cabell, then why did you seek my company?"

He shrugged. "Don't you think a man can seek your company for the pure enjoyment of it?"

She laughed, breaking the hard glitter of her eyes into a shower of brilliance. "Cabell, do you remember to whom you're talking?"

Cabell wondered why he'd never before noticed what truly beautiful eyes she had. They shone like the finest polished silver. "I'm talking to you, Nell. Who else?"

"Horse-face Blanchard?"

He flushed slightly. "You still remember that, do you?"

"A girl doesn't forget such a thing."

"It was a cruel name to call you. It didn't mean anything, though."

"Of course it did. I had a face that looked like a horse." She chuckled. "A fine Thoroughbred, I hope. The face hasn't changed much, and I suspect the other name—Spindleshanks I think it was—still applies as well. So you needn't try to flatter me into thinking you're pining for my sweet company."

"Ah, Nell." Cabell rolled onto his back, folded his arms beneath his head, and looked up at the blue sky. The grass beneath him was cool and refreshing, and truthfully so was the company. "We may have teased you cruelly, but I think your appearance wasn't truly what we aimed at. You were smarter and braver than any of us boys back then. I remember the piggyback races that one Fourth of July. You and Richard were paired up, and Richard whined that he didn't have a chance if he had to race with you on his back. So you carried him."

"He was smaller than I was."

"Yes, I guess he was. And doggone if you didn't win the race. Even beat me, and I prided myself on being the fastest sprinter in the parish."

"You were carrying Rachel, and she was always a dainty little thing."

"Yes." He wrenched his mind away from the path it wanted to follow. Rachel and rejection. His fist tightened, and he forced it to relax. "You taunted us with that victory for years to come."

"Just trying to keep you properly humble."

"Well," he said with a laugh, "you didn't succeed."

"That became obvious as time went by."

They reminisced about the things that had seemed so important when they were children together, recalling laughter, petty cruelties, childhood plots, secret fears, little victories that then had seemed so significant. It was pleasant to examine memories and laugh over those early days, even though Rachel kept intruding. She had been a part of those times, a redheaded elf, a cute little pest who'd grown into a beautiful obsession.

Sitting on the grass with Nell and listening to her poke gentle fun at herself and the others who had inhabited their innocent, pre-War world, he found it not so hard to slide smoothly and painlessly over those memories of Rachel. Before he knew it, they had talked the afternoon away. The ladies were directing children in the task of cleaning up the mess, and some carriages were already leaving.

"Can I see you home?" Cabell asked Nell.

"Thank you, but I came with David and Elizabeth."

"You could ride home with me. I'm sure they wouldn't mind."

"Well . . ." Her brow puckered in momentary doubt, then smoothed as she smiled. "All right. Their carriage is rather crowded."

They were the first to arrive at the Blanchard home. Cabell walked Nell to the door, where they were met by Samuel's rather surprised face. Tactfully the butler excused himself and left them alone to say good-byes in the entrance hall.

"It's been very nice spending the afternoon with you, Nell."

She raised a brow. "Even though you didn't get what you wanted?"

"What was that?"

"The whereabouts of Rachel and Peter."

His smile faded.

"Cabell, I'm not stupid. It was very pleasant being with you today. I truly did enjoy myself, even though I know what your motive was."

The old bitterness chilled the mellow mood the afternoon had given him. "I must admit it. You always were the smartest of us, Nell. But is it so wrong for a man to want his son?"

She simply looked at him. He didn't want to hear

those accusations from her lips again, but he did want to see her again.

"May I call on you, Nell?"

"Cabell, I'm not going to tell you what you want to know. I won't ever betray Rachel's trust."

"Perhaps I simply want to keep company with you."

"That's not likely, Cabell. We both know that."

Cabell sighed and opened the door, but before going out he turned to catch Nell's eyes with his own direct gaze. "May I come calling, Nell?"

She took a deep breath and eyed him dubiously, but the corners of her mouth pulled upward as though against her will.

"Yes," she answered softly, then closed the door behind him.

A barrage of wood chips flew from the cutting edge of J.C.'s ax as it bit into the dead tree. Rachel dodged the stinging volley.

"Watch out over there," J.C. called. "It's coming down any minute."

"Just shout when it starts to fall." She tossed a few more chips into the pouch she'd created by folding up the lower half of her apron. The woodchips were good fire starters. Especially these, as the wood had been dead and dry for at least a year. The tree had needed to come down for some months, but Rachel had been unsure how to go about cutting it without having it fall on the stock shed. Aldona knew no more than she. So when J.C. had offered to handle the problem for them, they took him up on it.

"How does a man from Kansas learn to fell a tree like a lumberjack?" Rachel asked J.C.

"Oh, I've been lots of places since I left Kansas, and

some of them had trees. Never can tell what a man's going to learn along the way."

Rachel squelched the urge to ask more questions. Just where had he been? What things had he done? Exactly what was he doing in a nowhere town like Tubac? She'd already done more than her share of prying, though, which was very bad manners here in the West. Too many people out here were trying to live down a past, just as she was.

J.C. swung his ax again. The dead wood creaked as he worked it free. Rachel wished Peter were here to watch this, but he hadn't yet come home from his sulk over the divorce. Too bad. He would enjoy seeing how an ax should be wielded.

To tell the truth, Rachel herself was enjoying seeing the ax so expertly wielded. Or perhaps not the ax itself, but the ax wielder. J.C.'s shirt was plastered to his skin by sweat. Well-defined muscles were sculpted in blue cotton. With every stroke and retreat of the ax those muscles rolled and swelled. His hair was damp and curly. Bright sunlight glinted among the tousled black mass and found reddish hues that gleamed like hidden fires.

Rachel had also noted that she was not the only one indulging in furtive watching. J.C.'s eyes had slid over her in more than one stealthy survey. She should have been embarrassed by the carnality of those quick looks, resentful even. But God help her, she wasn't. The glitter in his eyes made her ache in a way she hadn't ached in years. Juices that should have long since dried up started pumping into her blood. She wondered if something about divorce turned a woman into a slut. Perhaps that was why divorcées were shunned by decent folks.

"Timmmmberrr!" he called.

Rachel quickly jumped to a safe place behind J.C.,

but there was no need. The dead tree fell well away from the stock shed and well away from where she had been gathering chips—exactly, in fact, where J.C. had said it would. Rachel wondered how many women he had felled as easily.

She turned away, mentally kicking herself for the entirely inappropriate stab of jealousy that thought inspired. "I'm going to get a box for more of these chips."

"I'll start cutting this up into pieces small enough for Peter to split into firewood."

Rachel forced herself not to peek over her shoulder as the thunk of the ax started again. She was being utterly ridiculous, a grown woman getting as weak-kneed over a man as a giddy girl. Not that she could blame herself too harshly. After all, she'd been without the attentions of a man for three years. More, really, for she and Cabell hadn't exactly had a loving relationship when he returned from the War. Finding J.C. attractive was only natural; he was a splendid specimen of manhood. Moreover, he was a bit of a mystery—danger with hints of decency and gentle strength. What woman could resist such a combination?

When she got back with a box, the tree had already been stripped of most of its branches and J.C. was hard at work on the trunk. When she started gathering the wood chips, he straightened and wiped his sleeve across his brow. Exertion had deepened the bronze of his face, and his eyes truly did look like windows to the sky. One corner of his lips pulled upward in a half smile, and Rachel's heart performed a somersault similar to the acrobatics his kiss had inspired. Her own lips burned, feeling once again how his mouth had felt moving over her own.

Foolish woman, Rachel chided herself. Foolish, foolish, foolish. How quickly she forgot the valuable lessons of the past.

"Time for a break from this heat," J.C. declared. He swung the ax once more and left the blade stuck in the downed tree. "Got anything cool to drink inside?"

"Cool tea," Rachel offered. She could use a bit of cooling off herself, and not only from the sun. "It would go well with a piece of Aldona's pie."

"It surely would."

He smiled, and Rachel couldn't help but smile back. Suddenly she was very sure in her heart that J. C. Tyler, though a mystery, posed no danger. No man with such a smile could be anything but good.

"Let's go get that pie," he said.

Peter hunkered down in the brush that grew behind the stock shed. He didn't think he'd ever felt quite the way he felt now—angry, sad, resentful, confused, and hurt. All the feelings were rolled into a leaden ball that made his chest ache and his stomach hurt. Watching his mother and J.C. smiling, laughing, and doing normal, everyday tasks as if nothing were wrong, nothing had changed, made him feel even worse.

They ought to know how he felt and be sad for him. They ought to be looking for him, worried out of their heads. Never mind that he'd made all of Tubac his playground and often stayed away for hours. Never mind that he'd always resented his mother admonishing him to stay closer to the roadhouse. This was different. Peter wanted someone to be worried for him. He wanted someone to care.

But his mother and J.C. weren't thinking about him. They were thinking about each other. He could tell. J.C. looked at his mother as if she were made of sweet cream, and his mother looked back at J.C. the same way.

Peter's mood had been going downhill since he learned his parents were no longer married. His father had somehow put them both out of his life. Peter had never given the subject a lot of thought, but he'd always figured that someday they would all be together again. Now his mother told him they wouldn't. That wasn't right. That wasn't normal.

The way his mother and J.C. were acting made Peter feel even more down. He liked J.C. Any man who had a horse like O'Malley had to be all right. But even if he liked J.C., Peter's mother was, after all, his mother, and a mother shouldn't look at a man the way his mother looked at J.C.

Peter wiped away a tear that trickled down his cheek. He wanted to have parents like Manuel had parents— old and married and not looking at anyone with that kind of light in their eyes. He thought about his father. Memories were dim, and that in itself was upsetting. He could barely remember what his father looked like, or how his voice sounded, or if he was tall, short, fat, or thin. Flashes of recollection sometimes exploded in his mind—a smiling man giving him a pony with a silver bridle; a man lifting him high in the air and twirling him around as if he were a rag doll; a warm lap to sit upon while they swung upon a big swing and counted fire-flies—but he didn't know if they were real memories or dreams. Some other recalled images were not so nice, and he didn't want to think that those were true.

Peter screwed his eyes shut, as if that would eliminate the need to think. He wanted an everyday mother and father and a normal house with a big green lawn. Was that so much to ask? But his father didn't want him, and his mother would rather look at J.C. than come looking for him. He would show them all. He'd go to his favorite place and spend the night there. Maybe he wouldn't come back. Maybe he would take O'Malley and ride away from this place. He hated Tubac, and he hated everybody in it.

He stared at the door through which his mother and J.C. had disappeared, then turned and silently walked away.

 6

The first J.C. heard of the problem was the sound of doors slamming downstairs as he sat in his bedroom cleaning his boots late that night. Rachel's questioning voice floated up the stairs, then Aldona's, terse and worried. A flurry of steps thumped through the dining room and kitchen, then climbed the staircase. A door down the hallway from J.C.'s room opened and then shut. The stairs creaked once more beneath a hurried tread. Rachel's voice rose in a question and then trailed off into sobs.

"What the hell is going on?" J.C. pulled his boots onto his feet and started for the door. On second thought he went back and fastened his gunbelt around his hips before leaving.

Rachel and Aldona were in the kitchen pacing the floor as if someone had stuck a burr under their corsets. Not that either one of them was wearing such a contraption. Rachel, in fact, wore only a dressing gown over a thin linen nightgown. Her hair hung loose to her waist in a shimmering fall of fire. Boots peeked incongruously from beneath her hem and clumped to mark the rhythm of her worried pacing. Aldona was still dressed in the skirt and blouse she'd worn since morning, her apron soiled with contributions of all three of the day's meals.

"What's the problem?" J.C. asked.

Rachel's face jerked up at his entrance. Tears smeared her cheeks, making her look like a frightened, sad little girl. "J.C.! I thought you were asleep."

"Little chance of anyone sleeping with all the commotion around here. What's happening?"

"It's Peter. He hasn't come home."

"And you just noticed?" J.C. glanced out the kitchen window. The night had darkened hours ago, and the moon rode high over the Santa Ritas.

She moaned in frustration. "I took a rest before dinner and fell asleep. Aldona woke me just a few minutes ago to tell me that Peter hadn't come home for dinner. He's been gone since midmorning. Sometimes he stays away for hours when he's angry about something, because he knows it frightens me. But he always comes home for dinner. Always! He's never stayed away after dark."

Aldona handed him a cup of coffee while Rachel fought to stifle her rising sobs.

"At first I thought he was playing games with me, hiding somewhere in the yard or in a closet or under a table," Aldona said. "But we've looked everywhere, and he's not here."

"He's run away," Rachel quavered.

J.C. felt a twinge of panic himself. "Why would he do that?"

Rachel shook her head miserably. "He had a reason."

"What reason?"

"A reason to be angry!" she snapped. "A reason to run away! I thought the little imp had more sense. Oh, mercy!" Her eyes closed in pain. "When I think of all the things in this godforsaken land that could happen to a small boy . . . He could get lost. Apaches might . . ." Her face crumpled into tears.

"No, *mi amiga,*" Aldona comforted. "He is a smart boy. He will stay in town."

"I've got to find him!" She extricated herself from Aldona's comforting embrace and marched into the pantry. "Where's another lantern?" she demanded. Her desperate search sent a jar and bag of flour to the floor. "Damn! Goddammit! Where's a lantern when you need one?"

J.C. pulled her back through the door just as a stack of canned goods came crashing down in a small avalanche. He took her by the shoulders and turned her toward him. "Rachel, calm down. I'll find him."

"But—!"

He sat her firmly down in the nearest chair. "You stay put. If he comes back, you need to be here. Or someone might come with news of him. Aldona and I can search the town."

"But he's *my* son!" Her eyes were dark with pain, her face twisted in an agony of indecision.

"Do as I say. Stay here. We'll find him."

"Will you turn out the rest of the town to search as well?"

"Not yet. If you embarrass the boy, Rachel, he'll never forgive you."

"How do you know?"

J.C. smiled as Aldona handed Rachel a towel to wipe her tears. "I was once a nine-year-old boy myself. That's how I know."

It was no mystery to J.C. where Peter would hide to put a scare into his mother, and Rachel would have reached the same conclusion if her mind hadn't been in such a panic. He found Peter bedded down, fast asleep, in the empty stall next to O'Malley's. The boy didn't wake from the light of J.C.'s lantern, so J.C. hung the light from a hook in the wall and bent down to shake him.

"Peter!"

"Huh? What?" Peter came awake with a start and sat up as though he'd been launched with a spring. Straw hung from his shirt and was tangled in his hair—hair the exact color of his mother's.

"Peter, it's me. J.C."

The boy's eyes widened in alarm. He shot up and sprang for the doorway of the stall. J.C. was faster, however. He grabbed him by the waistband of his trousers and hauled him back.

"Do you know how worried and frightened your mother is?" J.C. demanded.

"I don't care!"

"Well, you ought to care, you little scamp."

Peter backed into a corner of the stall, glaring with hot, angry eyes. "I'm goin' away!" he announced sullenly. "I was gonna ride O'Malley, but he won't let me get on him."

"That's because O'Malley's thinking straighter than you are. Where the hell did you think you were going to go? And why?"

"My ma don't care! She'd rather make moon-eyes at you than think about me!"

"The hell she would!" J.C. made a face. "Moon-eyes?"

"You know." Peter rolled his eyes and oogled in demonstration. "You were makin' moon-eyes at her too. I saw you both while you were cuttin' down that tree. But you done it before then, and so has she."

J.C. had to laugh. "*That's* why you want to run away?"

The boy's bottom lip worked its way outward as he glared in sullen silence.

J.C. sighed. "Peter, sit down."

Peter merely crossed his arms over his bony chest.

"Sit, kid! Or I'll bring O'Malley in here to sit on you. And don't think he wouldn't. He's a very obliging horse, and he'll do anything I tell him."

Peter slid down the corner until his rear end hit the straw. J.C. hunkered down between the boy and the stall door.

"Peter, your mother's a young and attractive woman, and she doesn't have a husband. Men are going to look at her—make 'moon-eyes' at her—a lot. You can't tell me that I'm the only man who ever looked at your mother, and you haven't run away before now, have you?"

"She was makin' moon-eyes back!" Peter complained.

J.C. smiled with a certain amount of self-satisfaction. "And if she was, is that so bad?"

The boy's mouth tightened into a resentful line.

"Just because she looks at a man doesn't mean she cares any less for you."

"She shouldn't be lookin' at men. She's my ma."

J.C. sighed. Something was not quite right here. He settled himself more comfortably on the floor of the stall and cast his mind back to when he was an unruly, know-it-all kid.

"When I was a kid," he said, "I lived with my folks and my little brother on a farm in Kansas. I used to get mad at my folks a lot. I was in love with horses, just like you are. My dad loved horses too. He had some fine ones. I think he wanted to be a horse rancher instead of a farmer. But anyway, every time I did something wrong, I couldn't go near the horses. That was my punishment. If I didn't stack the firewood like my ma wanted me to, I couldn't go near the horses. If I whupped on my little brother, I couldn't go near the horses. If I talked smartmouth to my pa or cussed around my ma, I couldn't go near the horses."

"Geez!" Peter said, sympathizing with the severity of the punishment.

"Seems to me I was mad at my pa quite a bit of the time. My ma too. I'd get to feeling sorry for myself every once in a while and think they didn't love me like a ma and pa ought to love their son. Once I tried to run away, just like you figured to do."

"What happened?"

"My pa caught me and took his belt to my rear end. Said he was doing it for my own good, because he loved me. By that time I was big enough I could have whupped him back if I'd wanted to. I didn't, but I was madder'n hell at him.

"Two weeks later, while I was still mad at my folks, a couple of drunken saddle bums came along and shot up the place while I was in town buying supplies. They killed my folks and my little brother, then took my pa's horses and burned down the place."

Peter's eyes grew wide. "That's terrible!"

"Yeah. It was terrible." J.C. still didn't like to think about how he'd felt when he came back and discovered the slaughter. "It didn't take me long to realize how much my family had meant to me, and how much they'd cared about me in return. Sometimes, when you live with someone every day, you get so used to them loving you that you can't see it anymore. But when that love is gone, it leaves a hell of a hole in your life."

Peter bit his lip and plucked uneasily at the straw. "I guess so."

"I know so. And I know your mother really cares

about you, because I saw how frightened she is not knowing where you are."

The boy grimaced. "I guess so."

A silence crept between them, but it was an easy, companionable silence. Finally Peter sighed. "I wasn't really running away because you and Ma were making moon-eyes. Even though I didn't like it."

J.C. remained quiet.

"I can't remember what my pa looked like," Peter confided. "Ma says he's sad right now, and that's why we can't be with him. She says when I'm a lot older, I can go back and visit him, but I wouldn't know who he was, even if he was to come up to me and say hi."

J.C.'s heart jumped. He was on the edge of learning exactly what he wanted to know. He hadn't searched for Peter with that in mind, but things were certainly working out that way. So why did he feel like a stinking, lowlife skunk?

"Where is your father?"

"Georgia," Peter replied.

Georgia, J.C. reflected, was a long way from being killed by Comanches in Texas—the fate Rachel had assigned to her husband.

"He and my ma aren't married anymore. Ma told me this morning that my dad had gotten a . . . uh . . ."

"Divorce?"

"Yeah. Divorce. We're not ever going back, Ma says."

"You were running away because you want to go back to your father?"

Peter sighed. "I dunno. I dunno what I want."

"Do you remember why you left?"

Peter shrugged. "I remember Ma cryin' a lot—even after we left. I 'member goin' to Texas, to some lady who my granddad knew, but we didn't stay there, because the lady died. Since then we been all over. I hate it here.

I've hated everyplace we've been. I guess I figured to run away because I was mad at just about everything."

Peter's longing for a normal life, for his father, was obvious in every word. What had made Rachel take him away? Revenge against a husband who made her unhappy? She didn't seem capable of such malice.

"Do you miss your father?"

Peter's mouth twisted in thought. "Yeah. I guess. It'd be nice to have a father. One like Manuel's dad, or"— the boy glanced at upward at J.C.—"or someone who could teach me to ride and shoot and split wood with just a single thunk of the ax like you do."

J.C. had to stifle a laugh. First the kid whined about J.C. making eyes at his mother, and now he was practically inviting him into the family. Peter was one unhappy, confused boy.

"I think we should get back to your mother so that she'll know that you're all right. She's awfully worried."

Peter sighed. "Yeah. I'm sorry I was going to take your horse."

"I'll forgive you this time. Just don't let it happen again."

"It won't."

On the walk back to the roadhouse the boy's feet dragged more and more heavily the nearer they got to home.

"I guess I'm in real big trouble with my ma, huh?"

"Lots," J.C. agreed. "Maybe you should just explain to her what you feel, like you did to me."

"She's gonna be really mad. I'll bet I don't ever get to ride O'Malley again, even if you would let me."

"You'll just have to take it like a man," J.C. advised. "That's what we men have to do when the women in our lives catch us doing something stupid."

"Something stupid like running away?"

"Yep."

The boy stopped and gave a sigh worthy of a condemned man heading for the scaffold. "Ya know, J.C., I like you a lot."

"I like you, too, Peter."

"We're friends, right?"

"Right."

"Well, then, you don't have to call me Peter. You can call me Red. When I grow up, I'm gonna be called Big Red, and I'm not gonna be afraid of anything or anyone." He looked toward the roadhouse, pulled back his shoulders, and puffed out his bony chest. "Not even my ma."

"All right, Big Red. You ready to face the firing squad?"

"I'm ready."

J.C. watched Peter march toward the house. If the kid managed to be afraid of nothing and no one, then he was a better man than John Charles Tyler.

Rachel should have slept soundly after Peter returned safe and sound, but she didn't. She sat on the bench on the roadhouse front porch, watching the moon and nursing a restless, uneasy heart. A sense of guilt gnawed at her, making sleep impossible. Her mistakes in life had resulted in her son being so unhappy that he had tried to steal someone's horse and run away. When Peter had marched through the back door, dirty, rumpled, and decorated with straw, she had felt as though her very life had been returned to her. She'd been so relieved that a proper scolding had been beyond her.

But once Peter was safely in bed and asleep, the recriminations had come—not for him, but for herself. Peter's confession about where he'd been and what he had intended had confirmed her worst fears. For three long, difficult years she and Peter had been running, but one can never truly run from the past. Eventually the problems and mistakes of an earlier time catch up with the present. Now her past mistakes were catching up not only with her but with her innocent son.

The front door opened and a shadowy figure stepped onto the dark porch. Rachel knew immediately it was J.C., even though she couldn't see his face. Mr. Botts, the other boarder, didn't have J.C.'s height or breadth of shoulder. He stopped and leaned back against the wall.

"Nice moon," he commented.

"Yes."

"Couldn't sleep?"

Rachel sighed wearily. "It's been a difficult day."

"Peter all right?"

"He's upstairs asleep. I was so happy to see him that he got off scot-free. I don't think there are words to express how grateful I am to you for finding him."

"He was pretty easy to find. I just looked where I would have gone as a boy wanting to give my mother a good scare."

"I should have known he'd be at the stable. He loves it there. But the thought that he actually intended to take your horse and ride out on his own—that thought alone could keep me from sleeping for a whole year."

"Don't worry so much, Rachel. Peter's a good kid. Big Red—that's what he told me to call him. Seems like he doesn't know whether he wants to be a little boy or start growing into a man. Most kids go through that."

A twinge of guilty unease assaulted Rachel's gratitude. "Did Peter . . . did he talk to you about why he's so unhappy?"

"He and I talked a bit. I gather he still misses his father."

"Yes, he does." It was all right, Rachel told herself. She'd been hiding guilty secrets so long that she was beginning to see everyone as a threat. Even if Peter had told J.C. the true story, what did it matter? J.C. would hardly find her ugly past of interest.

"It's tough on a boy not having a father," he commented.

Rachel felt his eyes upon her, even though she couldn't see them. They searched through the darkness for her face, she was sure. Did he know that she hid the truth behind a much-practiced expression of innocent calm? What would he make of her past if he knew of it? Suddenly she was unbearably weary of lying and subterfuge.

"It is very tough on a boy not having a father," she admitted in a brittle voice. "Tougher still when a boy believes his father doesn't want him, when a boy's memories are a confusion of love mingling with nightmares."

J.C. was silent. She sensed his waiting and wondered if he'd known all along she'd been lying to him. Part of her railed against the urge to be truthful—the part that had been conditioned against truth by three years of running. The overpowering need to be open and honest was inescapable, however. If she couldn't trust a man like J.C., then whom could she trust? He'd just found her son and brought him home safe and sound. Despite the fact she knew so little of J.C., her heart told her that he was a good man, that he was in fact someone special who might touch her life in a special way.

"I've not been honest with you, J.C." she admitted in a soft, hesitant voice. "I'm not a widow. Peter's father is alive, in Georgia. We're divorced, he and I. Three years ago I left him and took Peter with me."

Rachel waited, glad of the concealing darkness. She didn't really want to see J.C.'s face, nor did she want him to see the naked bitterness on hers. The silence seemed to last and last. The porch boards creaked as J.C. shifted his weight. Then he sighed. The sound was weary and disappointed.

Rachel closed her eyes in pain, imagining what ran through his head to produce such a sound. He thought her a fallen woman, an irresponsible mother, a floozy, a lying bitch. Perhaps she was all of that.

"You don't talk like you're from the South," he said quietly.

She gave him a bitter smile. "Since I was leaving my past behind, I thought it best to leave the accent behind as well. Cabell wasn't happy about my leaving, especially about my taking Peter with me. He's sent detectives to find me off and on."

"You don't seem to me the sort of woman who would leave her husband."

"What sort of woman is that?" When he seemed reluctant to elaborate, she contined tersely, "How does it make sense for a woman to be punished the rest of her life for a mistake she made when she was sixteen? That's how old I was when I married Cabell—just as the War began. By the time he came back from the fighting, Peter was three. Cabell was a different man—not the one I'd married. Or maybe I didn't really know him when we got married."

J.C. was silent, and Rachel rebelled against the sudden need to excuse her behavior. This man didn't have the right to judge her. No one had the right to judge her unless he had endured the humiliation, fear, and pain that she had suffered at Cabell's hands. Even now she couldn't force herself to speak of it. After three years she was still bitterly ashamed—ashamed because a lingering bit of self-doubt still made her wonder if it wasn't something she had done to lead Cabell to hit her; shame because she had let the abuse go on for so long before she found the courage to escape. Never again, she vowed to herself. Never again would she become so dependent on a man that she buckled under to such treatment.

"My husband and I did not have a pleasant relationship," she told J.C. "To save my sanity, I ran away, and I took Peter with me." She gave J.C. a bitter smile. "I was wicked enough to leave my husband, but no power on earth would have made me leave Peter."

J.C.'s face was impassive. If there was no trace of sympathy, neither was there condemnation. His expression was as unreadable as a mask. "Have you seen your husband at all since you left him?"

"No. He doesn't know where I am. A good friend of mine wrote to tell me about the divorce. That's why Peter is so upset. I told him this morning."

"Does he want to go back to his father?"

Rachel sighed. "I don't know exactly what Peter wants." She smiled sadly. "I guess he wants the impossible. For everything to be perfect. For his father to be some sort of a hero and come riding into town declaring that we can be a family again."

"Have you ever thought of going back home and giving married life another try?"

"Married life wasn't what gave me the problem," Rachel said with a sour grimace. "My husband was what gave me the problem."

"Was he such a monster?"

Rachel shook her head. "I wouldn't call him a monster. I don't know exactly what Cabell is. But it would take a miracle to make things right between us, and I've long since stopped believing in miracles."

An awkward silence grew between them. Somewhere in the foothills a pack of coyotes sang to the moon.

Closer to home an owl hooted, lending the night a strangely peaceful feel. Rachel felt as though a weight had lifted from her heart, even though J.C. had not vociferously taken her side and declared her blameless. As she had said, she'd long ago stopped believing in miracles. But neither had he spat at her feet and hastened inside, too disgusted to bear her company. Telling the truth felt good for a change. It was liberating, exhilarating, heady stuff, the truth.

Suddenly needing to show her gratitude for everything, she got up, crossed to where he still leaned against the wall, and lightly kissed his mouth before better sense could squelch the impulse. Tonight was her night for impulsive and openhearted behavior, it seemed. His lips were cool and dry, but they left hers with a wicked tingle that was hotter than the midday sun.

Rachel hastily withdrew, a bit stunned at her own behavior. From what the dark allowed her to see of J.C.'s face, she concluded he was stunned as well. That was understandable. His face was devoid of any expression at all—an almost frightening blankness.

Suddenly J.C. came to life. The small distance she had put between them didn't quite put her beyond his reach, and he caught her arm before she could withdraw any farther.

"Come here," he commanded. His voice was quiet, husky, intense, and sent a strange thrill down Rachel's spine.

His mouth came down upon hers in a gentle attack from which there was no escape, even had she wanted to escape. The moon must have stolen her sense, Rachel concluded, for she met his assault with utter surrender. She dared even to respond to the gentle play of his tongue with hesitant caresses of her own. Her arms went around his torso and her hands explored his back. The hard thrust of him against her belly, the firm muscle of his thigh pressing between her legs, and the eager mating of their mouths created a sweet ache inside her.

When J.C. finally released her, Rachel staggered backward, dizzy with rioting sensations. He caught her before she stepped off the porch.

"Rachel . . . I—"

She pressed her fingers lightly to his lips, not knowing what he tried to say but unwilling to take the chance at spoiling the moment. What had happened between them was a fantasy, a brief cessation of reality in an all-too-harsh world. Rachel wanted to savor the moment before it shattered.

"It's late," she said softly. "I'll see you in the morning."

J.C. let her go. For a moment he stared at the door that had closed behind her, then he cursed softly.

He cursed nature for making men all too susceptible to women.

He cursed himself for still having a spot of softness in his heart after years in a heartless and jaded profession.

He cursed the doubts that ate at his conscience.

Damn it all! he thought. Rachel was a self-admitted runaway wife. Peter was a kid who needed a father if one ever did. And a duly appointed judge in the state of Georgia had declared that Peter Dorset belonged with his father, not his mother. The court wouldn't have done such a thing if it didn't have good reason, would it?

Don't be a fool! J.C. warned himself. *Four thousand dollars. A peaceful little ranch running with beautiful red foals that look like O'Malley. A home, a real life, peace. Don't throw it away because your brains are getting scrambled by a woman.*

In the storeroom off the kitchen he found some writing paper. Back in his room he resolutely sat down with pen and paper and wrote the words that would commit him once and for all to the road he had to take:

Have located your son, Peter Dorset, along with Rachel Dorset in Tubac, Arizona Territory. Apache problems make travel with boy too dangerous unless with escort. Please send funds for passage with freight wagons to Tucson or Mesilla. From there I will bring the boy by stage and train to Georgia.

Yr. obed srvt

John Charles Tyler

J.C. folded the paper and stuck it in the pocket of his shirt. He would mail the letter the next day, and then it would be done. Nothing could undo it. Not an alluring woman, a weak resolve, a soft heart, nor all the doubts in the world. Telling himself he was doing the right thing, he undressed and got into bed. Sleep would come, he told himself. All he had to do was visualize the beautiful green hills northeast of Santa Fe, a modest ranchhouse and outbuildings, a pastures full of pretty mares and O'Malley's lively offspring. He'd worked hard for his dream. He deserved it, and he was so close now that he'd be damned if anything would stand in his way.

The image of green hills and beautiful horses faded, though, and was replaced with the memory of how Rachel had looked when she was frantic over Peter's disappearance, how guilelessly she'd trusted him with the truth of who she was, and how artless had been the first brush of her lips.

Rachel Dorset was a woman whose memory could haunt a man for all his days. Just to prove it, when he at long last fell asleep, she haunted his dreams.

It was not a dream, however, but a nightmare that woke him at dawn the next morning as gunfire shattered the early-morning peace.

7

Tubac woke to the same nightmare that had come so often in its precarious history. Apaches swooped down upon the little town, the crimson dawn at their backs, a blood-chilling ululation announcing their grim intentions.

Dressed only in her nightshift and a hastily donned wrapper, Rachel barred the doors and fastened heavy wooden shutters over the windows that were designed to keep out not the wind and rain but arrows and war axes. This was not the first Apache attack she had endured, and if she stayed in Tubac, it probably wouldn't be the last. Still, the sound of shrill war cries and the sight of faces, bodies, and mounts so savagely painted filled her with sick dread.

Aldona burst from the kitchen carrying extra rifles and ammunition. She took a rifle for herself, stationed herself at one of the shuttered windows, and cocked the weapon with a look of grim determination.

"Damned heathen devils!" she muttered. "They'd better not get our cow again. She's the third cow we've bought in a year and the best milker we've ever had."

J.C. came down the stairs at a run, pistol in one hand and rifle in the other. His feet were bare, his shirt unbuttoned, his hair sticking out in all directions. The sight of him made Rachel smile, despite the grim situation, but seeing the person who followed on his heels wiped the smile from her face.

"Peter! I told you to stay upstairs!"

"I can fight!" Clutched tightly in his hand was the shotgun Rachel kept in their bedroom.

"No, you can't."

"I can shoot as good as anybody!"

"As *well* as anybody. And the answer is no!"

Aldona muttered a curse and fired through a partially open shutter. J.C., who had stationed himself at the front window, immediately followed suit.

"Peter!" Rachel shouted over the explosion of the rifle discharges. "I don't have time for this! Get under a table, and give me the shotgun."

With a defiant look Peter marched to the front window and took up station beside J.C.

Rachel didn't hesitate. She marched over to the boy, pulled him back from the window, and wrenched the shotgun out of his grasp. "You get under that table, young man, or by God, you'll wish the Apaches had taken you!"

Peter gave her a resentful look, but obeyed. Rachel imagined for an instant that J.C. glanced at her with an amused glitter in his eyes, but the next instant he was firing out the window, so she couldn't be sure.

Wallace Botts, their other boarder, was the last to stumble down the stairs. He'd taken time to don his boots and comb his hair, but his face was still creased with sleep.

"God in heaven!" he complained. "Why can't those cursed savages just leave us alone!"

"It's against their nature," J.C. commented.

Rachel handed Wallace her shotgun and pointed him toward the only unmanned window. The yips and howls of the Apaches rose and faded along with the thunder of hoofbeats as the Indians rode up and down the streets of the town and circled around the ruined walls of the old Spanish presidio. Aldona, J.C., and Wallace kept up a steady barrage of firing while Rachel went from window to window reloading weapons. She took J.C.'s rifle while he kept firing with his pistol.

"Thanks," he said, his concentration still out the window.

"I can't hit the side of a barn," Rachel commented. "But at least I can load."

"Wouldn't make much difference," J.C. told her. "Only thing I've hit so far is a couple of headfeathers. Shooting at Apaches is like shooting at shadows. One minute they're there and the next they're not."

Rachel's eyes stung from the gunsmoke. Her ears rang with the constant explosion of gunfire. Above it all was the savage, chilling cries of their attackers. When she darted a glance through Aldona's window, she saw Apaches galloping to and fro through roiling clouds of dust. They had gathered a small herd of horses at the near end of town. Some rode herd on the confused and milling horses while others galloped wildly up and down the streets, terrorizing the town with their shrieking, gunfire, and deadly arrows.

"Shit!" J.C. cursed. "They've taken O'Malley. Those damned sonsabitches! Now I'm mad." He fired into the street with renewed determination.

The warriors seemed oblivious to the return fire that issued from buildings along the street, the thickest from the saloon and the general store. Rachel could see no sign that Tubac's defenders had taken any toll on their attackers.

The Apaches' aim had been effective, though, for Will Horner, owner of the general store, lay in the street looking very dead. The Indians who rampaged up and down made a point of trampling the body.

Rachel covered her face with her hands. "Will! Poor Will!"

For the most part Tubac's citizens were fairly safe barred and shuttered within their adobe fortresses, but those caught outside during a raid often lost both their lives and their scalps.

Aldona let loose a string of Spanish expletives and shoved her rifle into Rachel's hands. "The *pendejos* are taking the livestock. Well, they won't take our cow!" She pulled Rachel toward the window. "Keep firing at them, *amiga*. I'm going to get Brownie."

"Aldona! No!" Rachel pleaded, but Aldona had disappeared through the kitchen door before the words were out of her mouth. Every colorful expletive in Rachel's limited cussing vocabulary ran through her mind as she ran after her friend. She hesitated only to turn around and prevent Peter from following her. "Get back under that table, young man! And stay there until I return."

"Rachel!" J.C. squinted at her through the gunsmoke hanging in the air. "What the hell . . . ?" His words trailed after her as she ran into the kitchen.

Aldona was halfway to the stock shed by the time Rachel reached the back door. She was afraid to call out for fear of drawing the attention of the Apaches, who were busy driving more horses from the livery barn and returning the concentrated gunfire that came from the saloon and Will Horner's store up the street. For a moment Rachel rocked back and forth in the doorway, wanting fearfully to return to the safety inside and at the same time desperate to help Aldona. The stupid cow certainly wasn't worth the risk. Brownie was a recalcitrant old creature whose chief pleasure in life was trying to kick the stuffings from whoever was trying to milk her. The ornery beast would never allow herself to be led out of the shed and into the house without throwing a fit. Aldona would need help.

The cow wasn't worth the risk of going out there, but Aldona was. Rachel muttered a hasty prayer and ran toward the shed.

J.C. got to the door just in time to see Rachel dash across the yard and disappear into the stock shed. "Goddamned senseless women!" he muttered to himself.

He checked the loading of his pistol, then cocked his rifle. The roadhouse yard was half hidden from the street, and so far the Apaches were busy rounding up horses and raising general hell. Could be, if there was a pantload of guardian angels assigned this morning to look after witless women, the Indians might not notice a cow being led from the shed to the house. Otherwise he and his rifle and pistol would just have to do the best they could.

The shed rattled with interior commotion, then the cow emerged, Aldona hauling away at its halter and Rachel pushing at the tail end. If the circumstances weren't so dire, J.C. would have laughed at the sight. Brownie was definitely getting the better of her two saviors. J.C. started to go to their aid, but before he could move, the cow bawled loudly, advertising her presence to the Apaches. In seconds a warrior galloped around the corner of the roadhouse to investigate. Alerted by his elated yips, two more followed on his heels.

Disaster broke with frightening speed. The terrified

cow lunged and broke loose. Aldona and Rachel ran for the house. More Apaches rounded the corner. J.C. downed one with a shot from his rifle, another with his pistol. Several warriors peeled away to chase the cow, but two came on, one notching an arrow in his bow, the other reaching for a rifle that hung in a scabbard on his back. The arrow flew, and Aldona fell without uttering a sound. As J.C. desperately reloaded his rifle, Rachel turned back to help her friend.

"Goddammit, run!" J.C. shouted at her.

The two grinning warriors bore down upon her, but she remained kneeling beside Aldona, who lay silent and still, an arrow through her throat. J.C. aimed his rifle carefully and fired. With a high-pitched screech, one of the warriors fell. His shriek seemed to jerk Rachel from her trance. She stood and turned to run, but before she went two steps, the other warrior lifted his rifle and fired. Rachel jerked as the impact of the bullet stopped her in midstride. Without uttering a sound, she crumpled to the ground.

J.C. screamed his anger in a cry every bit as savage as the attacking Indians'. His pistol was empty, his rifle only half reloaded. He ran forward and swung at the warrior with his rifle, using it as a club. Grinning like a death's-head, the Indian grabbed the butt end of the weapon. J.C. yanked hard, and the warrior toppled from his horse. He grabbed the Indian's own knife from its scabbard and drew it in a lethal arc across the man's throat. An instant of surprise registered on the Apache's face before he died.

J.C. quickly lifted Rachel's limp body into his arms. She stirred and moaned. "Aldona!"

She was alive! J.C.'s knees felt weak with relief as he ran with his burden to the house. Once he was inside,

Wallace Botts helped him gently lower her to the floor. J.C.'s shirt was wet and sticky with her blood.

"Aldona," Rachel whispered. Her eyes shot open, wide with pain and fear. "Where's Aldona?"

"Aldona's dead, sweetheart. She's gone."

"No! Don't let them . . . don't let them . . ." Her words trailed away in a weak plea, but she gripped his arm with the strength of desperation.

J.C. knew what she feared—that the Apaches would take Aldona's scalp. Most Mexicans believed right along with the Indians that a person so mutilated could not enter into heaven.

"I'll get her," he promised. "They won't have her."

Rachel's head whirled with pain and shock as J.C. gave her hand a squeeze. Then he was gone. She tried to concentrate through the confusion that muddled her thoughts. Fear for Aldona flooded through the muddy waters of her mind, along with a desperate need to call J.C. back. She'd sent him into danger, and she didn't remember why.

Her mouth moved, but no sound came out. Someone touched her brow and murmured something that she couldn't quite understand. Guns fired somewhere in the distance. Each shot exploded in her mind with a hurtful white light. She was cold, so cold, and here it was July. Or was it winter? The mist that seemed to enfold her was like a damp winter fog in Savannah. Somewhere at the end of a long tunnel was a boy's frantic voice. Peter, she remembered. Peter was calling her. She couldn't answer him. She couldn't even raise her hand from where it lay in something warm and sticky beside her.

The voice faded, and Rachel was no longer cold. Merciful blackness overtook her.

* * *

George Taylor Manchester sat in his library, his steel-rimmed spectacles perched on his nose, perusing the monthly accounting of Manchester Shipping. He had cause to be satisfied with himself. Many other Southern-based businesses had collapsed with the Confederacy or had died shortly after the War, strangled by a ruined economy. Not his business. His shrewdness had kept it alive during the War, despite Yankee blockades. After the War a cousin highly placed in Washington had seen to it that the Manchester holdings were not seized for taxes, treason, nor any of the other excuses that carpet-baggers used to steal property from a defeated people.

George Manchester was far from defeated. In fact the ledgers told him he was better off in the year 1870 than he had been in the years before the War. And now he had Serenity, a lovely plantation that had been postively squandered by that fool Stephen Barton. The man should have known better than to borrow so heavily against the land. Two years of crop failure should have taught him that the old ways had to be changed. If George hadn't bought the land, another piece of prime Southern property would have fallen into the hands of Northerners.

George did not intend to squander Serenity as Barton had. Some small part of the land would be sold to reduce his financial liability. The rest would be planted in a crop that was not so labor-intensive as cotton. Slavery was dead, and so was the economy it fostered. Southerners who could not adjust their thinking would not survive in this new world.

George closed the ledger and sighed. He wished his wife, Virginia, were alive to see how diligently he had preserved the Manchester fortune and status. He was pierced by a sharp pang of bitterness at the thought of how she had suffered that winter of 1864, coughing her life out with pneumonia, Yankees all around them, no medical help available. She had been an innocent in the whole disastrous mess of war, scarcely aware of the issues that divided North and South and longing only for a peaceful life with her husband. Rachel had labored desperately to save her mother, and had grieved unrelentingly when she died.

The thought of Rachel flooded George with regret. She was a constant part of his memories, but he shied away from thinking of her in the present tense. He had no daughter now, George reminded himself. At least he might as well not have one. Better that she had died alongside her mother than bring such disgrace to her family. The younger generation had no sense of decorum or responsibility, no moral fortitude, no values. He supposed it was the War that had made them so. Certainly he and Virginia had raised Rachel to be a proper lady and wife, to know her duty and to do it.

A discreet knock on the library door brought George from his woolgathering.

"Yes?"

Saul stepped into the room and closed the door quietly behind him. "Visitor, Massa Manchester. Massa Cabell's in the parlor."

"The devil he is!"

"Yassir! It's Massa Cabell all right."

George let loose a snort that made Saul retreat a step. "That wretched knave has a nerve!"

"You wan' me to boot 'im out?"

George considered for a moment. Throwing Cabell out would feel good indeed, and he certainly had every right to do it. But curiosity got the better of him. "No. Tell Master Cabell I'll be with him presently."

"Yassir. I'll do dat."

George was anxious to discover what Cabell wanted,

but attending him like some lackey called to heel—and that in his own home—was unthinkable. He could wait until George was good and ready to see him. For that devil to have the effrontery to call here was incredible, and the more George thought upon it, the more indignant he became. If Rachel's behavior had been irresponsible, Cabell's had been unthinkable. A man simply did not divorce his wife, no matter what her offense. One might separate himself from her company, forbid her name to be mentioned within his hearing, pension her off on a minimal allowance, or even lock her away in her rooms, but one simply did not seek divorce. To do so was to show weakness of character and a fatal insensitivity to one's responsibility to society. Worse still, to divorce a woman was to deal a deadly insult to a whole family for one woman's misbehavior.

Unthinkable. Unconscionable.

And Cabell Dorset—the cad!—had possessed the temerity to divorce a Manchester. If George were a younger man, and a better shot, he would have called the bounder out. Yet here the devil sat in the Manchester parlor just as though George owed him hospitality and shouldn't send him packing with a load of buckshot in his behind.

By the time he strode through the parlor doors and confronted his ex-son-in-law, George was fuming. He slammed the double doors behind him and glared at the interloper, grasping the back of a chair as though it were the only obstacle that kept him from going for Dorset's throat.

"Good afternoon, George. I'm grateful that I caught you home."

The very sight of his daughter's ex-husband made George somewhat ill. He'd always thought Cabell too handsome to be worth much as a man, and the full lips and almost feminine wealth of hair and lashes were a sign of soft character, as far as George was concerned. How true his instincts had been!

"I must say, Dorset, that you're the last man I expected to see sitting in my parlor, sipping coffee prepared in my kitchen."

"Excellent coffee it is, sir."

"What makes you think I didn't instruct the cook to lace it with cyanide?"

"No, George. You're too much of a gentleman to kill a man with something as underhanded as poison. If you wanted to send me to perdition, you'd do it in a more straightforward manner."

George's snort made him sound like a disgusted bull. "Suffice it to say that I don't hold a similarly high opinion of you."

"I suppose that's to be expected."

"You're fortunate I didn't have Saul toss you out of my house by the scruff of your neck. What do you want?"

"I want my son," Cabell said firmly.

"Really? Do you think he's hiding here at the Willows?"

"Don't be ridiculous. I don't have the foggiest notion of where Rachel and Peter are hiding. But I think you do."

George laughed contemptuously. "Cabell Dorset, you're a poor excuse for a man. First you allow your wife to get so out of hand that she takes it into her mind to leave you. Now, after three years, instead of having brought Rachel back and dealt with her in the manner of a man able to control his household, you divorce her, subjecting all of us to additional scandal and gossip. At this late date you decide you must have your son back, if not your wife, and whose help do you ask? The very man whose family you have held up to ridicule and contempt. You're not only a poor excuse for a man, you're an imbecile."

"I will ignore the insult for now," Cabell said in a tightly controlled voice, "as you are obviously overwrought."

"And you are a bounder through and through!"

"Perhaps, but if I'm a bounder, at least I'm a wealthy bounder who loves his son. Do you want to see your grandson raised by an irresponsible woman who has no respect for faithfulness or propriety? Do you want to see him raised without the advantages that wealth and status can give him?"

"By God, I didn't *want* any of this!" George snapped. He gripped the chair back with white-knuckled hands. He had renounced his daughter, yet the insults that Cabell flayed her with were bitter to bear. Wrong as Rachel had been, she was an innocent compared with her husband. "You're a fool to think I'd help you. Even if I could, I wouldn't."

"Dammit, man!" Cabell leaned forward and slammed his fist down upon the arm of his chair. "You must know Rachel's whereabouts! She's your daughter, for God's sake!"

"And she was your wife! Did that inspire her to obey or trust you?"

Cabell growled an imprecation.

"I helped her go," George admitted. "I gave her money and told her that if she must behave in such a manner, she could no longer consider herself my daughter. A distant cousin in Texas took her in."

"That much I know. I also know your relation died shortly after Rachel arrived. She is no longer where you sent her."

"If I thought she were, I wouldn't have told you. I

don't know where Rachel is, Dorset." For all its stern-
ness, his voice was desolate. "For all I know she may be
dead, and Peter with her."

"It's like she disappeared into thin air!" Cabell complained. "I've had three different damned detectives on
her trail at various times since she left, and not one of
them has come up with anything solid enough to chase.
The West is like a vortex that swallows fugitives whole
and leaves no trace."

"You'll never find them," George said with a hint of
satisfaction. "And I'm glad. I don't want my grandson
raised by a man such as you. Now, get out."

Cabell gave him a look that combined despair, frustration, and wrath. George almost felt sorry for the
man.

"You were a part of my family once," he told his ex-
son-in-law. "Not because I wanted you, but because my
daughter did. As you have seen fit to divorce her, you
are now only an unwelcome stranger. If you come calling again, I'll have Saul throw you out on your coat-
tails."

He opened the parlor doors and motioned Cabell
out. As he watched his ex-son-in-law's stiff-backed departure, George realized that he'd just thrown out the
last remnant of what had once been his family. His wife
and son were dead. His daughter and grandson might as
well be dead. He no longer had a family. No family at
all. He was alone.

Cabell halted at the sound of the door slamming behind him. He turned to glare at the fancy portico of the
Manchester mansion. Damn George Manchester, the
old goat! Damn Rachel! Damn the wide-open, trackless
West where she had disappeared with his son! And
damn himself as well. Rachel's father, useless, self-righ-
teous old fool that he was, had given him what he de-

served for being foolish and desperate enough to come here.

More than ever before, Cabell was feeling what he had lost. He was reaching the end of his options. His posters had yielded no result. Nell was impervious to his charm, loyal to Rachel as no one had ever been loyal to Cabell. And George Manchester was too steeped in bitterness to help him.

What he needed right now was a drink, Cabell decided.

Will Horner, Diego Sanchez, and Aldona Perez were laid to rest in the late afternoon of the same day they were killed. The heat being what it was in southern Arizona Territory, waiting more than a few hours to get the bodies underground was unthinkable. Rachel tried to rise from her bed to attend the burial service, but J.C. foiled the attempt.

"What do you think you're doing?" he asked as he firmly escorted her back to her bed.

A flannel nightshift was all that covered her, but Rachel was too miserable to be self-conscious. The room seemed to swim around her. Her back and right shoulder burned with pain, and every muscle in her body was watery and weak. She was so tottery on her feet, if J.C. hadn't supported her with an arm around her waist, she probably would have fallen.

"I want to go to the services," she insisted unreasonably.

"Yeah. You really look fit to get dressed and go stand in the heat."

Rachel closed her eyes as J.C. lowered her gently onto the bed and pulled up the sheet to cover her. The church bell at St. Ann's was ringing, mourning its own as it had done so many times since the Spanish had first built their presidio in Tubac over a hundred years before. Soon Aldona would be beneath the ground, and Rachel would never have a chance to say good-bye. She gritted her teeth and made another attempt to rise.

"Good Lord, woman! If common sense was gunpowder, you wouldn't have enough to blow your nose! Lie still! Look at that! You're bleeding again. Right through the bandage and onto your nightgown."

J.C. sounded like a fussy old woman—almost like Aldona, as a matter of fact. Rachel bit her lip to keep from crying. "I have to go. Someone should be there . . . who really knew her."

"You got yourself shot trying to help Aldona. You don't need to kill yourself trying to get to her graveside." With a roughened finger he scooped up the tear that ran down her cheek, and his voice softened. "Don't you think Aldona knows how much you love her? Don't you think she's kicking herself right now for going after that stupid cow and getting you shot?"

His unexpected understanding freed the flood of tears that ached for release in Rachel's eyes. Aldona had taken her in when she and Peter had first come to Tubac, uncertain of where to go or what to do, looking for a place to sleep and a meal to fill their stomachs. She had given them kindness, provided Rachel a job, and then finally offered her half interest in the roadhouse because, Aldona had sweetly lied, the work was too much for one woman alone. Poor place that it was, it had felt more like home than any other place since Rachel had left Savannah, for no other reason than Aldona's friendship.

Rachel tried to stop her blubbering, but she couldn't. She hated crying in front of others. Crying was a weakness, a plea for comfort and help, an opening for further hurt. She thought that over the last three years she had learned to be stronger than this.

J.C. fetched a clean towel to sponge her tears. "Better save some of those for when I change that bandage," he advised. "That's when you're really going to cry."

Rachel sniffed and took the towel from his hands, dabbing at her cheeks and nose with little effect. "I haven't stopped blubbering since I woke up," she complained.

"Losing a bucketful of blood and coming within a couple of inches of cashing in can do that to a person," J.C. told her with a smile.

"Sounds like you've had some experience with it."

"Some. Now, since you've managed to bleed all over that bandage again, I'd better change it." He took a dry towel and folded her fingers around it. "If you've got any tears left, try not to get them on the new bandage, eh? Sit up a bit."

Rachel turned her face away as he unbuttoned the top of her gown and gingerly threaded her right arm through the sleeve. Modesty was forgotten, however, as pain shot through her back and shoulder.

"Don't bite your lip like that or I'll have another hole to stitch closed," J.C. warned.

The only answer Rachel could manage was a growl.

"Yeah, I know it hurts. I've done this for others a time or two, and the most complimentary thing I've been called is ham-handed. Good thing you weren't awake when I was stitching you up the first time."

Rachel did have dim, nightmarish memories of nauseating pain and the sound of his voice soothing, encouraging, admonishing. She'd been near enough awake to remember the misery—and the care J.C. had taken with her, just as he was taking such care now. She ought to thank him, but her teeth were clenched so tight, she could only groan.

"You were lucky," he told her as he gently washed old blood from around her wound. "The bullet went into your upper back between your shoulder blade and spine and shot out your shoulder without hitting anything vital."

Rachel didn't feel lucky, but J.C. was trying so hard to cheer and distract her that she attempted a tight-jawed smile. She dared to glance down at her savaged flesh. "No more off-the-shoulder ball gowns."

Her halfhearted jest brought a smile to his face. "Don't worry. The rest of you is pretty enough that no man's going to notice a bullet hole or two."

Rachel started to smile, but something in J.C.'s eyes told her his comment wasn't meant as a joke. His eyes, those piercing shards of sapphire that seemed to bore right through to her soul, didn't leave hers, and the silence stretched. Before the awkwardness of the pause became unbearable, though, Peter knocked hesitantly on the bedroom door and peeked inside.

"Ma?"

"Peter!"

A mournful and frightened Peter had visited her bedside several times since she had first awakened, but she'd scarcely been able to talk to him.

"Are you better?" Peter asked.

J.C. wrapped a clean bandage around her shoulder. "She's well enough to complain about my nursing," he told Peter.

"Can I go to the burial, Ma? I . . . I wanna say 'bye to Aldona."

After what had happened that morning, Rachel wanted to keep her son locked in the roadhouse and never let him out of her sight, lest she lose him, too, but she couldn't do that.

"I'll go with him," J.C. volunteered.

Rachel's heart warmed toward him. "Thank you. I would feel better knowing that you're with him. Peter, you mind J.C."

"I promise," said the subdued boy.

"And will Peter's mother mind me if I tell her to get some sleep?" J.C. asked Rachel.

"I promise." She was fast asleep before they were both out of the room.

Rachel woke to the glow of the kerosene lamp and the smell of chicken soup.

"Good. You're awake!" came J.C.'s voice. "Are you hungry?"

Rachel turned her head and saw him sitting in the chair beside her bed. He looked tired. A two-day growth of beard darkened his cheeks and chin, and the wavering lantern light made the lines of his face seem more deeply etched than she'd ever seen them.

"Hello," she said softly, and sniffed. "Chicken soup?"

"I figured you could spare a hen, and my ma always swore that chicken soup could cure everything from a bullet wound to measles."

"I am a bit hungry. Did Peter eat?"

"Like a horse. He's fast asleep in Wallace Botts's room. Wallace decided to go up to Tucson with a few of the town's other citizens."

She glanced at the darkness beyond the window. The burial must have been over for hours.

J.C. seemed to read her mind. "Aldona's on her way to heaven, every bit as beautiful as she was in life."

"Thank you for bringing her in before the Indians . . ." She couldn't bear to think of what the Apaches would have done to Aldona's body, much less put it into words. "I had no right to send you back out into that."

"It's all right. You didn't have to send me. I would have gone anyway. Now, eat."

Self-consciously she allowed him to spoon soup into her mouth. It tasted as though he had simply thrown the chicken into the pot and let it boil, feathers and all.

"Good," she choked out.

He smiled. "No it's not, but it'll give you some strength. I'm afraid cooking isn't one of my talents. If you can't spit it on a stick and burn it over a fire, I don't know what to do with it."

She endured another spoonful. "Why are you doing this?"

"Because there's no one else to do it." J.C. shrugged. "There's not many women in this town, in case you haven't noticed, and what women there are are busy patching up their homes and their men."

The enormity of what had happened that morning settled upon Rachel with even more weight. Aldona dead. Peter so subdued that she scarcely recognized him. Even more people deserting Tubac. And herself lying in bed helpless, so weak that she was allowing a man who was the next thing to a stranger spoon-feed her horrendous-tasting soup. Suddenly she lost what little appetite she had.

"That all for now?"

"Yes. Thank you."

She looked up into J.C.'s face—a face in which a week ago she had sensed danger, mystery, and an instant attraction, all of which made her wary. Now she could only be grateful that he was here. Without him she would doubtless be dead, and Peter would be on his own in this lethal country that she had dragged him into.

"You saved my life," she said softly. "Thank you."

J.C. actually looked embarrassed.

"And now you're taking care of me and Peter when you really don't have to. You could have ridden off with the others today and no one would have thought the worse of you." She reached for his hand. It was hard and warm, and his fingers curled around hers without hesitation. "It's like you were sent straight from heaven to help us. Thank you so much." She sighed, and her eyes closed.

J.C. watched as Rachel drifted slowly back to sleep. Her hand still rested in his, and the peaceful look on her face made his conscience flinch. This was certainly the first time J. C. Tyler had ever been perceived as an agent from anything but hell.

"Rachel, Rachel," he said softly. "Heaven sure isn't what sent me here."

Heaven hadn't sent him, and heaven most likely wouldn't take him in when all was said and done. He'd spent the last fourteen years in an occupation that was about as unsavory as it could get and still be on the right side of the law, and this late date was a hell of a time to grow a conscience.

 8

The bench on the roadhouse porch afforded a wonderful view of the sunset, and on this evening, a week after the Apache raid, the sunset was a spectacular one. A line of thunderheads over the Sierritas caught the last rays of the sun. Their glowering gray underbellies almost touched the mountains, while their tops towered upward in soft, glowing shades of pink. To the north a high layer of scattered clouds glimmered a bright molten orange that lit the whole Santa Cruz Valley with a golden radiance.

As J.C., Rachel, and Peter sat together watching nature's show, J.C. stole a glance at the woman who sat next to him. The glow of the sunset softened the lines of pain that the last week had etched around her eyes and mouth. Even without the help of the deceiving light, those lines had been fading these last two days since she'd been on her feet. Rachel Dorset, alias Rachel Manchester, was one hell of a strong woman, J.C. mused. He'd had to use every trick he could think of to keep her in bed as long as he had, which probably hadn't been long enough. She'd constantly been popping up to see to one thing or another. J.C. had made sure that there was little for her to see to, however. With Peter in close attendance, he had repaired the bullet-holed window shutters, cared for the chickens—the stupidest, dirtiest birds on the face of the earth, in his opinion—chopped wood, cooked meals for Peter, Rachel, and himself, and hauled water to Aldona's pathetic little vegetable garden. Rachel had enough to worry about just getting well, he figured. And in moments when he was honest with himself, J.C. admitted he was grateful to put off confronting the reason he had come to Tubac.

After five days had passed, however, God himself couldn't have kept Rachel from getting up. J.C. hadn't objected too strenuously; he and Peter were both tired of their own cooking. And Rachel did look well, even though her arm was still in a sling. In fact, J.C. thought, Rachel looked better than well. Every day she seemed to grow more beautiful, or maybe he just noticed more things about her that were beautiful. Did any other woman have a smile that conveyed such wealth of feeling? It could be gentle, mischievous, tolerant, bright, gay, sad, even stubborn. And her eyes ran the full spectrum of green—sometimes cool and deep like a forest pool, other times glittering like cut emerald, and in rare moments that seemed to come more and more often over the last week, warm and inviting as new spring grass.

J.C. didn't want to admire Rachel, but he did. She had too much courage, too much determination, too little self-pity, and too much concern for others not to be admired. He didn't want to dream of her at night or feel desire stir when she was near, or even when she invaded his thoughts, which was too often.

It was the situation that was softening him, J.C. told

himself, not Rachel. Having someone other than himself to care for dredged up old memories of a long-ago youth. He'd forgotten how having a family around filled out the shell of a person's existence. Not that Rachel and Peter were his family or ever could be, but for this past week they'd been thrown by circumstances into a dependency that seemed like family.

What a picture they made together, J.C. thought as he regarded Rachel, who was now catching the last light of the sunset to finish a piece of mending. During the last week the reserve around her had melted, revealing a woman who was soft as she was strong. What might happen between them if she were not a woman with her past and he were not a man with his? He had tried not to think of Cabell Dorset, the reward poster that was still folded in one of his saddlebags, and the property that called to him from Glorieta. The time was very near when he would have to think about those things, have to make up his mind. He wondered if he could go through with taking Peter, knowing how much the boy meant to his mother, knowing how much she had already lost, and falling more under her spell every day.

The silence between them all was comfortable. The spectacular surrender of day to night inspired a reverent quiet similar to the respectful hush inside a church. The show was ending now, however, and the valley had darkened to the dusky blue that preceded night. Rachel had given up on her mending, and Peter was beginning to squirm.

"Hey, J.C.?" the boy finally said.

"Yeah?"

"You think you'll ever find another horse like O'Malley?"

J.C. grunted. The thought of his beautiful stallion in the hands of the Apaches hurt like hell. O'Malley had been his friend, his family, his hope for the future. "There aren't many horses out there as good as O'Malley. And if there were, I couldn't afford their price."

"Oh," Peter said in a dispirited tone.

"But I stumbled onto O'Malley out of luck. Maybe I'll have that kind of luck again someday."

"He was a beautiful horse," Rachel commented. "Not that I know that much about horses, but anyone could see he was special. I imagine he was the centerpiece of your entire ranch."

"Yeah." J.C. didn't want to talk about it, or even think about it. Right now there were a lot of things he didn't want to think about.

A lone rider trotted down the street slowly, looking left and right in the manner of a man newly arrived in an unfamiliar place, a cautious man at that.

"My goodness!" Rachel said. "A stranger. With everyone making plans to leave Tubac for someplace safer, I hardly expected any newcomers to pass by. Maybe he'll stop for supper or a room. I'd better go check the fire out back."

J.C. squinted at the stranger as he came slowly up the street. The man was uncomfortably familiar, though in the gathering darkness it was hard to see his face. The way he sat his horse—the horse itself. Damn! It was Chester Williams!

"Peter, you'd better go help your mother. She's still only got one arm, and she shouldn't be lifting much."

"Awww!"

"Go on."

J.C. followed the boy inside, mind churning. There was little doubt that Williams was pursuing the same prey J.C. had followed here. Why else would the man come to this hole-in-the-wall mud-hut town? If he saw

J.C. on the porch of the roadhouse and came in to say hello—well, Williams could jump to a conclusion just as well as any other man.

They found Rachel in the kitchen struggling to flute the crust of a pie with the fingers of her one useful hand. She looked up at J.C. and smiled one of those smiles that could make his heart skip a beat.

"Do you think we'll have a customer?"

"Don't know. Think I'll take a little walk—stretch my legs. You all right here alone with Peter?"

"Of course."

"If that fella stops by, just be careful. You can't tell what a stranger might turn out to be."

"Some strangers turn out to be very nice."

There was that smile again. Suddenly J.C. wanted to grab Rachel and Peter and run with them both to a place where beautiful smiles and courage could wipe out ugly truths. But no such place existed. The real world had just come to pay a call in Tubac.

"I'll be back soon," he said. He tried to return her smile with one of his own but found he was beyond smiling.

J.C. cautiously came out from behind the roadhouse to discover that Williams had passed them up and continued on to the cantina, or what passed for a cantina in Tubac. He decided to follow him there.

Tubac's cantina consisted of two small rooms. The main door through which Williams entered led to the saloon, which held all of three tables for customers and a longer table that passed as a bar. Off the saloon, with an inconspicuous back entrance of its own, was an even smaller room that boasted one table that was used for gambling. J.C. watched Williams go in through the main entrance, then slipped through the back entrance into the poker room. There was no true door between the two rooms, just a wide adobe archway, but this was enough of a barrier to let J.C. listen to Williams's conversation with Jesus Gallegos, the proprietor, without being noticed.

"Got beer?" Williams asked.

"Sí. Ten cents."

Williams put his money on the table and looked around while Gallegos got his drink. "Nice place," the bounty hunter lied.

Gallegos grunted noncommittally.

"Town looks a bit dead, though. You don't have much business."

Indeed the cantina was empty. Williams was lucky that Gallegos hadn't closed the doors and gone upstairs to his wife and six children.

"How many people you got in this place?" Williams asked.

Gallegos looked around the room. "One. You."

"Not in here," Williams said with a sigh. "In the town."

Gallegos shrugged. "Fewer today than yesterday. Fewer still tomorrow. Sooner or later there won't be no one left."

"Not a whole lot of folks left here, eh? Fella up in Tucson told me there's a redheaded white gal lives down here. Got a kid with 'er. You know the one?"

J.C. emerged slightly into the archway. Williams had his back to him. He shook his head at Gallegos, and placed a finger to his lips. The proprietor gave no indication he'd seen J.C.'s cautionary signal, but he gave Williams a suspicious look, then shook his head. "People come and they go. I dunno. Women don' come in here much. If you wan' a woman, Rosalie Mendoza will do it for cheap. She's out back doing chores."

J.C. could see frustration in the set of Williams's

shoulders. "You don't remember ever seeing a redhead with freckles and green eyes? Gal with color like that would be hard to miss. 'Specially around here." Williams placed a greenback on the table.

Gallegos looked at the money, then at Williams. J.C.'s jaw tightened until his teeth ached while he awaited the answer. Finally the proprietor shrugged. "Don' remember anyone like that."

Williams's exhaled breath sounded like a curse. "You know where in town I can get a room for a couple of days?"

"There's a place up the road that rents out a couple of rooms, but I think they're full up. I got a room upstairs, but the bed and curtains caught fire during the last Apache raid. You can have it if you don' mind sleepin' on the floor and don' care that ever'thin' smells like smoke."

"Shit!"

"Other'n that there's the stable, if'n you don' mind the flies. They're thick this year."

"Damned backwater, fleabitten . . ."

While Williams complained about the lack of amenities in Tubac, J.C. slipped out. He felt slightly sick to his stomach, but the queasiness had nothing to do with the musty odor of the cantina. Williams wasn't stupid, and Rachel stood out among the citizens of Tubac like a flame burning on a dark night. Williams would find Rachel and Peter, and he wouldn't waste time shilly-shallying the way J.C. had.

The time had come to finish the job he'd come to do, J.C. acknowledged. Better him than Chester Williams. The logic of it didn't prevent him from exhausting every one of his considerable vocabulary of swear words.

* * *

How long had it been? Cabell wondered. Hours? Days? A week? He had lost all sense of time. Sweet Nell, if she were here, would tell him that he'd lost all sense, period. Cabell chuckled aloud at the inane attempt at humor. The sound came out as a hoarse cough, hurting a throat burned raw by too much liquor. He took another swallow from his current bottle. The liquid spirits soothed and stung at the same time. He had forgotten just what it was he was drinking. It didn't matter. He didn't care how it tasted. He just wanted the buzz to continue, on and on and on forever. With sobriety would come guilt, and the price of clarity was pain. To hell with living in reality. Give him the shadowland of intoxication any day. If the alcohol killed him, he didn't care. Death would be no great loss.

Sobriety was a persistent suitor, however. The more Cabell drank, the more he had to drink to keep real life at bay. Even now the buzz of his brain was insufficient to erase the memories and unpleasantness that kept popping to the surface of the sludge that was his mind. He could still hear George Manchester's voice. *You're a poor excuse for a man,* it repeated again and again. *A bounder, bounder, bounder.* Well, that was true enough, Cabell acknowledged. Indeed he was a poor excuse for a man. Nell had said it also. *What kind of man raises his hand to a woman . . . ? You've always been an expert at pulling the wool over people's eyes.*

His own eyes as well, but it took liquor to do it. And lately it was taking more and more liquor. The interview with Manchester had driven home the magnitude of what he had thrown away, of what he had lost, of what he would probably never recover.

Why? To whom or what did the blame belong? The War? The Yankees? Rachel? The liquor? Was it his own fault? God help him, was it his own stupid fault?

Cabell cursed and pushed himself up from the chair in which he lounged. "Damnation!" he shouted at the top of his ravaged voice. Woozily he looked around him, realizing that he was not in a drinking establishment, but in his own library. That he recognized the room was a bad sign. He wasn't nearly drunk enough. From a painting that hung above the massive oak desk, Cabell's grandfather frowned down upon him in patriarchal judgment. Stiff-necked old bastard! What did he know of pain, guilt, anger, betrayal?

In a sudden fury Cabell threw his bottle at the painting. The glass shattered with a satisfying explosion and spattered brown liquid over his grandfather's stern face. "It is not my fault!" he shouted at the portrait. "Not my fault!"

The figure above the mantel simply continued to gaze down upon him in contempt. Cabell collapsed back into his chair, narrowly missing plunking his rear down upon an ornately carved wooden arm instead of the cushion of the seat. For a moment he stared blankly at the shards of glass lying on the hearth below the mantel, regretting the waste of liquor. His eyes fastened upon the jagged neck of the broken bottle and lingered there with morbid fascination. The edges appeared deadlier than a well-honed blade. Drops of amber liquid clung to the inner surface of the glass. Whiskey? Rum? Port? Which was it that he wallowed in tonight and for the nights and days past? His palate could no longer discern. The liquor had ruined his taste, his character, his life.

Cabell sobbed and looked once again at the jagged glass. Wouldn't it be fitting in a ghastly sort of way if the bottle that had ruined him was the instrument to end it all—all the pain and struggle? The bottle neck grew in his blurred vision, glittering edges like a jumble of razors. He could almost feel the clean pain of those edges slicing across his throat, the warm gush of blood, the peaceful slip of his tortured mind into the ultimate shadowland.

A cry rose up from his very soul and broke forth into the musty air of the library. Cabell heard the sound as if from a great distance. It went on and on, weeping, mewling, blubbering in misery. Still staring at the broken glass, he wrapped his arms around himself and rocked back and forth, back and forth, back and forth in time to the cries. A woman's face filled his mind, comforting and shaming at the same time. Not the woman who had taken his name and borne his child, but another. Nell.

Nell was about to retire when Magnolia tapped shyly on her bedroom door.

"Miz Nell, ma'am. Are ya there?"

Nell opened the door to see the youngest member of her brother's household, the cook's teenaged daughter, wide-eyed and looking like she would burst any moment with the excitement of what she had to say. "Miz Nell! Ol' Theo from Massa Cabell's place is at the back door! He's acarryin' on somethin' awful an' saying he's gotta talk to ya. I tol' 'im it's too late, but he won' go 'way, Miz Nell!"

"Very well, Magnolia. Show Theo into the parlor."

Magnolia's eyes widened even farther at the notion of showing Cabell Dorset's black valet into the family sanctum. "The parlor?"

"Yes. And don't make such a commotion that you wake the family, please. It's very late. Are all the rest of the servants in bed?"

"Yas'm! My mam's in 'er cabin, and Samuel's in 'is room. Ain't no one about but me."

"Then no one but you needs to know about our late-night caller. Now, do as I told you."

"Yas'm!"

Magnolia bounced down the hall, her face shining with the enormity of her mission. Nell smiled slightly as she watched her go, but the smile faded as she pulled on a wrapper over her nightdress. She couldn't imagine what could bring Cabell's man, Theo, out into the night to call upon her, of all people, but whatever it was, it couldn't be good.

Theo greeted her with noticeable relief. His hat was a twisted mess tortured by nervous hands. His handsome ebony face glistened with a fine sheen of perspiration. "Miz Nell!"

"What is it, Theo?"

He gave Magnolia an anxious look.

"Magnolia, you can go to bed now," Nell told the girl. The girl's face fell.

"Go on, now," Nell urged. "Everything is fine."

"Yas'm."

"Now, Theo," Nell continued when the door had closed behind Magnolia. "What's wrong?"

"It's Massa Cabell. He's gone crazy, I think, moanin' and rockin' and cryin'."

Nell sighed. "He's drunk."

"Yas'm. He be drunk all right. For a week he been suckin' on that bottle like it was his mama's . . . uh . . . well . . . he been suckin' on the bottle somethin' fierce. But it's more. I'se afraid he's gonna do somethin' awful, Miz Nell, and he keeps callin' fer you. I wouldn't ha' come here 'ceptin' for that. He keep callin' your name."

"Are you sure he's calling *my* name?"

"Yas'm. 'Nell!' he call. 'Nell!' Then he be mumblin' all sorts of nonsense an' cryin' like a babe. I tried to get 'im up to 'is bed, but he took after me like a wild man. The devil done got him by the throat this time, Miz Nell. Maybe if Massa Cabell see you, he'll calm down."

"Where is he?"

"At the house. In the library. Same place he's been all week. Hasn't stirred from that room, he hasn't."

Nell shook her head. Theo asked the impossible. No decent woman would leave her house in the middle of the night to pull a drunkard from a liquor-induced tantrum. It wasn't fair of Theo to ask. It wasn't fair of Cabell to call out her name. It wasn't fair of her heart to melt with pity for the scoundrel.

"All right, I'll come. Give me a few moments to dress."

Theo looked as if he might drop to his knees in gratitude. "God bless you, Miz Nell. You're a holy angel is what you are."

"No doubt," Nell agreed with a wry hint of a smile. "Wait for me on the front veranda. I'll just be a moment."

Magnolia was on the other side of the parlor door when Nell opened it. The impish grin she gave Nell held not a trace of guilt.

"Magnolia, you scamp! Not a word of this to anyone, you hear?"

"Yas'm! Ma mouth is shut tight!"

"You keep it that way, or I'll take the switch to you right after Master David takes the switch to me."

"Yas'm!" Magnolia giggled. The girl knew that neither switching was likely.

Thirty minutes later Nell walked through the servants' and tradesmen's entrance of Cabell's grand three-storied mansion—the house that he'd bought right after he wed Rachel, the house where Rachel had given birth to Peter, the house that Rachel had fled one dark night three years ago. Nell had been here often enough visiting her best friend, both during the War, when Cabell was gone and Rachel had been melancholy with missing him, and then after the War, when Rachel had been melancholy for other reasons. Now, if Theo was to be believed, Cabell was turning the house into a tomb for himself.

If these walls could speak, Nell mused, how they might cry out against humankind's inhumanity to others, and to themselves.

The kitchen was dark and musty. The hallway was dark as well. A crack of light shone beneath the library door.

"I'll come wit' you," Theo offered.

"No. It might be better if I see him alone. I'll call you if I need you."

"Be careful, Miz Nell. Massa Cabell be strong as a bull when he be riled, an' he riles easy when he's got the liquor in 'im."

The first thing that struck Nell as she entered the library was the stench. The sour odors of stale liquor, sweat, and vomit combined with enough power to make her want to retreat from the room and shut the door behind her. Then the soft sound of Cabell's voice transfixed her. He was calling her name. Soft and slurred, but it was her name. In the dim light of the room's one lighted lamp, she could scarcely see beyond the shadows and dark shapes of the untidy library. Cabell was not immediately apparent.

"Nell," came the sound again. Weary, hoarse, despairing.

"Cabell?"

Nell's query rang like a clear bell through the sour silence. A large chair that was situated with its back to the door jumped, its carved wooden claw feet scraping across the parquet floor. Slowly a figure rose from the chair and turned, swaying slightly, to face her. Cabell looked like he had risen from his own grave. The soul that looked out from too-bright eyes had spent the last few days previewing hell, Nell conjectured.

"Nell?" he croaked.

"Cabell, what are you doing to yourself?"

"Nell?" The pasty face grew paler, if that were possible. The blond hair that usually framed it in carefully combed waves clumped together in rumpled, greasy strings. Cabell's shoulders slumped beneath a shirt that was stained with things best left unidentified. The shirt was unbuttoned from neck to waist, baring skin that glistened with sweat and was smudged with dirt and God only knew what else. The top two buttons of his trousers were unfastened as well.

Nell closed her eyes. The proper thing to do at this point, she knew, was faint. Any proper maiden lady would have no trouble doing so. But if Nell truly had been proper, she would have never come into this room.

"Nell! My God! What are you doing here?"

Nell clenched her jaw and took a determined breath of the fetid air. "You should be careful what you call for, Cabell, for you may just get it."

Cabell's eyes rolled up into their sockets and he folded into an alcoholic heap on the floor.

Bright sunlight stabbed painfully through Cabell's bedroom window when he woke. A warm breeze belled the sheer draperies and stirred the air in the room, scenting it with the perfume of late-summer flowers. The smell was enough to make him want to throw up.

"Good morning," came a musical voice.

Cabell groaned. It hadn't been an alcoholic hallucination. Nell was here.

"Drink this," she instructed, and held a cup to his lips. A vile-smelling brew poured down his throat. His stomach lurched, then grew still.

"What're you doing here?"

"You called for me. Remember?"

"I was drunk!"

"You certainly were. Disgusting, actually. Theo feared for your life, and he was brave and loyal enough to persuade me to help you."

"Oh, God."

His skin hurt. His bones ached. His guts felt like a herd of elephants had trampled through his innards.

"Drink some more," Nell urged.

He would have pushed the cup away, but he was too weak in both body and spirit. The warm concoction was bitter, but strangely soothing. Sleep overtook him.

When he woke again, she was still there, sitting by his bedside, regarding him as a schoolmistress might regard a disappointing child. The light streaming through the window was muted and golden. Late afternoon, Cabell guessed. Considering that he had swilled liquor in mind-numbing quantities for a long stretch of time—just how long a stretch, he was afraid to ask—he felt quite well.

"I can't believe you're really here," he half whispered.

"I can't either. I sent a note to David and Elizabeth saying I've been called away to tend a sick friend. When David finds out who that sick friend is, I'm afraid we'll both be in for it."

"Don't tell him."

"I don't lie, Cabell."

Stiff-necked, prim, and proper as always. Cabell couldn't believe he had really called her name in his drunken raving. He couldn't believe she would place herself in such an untenable position by coming to him. "I'm glad you're here," he said, surprising himself. The words had slipped out before he had known they were there.

If he expected her to respond in kind, she didn't. A frown drew her face into a pucker, making her look even more like a disapproving spinster schoolmistress. "You know that you are killing yourself, don't you, Cabell?"

Cabell chuckled sourly. If memory served him right, he might have gotten the deed done the night before in a fashion much more certain than whiskey's dull threat. Then again, he probably wouldn't have had the balls to go through with it. "Don't worry about it," he advised her.

"I don't know why I should worry about it," Nell snapped, "except that it seems such a waste for you to take all the gifts God has given you and treat them with such disdain."

The sharp anger in her voice brought him more fully awake.

"Really, Cabell, do you think that this sort of destructive self-pity is worthy of a man like you? When we were children, you were always the one out in front, always the one leading, wanting to brave the world, taking chances. Sometimes you were self-centered and thoughtless, but you stood up for the rest of us when you had to. I remember you flattened Robert Danewood once for calling me a hurtful name"—she gave him a small smile—"even though you teased me with names a time or two yourself. When Rachel's dog died of the distemper, you went all the way to the next county to get her another hound puppy just like the one that died. You were a good boy, and I thought, in spite of your being too charming and too rich, that you grew into a good man. But during these last years I don't know you anymore."

Where Cabell had expected sympathy, he got judgment. His jaw tightened in resentment. "You don't know anything."

"I know that each man and woman on this earth has to find the strength to live life with honor and kindness, no matter how unkind the world is."

"You don't know anything!" he repeated more loudly. "Do you think I want to feel like this? Do you think I enjoy pickling myself in liquor? I can't stop drinking!"

"Cabell . . ."

"No!" He started to rise from the bed but thought better of it when his head began to swim. Instead he sank back and challenged her with his eyes. "Don't you dare sit there with your lily-white hands and lily-white soul and tell me that I can somehow find the strength to stop drinking. I drink to forget what I have to forget. Do you know what it feels like to point a gun at some boy's face and blow it off, see his blood and brains blow out like juice and pulp from a rotten fruit? Have you ever looked into someone's eyes at the moment you shove a sword into his belly, seen the surprise, then the pain, then the horror and fear? Have you?"

Nell had taken his hand. He didn't resist her attempt at comfort. In truth he scarcely noticed it.

"Have you ever seen a dry and dusty field turn to mud from the blood that's spilled upon it? Or breathed in the stink of a thousand bodies left to rot in the sun, bodies that once were young men with mothers, sisters, wives, sweethearts?" He shut his eyes against the images, but they kept marching across his brain. A drink was what he needed. Right then he would have given his soul for a drink, if he hadn't already given it.

"Then I came home, and I wasn't the man Rachel married." His mouth twisted bitterly. "A crippled leg and a crippled soul. She was so sweet, so brave, so . . .

pitying! Every time she looked at me, the thought of her pity made me angrier."

"Cabell . . . I don't think Rachel ever pitied you. I think the pity was all in your mind."

"What do you know?" he snapped. Then his voice gentled. "I never meant to hurt her. But when I drink, some devil gets a grip on me. Some devil who claws at my soul and wreaks havoc on everything and everyone in my life." His agony surfaced in tears that burned the back of his eyes and demanded release. He fought it, for men didn't weep like babes, but the misery was too much for him. Hot, disgraceful tears flooded his eyes and ran down his cheeks.

Nell dabbed at his face with a handkerchief.

"Get out of here!" he demanded.

"No. I won't leave you alone right now."

Cabell wept like a frightened child, hating himself for the weakness but somehow relieved to let the pain take its course. He hated Nell for being there to see his frailty and in the same thought loved her for trying to comfort him. Lord but he needed a drink!

"Go ahead and cry," Nell encouraged gently. "Beneath all that brashness you were always such a gentle man. You have every right to howl at the horror of war."

He didn't resist when she sat on the edge of the bed and brought his hot, wet face against her shoulder. The comfort she offered flowed like a balm over his writhing soul. Her fresh, clean scent reminded him that some things in the world were still untainted; her soft voice affirmed that gentleness and loyalty did still exist; and finally, the firm female flesh that pillowed his cheek, so temptingly close to his mouth, inspired his body to recall that he was, in spite of everything, still a man.

"Cabell, you're stronger than the horrors you lived and you're stronger than the whiskey," she told him.

"Scream at fate and shout out your anger, if you must, but please don't let them destroy your life."

Right now Cabell didn't feel like screaming and shouting, and the need to weep had passed. The need for something else was rising. "Nell, you must go."

"I've said I won't leave you, Cabell. Not until I'm convinced you're no longer a danger to yourself."

"I'm not a danger to myself right now," he told her. "But I'm very much a danger to you."

She laughed softly. "You put too much importance on my reputation. Believe me, Savannah's wagging tongues have juicier things to gossip about than a dried-up spinster who's been on the shelf half her life."

Cabell was suddenly angry at the words she used to belittle herself. Any woman with Nell's beautiful smile would never "dry up." A beautiful smile, smooth skin, and eyes that seemed to hold the wealth of womanly wisdom at the same time that they shone with innocence.

"You're not a dried-up spinster," he insisted. "Anything but."

"Cabell, what are you doing?"

Of its own accord his hand had moved to the fullness of her breast. He could feel her heart race at his touch, and the need in him rose higher and hotter.

"Nell, you should go. Now." His voice warned and demanded, but his hand pleaded differently.

"Cabell, don't. . . ."

He didn't want to desecrate the only friendship he had left in the world. One part of him wanted to shout at her to escape, but another, stronger part longed to beg her to stay. "You're beautiful, Nell."

"No . . ."

He pulled her down beside him and started to work on the ridiculously tiny pearl buttons that fastened her bodice. Her hands pushed hesitantly at him, then stilled. Her eyes closed as he unlaced her corset and pushed the lacy straps of her chemise from her shoulders, peeling the gauzy fabric down to reveal the bare flesh of her breasts.

Cabell's eyes worshiped her, then his mouth, his tongue, his teeth. She wept at his caresses, half fear, half awakening desire, but his need was so great that he scarcely heard. All he knew was that the woman who had come to fill his mind now lay still and compliant beneath him. He whispered sweet phrases against her soft skin, gentled her with his hands.

Her very proper and ladylike clothing was a fortress that sought to defy him, but Cabell managed to find his way through the skirts, petticoats, and pantaloons to the paradise that beckoned between her thighs. She buried her face against his shoulder and moaned when he urged her tense legs apart, but when he slipped a finger inside the incredibly tight, wet sheath, her body arched toward the caress. Impatient, desperate with craving, Cabell could not afford the time to court her as a virgin should be courted. Every sense, every nerve vibrated with urgency, driving him beyond gentleness. She cried out in pain when he plunged inside her.

"I'm sorry," he grated out as he pumped into her once, twice, thrice. "God, Nell, I'm sorry!"

He was horrified and sorry, but beyond his own control. With great effort he slowed the rhythm of his invasion, kissed the top of her head where it pressed against his shoulder, smoothed his hands over her silky buttocks in a soft caress.

"Nell, my love, relax. Relax."

Amazingly she did. Her legs opened wider to receive him. Her little cries of pain gradually became soft gasps of awakening wonder. She began to meet his thrusts in a way that drove him quickly to a gasping climax. He felt like a consummate villain and an invulnerable hero at the same moment.

"Nell," he panted as he labored for breath, "you make me strong. You're the first woman who has moved me to passion since the War. God bless you, and God help you. You make me strong."

 9

Early morning was Rachel's favorite time of day, when the world was just awakening, the air still and cool with the night's kiss, the colors of land and sky vibrant and fresh, not yet paled by the glare of the Arizona sun. Being up and about was a relief after a week spent moldering in bed, and although Aldona's death was still a tender ache in her heart, she could feel the return of vitality like a tonic coursing through her veins.

The mesquite on the hearth had burned down to a good cooking fire. Rachel used a small shovel to transfer some of the coals to the raised horseshoe on one end of the adobe platform, then set a heavy iron plate on the horseshoe to cook the morning's tortillas.

"Peter! Go fetch the eggs from the henhouse if you want breakfast!"

Peter looked up from where he sat with J.C. on a tree stump near the woodpile. They were whittling—an art that J.C. had taught Peter over the last week. Peter had taken to following J.C. like a puppy hungry for treats, and every morsel of attention he gleaned from the man was eagerly gobbled up. Rachel was glad to see her son happy. He was no longer sullen and defiant. Neither was he eager to break away from his newfound hero to pay attention to his mother's needs, but that small thing was easy to forgive. Peter had needed a man's attention for a long time.

"Peter? Did you hear me?"

"Uh . . . yes'm! I'm goin'."

He bounced up and ran to the henhouse. For the past few days it seemed a dead run was his only way of getting places. Rachel smiled at his bouncing energy as she smeared a dollop of bacon grease in a cast-iron skillet and set it on the grill over the fire.

"Need more firewood?" J.C. asked.

"I could use a bit more. How many eggs do you want?"

"Four or five ought to do it, if the hens cooperate. And a couple of those good tortillas."

"Coming up."

"I'm glad you're cooking," J.C. said with a grimace. "Peter and I were getting mighty tired of my grub."

"Ah well, you have other talents."

"Yeah, but they don't have anything to do with food. How's your shoulder?"

"It's good. See, I even have my arm out of the sling."

"You shouldn't."

"Quit being an old woman," Rachel admonished with a smile. "I'm not going to undo all your good patching."

"See that you don't."

It was the first they'd spoken that morning except for a brief hello. J.C. seemed distracted. Usually he was ready with a wry comment or idle conversation, but since last night he'd been as broody as an old hen. Rachel wondered what was wrong. Likely he was fretting about his stolen horse or whatever business had brought him to Tubac in the first place. He would probably be on his way now that she was back on her feet, and he certainly had every right to. He'd already done more for them than she had any reason to expect—carrying the load of hero, nurse, friend, and surrogate father for Peter.

She was getting spoiled, Rachel admitted, and J. C. Tyler was too good to be true. He wouldn't be around forever. Rachel needed to pick up the pieces of her life and take Peter somewhere safe, someplace where they could make their own way again. Tubac had become a playground for the Apaches. Soon it would be deserted if the present exodus continued. She'd heard the rumors about General Crook coming to the Southwest to deal with the Indian problem, and other rumors about planned attempts to treat with Cochise, but the Apaches didn't seem to be in the mood for peace. She wasn't sure they even understood the concept. The Americans and Mexicans who shared the Southwest with the Apaches weren't in the mood for peace either. Their hatred of the Indians ran deep and hot. Arizona was going to see a lot more bloodshed before it knew peace.

J.C. dropped an armload of wood beside the hearth. "Anything else you need?"

"You can see what's keeping Peter in the henhouse. He's got a running battle going with the big speckled hen. She doesn't want anybody taking her eggs."

"I'll see if I can't even the odds a bit," J.C. said with a smile.

Rachel watched him walk toward the henhouse and let her mind drift to more pleasant subjects than Apaches and generals and the necessity of fleeing to yet another place. Since leaving Cabell, she'd regarded every man with suspicion. J.C. was the first man who had won her trust, and he'd done it without even trying. He'd won more than her trust, she acknowledged. He smiled at her and she glowed inside. The most casual touch made her feel as weak as a giddy girl. She looked forward to seeing him first thing in the morning and missed him when she retired to her solitary bed at night.

Dangerous feelings, those were, for she knew very little of J. C. Tyler, nothing of his past or his plans for the future. She knew nothing of him in fact other than what she could see with her eyes and feel with her heart. She saw his patience with Peter, his gentle care of his prized horse, his gallantry toward her. A time or two she'd seen a less-than-gentlemanly gleam in his eyes, but he was a man, after all, and he'd never leered, pawed, importuned, or made a jackass out of himself as so many other men might. What little intimacy they'd shared had been at her consent, if not her open invitation. Her heart told her that J. C. Tyler was a good man. Better than a good man. He was a man she might love if she let herself.

Rachel told herself sternly that she must not let herself—not unless he indicated somehow that they might have a future together. After three years of painful, hard-won independence she certainly didn't need to turn to jelly over a pair of sky-blue eyes and a chiseled jaw.

Peter came out of the henhouse with J.C.'s hand on his shoulder. The boy had made a pouch of his shirttails, and that pouch was lumpy with eggs. When he noticed his mother looking at him, Peter grimaced, holding up a hand that bore evidence of the speckled hen's ire.

"That old biddy needs to go into the stewpot," Peter declared.

"Not as long as she produces more eggs than any of the others." Rachel smiled and tousled her son's bright hair. "You'll live, I think. Are you hungry?"

"I'm starving!"

"Then wash up."

Rachel took the eggs from Peter and cracked them into the hot skillet, then laid tortillas to cook on the iron plate over the horseshoe hearth. No sooner was breakfast cooked than it was devoured by J.C. and "Big Red," as Peter had taken to calling himself. Both of them were walking appetites, Rachel mused with fond indignation. She scarcely managed to save anything back for herself.

"Will you show me again how to whittle that chain?" Peter asked J.C. as he wiped the last remnant of egg from his mouth.

"Maybe later," J.C. told him. "I thought you told Manuel you'd go fishing with him."

"I'd rather whittle with you."

"A mess of fish would sure be good for dinner."

Peter looked thoughtful. "Yeah. I guess they would."

"I might come down to the river and share your fishing hole in a bit. You'd better catch what fish you can now, before I get there and all those fish swim over to my hook."

"No, they won't!" Peter said with an impish grin. "We'll catch them all before you come!"

"You'd better get to it, then."

"I will!"

The boy ran inside and emerged seconds later, fishing pole in hand.

"You go straight to the fishing hole and don't wander off anywhere else," J.C. called after Peter as he bounded in the direction of the river.

"I wish I could get him to do things that easily," Rachel said. "You certainly do know how to deal with small boys."

When J.C. turned to look at her, the smile that had been on his face had turned into a grim, stony mask. Rachel's instinct was to take a step in retreat. She re-

membered that flat black look of his. He'd turned it on
Bull Larsen the night he'd thrown Bull out of the roadhouse. It had frozen his face at other odd moments as
well, flickering across his features like a cold wind, then
leaving before Rachel could even wonder about what
had brought it on.

This was not a passing moment, however. All the
warmth had left his eyes, which were as chilling as blue
glacial ice. His mouth was a flat line that looked incapa-
ble of softening to a smile.

"Rachel, I have something to tell you."

The bubble was about to burst, Rachel sensed. His
tone promised the worst. He was leaving, she conjectured. Just when she had decided she could trust him,
could safely depend upon him, he decided to leave. Or
worse, he was married and going back to his wife. Or
maybe he was running from the law—a gunman or bank
robber. Her heart constricted in her chest. Fool that she
was, she didn't want to know.

"Let's go into the kitchen and sit down," he suggested.

Lord help her, but it must be bad! As if delay could
change the inevitable, Rachel cast about for any excuse
to put this off. "I . . . I have to feed the chickens, J.C.,
and then do the dishes. Can't it . . . wait a bit?"

"No." His refusal was flat and dark, and his hand
landed heavily on her uninjured shoulder to guide her
through the back door.

"Do you want some of yesterday's biscuits?" she
stalled hopefully. "There's prickly-pear jelly still in the
cupboard. It's really—"

"Rachel, be quiet and sit down."

She sat, her heart hammering.

"Rachel . . ." He sighed disconsolately. "There's no
easy way to tell you this, so I'll just bust ahead and say it.

I came to Tubac for a reason, and that reason was to find you and Peter. Your husband put out a passel of posters offering a reward to anyone who could get Peter back for him. I need the money, so I tracked you down."

Of all the dire things Rachel had imagined J.C. might be, one of Cabell's vultures was not one of them. She stared at him in mute astonishment, so stunned she could scarcely speak.

"Cabell sent out posters?" she said weakly.

J.C. took a folded paper from his shirt pocket and handed it to her. She opened it gingerly and read through the dirty creases and worn folds. She couldn't believe Cabell had done this —laid out their personal family problems in black and white, put a hefty reward on Peter's head that was bait for every lowlife piece of scum who wanted to make an easy buck.

Shock crystallized to fury. "The wretch! The miserable wretch! He hired a couple of detectives over the years, but this! To print up a . . . a *wanted* poster as though we were common criminals! For every lowlife gunman, bum, and bounty hunter. . . ." Rachel rose slowly from her stool, her hand white-knuckled, fingers curling around the edge of the table in a death grip. "Bounty hunter! That's what you are, isn't it? You live by hunting down poor miserable rogues and bringing them back to hang! You live off other men's evil and misery, and now you've decided that a woman and little boy are easier to hunt down!"

"Yeah," he said in a flat voice. "I'm a bounty hunter. I know it's hard on you, Rachel, and I'm sorry for it. I really am sorry for it. But I'm going to take the boy back to his father. Peter's better off going with me than some others who might come for him. I'll make sure he's safe."

"You're sorry for it? Sorry, you say? You belly-crawling snake! You piss-brained, stone-hearted, lying sonof-abitch! You touch my son and I'll make you sorry, all right! I'll make you sorry your mother ever birthed you! I'll make you sorry you ever gave a thought to doing Cabell's dirty work!

"Calm down, Rachel."

"Not on your life! I've met some low-down skunks, but you beat all, passing yourself off as a friend, playing up to my son, playing the Good Samaritan as if butter wouldn't melt in your mouth while all the time you were stalking us. How do you sleep at night? How do you live with yourself? How do you hide the rotten smell of your putrid soul?"

The grim line of J.C.'s mouth got a bit harder. "Take it easy, Rachel. I'm not the one who got you into this mess. If you want to fight this, don't fight me. Take it up with Cabell Dorset. Take it up with the court. I'm just doing a job."

"Your job can roast in hell with the rest of you!"

He half sat on one corner of the work table and folded his arms across his chest. "And to think that you once told me I was a saint straight from heaven!" he recalled sardonically. The flare of his nostrils and set of his mouth signaled a temper about to boil, but Rachel didn't care. Her own had already boiled over and steamed away her caution. She didn't care how mad the villain was, she was madder.

"Why did you wait so long to make your move, Mr. Bounty Hunter? Do you enjoy toying with your prey and watching the pathetic little lives you're about to destroy? Or maybe winning their trust and affection—yes their goddamned stupid affection—makes it that much more fun when you shatter them. Is that the way it is?"

His mouth twisted, and he dragged one hand over his face. When his face was revealed a second later, the passionless mask had reappeared. "You're lucky I have the honesty to tell you what's going on, Rachel. It would have been easier to take the boy without you knowing. No good-byes. No nothing. You wouldn't have had a clue about what happened to either of us. I could have let you live out your days wondering, thinking Peter was dead, or taken and tortured by Indians. Is that what I should've done?"

"Spare me your noble charity! You're enjoying the gloat! I can see it in your eyes."

"And you're standing there whining and snarling without even stopping to think what's best for your son."

"I always think first about what's best for my son!"

"Is that so? Let me tell you something, Rachel. There's posters about you and Peter littering every barroom between here and the Mississippi, and there's no shortage of scum who don't mind tracking down a woman and kid for the price your husband's offering."

"So I noticed," she inserted acidly.

"That stranger who rode into town last night is Chester Williams, a skunk who makes me look like a goddamned lily-white angel. You don't want Peter falling into the hands of him or some of the others who'll be interested in that four thousand dollars."

Rachel gave him a sour smile. "I don't see how we could get much lower than the present company."

"If you think that, sweetheart, then you don't have much acquaintance with the world you live in. I came after Peter because I need the money, but the boy means a lot more than money to me now. He's better off going back to Georgia with me than anyone else who might come after him."

"Peter is better off staying with me!" she declared in a tight voice.

"That's not what the law says," J.C. shot back, his voice dark, angry, and colored with the hurt of her insults.

"The almighty law, written by men, administered by men, for the protection of men!"

"It's wrong to deprive a boy of his father, and deprive a father of his son."

"And it's right to deprive a mother of her child?"

"It was your choice to leave."

"My choice! You don't know Cabell Dorset like I do," Rachel said bitterly. "Do you think I ran away from my husband for the fun of it? That I've fled across the continent, living in places that make hell look like a holiday resort, as a mere lark? Would I give up life in a mansion with servants and fine clothes and easy living unless I had to? Would I drag poor Peter to a place like this unless there were a greater danger waiting for us back in Georgia?"

J.C. couldn't hold her earnest, pleading gaze. Hope flickered in her heart that he had doubts about what he was doing.

"J.C., believe me, taking Peter back to his father is not the best thing for him. Cabell is a violent man, a drunkard. When he gets angry, he uses his fists on anything that riles him."

J.C. hesitated for only a moment. Rachel could see the disbelief in his eyes. "That's not what Peter tells me," he said with calm resolve.

"Peter is a nine-year-old boy! I've let him go on believing his father is a good man."

"Maybe he is a good man. You can't fault him for not being interested in his son."

She dropped her head into her hands, desperate to convince him, but not knowing how.

"If Cabell is such a villain," J.C. asked reasonably,

"why didn't you tell that to the judge and ask him to give Peter to you?"

Rachel had difficulty holding back tears. The climbing hysteria in her voice did nothing to add to her credibility. "Dammit! I didn't know Cabell had filed for divorce! Do you think I can buy the Savannah newspaper notices in the places I've lived over the past three years?"

J.C. shook his head, and the flat, hard expression once again chilled his eyes. "It's not up to me to decide if Peter goes back. The law's already decided that. The only thing I can do is make sure he goes back with a friend, not some stranger who scoops him off the street someday. I was going to wait until I could buy passage with a string of freight wagons or hire an escort, but now that Williams is here, it's important that I get Peter out of town fast. There's a string of freight wagons due through here today or tomorrow. They're headed for Mesilla, and they've got enough men along to make the trip pretty safe. I'm going to hitch on with them, taking Peter with me. You can come with us if you want, Rachel, and take this up with your husband in person."

"Damn you! You're not!" Rachel lunged for the shotgun that was propped in the corner of the kitchen. Since the last Apache raid, every room in the roadhouse had a resident weapon. Rachel had never dreamed she would have to use one against J.C.

If he was caught off guard by Rachel's sudden move, J.C. didn't show it. His only acknowledgment of the shotgun pointed at his chest was the slight lift of a brow. "Just how do you think that's going to help you?" he asked calmly.

"That should be obvious. You're not taking Peter. No one on earth is going to touch my son as long as I'm alive to defend him."

"You don't need to be so dramatic, Rachel. I'm not going to hurt Peter. I'm just taking him back where he belongs."

"He belongs with me! Now, raise your hands above your head." Rachel didn't quite know what should come next. She couldn't hold the shotgun on him forever. Neither could she tie him up while holding him at bay with the weapon.

"I think the next thing you say is throw down your guns," J.C. offered.

Rachel chewed on her lower lip as she looked him up and down. "You're not wearing your guns."

"Right. So why am I holding my hands above my head? Just what threatening thing do you expect me to do with my hands?"

"Uh . . ." Her heart hammered in her chest. How could it be that she held the shotgun and yet he seemed to be the one in charge? She couldn't order him to leave; he'd just snatch up Peter on his way out of town. She couldn't club him senseless, for that would require coming within reach of those dangerous arms. Shooting him down in cold blood would solve the problem, she reflected wryly. Could she do something like that to save Peter? Rachel didn't want to think about it.

"Rachel, this is stupid." J.C. let his arms drop. Rachel jumped at the sudden motion. Her finger jerked against the trigger, and one barrel of the shotgun fired. Lead pellets slammed into the ceiling above J.C.'s head and sent a rain of adobe, wood, and plaster down about his ears.

"Goddammit, woman! What the hell are you doing?"

"Don't move," Rachel cried, but the command came out as a frightened squeak.

"Give me that damned shotgun!" He stalked toward her, his eyes glittering with anger.

"Stay away! I'll shoot! I've still got one load!"

He paid no attention as she leveled the shotgun at his heart. "The only way you're going to shoot me is by accident. I know you, Rachel. You wouldn't swat a fly."

"I'll swat you!" Her voice quavered as she backed away from his advance. The shotgun was heavy, and her hands slick with sweat. Her injured shoulder was on fire.

"Give me the shotgun, you little idiot!"

He reached for both her and the gun. Rachel twisted away in a panic. They struggled for the weapon. J.C. shoved it upward as it fired. The ceiling suffered another casualty.

J.C. wrenched the now-useless shotgun from Rachel's hands and flung it away. "You crazy woman! You want to kill us both?"

Rachel tried to dart beneath his arm, but he caught her and pinned her against the wall. "Goddamn! If your poor husband is a drunkard, I can see why he turned to drink!"

Fury lent Rachel the strength to free her good hand. She used it to land a vicious blow to his face. He caught her arm before she could do more damage. Rachel struggled, then stilled, realizing the futility of pitting her strength against his. She looked up into his grim face and blazing eyes, and for the first time since she'd left Cabell she felt total despair.

Peter stared with wide eyes at his mother and J.C. Halfway to the river he'd noticed that he didn't have his can of bait. When he'd run back to fetch it, the raised voices inside the kitchen had inspired him to pull the back door a tiny bit ajar and look inside before he proceeded. His mother and J.C. stood stiff-legged and mean-eyed as two dogs ready to rip out each other's throats. Uncertain what to do, Peter had crouched at the door and listened. Each word he'd heard snapped another thread in his childhood tapestry of trust and dreams and happy endings. The things his mother said about his father—drunkard, violent, his father? And J.C.! J.C. was not a friend; every bit of attention he had given Peter, the riding lesson, the whittling lessons, the man-to-man talks, had been a lie. He didn't care about Peter or what Peter wanted. And he was shouting at Peter's mother. He didn't care about her either.

The shotgun blast had startled Peter off his feet and set him on his backside in the dust. He'd gotten up and lunged for the door, but the two within had been so riveted on each other that they didn't notice. To Peter's surprise neither of them was dead or even bleeding, but J.C. was advancing on his poor mother with murder in his eyes. They struggled. The shotgun fired again, and J.C. ripped it from his mother's hand and flung it aside. Peter's mother looked frightened and hurt.

All the time he'd watched and listened, Peter hurt inside for himself. Now as he stood in the doorway and saw the look in his mother's eyes, a very unchildlike anger shook him, not on his behalf, but on his mother's. It was an old anger, one that recalled nightmare flashes of shouting and cries, bruises on his mother's face, tears in her eyes. He didn't know where the images came from, hadn't remembered the anger until now. It had been buried somewhere deep inside him, beneath the loneliness and hardship of their nomadic life and his resentment at not having a normal family and a normal home. The sight of his mother imprisoned against the kitchen wall by a furious J.C. freed that long-buried anger, though. And now it burned brighter than ever.

Peter acted from instinct, letting the anger guide and goad him. He flew across the room and launched himself onto J.C.'s back.

"I'll git 'im, Ma! I'll git 'im for ya!"

Rachel's startled exclamation and J.C.'s curse collided. J.C. staggered backward with Peter's fists flying around his head and the boy's feet kicking at every place they could reach.

"Git 'im!" Peter shrieked.

Rachel grabbed the iron skillet that hung from a nail on the wall and swung it at J.C.'s head. His hands more than full with Peter on his back, J.C. couldn't dodge. The skillet connected with his skull, and he dropped like a rock.

"Oh, mercy!" Rachel whispered as she gingerly turned J.C.'s limp body onto its back.

"Is he dead?" Peter panted. "Did we kill him?"

Rachel felt for the pulse at his throat. "No. He's alive. Thank God!"

Peter gave her a despairing look. "We have to go again, don't we?"

"Yes, we do. And very quickly. Fetch me a rope from the shed so that we can tie him up."

While Peter ran for a rope, Rachel wiped the blood from the gash she'd inflicted above J.C.'s temple. She didn't know why she should bother, but it seemed necessary, somehow. The fury had left her. In fact all feeling had left her except self-condemnation. She had let her guard down. Weak and foolish, she had longed to trust, to depend upon, to love, and once again she'd been betrayed. She should have learned by now that a woman had to take care of herself and hers. Looking to a man for support and comfort only led to disaster, at least for her. The worst part of her lapse was that she'd almost led Peter into disaster as well.

"You almost made me forget the way the world really works," she told the unconscious man. "But you reminded me before it was too late. I suppose I should thank you for that."

She touched her finger lightly to his lips, remembered how his mouth had felt on hers, and sighed.

When J.C. came to his senses, he wished he hadn't. Pain throbbed through his head with every pulsebeat. His shoulders were on fire, and his hands were so numb that they might as well not be at the ends of his arms. He sorted through the chaos of his brain. Even thinking hurt. When he remembered the last moments preceding his lights going out, it hurt even more.

"Damn!" he groaned. Who could've guessed that such a small woman would be a hell of a fighter? Bested by a woman who could be blown away by a stiff breeze and a puny nine-year-old boy! Bad enough that he'd let Emilio Gonzales get the drop on him, now this. He really was losing his edge.

J.C. lay on his stomach, his hands tied behind his back and his bare ankles roped together as well. He was the one who'd told that imp of the devil the trick about taking off a man's boots and stockings before tying him up. Too many prisoners escaped by pulling their feet out of their boots. Little did he know that the boy would use it on him! The knots were secure. They didn't yield an inch when he strained against them.

"Goddammit!" he muttered into the floorplanks. *Just wait,* he promised Rachel silently. *Just wait until I catch up with you.*

Not that he could blame her too much.

"Hey in there!" came a man's voice from the front of the roadhouse. "Anybody here?"

J.C. cursed to himself when he recognized the voice. He kept silent, hoping Williams would pass on by, but luck was not with him. The front door creaked open.

Boots clumped on the dining room floorboards, crossing the room several times, then they came toward the kitchen. J.C. managed to turn on his side so that he was looking at the door into the dining room when the bounty hunter walked through it. Williams stopped. A hand reflexively went to his gun, then relaxed when he realized that J.C. was the only one in the room.

"Well. What have we here? My old friend, John Charles Tyler."

J.C. grunted churlishly.

"What kind of a mess have you gotten yourself into, boy? Could it be that we're chasin' down the same villains once again?"

"Untie me, Chester."

Williams laughed, grabbed a stool from the table, swung it under his backside, and sat. "I kinda like you just the way you are, John Charles. Seems like you almost got the best of me again. I would'a ridden right outta town if I hadn't heard that big fella in the saloon this mornin' complainin' about some redheaded gal who ran this here roadhouse. Now I find the lady's left me a little sign that she was here."

J.C. closed his eyes from the sheer mortification of the situation.

"You're losin' your touch, boy. I had to clean up after you with Gonzales. Right before they hanged 'im, he told me I should give you his regards. Looked like he was laughin' even right when they sprung the trap from beneath his feet. Now I find ya trussed like a plucked turkey by a gal and a little kid. Bedamned! I'll bet if 'er husband had known the lady was such a dangerous sort, he'd a offered a bigger reward for gettin' the kid back. Whaddaya think?"

"Dry up, Williams!"

"Looks like I've gotta clean up after ya again, John

Charles. I don't suppose you'd like to tell me which way the lady went."

"Goddammit! Untie me!"

"Or how long ago they left?"

"Would you please untie me?"

"Reduced to beggin'! It's a damned shame, John Charles. You were mighty good once. Fast with a gun and cool on nerve. But even the best of us runs into someone too tough to handle someday. Didn't figger yours would have tits and wear a skirt!"

Williams slapped his thigh and gave a loud belly laugh. "I'll see ya around, John Charles, and I'll tell the redhead hello for ya. Lucky for you she's not the killin' kind, or you'd be laid out on the floor stiff as a board."

J.C. cursed Williams, fate, and Rachel Dorset—especially Rachel Dorset, as the rival bounty hunter sauntered out the door whistling a merry tune.

10

The valley of the Santa Cruz seemed to undulate in ripples of heat. Shimmering in the far distance, silvery mirages beckoned the unwary with false promises of water, but the group traveling up the valley knew the tricks of this treacherous land, knew that the only water to be had was the muddy trickle of the river. The little cavalcade of Ochoa wagons stayed on the scorching road, trudging toward the Mexican border in the morning heat, horses and people alike sweating and dusty. Outriders watched the terrain forward, rear, and to either side while a phalanx of heavily armed men surrounded the wagons.

At midday they rested beneath a small stand of cottonwood trees, the people eating a sparse noon meal, the horses drowsing in the shade, tails switching at flies. Peter begged to help unhitch and water the horses and feed them their noon ration of grain. Robert Ochoa, a bluff, good-natured man for all that he was tough as sunbaked leather, patiently tolerated the boy's sometimes bumbling help. Rachel set to work helping Ruth and Ruth's two maids—one Mexican and the other

Pima Indian—prepare the noon meal. Even though it was a simple, cold repast, an army's worth of food was required to satisfy all the men who guarded them.

Finally Rachel filled a tin plate for herself and Peter, and they sat down on a patch of grass to eat their meal of bread, cheese, and cold beans. Ruth Ochoa joined them.

"Do you have enough to eat?" Ruth asked Rachel.

"Oh, yes. Thank you," Rachel replied.

The older woman smiled at Peter. "Boys your size need a lot to fill them up. There's a berry pie in the wagon to cheer up tonight's supper. You'll like that, won't you?"

"Yes, ma'am," Peter answered politely. "Ma, I'm finished. Can I go back to the horses?"

"Don't get in the men's way," Rachel warned. "And don't stray from the wagons."

"Yes'm."

Rachel watched her son walk off. The bounce was gone from his stride, and a walk now sufficed where the day before he'd not gone anywhere at less than a run.

"He's a fine lad," Ruth said.

"Yes." Rachel sighed. "I can't thank you enough for letting us come along with you, Ruth."

"But of course you had to come, dear. You certainly couldn't make the trip alone, and the stagecoaches have all but stopped service. Not that I blame them. Since the troops left Tubac, there's no protection for man nor beast from Cochise and his devil Chiracahua."

"Are you sure you won't reconsider taking some payment, at least for the food we eat?"

"Rachel, dear, compared with my husband, sons, and the *caballeros,* you and Peter don't eat anything at all. I'm only sorry you didn't have time to arrange for your own wagon. The baggage wagon isn't a very uncomfortable place to ride."

"It's not so bad. I don't think Señor Ortega had anything at the livery that he could give us. The last Apache raid almost wiped him out. I fear I didn't plan very well for this. Our decision to leave was very sudden."

"I understand, dear. This latest spate of violence from the Apaches has everyone poised to leave the area."

"You must be very sad to leave your beautiful ranch after you and Mr. Ochoa have worked so hard there for so long."

Ruth's sigh was resigned. "My heart is broken, and Robert's also. But a piece of land, beautiful as it is, is not worth our lives and the lives of our sons. We have already driven most of the cattle to our property west of Magdalena, though we lost a few of them to Apaches on the way. We lost a good cowboy as well to an arrow in the back. Robert is furious. He says the government in Washington should either send troops to protect us or give the whole southern part of the territory back to the Indians. That's why he is anxious to return to Mexico, to his family's property. But you know, my dear. You have lost much as well. You were very close to Señora Perez, were you not? And now you lose the roadhouse as well."

"With everyone but the Apaches leaving the area, the roadhouse would have done me little good. Tubac will soon be a ghost town."

"In truth, Rachel, I'm very happy to have your company on this journey. In this country it's so rare to have another white woman's companionship. I hope you'll consider staying with us in Magdalena until you can decide what you're going to do."

"That's very generous of you."

"We women must stick together, you know. Well, I

see Robert is summoning me. I should find out what it is he needs. We'll talk again this evening."

"Thank you, Ruth." Rachel sighed. Mexico. Once again she was dragging Peter into the unknown, but perhaps crossing the border would throw Cabell and his bloodhounds, like J. C. Tyler, off the scent.

J.C. . . . It hurt to think about him, about how foolish she'd been. If she'd been Eve in the Garden of Eden, any forbidden fruit she picked would have been rotten.

She glanced around to locate Peter. He was with the horses, as she had expected. Leaning against the muscular shoulder of one of the big, stolid draft mares, the boy looked like he had lost his best friend. In a way, Rachel reflected, he had. She got up and went over to him.

"Hi." She laid a gentle hand on his shoulder.

"Hi." He looked at the distant mountains, then down at his dusty boots—anywhere but into her eyes. "Do you . . . do you figure J.C. got out of the ropes yet?"

"Someone will come by the roadhouse and find him."

"You don't think I tied the ropes too tight, do you? I wouldn't want his hands to turn black and fall off."

"I don't think that will happen."

Peter absently rubbed the mare's shoulder with his hand. "I didn't have J.C. figured for a skunk. Did you, Ma?"

"No, Peter. I didn't figure him for a skunk either. Sometimes people turn out different from what we figure them to be."

He lifted his head and looked her full in the eyes. "Is that what happened with Father?"

Rachel couldn't move her gaze away from her son's. Those wide blue eyes that had once been so trusting were more cautious and world-weary than a child's should have been. At the tender age of nine he was growing up all too fast. She had tried to keep him co-cooned. In her heart she still longed to, but the real world kept intruding.

"I heard what you said to J.C. about Father," Peter said soberly.

"I thought you probably had." Rachel sighed. "Peter, I didn't tell you the truth about your father because I thought you were too young. But now that you're growing up, perhaps you can understand."

"He's a drunk?"

"*Drunk* is a very harsh word, Peter."

"That's the word you used."

"Yes, it is, but maybe I shouldn't have used it. Your father was a fine man, the handsomest, smartest, bravest man in all of Savannah. But when he came back from the War, he took up drinking. The whiskey made him mean. It's like he became somebody else who wasn't really your father."

"Like Mr. Larsen when he drinks?"

"Very much like Bull Larsen," Rachel agreed. Despite the seriousness of the discussion, she almost laughed to think how fastidious, aristocratic Cabell would react to being compared to the crude cowboy. "That's why I left and took you with me, Peter. Your father got very angry at me whenever he drank, and I was afraid he might get angry with you as well."

Peter closed his eyes, as if retreating into another world. For what seemed like a long time he was silent. "My father would never hurt me."

"Your father loves you, Peter. I'm sure he does. And I hope he wouldn't ever hurt you. But I wasn't sure. I'm still not sure."

"Why doesn't he just stop drinking?"

"When you're a grown man and go to visit him, why don't you ask him that?"

"I will!"

Rachel touched his cheek. A tear trickled from his eye, wetting her finger. "Peter, don't judge your father too harshly. Though he would never tell me about it, I think he had a very hard time in the War. And once whiskey gets a hold on a person, it doesn't let go very easily."

"Well, I think he's a bigger skunk than J.C.! If he comes to get me, I'll send him a-runnin'. J.C. too. You don't need to worry about any of them as long as I'm around!"

"I'm not worried, Big Red," Rachel said with a smile. "I'm just glad we're still together."

The party delayed getting on the move again while the men had a conference over the state of one of the wagon wheels. The wheel had to be repaired, they decided, before moving on. They had just gotten it off the wagon when a stranger rode in. Behind his own horse he led a big rawboned buckskin, saddled but riderless, that looked as if it had seen better days. The stranger was armed to the teeth with pistols riding both hips and a shotgun and rifle each scabbarded on the saddle.

"That isn't one of your cowboys, is it?" Rachel asked Ruth.

"No. I haven't seen him before. Probably someone who wants to ride along with us. He's taking a chance with his scalp, traveling alone in this country."

Something about the stranger struck a spark of apprehension in Rachel. She told herself she was being silly, that her experience with J.C. had her jumping at shadows. But she didn't like the looks of this man. Broad-shouldered and beefy and his face so weathered that his age was indiscernible, he had a coldness about him that could be felt rather than seen. Rachel could scarcely make out his features in the shadow of his hat, but she knew his eyes were icy, his mouth a thin, grim seam in his face. She didn't have to see it; she felt it.

The newcomer stayed mounted and talked to Robert, but his gaze roamed the camp. When he saw Rachel, the stranger grew still, and a tight, satisfied smile cracked his face. She'd been right. His mouth was thin-lipped and grim, his eyes two shards of ice. Rachel felt a pang of fear knife through her when the stranger took a leather wallet from his shirt pocket and flipped it open in Robert's face, briefly showing a badge before flipping it closed. Robert looked toward Rachel and frowned.

"Now, what do you suppose that is all about?" Ruth asked.

J.C.'s warning echoed in her head. *Peter's better off going with me than some others who might come for him . . . some others who might come for him . . . some others who might come for him.* Rachel looked quickly to where Peter had been holding one of the cowboy's horses. He was still there. She had a brief, desperate desire to mount that horse with Peter and gallop off into the desert, but immediately recognized the futility of such a move. Neither she nor Peter rode well and they would be easy to catch—if they could both manage to stay on the horse.

"What is it, Robert?" Ruth stood as her husband came over to where the women sat. The stranger, still mounted, still leading the riderless horse, followed him.

"This man's a U.S. marshal," Robert said. "Name's Williams."

"Hello, Mr. Williams."

"Ma'am." Williams touched his hat and nodded in Ruth's direction, but his gaze never left Rachel.

Ochoa looked uneasy. "The marshal's here about Miz Manchester. He has a poster about a woman who's wanted for running off with a kid. Says Miz Manchester's name is really Miz Dorset."

Rachel stood. Her heart pounded, and her palms were cold and moist with sweat.

"My goodness!" Ruth exclaimed. "How bizarre. I'm sure he must be mistaken."

"He's got a poster right here," the rancher confirmed. "Red hair and green eyes, it says, and the boy with red hair and blue eyes. Rachel Dorset. That you, Miz Manchester?"

Rachel struggled to find her voice. "I certainly never kidnapped anyone."

"Begging your pardon, ma'am"—Williams pinned her on his cold gaze like an insect skewered on a pin—"but the court said the boy was to live with your husband after the divorce. And since you won't hand him over to your law-abidin' husband, the law figures that's kidnappin'."

"Divorced!" Ruth exclaimed. "Rachel? You're divorced?"

Peter had joined the group by now. His fists were balled and his jaw clenched. "I ain't goin' back to my father! He's a drunk!"

Rachel's heart plummeted. Peter had just effectively cut the thin thread of hope that she could brazen her way out of this with a denial.

"You're divorced?" Ruth repeated, as if the concept was so outlandish that she still couldn't believe it.

"You're goin' to have to come with me, ma'am," Williams asserted. "The boy's father wants him back, and the law would like a word or two with you."

"This is ridiculous!" Rachel declared. A nightmarish sense of unreality clouded her mind. She had known Cabell hunted her, but the law? A U.S. marshal, for heaven's sake?

"No, ma'am. It ain't ridiculous. I'm sure these good people here, bein' law-abidin' folks, would advise you to come peaceful like."

Suddenly she remembered. J. C. Tyler had told her that another bounty hunter had ridden into Tubac, and his name was Williams.

"You aren't a marshal!" she accused. "You're a low-down skunk of a bounty hunter."

He sighed, reached into his shirt pockets, and brought out the badge. It looked real enough. Perhaps J.C. had lied. It wouldn't have been the only thing he'd lied about.

By now the whole camp had gathered around to listen. All eyes were on Rachel. The people who moments before had been her friends looked at her with pity, contempt, accusation, disgust. Peter pressed himself against her side and clutched her arm.

"Now, Miz Dorset, let's not trouble these good law-abidin' folks any longer. Get whatever you need to bring and sling it on the buckskin. The boy can ride with me, and you can ride the buckskin."

"Ma!"

Do something! Rachel heard in her son's voice. Her own frantic mind demanded the same, but she could think of nothing to do. Ruth Ochoa had turned her back, her spine stiff with betrayed trust. The two maids whispered to each other behind their hands. A cowboy expressed his opinion of her by spitting in the dirt, and his *compañeros* appeared to be in agreement. Robert Ochoa looked uneasy and disapproving. His two sons, both of whom had spent a good part of the morning lingering around the baggage wagon to flirt, wore faces that were chillingly blank.

"It's not a good idea to travel this country alone, marshal," the rancher said with a sigh. "Why don't you travel to Nogales with us?"

"Thanks, but I move faster on my own. We'll make out all right."

Rachel's last hope was an appeal to Robert Ochoa's gallantry. "You can't let this stranger force me and Peter to go with him, alone, without any protection. The mountains around this valley are crawling with Apaches."

"I been around these parts a lot, Miz Dorset, and I ain't been outsmarted by no Injuns yet. Like I said, we'll make out all right."

"No! I don't think you're the law at all, Mr. Williams. I'm not going with you. Neither is my son."

"I showed you the badge."

"I'm not convinced."

"Well, that's just too damned bad."

"Now, marshal—" Ochoa began when Rachel turned pleading eyes upon him.

Williams spoke a tight-voiced challenge. "You sidin' with a fugitive against the law?"

"Well, no . . ."

"Then keep out of it." He turned back to Rachel. "Get your things, missus, or you and the boy'll go without 'em. We've got a long way to ride before dark."

Ochoa looked at the ground. The cowboys began to drift away. Ruth had shooed her maids toward the women's wagon. Rachel felt as though she and Peter had suddenly ceased to exist. Williams grinned at her, and a chill went down her spine. *A skunk who makes me look like a goddamned lily-white angel.* That's what J.C. had said about Chester Williams.

"Ma?" Peter burrowed into her side, his manly declarations of protecting her forgotten.

"Go to the baggage wagon and get the valise," she said softly. "Don't worry. Everything's going to be fine."

"That's right," Williams agreed, still grinning. "Long as nobody makes trouble, ever'thin's gonna be fine."

Robert Ochoa once again urged Williams to stay, but the man declined brusquely. Rachel's last hope disappeared when Williams searched their valise and tossed out the loaded pistol that Peter had stashed between Rachel's two clean dresses and his own spare britches.

Williams grated out an unpleasant laugh when he found the gun. "Boy, your daddy's gonna have his hands full with you once we get you back to Georgia, ain't he?"

As they rode away, Peter on the front of Williams's saddle and Rachel mounted precariously on the buckskin, Robert Ochoa looked after them with a worried frown, but Ruth did not so much as glance Rachel's way.

Once out of earshot of the Ochoa wagons, Williams dropped all pretense of civil behavior. He jerked Rachel's horse up beside his own, grasped the chin of the boy who rode in front of him, and turned Peter's head toward Rachel.

"You see your momma there, boy?"

Peter answered with sullen silence.

"Your pa wants you back to the tune of four thousand dollars. But he's not offerin' a single cent for your ma. You act up on me, and she's gonna suffer. You understand?"

Reluctantly Peter nodded.

"And you, Momma. I brought you along so I don't have no trouble from the boy. But I don't need you that much. You got it? First time you try anything, the boy gets a switchin'. He probably needs one anyhow. The second time you act up, I'll put a hole in ya. No one's gonna think a thing about me shootin' you in self-defense. It's plain in most people's mind that any woman who'd run away from her husband and steal a kid doesn't have a full load in the barrel anyhow. No one'll give it a second thought. So you behave yourselves, and we'll all get along fine. That clear?"

Rachel returned Williams's glare with one of her own.

"Answer up. Both of ya."

"It's clear, Mr. Williams. Peter won't make any trouble, and neither will I."

Unless I think I can get away with it, Rachel added silently.

J.C. knelt on the ground examining the track of a shod horse that ever so slightly dented the hardpan surface. He'd lost the trail a half mile back, but luck had carried him in the right direction, and now here they were again. The imprint was distinctive to a discerning eye. The right hoof of the horse wore a shoe that had an off-center nail toward the rear, and the horse had a habit of flinging its left foot out as it picked it up, which blurred the left edge of the track. J.C. could have followed this particular horse to hell and back if he'd had to, but today the only place the track had taken him was on a southward path from Tubac in a direction parallel to the Ochoa wagons. He hoped the rider following the Ochoas was some innocent fool who didn't know any better than to ride out alone in Apache country, but it was a dim hope. Who besides Chester Williams had better reason to follow Rachel Dorset? Besides J.C. himself, that is. Who besides a bounty hunter would be riding one horse and leading another that carried neither rider nor packs, as the tracks showed? Williams was going after Peter, and Peter would need a horse to ride.

"Damn!" He got up slowly, arching his back to stretch muscles that were still sore from several hours spent lying trussed on the hard floorboards of Rachel Dorset's kitchen. His wrists and ankles were chafed raw by his struggles to free himself—an impossible task, for he himself had taught Peter the nearly foolproof knots he'd tied him with. If Señora Sevilla had not come to buy eggs from Rachel, as she did every Thursday, he might be lying there still. As it was, four hours had passed before he was discovered. Every muscle in his body ached, not to mention his ego.

For all her efforts Rachel had hopped herself from the frying pan right into the fire. She was one hell of a fighter, but she was going to lose—either to Williams or to himself. He prayed it wasn't Williams. Characters like Ramon and Emilio deserved to deal with Chester Williams. Probably J.C. himself deserved to deal with Chester Williams. But Rachel and Peter did not.

J.C. squinted into the distance, where the valley faded into a wash of pale green and purple. The air was shimmery with heat even though the afternoon was mostly spent, and a slight haze of dust might have been raised by the passage of wagons that had since passed out of sight, or it could be the remnants of a fitful wind that whirled off the line of thunderstorms that towered above the mountains. J.C. sighed and climbed back into the saddle.

"Come on, old girl." His mount was a dilapidated sorrel mare that he'd coaxed out of Señor Ortega at the Tubac livery. She was one of the few the Indians hadn't bothered to take. Apaches knew good horseflesh, and they hadn't wanted this beast. "Keep on going till I get my hands on that woman, and I promise you'll spend your last years grazing in the prettiest pastures you ever did see."

The mare plodded on. She didn't hold a candle to O'Malley, but for an old nag she had heart. There was something about females with heart and guts that got to him. Heart and guts. Rachel and the sad sorrel mare.

The sun was nearly on the horizon by the time J.C. came upon the Ochoa wagons. He'd found the spot miles back where Williams's tracks had merged with the rancher's, and he hoped the bounty hunter and Rachel might still be with the larger party.

"Strangest thing I ever did see," Robert Ochoa told him. "Fella was a right hard case all right, U.S. marshal or not. Wouldn't travel along with us. I was inclined not to let him take her and the boy, but there wasn't much I could do. He was the law, after all, and it wasn't none of my business. She didn't exactly deny all that stuff on the poster. My wife was right put out about findin' out she'd been offerin' friendship to that kinda woman. I was surprised at it myself. She seemed like a decent gal to me."

"Well, sir, Williams isn't the law. He's a bounty hunter." So was J.C., but he wasn't going to admit it to Ochoa. Right now his profession left a sour taste in his mouth. "When did they take off on their own?"

"'Bout three hours ago."

"Which direction?"

"Northeast, toward the mountains. Don't think he was headed back to Tubac."

J.C. cursed silently. There had been tracks diverging from the Ochoas' as well as converging, and he had missed them. On this rocky surface it wasn't surprising, but he'd certainly picked a hell of a time to make a mistake.

"If I was him," Ochoa continued, "I'd find myself a nice, out-of-sight wash to bed down in for the night. Something away from the road so as not to be so noticeable to the Apaches. They'll have to stop before long. Moonlight ain't no good to ride by, and you can't ride where you can't see."

J.C. squinted in the direction that Ochoa pointed. Daylight was fast fading into dusk. Ochoa was right. A man was likely to break both his horse's neck and his own riding this country in the dark. The image of Rachel and Peter enduring a night in Williams's company made knots rise along J.C.'s jawline. He had to find them before dark. Williams wouldn't be stupid enough to build a campfire whose glow and smoke might lead him—or the Indians—to their camp.

"You're welcome to bed down with us for the night," Ochoa offered.

"Thanks, but there's some light left. I figure I'll push on."

Ochoa shook his head. "Suit yourself."

J.C. read an itch for the complete story in the rancher's tone, but Ochoa didn't ask. In the West a man didn't pry into someone else's business.

"When you catch up to 'em, you tell that little lady . . . well, you tell her I'm sorry she's got such a heap of trouble. Tell her I'm sorry."

"Thanks for your help. I'll do that."

Not that she'd hear him. When he caught up with them, if he caught up with them, Rachel wasn't going to be any happier with J. C. Tyler than she'd been that morning. If he managed to get past Williams in one piece, likely she'd try to tear him limb from limb and feed him to the coyotes.

Bringing in bank robbers and murderers was an easier task.

He kneed the mare into a jolting trot, angry with himself for letting things go this wrong. If he hadn't underestimated Rachel, she and Peter wouldn't be alone in the desert with a man who picked his teeth with rattlesnake fangs. If he'd done things right, they wouldn't all be Apache bait in this stupid cat-and-mouse game. As

he headed back north, J.C. thought of Rachel and wondered whether a few *ifs* might be running through her
mind as well.

Rachel sat beside Peter, her back propped against an
acacia tree, weary in every muscle, bone, and fiber of
her being. Eating was out of the question; she had absolutely no appetite. Who could have an appetite with
Chester Williams not ten feet away? He sat propped on
his saddle, drinking from a bottle of liquor he had gotten out of his saddlebag and chewing a mouthful of
jerky. He stared at her with an unnerving intensity, and
the weight of his eyes made her want to scream. Those
eyes were the most chilling thing about the man. They
were cold as a snake's and just as passionless. No sympathy softened them. Not even lust, greed, hatred,
pity—no human emotion at all. She suspected that
Chester Williams could kill a man without twitching an
eyelash. A woman as well.

J. C. Tyler, for all his deception, had not been the sort
of creature this man was. J.C. at least was human. He
might be a low-down skunk of a bounty hunter, but he
possessed a bit of human decency. He had saved her
life, cared for her and Peter, made her laugh, made her
remember that she was a woman. All his small kind-
nesses and seeming heroism had been a treacherous
plot, it was true. He was a lying, deceiving piece of
scum, and she was ashamed and embarrassed that she'd
allowed herself to be duped. Still, Rachel hoped that
someone had found J.C. before he'd spent too many
hours on the floor of the kitchen. Not that she was truly
worried about him. Of course not! Why would she worry
about a man who had deceived and betrayed her, who
had thrown her affection back in her face with treach-
ery? J. C. Tyler deserved whatever he got!

"If you're not gonna eat, you'd best go to sleep, missus," Williams said around his mouthful. "We're gonna be ridin' hard tomorrow."

"I'm not sleepy."

"If you're thinkin' to stay awake and slip out tonight, you better think again. I'm a light sleeper. And if you try anything, that boy of yours is gonna get the thrashing of his life."

"I'm not plotting escape," Rachel told him. "I just can't sleep."

When they had first stopped here, Rachel had considered grabbing Peter and making a run for it. The mere thought in her head had earned Peter a painful pinch on the arm. However Williams had known what was on her mind, he seemed frighteningly good at it.

"Suit yourself," Williams conceded. "But if you can't keep up tomorrow, I'm likely to leave you for Apache bait. Like I said before, t'aint you the gent wants."

There had to be some way to escape this nightmare, Rachel told herself. If not on the desert then perhaps in Tucson or Mesilla or wherever Williams took them.

Dusk deepened into night. Peter huddled against her side, silent and frightened as Williams continued to drink. The moon rose and bathed the terrain in its milky light. The pale radiance made the valley look cold, even though day's heat lingered well into the night. The occasional *whuff* from one of the horses, the hoot of an owl, and the distant song of a coyote only emphasized the stillness. The odor of Williams's whiskey stung Rachel's senses, calling up unpleasant associations that made the night even more frightening.

Finally Rachel drew the corners of her blanket around her and closed her eyes, unwilling to continue watching Williams sink closer and closer to drunkenness. Before she could doze off, a voice came out of the darkness.

"Up and at 'em folks! The night's still young!"

Rachel jerked from a light doze. Williams reacted like lightning. He had a gun trained on the intruder before Rachel found her senses. Her eyes shot wide open at the sight of J. C. Tyler sitting casually on a rock beside Williams's bedroll. He didn't look a bit bothered by the pistol Williams had pointed at his chest. His own pistol was in his hand, aimed with unwavering steadiness at Williams's head.

 **11**

"How the hell did you get here?" Williams growled.

"Just walked right in behind you and made myself comfortable," J.C. told him with a smile. "You're slipping, Chester. There was a day when you had eyes in the back of your head, when not even a gnat could fly into your camp without you knowing it. Too much whiskey'll dull your senses, you know."

Williams's face cracked in an imitation of a smile. He lowered his gun and sat up. "Hell, a man's gotta relax sometimes. Ain't no one here to worry about 'ceptin' a woman who don't come up to my chin and a whelp who looks like he cain't work up enough grit to spit. And if any Injuns come around, I figure the missus there will squeak about it. She's been in a tizzy since I met her. Even an Injun cain't sneak up on a woman in a tizzy."

"I did," J.C. reminded him.

Though Williams had lowered his pistol, J.C. hadn't backed off with his.

"Well, now, John Charles, you don't exactly count."

"How so?"

"You're a friend."

J.C. lifted his pistol until the muzzle looked up Williams's nose. "I didn't notice that we were friends when you left me lying in that damned kitchen."

Williams's strained smile faded as he looked into the gun's snout. "You ain't gonna hold that against me, are you, boy? Hell, there's four thousand dollars at stake here. Besides, I figured that lying there thinkin' about how you went wrong might do you good. Any man who lets these two get the drop on him needs some time to think about how he should be doin' things different."

"As a matter of fact I am going to hold it against you, Chester. I've always found retribution to be a good philosophy to live by." He shot a quick look at Rachel, who could read nothing in his eyes but the opaque reflection of the night's darkness. She was immensely relieved to see him and at the same time apprehensive. The look he gave her wasn't exactly reassuring. But then, all things considered, she could scarcely expect him to shower her with roses.

"Is that lump beneath the blankets Peter?" he asked her.

Rachel nodded.

"Wake him up. We're going."

"Just wait a damned minute!" Williams brought up his pistol again, but J.C. knocked it out of his hand. "Dammit all, J.C.! Whaddya think you're doin'? These two are mine, fair and square!"

"They were mine before they were yours, and I'm taking them back."

Rachel was beginning to feel like a bone being fought over by two dogs.

"Whazgoinon?" Peter poked his head from beneath the blankets, yawned, and looked around groggily. His eyes brightened when they lit on J.C. "J.C.! You're here! We didn't kill ya!"

"Not this time." A brief smile touched J.C.'s face as he glanced at the boy—a softening of his features that made Rachel think of the affable stranger she'd known in Tubac. The transformation was only momentary, though. "Get up and put your boots on, Big Red. Then get your things together. We're riding out together, you, me, and your mother."

Williams shook his head. "You're not playin' by the rules, John Charles. I got these two fugitives in my possession. The game's up, and I won. Bounty hunters may be a sorry lot, but we don't poach."

"This isn't a game, Chester. These two aren't run-of-the-mill fugitives, and I've got sort of a special interest in them."

"Is that so?"

"That's so. If you've got a beef with me taking them, we can settle up later, when we don't have a woman and kid watching."

Williams slowly got to his feet. "You're not takin' 'em unless you shoot me down, John Charles, an' you better shoot to kill, 'cause if you leave me kickin', I'm gonna follow your trail and make sure you're sorry the missus here didn't kill you in Tubac instead of tyin' you up like a hog. You're gonna have to grow eyes in the back of your head and stay awake the whole way between here and Georgia. Think you can do that, boy?"

J.C.'s pistol cautiously tracked Williams's every move, but the bounty hunter paid no mind to the weapon. His eyes locked with J.C.'s, his arms spread wide to taunt him with a better target. "I know you, boy. You couldn't no more shoot a man in cold blood than fly to the moon. But you're gonna hafta if you want that four thousand dollars the kid's daddy put on his head."

"This has gone way beyond four thousand dollars, Chester."

"Not for me it hasn't." His craggy face grew sly. "I suppose I could let you have the woman, if it's a hankerin' for her that's got your back up. Skinny redheads ain't my type, but from the way you was lookin' at her a while back, I figger she's yore type, all right. That sound like a fair deal?"

Rachel held her breath when J.C. didn't immediately answer. She gave Peter a look that she hoped was reassuring.

"I've got a better deal," J.C. finally said. "How about we fight for the both of them in a fair contest?"

Williams's eyes glittered. "What sorta contest?"

"Fistfight. Winner takes all. Loser minds his manners and gives up the chase."

"John Charles, you're a bigger fool than I gave you credit for. You're askin' for a beatin'."

J.C. merely smiled. Rachel didn't know why. Chester Williams was taller and heavier than J.C. and, unless she missed her guess, a good deal meaner.

"Anything goes?" Williams asked with a grin.

"Anything except guns or knives."

"Fine by me. 'Ceptin' those two get tied up. Don't want them skippin' out while we're decidin' who they belong to."

"Agreed." J.C.'s gaze shifted to Rachel. It glittered with a malicious light that made her breath catch. "I'll do the honors."

Williams chuckled unpleasantly. "Give a little of their own back? Sounds right to me. Git a rope."

Five minutes later a seething Rachel jerked her hands against the knots that held her arms behind her back. Peter had been tied in a similar fashion. J.C.'s grin was infuriating.

"Are my hands gonna turn black, J.C.?" Peter asked, more excited than afraid.

"Not unless you keep wriggling around like that."

"I'm wriggly 'cause I gotta go!"

"You should've told me before. Now you'll have to wait until after Mr. Williams and I settle a few things."

"You're gonna beat him up, huh?"

"Yep."

Williams snorted his contempt at that, but J.C. merely grinned.

"You're enjoying this!" Rachel hissed.

"You bet I am. All I need now is an iron skillet to crown you with, and I'd enjoy myself even more." J.C. reached around her and gave the knots at her wrists a final tug. He was close enough for her to feel the heat of his body.

"I hope he knocks you senseless," Rachel said spitefully.

"You're welcome, I'm sure. Don't worry." His lips were close to her ear, his breath and the words a warm tickle on her flesh. "I'm not going to let him win."

She gritted her teeth. "I couldn't care less."

"You should."

When Peter and Rachel were both securely bound, J.C. drew a circle in the dirt. It was barely visible in the moonlight. "First one that steps outside the line with both feet is the loser. Fair enough, Chester?"

"Fair enough." Williams pulled a knife from inside his boot and threw it aside. "Hope you're goin' to enjoy this little lesson I give you, boy."

J.C. tossed his gunbelt away and stepped inside the circle. At first the two men circled cautiously, each looking for the other's weakness, each looking for an opening. Rachel watched with a feeling of dreadful fascination. Since she had come west, her once-delicate sensibilities had toughened. She'd seen drunken brawls, Apache attacks, Mexican bandit raids, and once even witnessed a lynching. But violence still made her breath catch and her skin crawl, and these two looked more than capable of doing serious violence to each other.

Peter seemed as mesmerized as she by the sight. His eyes were wide, his face flushed with excitement. "Get 'im, J.C.," he yelled. "Go git 'im!"

Rachel felt like echoing the sentiment, but she'd be damned if she'd give J.C. the satisfaction of knowing that she'd far rather try to escape from him than from Williams.

Suddenly the fight was on. Williams lunged forward, leading with his fists. J.C. ducked and landed a blow in Williams's midsection, but Williams managed to come back with an uppercut to J.C.'s chin. The two men swung, dodged, grappled, and struggled to keep their feet within the circle. Williams was bigger and heavier, his reach longer. When they landed, his punches sounded like hammer blows. When they missed, Rachel could hear the wind of their passing even from where she sat. J.C. had the advantage of being younger and better conditioned. Where Williams wore a slight gut, J.C. had a flat belly chiseled with muscle. Where after only a few blows Williams panted and blinked his eyes against the flood rolling off his brow, J.C. had scarcely broken a sweat. His movements were fluid and sure, and even though his nose was bloody and one lip was split, a grin still spread across his face as he taunted his opponent.

"Give up yet, old man?"

Williams panted for a moment before he could regain enough wind to respond. "Old man my ass! I'll dance on your grave someday, boy." He bulldozed forward, using his head as a battering ram and slamming into J.C.'s middle. J.C. stumbled backward. One foot came down out of the circle.

Rachel gasped, but J.C. hung on and came back at Williams with a blow to the jaw that sent the other man crashing to the ground. J.C. followed him down. The two of them grappled viciously, punching and jabbing, until Williams managed to shoot his knee upward into J.C.'s groin. J.C. grunted and rolled away, doubled up in pain. Williams got to his feet and kicked him in the ribs. On the second kick J.C. grabbed his foot and brought Williams crashing down outside the circle.

Panting, J.C. bent over and braced himself on his thighs while Williams regained his feet. "Fight's over," he announced.

"Like hell!" Williams stumbled to his pistol and grabbed it.

"J.C., watch out!" Rachel and Peter both screamed at the same time.

J.C. kicked the pistol from Williams's hand before the man could bring the weapon to bear. Then he grabbed Williams by the front of his shirt.

"You forgot the rules, Chester. I win." J.C. punctuated his statement with a sharp punch to Williams's nose, which was already running scarlet. Then he released his shirt and hit him again. Williams sank to his knees. J.C. collected his pistol and slung his gunbelt around his hips. "Pick up that gun of yours again before we're out of here and I'll put a bullet in you, Chester. I swear it. Follow us and I'll take your weapons and horse and leave you out here as Apache bait. Understand?"

His hands cradling his gushing nose, Williams choked out a yes.

Pistol trained cautiously on his rival, J.C. dug into the saddlebags on his dilapidated mare and came up with a gold coin that he tossed into the dirt in front of Williams's knees. "That's for the extra horse. Thanks for bringing it along."

Williams glared up at J.C. from over his bloody hands. "Enjoy that four thousand while you can, John Charles, 'cause next time I see you, I'm gonna flatten you good."

"You can try," J.C. told him with a grin. He sliced Peter's bonds, then Rachel's, and pulled her to her feet. For a moment they were so close, Rachel could hear his heartbeat. Blood smeared his chin from where he'd wiped it from the corner of his mouth. His lip was split and swelling, and one eye was going to have a magnificent shiner. "If you'd rather ride on with Chester while Peter goes with me, just let me know," he offered with a twisted grin.

The sympathy she had started to feel for him evaporated. "You won't get rid of me that easily."

"A man can always hope." He pulled her toward the buckskin.

Rachel wrenched her arm out of his grasp. "Can't I walk?" She and this horse had already come to an agreement of mutual dislike.

"No. You can ride sitting up or tied backside up over the saddle. It's your choice."

Rachel guessed from J.C.'s tone that the horse liked her better than J.C. did at this moment. Cooperation seemed to be the best option.

J.C. mounted his bony mare and swung around to look down at Williams, who was still on his knees, panting for breath and bleeding from the nose. "I figure I owe you a cut of that four thousand, Chester. If you want to collect, you'll be able to find me raising horses on the prettiest piece of land north of Santa Fe."

They made a cold camp after an hour's ride, with Rachel clinging to the saddle of the led horse and Peter riding in front of J.C., who rode slowly, letting the old mare feel her way through the deceptive and shadowy moonlight. J.C. stuck to the foothills and halted in an arroyo that provided a bit of shelter against hostile eyes that might note their presence. Rachel peered into the dark anxiously as J.C. helped her slide down from the saddle.

"We'll be all right here," he assured her. "The Apaches mostly watch the road along the river or the tracks coming out of the mountains."

Rachel would have liked to cut him dead, not speak to him at all, but she was uneasy enough to let her worry overcome her pride. "What if your friend Williams comes after us?"

"He won't."

"What makes you think so?"

"I've known Chester a long time. He's a tough customer and a snake, but he's smart. He'll leave us alone until I get that reward from your husband, then he'll come after me with blood in his eye."

"I wish you both well in beating each other to a pulp," she said archly. "Williams may be a snake, but at least he has the honesty to look and act the part. He doesn't slither into people's lives under the pretense of friendship."

"Yeah!" Peter agreed. "You old buzzard turd! I'm glad you lost O'Malley. I hope every horse you ever get is as ugly as the one you're ridin' now!"

"Peter, hush!" Rachel admonished. "There's no reason to insult that poor old horse." She took a blanket from where it was tied to the back of J.C.'s saddle and marched off to spread it on the sandy bottom of the arroyo beneath a mesquite tree. Now that they were safe from Williams, her anger at J.C. had returned in full bloom. He might have rescued them from that nightmare of a bounty hunter, but he'd done it for his own mercenary purposes, not out of any regard for their well-being. And while he might be preferable to Williams, he was still a lying, deceiving son of a skunk.

"Peter, come help me fix a bed."

Peter sulked his way over to her. The excitement of the fight and escape were over, and his brief resurgence of hero worship had slipped once again into disappointment. Tired and scared as he was, his anger targeted Rachel as well as J.C.

"I'm hungry." He glared at both Rachel and J.C. as Rachel shook the blanket out.

"There's jerky in the saddlebags," J.C. told him.

"I want something hot. I want a fire."

"No fire, unless you want Apaches dropping by for supper."

"I ain't scared of Apaches."

"Is that so?" J.C. held out some strips of jerky to the boy, who made a disgusted face as he took them. He sat on the blanket Rachel had spread and continued to glare at J.C., Rachel, the sand, the thornbushes, the mesquite trees, and anything else that crossed the path of his vision.

Rachel declined J.C.'s offer of the dried and salted meat. She still had no appetite. She sat on the blanket beside Peter and watched as J.C. sat down on a flat rock with a canteen and his share of jerky. She was so weary, she could cry. Her shoulder ached abominably; her legs were chafed from the saddle; and she was sore in places she didn't even want to think about. Night sounds of the desert chittered and chirped all about their dark camp. A faint scream echoed far up the canyons to the east—a mountain lion making a kill or protesting prey that got away. Without the security of adobe walls around her, Rachel discovered a wildness in the land that she'd never before noticed, and without even a fire for comfort, the night seemed wilder still.

J.C. didn't seem to notice, however. He seemed perfectly at home without walls around him. The untamed darkness suited him, and he looked more at ease sitting on a rock in the middle of nowhere than he had sitting in the roadhouse dining room.

"It's very lonely out here," Rachel finally said, more to hear the reassuring sound of her own voice than to begin conversation.

"Lonely is good," J.C. replied. "When you get company in these parts, they're usually wearing war paint and carrying war lances."

"Are we close to Tubac?"

"Couple or three hours' ride," he told her. "We should get there midmorning."

Hope flared briefly. "You're taking us back?"

He shot her a brief, inscrutable look. His eyes were dark and cryptic as the night, and the only thing Rachel could read in them was grim determination. Her heart fell.

"I'm hoping those freight wagons are still there."

"You're still taking Peter."

"Hell yes. I just won you both in a fair fight. Didn't you notice?"

Rachel felt helpless. Fate was closing in on her. She wasn't above begging, if begging would make any difference. "Please, J.C. Please don't do this."

Her plea, made from the depth of her heart and over the protest of her pride, seemed to have no effect. "Give it up, Rachel. Be grateful I'm still willing to let you come along. After that knock you gave me on the head, you're lucky I don't forget my more decent impulses."

"You don't know the meaning of decent!"

"You'd better hope that I do." His voice rose to match hers. "Damn but I'm tired of fighting with you! Dorset doesn't want you, Rachel. He wants Peter. Right now, leaving you behind is a real temptation. Behave yourself or you'll find yourself stranded and alone in Tubac."

"Do that and I'll find a way to follow and make your life a living hell. Believe me."

J.C. sighed and shook his head. "You're just the woman who could do it too. I suppose you'd rather I'd left you two with Williams."

"Do you think there's a difference between you and him?" She longed to hurt him the way he was hurting her, to stab through that iron armor around his heart— if he did indeed have a heart. "I can't see any difference."

"Maybe there's not," he admitted softly.

Peter threw in his two cents' worth. "I hope your horse ranch burns in a fire. I hope you get bit by a rattlesnake and scalped by Apaches. I hope—"

"Peter, that's enough!" Oddly J.C. looked more hurt by Peter's childish vitriol than by Rachel's calculated insults, but he quickly regained the impenetrable mask she was beginning to think of as his bounty hunter face. If she hadn't known there was a man beneath that mask, she would find him a good deal easier to hate.

"Time to turn in," J.C. announced when he'd finished his jerky. "Do you and Peter need to visit the bushes?"

Rachel's face heated. During her bedridden recuperation, she'd had to endure things much more embarrassing than a trip to the bushes within J.C.'s sight, but then he'd been a friend. Now he was foe. "Come with me, Peter," she snapped. "And I'll thank you to turn your back," she shot at J.C.

She may have merely imagined the amused smile that

curved his mouth as he turned around, but imaginary or not, it made her flush even hotter. Her freckles were burning holes in her cheeks.

"Don't go more than a few steps," he cautioned. "There's things out there unfriendlier than I am."

"But not more loathsome!" she replied.

When they returned, J.C. directed Peter to the blanket beneath the tree. "You sleep here." When Rachel started to join her son, J.C. shook his head. "You sleep over here." He pointed to another blanket five feet away.

"Peter will be frightened without me. He won't sleep."

"He's so tired, he'd sleep in a camp full of rampaging Indians. You'll only be an arm's length away."

Having little choice, she resentfully gave in and sat down on the separate blanket. But she cried a protest when J.C. tied her wrists together.

"What are you doing?"

"You think I trust you?" He checked the ropes to make sure they were tight enough but not too tight, then strung a rope from her wrists to her ankles and tied them. "That's so you can't get your wrists up to your mouth and undo the knots with your teeth."

"I'll undo *you* with my teeth."

He grinned. "I believe you would."

Peter glared to protest his mother's treatment, but he was so sleepy that the glare didn't last past the time J.C. pushed him gently back on the blanket and wrapped it warmly around him.

"You're not going anywhere tonight without your mother, are you, Peter?"

"No," the boy admitted.

"That's good, because she still needs your protection."

"You're a bad man, J.C."

"Yeah," he said softly. "I'm a bad one, all right."

When he returned to her blanket, Rachel gave him a look designed to scorch the hair right off the devil's head.

"Peter'll be fine," J.C. assured her. "You can lie there all night and watch him sleep, if you want. Move over."

"What?"

He shook out another blanket. "Move over. There's only one blanket left." Sitting down beside her, he draped the blanket around them both.

"What do you think you're doing?"

"Be quiet. You'll wake up Peter." He drew her down beside him and cradled her body within his, spoon fashion.

She sputtered a protest. "I will not stand for this!"

"You're not moving without me knowing it, Rachel. You're as slippery as a she-coyote, and I'm not taking any more chances."

She sputtered again as his arm wrapped around her and settled her more firmly against him.

"You don't have to worry about your virtue. I'm too tired to do anything but sleep. Besides, I have a headache."

She lay stiffly against him until weariness got the upper hand. Slowly Rachel relaxed. As the night got cooler, the warmth of him curled around her, lulling her to sleep. The hard bulwark of his body was a comfort of sorts, security against the vague threat of mysterious desert sounds.

As she drifted toward sleep, Rachel mused how foolish she was to be fearful of things that go bump in the night when the biggest danger of her world lay right beside her.

They arrived in Tubac midmorning of the next day.

Rachel was glad to reach the haven of her own room, though it was stripped of her personal things and a two-day layer of dust—which in this country was considerable—coated the meager furniture. She had endured the day's ride in nervous silence, nervous because she was sure that the buckskin gelding was plotting to toss her off and then kick her just for the fun of it. Nervous because she imagined hostile Apaches hidden in every wash and behind every bush. Nervous also because, as hard as she pondered the problem, she could think of no way to get Peter away from J.C. She had tried again in the morning's rational light to persuade him to leave them be, but he was adamant. He wouldn't even look at her, much less listen to her, the pig.

Now as she looked out her bedroom window at the little village baking in the midday heat, the situation seemed frustratingly hopeless. She pounded the window frame with her fist, then pressed her forehead to the adobe of the wall.

"Damn! Damndamndamn!"

No one was going to rescue them from this mess except her. She had to do something.

"We're goin' to the stable," Peter called up the stairs.

"Wait a minute!" Rachel hurried down to the dining room, where Peter practically hopped up and down with impatience. "J.C. says that I can take care of that buckskin you were riding, and if Señor Ortega has a saddle that fits me good, I can ride him this afternoon."

"Fits me *well*." A flash of annoyance made her voice sharper than she'd intended. To win her son's affection, it seemed, all J.C. had to do was let him ride a horse. Never mind that J.C. intended to take him away from his mother forever.

Just then J.C. himself walked in the front door. "What's the holdup, Big Red?" When he saw Rachel, his face hardened into the mask. "Hello, Rachel." he said cautiously.

She didn't bother to give him a civil greeting. "I'm going out," she said, brushing past him with a cool look.

One brow slashed upward, but other than that he didn't seem alarmed. "Have a nice walk."

His lack of concern over what she might do added to her annoyance. "I don't suppose you would let Peter come with me."

"Peter and I are going to the stable. You're welcome to come if you like."

"No, thank you." Jaw clenched to hold back the growl in her throat, she marched out onto the porch, carefully shutting the door behind her. She would have liked to slam it so hard it jumped from its hinges, but she wouldn't give J.C. the satisfaction of seeing her reduced to such a childish display.

An hour later, after canvassing the people of Tubac— the few that remained in what was rapidly becoming a ghost town—she discovered that the only help she could expect was from herself. Her desperate situation could only be explained by telling the truth, and once they learned the truth, these people who had known her and Peter for a year, who had eaten in the roadhouse dining room, done business with her, endured with her the dust, heat, and Apaches, had no sympathy for a divorced woman who was trying to keep her child. Even Señora Sevilla, who had bought eggs from her every week, gave her a cold shoulder. Señor Ortega's kindly Pima Indian wife was concerned and sympathetic to her situation, but her husband plucked her from their conversation, gave Rachel a brusque greeting, and closed the door in her face.

No one would help her but herself, Rachel concluded as she headed back to the roadhouse. Herself. Alone.

Since leaving Cabell, she had done things she'd never dreamed she would do in her whole lifetime. She alone had made a place for herself and her son wherever they'd gone. She had dealt with hardship, poverty, wild Indians, and rowdy drunks. She didn't need someone to rescue her and Peter from J. C. Tyler; she could do it herself.

And she would do it, no matter what it cost her. Nothing could be worse than letting her son return to the horrible life they had fled. Perhaps Cabell loved Peter. He probably did. Perhaps he would be patient and restrained, as he had not been with her. She didn't think so. Intellectually Rachel knew there had been a time when she'd known her husband as a kind, gentle, and understanding man. Her emotions remembered only the fear and violence, however, the sick feeling she'd always gotten inside when he started to get angry, the lengths she would go to to hide things she thought might set off his temper. Now she would go to the same lengths to ensure that Peter would not have to live with that nightmare—any lengths at all.

Her determination had solidified to concrete by the time she got back to the roadhouse, and when J.C. looked up as she came into the kitchen, her face, she was sure, was as set in stone as his was. She fixed supper in silence. There was not much in the roadhouse to eat. The hens had laid a few eggs and there was cornmeal for tortillas. It didn't matter. None of them were very hungry. Peter's earlier ebullience had faded. He sulked through the meal and went to his room as soon as he'd eaten.

Rachel gathered her courage while she washed the dishes. J.C. sat silently at the kitchen worktable where they'd eaten, his eyes boring into her back. The very thought of what she planned to do turned her insides to mush, her knees to jelly.

It would work, she told herself. It had to work. When J.C. had kissed her in the horse corral, that hadn't been a lie. When she'd caught him looking at her with desire in his eyes, that hadn't been a lie either. Sex was a potent weapon. It could melt men's resolve, turn cowards into heroes and decent men into derelicts. It was a weapon every woman possessed, but one a decent woman would never employ.

Rachel tried to ignore her conscience. She was no longer a decent woman, she reminded herself. A divorced woman had no virtue to protect as far as the world was concerned. Peter's future was at stake. No sacrifice was too great. Words and pleas had not moved J.C. Perhaps something more basic would.

When the last dish was dried and put away, she caught her lower lip in her teeth and almost drew blood. Then she took a deep breath and turned to face the man sitting at the table.

"J.C., if I could make you a more tempting offer than Cabell's reward, would you forget you ever found Peter and me?"

His face could have been cast in iron. "There's not much in this world more tempting than money, Rachel."

She wet her lips and did her best to put lurid suggestion into her eyes. "Nothing, J.C.?"

12

J.C.'s face was carved from stone. He labored to keep it that way in spite of the interested alertness of every nerve in his body. God help him, Rachel was pulling out the heavy artillery now!

Rachel's face was flushed, the freckles on her nose and cheeks swarming together in high color. Embarrassment somehow made her even more appealing. "What would it take to persuade you to forget you ever found me and Peter?"

His teeth ground, and he felt the muscles at his jawline twist into knots. "Just what are you offering?" Play innocent, and maybe she would give up before he did something they would both regret.

"I haven't got money," she purred. "But anything else I have I would give. Anything. You name it."

Damn she was good at this! Did women come by this sort of thing naturally, or did they have to practice? "Rachel . . . ," he protested.

"You can earn money by going after someone else, can't you?" She hurried on before he could stop her. "There must be lots of villains in this territory heading for the border, villains who deserve attention from a man like you."

"Yeah." But they didn't have hips that swayed so enticingly or breasts that curved so temptingly against the soft cotton of her bodice.

"So you wouldn't really lose anything by going after someone else."

"Still haven't convinced you that I'm your savior, huh?" He tried to take refuge in sarcasm, but the ploy didn't work. Her eyes flashed with momentary anger, but she didn't let it deter her. She glided forward and laid a hand on his shoulder. The heat of her touch scorched through shirt, skin, muscle, bone, and marrow. In a few moments he was going to have steam coming out his ears.

"Rachel, you don't know what you're doing."

"I know exactly what I'm doing, J.C." To demonstrate, she leaned down and kissed him on the mouth. With superhuman effort he turned himself to stone, unmoving, cold, but with a center of molten desire. It seemed that he'd desired this woman since the beginning of time. Over the past few days he'd tried to bury that desire with anger, with bravado, with icy reason and calm determination. But Rachel's lips, soft, sweet, and yielding, were making his best efforts look like dandelions in a stiff wind.

Somehow he found the strength to push her away. "Stop it! You're not a whore. Stop acting like one."

"I'll be a whore. I'll be anything you want, J.C., if you'll forget Peter and go on about your business."

"You think it's that easy?" He stood, suddenly angry—angry that he had let himself get involved in such a no-win situation, angry that he'd broken a cardinal rule and let his emotions run loose, angry that a good and decent woman was demeaning herself in such a low way, angry that he was on the verge of responding.

"It's easy," she said temptingly. "Just say the word."

Goddamn! This had seemed like such a simple task when he had started out. But he'd ended up being jumped by a kid, conked over the head by a woman, kicked, smashed up, and threatened by Chester Williams, and cursed as a kid-eating troll by the very kid who'd come to mean more to him than the four thousand dollars riding on his head. Now this! Rachel already haunted his dreams. Now she thought she could get her way by offering herself as a sacrifice to his lechery. No doubt she blamed this on him too. And goddamn if the woman didn't know how close she danced to the edge of the cliff.

"You don't know what the hell you're getting yourself into."

"Really?" Her eyes glanced downward to where the bulging evidence of his response had become obvious. Face growing even hotter, she still managed to drag her gaze upward to meet his in challenge.

Her determination to lure them both down that path made him even angrier. "Prepared to sacrifice yourself, are you? Is this what I'm supposed to do?"

In a sudden movement he backed her up against the table. He reached for her, ignoring her surprised gasp, cupping his hands on her buttocks and lifting her against him where she could feel every hard inch of what she had done to him. A bolt of heat tore through him, warning him that he, also, was dancing on the brink of a precipice. He saw her trying to gather her courage for the ultimate sacrifice, and somehow the combination of fear, determination, and desire in her eyes touched him past resisting.

He hadn't intended to kiss her, but he'd come too

close to temptation. It reached out and grabbed him, and before he knew it, he was laying siege to her mouth. She stiffened against him, then yielded. For a moment he forgot he was angry, that Rachel would rather curse him than kiss him, and that he was locked in a dilemma for which four thousand dollars was not nearly enough payment. Rachel was warm and soft against him, smelling of aroused woman, her breasts pressing against his chest, her firm buttocks filling his hands. He wanted nothing more than to lay her back on the table, lift her skirts, and take her up on her devil's bargain.

He wrenched himself away. "No, goddammit!"

Rachel fell back against the table when he let her go. She was disheveled and flushed. Her eyes looked stunned. J.C. couldn't resist the temptation to brush back the bright strands of hair that had fallen over her face.

"I'll say it again, Rachel. You're not a whore, so stop acting like one. You're too good for this."

She came to sudden, furious life and pushed him away. "You kissed me just to make a fool out of me!"

"No. I kissed you because you hawked your wares just a bit too well."

Her hand curled into a fist, and she shook with the desire to hit him. "You're the lowest kind of worm. And I am a fool to have thought for even a minute that you had a heart!"

"A heart," he echoed, one brow raised. "Is that what you were appealing to?"

"Obviously I should have known better."

He looked at her for a moment through cold eyes. Her face burned so brightly, the very roots of her hair looked to be on fire.

"You're probably right," he finally admitted. "I don't

have much of a heart. In my business it just gets in the way."

If he didn't have a heart, why was he faltering? J.C. suddenly realized he would never be able to walk away from those blazing eyes.

"You're a fool, Rachel Dorset. You're the kind of woman who doesn't know when to give up. Why don't you stop beating your head against a stone wall and accept that Peter's going back to his father? If I don't take him, someone else will. Accept it."

She clenched her jaw and lifted her chin.

He felt heavy with unquenched desire and morose with the certain knowledge that he was asking for a heap of trouble by letting her come along. She was going to be a constant temptation, and a troublemaker to boot. But there was no help for it. He could justify taking Peter, but he couldn't wrench the boy away from his mother, not now that he knew them both.

"I want you to listen and listen well, Rachel. There'll be no more of this. The first peep of trouble from you and I'll leave you behind," J.C. threatened. "Understand?"

"Understand," she said tonelessly.

"Good. And Rachel?"

"Yes?" she said cautiously.

"Tempt me like this again, and you'll get more than you bargain for. Don't do it."

She gave him a twisted smile that mocked him and herself at the same time. "I wouldn't dream of it."

J.C. sighed. Lord how he wished he'd never seen that damned poster! "Get your things together. We'll be leaving in the morning, one way or another. I'm going to find the drivers of those freight wagons. I'll take Peter with me."

"He might be asleep. Leave him here."

J.C. shook his head. "Right. And how long would it take you to be gone with him? Rachel, Rachel, I may not have a heart, but I'm not that short on brains."

Next morning before dawn Rachel and Peter loaded the last of their meager belongings into the wagon that J.C. had gotten from the livery in exchange for the buckskin gelding Rachel had reluctantly ridden from Williams's camp. The bony old sorrel mare that J.C. had ridden was tethered to the back of the wagon.

"I promised I'd take her to greener pastures in New Mexico," J.C. said brusquely when Rachel commented on him bringing the mare.

He had scruples about not betraying a horse, but none where she and Peter were concerned. She would have made a bitter comment, but didn't, because his long-suffering expression showed he expected it. Instead she smiled sweetly at the mare. "Don't trust him, girl. He's a snake."

"Damnation!" J.C. muttered. "This is going to be a long trip."

Their wagon was small and poorly sprung, hitched to two mules that up until the night before had belonged to the train of freight wagons they were to join. J.C. had found the mule skinners in the saloon the night before and had won the mules in a poker game. He'd won himself a job as well: J.C. would help with the big freighters in exchange for his own wagon being able to tag along with the train for protection. To sweeten the deal, he'd promised to give back the mules at journey's end.

J.C. opened the storage box under the driver's seat and tossed in the rifle and two shotguns he'd confiscated from the roadhouse when they'd arrived the day before. "Throw that under here," he told Peter as the boy came out the front door with a box of cooking and eating utensils. "There's plenty of room, and it'll give us more space in the back."

Peter stuck his head in the wagon box. "How come it's got so much room in here?"

"Someone probably built it for hauling contraband across the border."

"Wow!"

"Got everything?"

"Yeah."

"Did you get the iron skillet?" Rachel asked.

Peter gave a long-suffering sigh.

"Go get it," Rachel told him.

"I'm not sure I should let you bring that skillet," J.C. commented with a grimace.

Rachel bit back a sharp comment, remembering what J.C. had threatened about leaving her behind. She had to behave herself, at least until it was too late to put her off the train.

"Glad to see you've put a bridle on your tongue." J.C.'s smile told her he knew exactly what was going through her mind. "Because you're going to have to be civil to me for a while. I told the train captain that we're a family. You're my wife and Peter is my son."

"What? Why on earth did you do that?"

"Saves some questions and explanations."

"For whom?"

"For both of us."

Rachel longed to wipe the twinkle out of his blue eyes and the superior look off his face. "If you think I'm going to pose as your wife—"

"Ah, ah!" J.C. warned. "No trouble, remember?"

"This is unreasonable and unnecessary!"

"Really?" he inquired with exaggerated courtesy. "Would you care to explain the real situation to the men on the wagons? Some of them haven't seen a white woman for a long time. I'm sure they'd be interested to know the pretty redhead traveling with them is a divorced woman with no father, husband, or brother to stand up for her."

Rachel's lips tightened. Being divorced and alone would make her fair game to men who otherwise wouldn't think of bothering a "decent" woman.

"Don't look so sour," J.C. advised. "It's only until we get the stage at Mesilla. If I can act like I was fool enough to marry a redheaded shrew, then you can act like the long-suffering wife of a good-for-nothing snake. It's not going to kill you."

"You admit you're a snake?" she inquired smugly.

"I admit that you think I'm a snake."

She regarded him sourly. "Very well. You win. But if we have to be married, at least we don't have to be on speaking terms."

"Fine by me"—he grinned suddenly—"Mrs. Tyler."

When J.C. introduced her and Peter to the wagon captain, Rachel swallowed her pride and tried to be demure and wifely, things that had been natural before she'd left Georgia. During the last three years she'd gotten out of practice. It was harder than she remembered, or maybe it was difficult because J.C. stood beside her, cupping her elbow in his large hand, jangling her nerves with an absurdly possessive smile.

"Howdy, Miz Tyler. Hope you and the young'un don't mind bein' in the rear. I know it's dusty, but it's the safest place in the train."

The "young'un" had been briefed. Peter held his silence. His mouth, however, pulled down sullenly at the "Miz Tyler."

"We're grateful you're letting us travel with you, Mr. Coates," Rachel said at J.C.'s subtle squeeze on her arm. "We wouldn't want to make the trip alone." Not alone, no. Without J.C. would be fine, but not alone.

"Well, now," Coates said, his weathered face creasing with a smile, "havin' a lady like you along will be a pleasure, missus. It surely will."

The pleasure would be all theirs, Rachel mused as she peered through the day's first light at the mule skinners. They were hard and tough-looking as jerky that had been dried in the sun too long. There wasn't one of them, including the captain, that she would want to meet on the street at night, or even in the daylight. Several of the men nodded politely and touched their hats. One or two gave her a brief look, then averted their eyes. If her true status were known, those looks would have been longer and a good deal less polite, and the gallant salutes would have been replaced by speculative leers. Rachel would never have admitted her feelings to J.C., but the situation being what it was, she was glad enough to hide behind the shelter of his name.

They were on the road by the time the first rays of the sun shot from behind the mountains to the east. The huge freight wagons jolted along at a good pace, with the whips often snaking out over the backs of the mule teams to urge them to a faster pace. The wagon captain was in a hurry to get to Mesilla, J.C. told Rachel. He was hauling a load of yard goods, tools, and good liquor from Mexico that was fetching a top price there. To cut off time, they were going to bypass Tucson, cut through the broad valley between the Santa Rita and Rincon Mountains, and from there head straight for Apache Pass and on to the Rio Grande. If they pushed hard, they might make the trip in a week or so.

The thought of a week or more eating the dust of the fifty mules and five wagons in front of them did nothing to improve Rachel's mood. It was almost impossible to recall how it had felt being a gently reared and thoroughly pampered belle at the Willows in Georgia. Not a callus had marred her palms, her skin had never reddened from sunburn, and she'd certainly never had dust grinding between her teeth and scratching her eyes every time she blinked. She couldn't have imagined the desperation of not knowing what her future held, living from hand to mouth, or being so helpless that she would offer her body, her very soul if need be, to keep safe what she loved most. She wondered if there had been a point somewhere along the line of her descent to these desperate circumstances when she could have saved herself from sliding down this far, some opportunity for redemption that she had missed, some decision fatally flawed.

The sun soon rose high enough to be a white-hot furnace. Rachel could scorch her hands by merely touching the wooden wagon seat beside her. Even the dust couldn't soften the glare of sand and rocks. J.C. was moodily silent as he drove the wagon; he certainly didn't need her company, Rachel thought morosely, so she climbed into the back of the wagon where he'd rigged up a canvas tarp to keep rain and sun off both them and their baggage. Peter sat on a pallet of blankets and whittled idly at a stick. He looked up as she sat down beside him. Rachel's heart lifted a bit, and she knew for sure that Peter made all the dust, desperation, and drudgery of the past three years worth it.

Peter glanced at his mother's face and decided he would be better off up front. She'd climbed into the back of the wagon, looking like a storm cloud, then she'd spied him, and her face got all soppy. She was going to get motherly and mushy on him, he could tell. He would rather endure the heat and dust in the open.

"Put your hat on," Rachel called after him as he climbed out onto the driver's box beside J.C. Peter muttered and dove back beneath the tarp to grab his hat. J.C. glanced at him as he settled onto the hard seat and jammed the hat on his head, but the bounty hunter didn't say anything. Peter was glad, because he didn't want to talk. He especially didn't want to talk to J.C.

The last few days had been confusing enough to make Peter wish he could dig a hole in the ground and hide until he was grown enough and tough enough to tell people to go to hell when they started pushing him this way and that. His mother would scold him if she knew he was thinking words like hell, but that was how he felt. He wanted to tell the whole world to go to hell, because the world was full of shit—another word his mother wouldn't let him use.

He had really gotten to like J.C. before all this happened. Now he hated him—sometimes. He'd been happy enough to see him when he showed up and fought Mr. Williams. The other bounty hunter had been mean as an Apache and ugly as an old molted snakeskin. He'd given Peter a switching when his mother had made trouble. Was that fair? Not that he would want his mother to get the switching. The mean old snake had threatened to do worse. Peter had heard him say he'd shoot his ma if she got too far out of line. He would have liked to grab the bounty hunter's pistol and shoot him, but he wasn't fast enough and didn't have arms long enough to get the gun. Damn he wished he was bigger! Damndamndamn! Another word his mother would thump him for using.

Peter didn't think that J.C. would take a switch to him, and he surely wouldn't shoot his mother, even though he sometimes looked as though he'd like to give her a wallop or two. J.C. wasn't as mean as Williams, or as ugly, but he was still making his mother really mad taking them back to his father like he was.

For a long time Peter had thought he wanted more than anything in the world to see his father again. After what his mother had told him, though, he'd changed his mind. More and more often, memories of the time before they left Savannah leaked into his mind. Some of them were a lot like nightmares. They shouldn't have to go back to Georgia if they didn't want to. J.C., Peter decided, was almost as much of a *pendejo* as that awful Chester Williams.

Still, it was hard for Peter really to hate someone who loved horses as J.C. did. And J.C. had taught him to whittle, even if he was a lying skunk.

Peter sighed dramatically. Life was very confusing.

"Want to take the reins?" J.C. asked.

"Don't know how to drive."

"You can learn, can't you?"

Peter gave him a sour look.

"You'd better learn, unless you want your mother to do all the driving on this trip. Once things get settled down, I've got to help with the big wagons. They need a relief driver. That's why they're letting us come along."

Peter looked at the two mules pulling their wagon. They were sleek, handsome animals. A mule could never hold a candle to a horse, but for mules these were good-looking beasts. His hands itched to hold the reins, if the truth be told, but he was reluctant to let J.C. see that he wanted anything the bounty hunter had to offer.

"I could learn if I had a mind to." The look he gave J.C. said plainer than words that it wasn't the lesson he didn't like but the teacher.

J.C. handed him the reins. Peter felt an instant elation as they vibrated in his hands in time to the mules' pace. One of the mules started tossing its head.

"Loosen up a little," J.C. advised. "You're pulling on the bit. You don't need to do much as long as we're following the other wagons. They're good animals. They know what they're doing."

Peter couldn't help but smile as the wagon jolted along. The day was suddenly brighter, the dust less irritating, the heat more tolerable. His hands communicated with the mules through the reins, and they seemed to talk back to him. Mules were almost as good as horses for making a body feel better, he decided.

"Is that a smile I see on your face?" J.C. asked.

"No." Peter made haste to scowl.

J.C. let him brood for a moment, then spoke again. "Peter, you're going to be fine with your father. He wants you back real bad—bad enough to pay a heap of money to get you back."

"What about my ma?"

J.C. hesitated. "Maybe your mother will make up with your father."

Peter didn't think J.C. looked entirely happy about that.

"Do you remember much about your pa?"

Peter dredged through the confused memories that had just begun to surface. "No," he admitted. "Ma says he drinks too much."

"A lot of men drink. That doesn't mean they don't love their children."

Peter didn't like trying to look at two sides of an issue. One side was confusing enough. "I don't want to go back to Georgia."

"Didn't you tell me once that you hated Tubac? That you hated it everywhere your mother had taken you?"

"No," Peter denied. It was true enough, but now he regretted telling J.C. those things. Seems like every time he opened his mouth to an adult, whatever he said got turned around and used against him. "I want to stay. I don't want to go back."

J.C. gave him that disconcerting stare that seemed to see right through a person. Peter felt like squirming, but he didn't. He tried to concentrate on the mules.

"Sometimes life just doesn't turn out the way you want it to," J.C. finally told him. His voice sounded sad, though Peter couldn't figure out what he had to be sad about. "Even when you're a kid. Especially when you're a kid. Somebody's going to end up taking you back, Peter—me or someone else. You just have to make the best of it."

Peter snorted.

"Not only that, you should try to make it easier on your mother. This is hard for her."

"Then let us go."

J.C. shook his head. "Like I said, if it's not me, it'll be someone else."

Peter felt the finality of his fate in a way he hadn't before. He scowled and tried to hand the reins back to J.C., but J.C. wouldn't take them. "I don't want to drive anymore," Peter protested.

"Don't sulk," J.C. commanded. "Drive."

Peter drove. As the morning progressed, J.C. showed him how to slow the team and how to liven them up. When they stopped at noon, Peter learned how to turn them in a circle, how to back them, and then how to check the harnesses for places where the leather straps might rub the animals and create sores. He loved every minute of it, which made it difficult to retain the sullen manner that he thought J.C. deserved. He wasn't stupid, after all. He knew the bounty hunter was trying to get on his good side.

The noon meal was tense. J.C. and Peter's mother didn't talk much. The only food was the ever-present jerky, warm water from their canteens, and a few dried-out tortillas from last night's supper. J.C. promised he would bring down something for supper. He would be driving one of the big wagons up front for a while in the afternoon, but when he was relieved, he would ride out on the old mare and do some hunting.

"Does that mean I can drive the wagon alone?" Peter asked. He tried to keep the enthusiasm from his voice. It wouldn't do, after all, to let J.C. know that he was happy about anything.

"I figure you can," J.C. said. "You've got a knack, and I'm sure you'll do a better job than your mother."

Rachel gave J.C. a scowl, but Peter couldn't tell if she was mad because J.C. didn't think she could drive the wagon or if she was mad because Peter was talking to J.C.

J.C. returned his mother's scowl with a smile that looked more threatening than friendly. "I won't be going out of sight, so don't get any wild ideas."

"Enamored little wife that I am, I wouldn't dream of it," Rachel replied with sugary sweetness.

"And a coyote wouldn't dream of howling either," J.C. said sourly.

She pointedly turned her back, and Peter watched J.C.'s expression as he absorbed her disdain. The smile faded, and the cockiness left his face. The bounty hunter looked as unhappy as Peter felt. Maybe, Peter decided, J.C.'s life wasn't turning out quite as he'd planned either. Served him right.

The freight wagons finally circled to make camp as the sun was setting. For the last two hours before stopping the going had been rough, for they had forked off the main road onto a less-traveled track that hugged the foothills. Rachel was exhausted. She was accustomed at the roadhouse to working from before dawn to long after dark. How she could be so tired after doing nothing all day besides sit in a wagon was beyond her. Of course not too many days before she'd been confined to her bed, compliments of an Apache bullet. That might have something to do with her weariness. Or it might be that all the emotions clanging around inside had worn her out.

She looked at the two fat hares that J.C. had brought in for dinner. Feeling about as done in as the poor rabbits looked, she took a knife and prepared to skin them. Too bad she couldn't do the same to J.C.

"Want me to do that?" J.C. asked.

Rachel turned a level gaze upon him as he squatted beside the fire. She speculated that the look he gave the knife in her hand was just a bit nervous. "Afraid I'm practicing up for you?"

He grinned. "You were looking at those rabbits with blood in your eyes."

"I've got nothing against the rabbits."

"I know."

"Don't worry, Mr. Tyler. Your skin is in no danger. I'm too tired."

"Glad to hear it." He got up and took the knife from her hand. "Sit down. I'll cook the rabbits."

She didn't protest. "Where is Peter?"

"Talking to the mules. Where did you think?"

She had to smile. All afternoon long she'd sat beside her son on the wagon box, listening to him talk to the mules. He'd said scarcely a word to her, but he'd had quite a conversation with his long-eared friends. John and Sam is what he'd named them. If they'd had names before, they undoubtedly answered to John and Sam after listening to their pint-sized mule skinner addressing them by those names for so many hours.

"Maybe his father will buy him a horse of his own," J.C. commented.

Rachel's face immediately fell, and J.C. cursed. "I'm sorry. I shouldn't have said that. I just thought . . . maybe if you pictured Peter being happy in Georgia . . . it would make this easier for you."

She heard genuine regret in his voice. J.C. didn't like what he was doing, Rachel realized suddenly. The insight made it hard to hate him, and Rachel wanted to hate him, wanted that hatred as a focus for her misery, a constant goad to her determination. But the sorrow was there in his voice. Sorrow and sympathy. He probably did actually believe Peter's return to Georgia was inevitable, and that he was the best man to take him there.

"I'm sorry too," she said quietly. Sorry for a host of things.

As darkness fell, the little camp with its circled wagons and flickering campfires became an almost cozy place, and J.C.'s fire was the center for that coziness. One after another the drivers found an excuse to drop by—to mooch a cup of coffee ("Cain't nobody make coffee like a woman," one claimed), to compliment Peter on his driving ("This one's gonna grow up ta be the best mule skinner in the West!"), to talk to J.C. about one of the mules on the team he was to drive the next day, to ask Rachel if she knew a remedy for toothache. For freight drivers on the trail they looked suspiciously washed up, slicked down, and dust free. No matter what pretense they used, each visitor stared at Rachel as if she were a deep, cool draft of water in a hot and dusty desert. It was the same look she'd been getting from men since she came west, especially in Arizona Territory, where white women were scarce as water.

How differently they would treat her, Rachel thought cynically, if they knew she was a divorced woman. In the

West, more than any other part of the country, "decent" women were revered. A man could as soon be shot for mistreating a lady as for robbing a bank. Decency was fragile, however. By the act of running away from her husband's abuse, protecting herself and her son, Rachel had permanently removed herself from the feminine pedestal. Divorce branded her as no better than a whore, even though she'd never so much as kissed a man other than her husband.

Except J.C., Rachel remembered. J.C. had kissed her, and she had kissed him back. What's more, she'd enjoyed it, fool that she was.

Shortly after dark had fallen, everyone in the camp had migrated to Rachel's and J.C.'s fire. Much to Rachel's surprise J.C. pulled a harmonica from his pocket and began to play. He was good. The simple tunes were haunting, as fitting to this wild country as a coyote's howl.

After the last visitor had left to seek his blankets, Rachel dumped the coffee and banked the fire. "I would never have guessed you played the harmonica," she told him.

"My father taught me. The mouth organ was his."

"Oh. You never played in town."

"Harmonica tunes don't sound right in a town. You need lonely country for that music. Wide, wild spaces and skies full of stars."

A cynical smile twisted Rachel's lips. "A bounty hunter with poetry in his soul?"

"Bounty hunters don't have souls. Not if they do the job long enough."

She didn't want to feel for him; she wanted to feel only for herself and Peter. But it was hard to hate a man who could translate loneliness into music. It was hard to hate a man whose soul was in his eyes even while he claimed the lack of one.

It was also hard to hate the man who resisted the temptation to take advantage of their "married" state when he joined her in the wagon to sleep.

"I assumed you would sleep with the other men," she whispered sharply.

"We're married. Remember? You think any one of those men would believe I could be married to a woman like you and let you sleep alone?"

"We're not really married," she reminded him in a worried whisper.

J.C. smiled at the apprehensive set of her face, but that was as far as his teasing went. Preserving his husbandly dignity and putting her fears to rest at the same time, he called Peter to join him from where the boy had bedded down beneath the wagon. For the rest of the night the three of them slept, curled as closely as a pile of puppies against the cool night air.

As she fell asleep, Rachel lamented to herself again the difficulty of hating J. C. Tyler. But in a way she was glad for it. Hatred could be such a waste of energy, and she was going to need all the energy she could save to get her and Peter out of this mess.

At the first pale hint of dawn Rachel woke with a start to a bloodcurdling scream. J.C. shot up beside her, grabbed his rifle, and pushed her back down in the wagon with Peter. "Woman, you are a goddamned jinx! Do Apaches follow you everywhere you go?"

 **13**

"Get in!" J.C. commanded. The wagon box under the driver's seat opened to the back as well as the front, giving access to the box from the bed of the wagon— another innovation by smugglers, no doubt. The goods that J.C. was trying to hide were Rachel and Peter. He had hastily emptied the storage compartment of its contents to make room for both of them.

Rachel's heart raced. The predawn had exploded into chaos. War cries and dust roiled around the little circle of wagons, and J.C.'s face, looming above her, was taut with urgency as he pushed her toward the box.

Three years of seeing to her own defense—her own and Peter's—was a habit hard to break. "No! I can't just sit in there! Give me a gun! I'll fight!"

"Like hell! You'll hide with Peter. Now, get in! Peter, go in after her."

"I can shoot!" Peter's voice quavered, despite his attempt at bravado. "Let me shoot the Indians."

"I know you can shoot," J.C. said with a heroic attempt at patience. "That's why I'm putting you in here to defend your mother. She can't shoot worth a damn.

We'll let your mother hold the gun," J.C. told the boy as he crawled into the box. "It'll make her feel better."

J.C. handed Rachel a loaded pistol. "Stay in here until I come for you, or until the Apaches are gone." He reached for her hand and curled her fingers around the butt of the revolver. "Don't let the Indians take you or Peter, Rachel. You understand?"

Her eyes looked up into his. Unexpectedly J.C. leaned down and kissed her, hard and quick, his lips branding hers with emotions that no spoken words could convey. His hand tightened over hers and squeezed as he admonished Peter, "Take care of your mother, Big Red."

The hatch to the box slammed shut, and Rachel could hear the rustle of a tarp being dragged over it. The darkness seemed absolute and smothering. Already Rachel ached from the cramped position.

Peter squirmed. "I wanna go out. I can fight!"

"Be still," Rachel warned. "Do you want to leave me alone with no one to protect me?"

"No. I'll protect you, Ma."

She ran her hand gently over his hair. "Thank you, Big Red. Now, let's be quiet."

Why they needed to be quiet Rachel didn't know, for they seemed to be in the vortex of a maelstrom of noise. Gunfire, yips, screams, and shouts whirled around their little universe of darkness. Smoke stung their eyes and clogged their nostrils, and as the hours passed and the sun climbed, the box became an oven. The air inside became fetid with their terror and their sweat.

Just as Rachel thought they would die of the heat, the gunfire and screaming ceased. Silence descended in an ominous curtain, broken only by distant snatches of laughter, guttural words, an occasional shriek of victory. The Apaches had won.

Terror had become Rachel's familiar companion during the last hours. Now grief joined it. She closed her eyes and grieved for the mule skinners who'd made their silly excuses to visit her fire the night before, with hair slicked down and faces washed for probably the first time in days. She grieved for the wagon captain, Mr. Coates, for his teenaged nephew who'd been along to help tend the mules and learn about driving the big wagons.

Most of all she grieved for J. C. Tyler. In this extreme she didn't bother to analyze the pain of his loss. In spite of what he was, what he'd done, her stubborn heart had held on to its affection for him. At that moment all she could remember was how he'd looked tossing Bull Larsen out of the roadhouse, chopping down that tree beside the stock shed, patiently teaching Peter how to whittle, talking with her on the bench by the front door and watching the Arizona sunset. She also remembered the wicked look in those blue eyes just before he'd kissed her in that dusty horse corral, standing next to a sweating and bemused O'Malley. And the wild desperation in his face when he'd crouched over her on the floor of the roadhouse kitchen. Her blood had been all over his shirt, and in his eyes she'd seen the reflection of her own pain. What had prompted that last desperate kiss before he'd shut her into the wagon box? What had been the imperative message in those burning blue eyes? She would never know, because J.C. was dead, alongside Aldona and the mule skinners and wagon captain and the host of others, American, Mexican, and Indian, who had been slaughtered in this bloody land. She would soon be dead also. Then she wouldn't be afraid anymore, and there would be no more grief. Soon . . .

"Ma?" Peter's uncertain voice brought her mind back into focus. "Ma? What's happening?"

Triumphant shouts erupted somewhere close, followed by yips and almost inhuman howls of glee. A frenzy of pounding and ripping was followed by more cries.

"I don't know what's happening, Peter. Try to be quiet."

The smoke in their tiny prison had thickened, and it had a singed, charred-meat odor that made Rachel's stomach rise. Breathing was torture, and the air was so hot, her head swam. Somewhere close by, a mule screamed in agony. The sound was chilling.

"I want to go out," Peter sobbed.

"Shhh! Shhh! I know. Not yet." Rachel hugged the boy to her, in spite of the heat. How did she tell her son that their chances of survival were almost nil? She could hear the Indians ransacking the wagons, one after the other. If she and Peter were discovered, would she have the courage to use the pistol J.C. had given her? *Don't let the Indians take you or Peter.* Those words were the last he had spoken to her, and when he'd said them, his eyes had bored into hers, as if to impress them onto her very brain. Rachel knew why. But could she pull the trigger?

The wagon shook suddenly as an Apache warrior jumped on board. Tinware and pots clattered onto the floorboards. The sound of ripping fabric told them the fate of their clothing. Peter whimpered, and Rachel pressed her fingers over his mouth. Another jolt shook them as someone else leaped up to the wagon bed. They seemed to linger forever, arguing loudly over one thing or another. Once it seemed that someone jumped up and down on the wagon, out of either fury or high spirits. Rachel hugged Peter to her with one hand, clutched the pistol with the other, and prayed.

The wagons springs creaked as the Apaches finally jumped off. Rachel breathed a sigh of relief, then caught her breath as a scream shattered the hot darkness. Apache laughter. More screams. They'd found a survivor among the mule skinners, she realized with horror. Minutes seemed like hours as the torture continued. The sounds coming from the victim became higher pitched, less human, more garbled.

Rachel's stomach threatened to heave. Now she knew she could pull the trigger if need be. She wished desperately that she could perform such a mercy for whoever was providing grim entertainment for the savages.

The screams finally stopped. An eternity passed. Rachel's imagination ran wild. She pictured warriors stalking around the wagon, laughing at the thought of the two victims hiding in the box, planning the tortures that would make their deaths entertaining. Unable to wait in ignorance any longer, she opened the forward door of their prison just a crack and peeked out. The carnage that met her eyes was sickening, and she pushed Peter back when he would have followed her example. Within the narrow range of her vision alone lay four bodies, all missing their hair. Mutilated as they were, the corpses were hard to identify, but she didn't believe any of them were J.C. She would have recognized him, Rachel was sure, no matter what the Apaches had done to him. Much worse than the scalped bodies was the poor man tied to the huge rear wheel of the wagon in front of hers. He'd been stripped naked and was positioned head down over a small fire that now winked as coals in the dust.

Rachel drew back, her hand to her mouth, trying not to throw up.

"Ma, what's out there?" Peter asked in a thin voice. "Can we go?"

She shushed him, whispering, "Not yet. Be brave, Peter. We both have to be brave."

She forced herself to look out again. Every once in a while an Indian crossed her field of vision. One staggered and laughed. He had a bottle in his hand. Rachel deduced that the raiders had found the liquor Mr. Coates had been hauling to Mesilla. Another trotted by, laughing, calling out to someone else. He, too, had a bottle. A moment later a gray-haired, grandfatherly-looking fellow wearing elaborate war paint came into view yipping and dancing. He danced around one of the bodies, took a couple of deep pulls on his bottle, and fell over, drunk.

Rachel carefully closed the door to the box and squeezed Peter's hand. "The Indians are getting drunk."

"The Indians won?" Peter asked softly.

"I'm afraid so."

"Is everyone . . . is everyone . . . ?"

There was no way she could soften it. "Everyone's dead. Everyone except us. But we're going to live," she whispered grimly.

If luck was with them. If they had a guardian angel somewhere in heaven who was looking out for them. If they could wait undiscovered in this broiling box until the Apaches got falling-down, dead drunk.

Cabell was at breakfast when the letter came. Dirty and creased, it stood out from the other mail that Theo offered him on the silver salver. The valet had placed it apart from the other envelopes so that their pristine whiteness would not be soiled by its proximity.

"Good heavens! What's that?"

"Whatever it is, Massa Cabell, it look like it been around da world a couple a times."

"Being dragged behind an oxcart at that. Probably a prank." He'd received more than one hate letter from zealous Southerners who thought his successful import-export business catered too much to the interests of Yankees. Five years after the South had been defeated, old animosities still ran high. Perhaps this time they had put dirt on the outside of the missive as well as on the inside.

"Just leave it, Theo. I'll get to it after I've eaten."

He finished his sausage and biscuits without much gusto. He wouldn't have eaten at all if not for Clara's insistence. The old cook would subject him to a fifteen-minute lecture if he spurned the meal she'd prepared for him, then she would spend the rest of the day in a wounded huff. When she'd been a slave, she'd done the same. Even when his mother had been alive and Clara had cooked at River Oaks, the Dorset family plantation, Clara had been more the ruler of the house than Melissa Dorset had been. Now that Cabell's parents were dead, Cabell divorced, and Clara freed, she was even more the queen bee.

Just as well. If not for Clara these past few days, Cabell wouldn't have eaten anything. Unless he was very careful, what he did eat didn't stay down very long. Sometimes he had the shakes so bad, he thought he might fly apart. Every muscle in his body, every bone, every joint hurt. He was tired all the time, but sleep gave him no rest, for nightmares sprang to life the moment he closed his eyes. There was more than enough muck in his soul to provide years of nightmares.

He could relieve all these problems with a drink, Cabell knew. His mind, his body, his very soul craved the stuff. Cabell hoped he wouldn't take that drink. He didn't know if he had the strength; he only hoped, and lived minute by minute, hour by hour, painfully sober, nauseated, hurting in every fiber, but determined.

The mail consisted of a letter from his agent in Raleigh, another from an agent in Edinburgh, a bill from his tailor, and two invitations to social affairs. A few society matrons had chosen to ignore the stigma of his divorce and, considering the dearth of financially sound, eligible bachelors in the area, decided that Cabell Dorset was acceptable after all. He tossed the invitations aside. He was in no mood to meet a covey of marriageable females.

Gingerly he picked up the dirty envelope and opened it, wondering whom he had offended this time. He scanned the lines quickly, then again, scarcely believing his eyes.

"My God! Finally!"

Bless John Charles Tyler, whoever the fellow was! The moment's elation made Cabell's hand shake from more than lack of a drink. He was going to have his son back at long last. Sending money for the passage was no problem. He would pay the devil's way to hell and back if he could deliver Peter to him.

"Theo! Get in here!"

Theo appeared, eyes wide with alarm. "Yassir! What's wrong?"

"Nothing's wrong!" Cabell paced across the dining room and back, feeling better than he had in days, in years. "Theo, something has finally gone right! Have my horse saddled and brought around. I need to go to the bank. How much do you suppose it costs to get to—where the hell is Tubac, Arizona?"

"Tobacco, Arizona? I don' know."

"Are there rails into Arizona Territory yet? No, of course not. Who would want to go there? Stage lines, then. I need to find a booking agent to determine the amount. Wait!"

"Yassir?"

"I'll go to Tubac myself!"

Theo rolled his eyes.

"Don't give me that look!" Cabell warned.

"Massa, you still be sick. You can hardly sit yo' horse to ride to church! Now you gonna go all the way to this place? Mus' be at least a hun'red mile away!"

When the idea first popped out of his mouth, it had seemed wild to Cabell as well, but Theo's low opinion of his fitness spurred him to rise to the challenge. "I am not sick. When I fell off my horse on the way to church that day, I . . . I hadn't had enough to eat. It was just a small dizzy spell is all. But that's over. Right now I'm just tired."

"Yassir." Theo's voice was rich in the understanding of what kind of effort was making his employer tired. Cabell shot him a look full of affection.

"Besides, I'm certainly not going to be riding a horse all the way to Arizona. There are steamers, trains, stagecoaches. It's modern days, Theo. A man can cross the country now in weeks instead of months."

"Yassir."

"Now, go have my horse brought around."

"You still goin' to the bank?"

"No. Just do it."

Somewhere between the time he'd read the glorious news in Mr. Tyler's letter and the moment he'd fastened on the determination to fetch Peter himself, some subconscious part of him had decided to visit Nell. At the very thought his palms began to sweat. She deserved to hear that Rachel and Peter had been found. For good or ill, Rachel had been the bond tying them together these past weeks. If he set off on this course of action without telling Nell, she would have one more thing not to forgive him for.

It was just an excuse to see her, Cabell chided himself. Hadn't he already made enough of a fool of himself? It had been four days since he'd awakened to find her gone from his bed. The remnants of history's worst hangover hadn't kept him from remembering the inexcusable way he'd taken advantage of her soft heart, and her soft, untutored, and wholly delectable body. Not until a full day had passed had he mustered enough courage to apologize. He'd tried to find her at her brother's home, but she had been out walking, he was informed by old Saul. Cabell had managed to find her in a nearby park, sitting beneath the branches of a huge oak and looking more beautiful than he would have believed possible. How had he not realized, all these years, that Nell was beautiful in a way that no other woman even approached?

What a chastening interview that had been! Not that Nell had castigated him. Just the opposite. She had taken the responsibility upon herself. She'd been matter-of-fact and gracious, if a bit distant. Her brother knew that she'd cared for Cabell in his "illness." David had scolded her thoroughly for her foolishness, though she'd not told him the whole of it, Nell had admitted, and a twinkle of wry humor had momentarily relieved the sober darkness of her eyes.

God, what a cad he'd felt himself to be! Not only had he debauched an innocent woman—as good-hearted and pure a woman as ever lived—but she was being a sport about it. He'd have preferred her to rail at him, weep, demand satisfaction. Anything but look at him so calmly with that hint of disappointment in her eyes.

Still, he had to see her again. Maybe this time she'd be decently mad.

Theo announced disapprovingly, "Yo' horse is ready."

Marching as if to battle, Cabell jammed his hat upon his head and went out the front door.

Nell tried to maintain her composure when Saul came to the solarium door and announced to her and her sister-in-law, Elizabeth, that Cabell Dorset had come to call. Elizabeth looked up from her sewing and scowled her disapproval. While David had been concerned and mildly shocked that Nell had "sat with" Cabell during his illness—as Nell had phrased it—with only Theo and Clara as chaperones, Elizabeth had been horrified. She would not have approved of Nell risking the family reputation by such behavior with any man, but the fact that Cabell was divorced and known to be rather immoderate in his drinking habits made the situation even worse.

And now the libertine had the effrontery to call at their house. "We are not receiving," Elizabeth said tersely.

"Saul, wait!" Nell stopped the butler before he could turn away. "Elizabeth, Cabell is a friend. He's done nothing to deserve such rudeness." Not quite true, but she certainly wasn't going to confide the whole of it to her sister-in-law.

Elizabeth drove her needle into her embroidery with a vicious jab. "Nell, you are chasing disaster by letting this man court you."

"Court me? Elizabeth, I assure you, Cabell is not courting me."

"I don't know what you would call it if not courting. He spent all afternoon with you at the church picnic, and he's called here for you at least twice. Emily Baxter saw the two of you walking together in the park just two days ago, and the way servants talk, I'm surprised that the whole city isn't gossiping about you being in his house, alone, all that time—"

"Elizabeth, I'm a grown woman, a spinster, not some green girl who needs guarding every moment of the day."

"Just because you're no longer young doesn't mean you're not vulnerable to gossip!" Elizabeth snapped. She tossed an exasperated look toward Saul. "Very well, take Mr. Dorset to the formal parlor and tell him we will be there shortly."

Nell started to rise, but Elizabeth chided her: "Stay where you are. You don't want the man to think we are scurrying to greet him. He can wait on our pleasure. If you ask me, Cabell Dorset has too much money and too few scruples. But obviously you are not interested in my opinion."

Nell contained her impatience with a sigh. Her stomach was doing flip-flops, her heart beating double time. Since being with Cabell in that most forbidden, unexpectedly sweet way, her world had changed. Her skin had become exquisitely sensitive to the light caress of the wind, the stroke of a brush through her hair, the butterfly touch of her own fingers when she dressed or undressed. Colors seemed more vibrant, scents sharper. Everything somehow reminded her of Cabell, of the wondrous thing they'd done together that racked her with both joy and guilt.

She had been a coward at the last, unable to face the aftermath, leaving before he woke. Perhaps her foolish heart had nurtured some hope that their spontaneous union had been special, that he would come after her and declare his love. Foolish woman! When he finally had come after her, he'd stumbled all over himself apologizing, then told her what a grand sport she was. The fool!

Elizabeth finally set her sewing aside and rose imperiously. "Now we can go. Come, Nell."

Cabell was leaning against the fireplace mantel looking down onto the swept grate when they walked into the parlor. He straightened and turned at their entrance.

"Good morning, Mr. Dorset." Elizabeth's greeting was chilly.

"Mrs. Blanchard," Cabell replied, nodding politely to Elizabeth. Then the full weight of his gaze shifted to Nell. "Both of you ladies are looking lovely this morning."

Elizabeth sniffed. "This is an unusual time of day for a call, Mr. Dorset."

"I apologize for the unfashionably early hour, Mrs. Blanchard, but I needed a word with Nell."

"Yes? And what word is that?" Elizabeth prompted, one brow raised.

"Alone, if you don't mind," Cabell said.

"Mr. Dorset, my husband's house is not a house of assignation."

"Of course it isn't. And Nell is not a woman who would permit an assignation, Mrs. Blanchard."

As Cabell's voice took on a steely tone in her defense, Nell couldn't help but smile. "Elizabeth, it's all right. I'll speak to Cabell alone."

"Not in my house," Elizabeth said with quiet determination.

"Then we'll simply walk together," Nell suggested. "Surely there's no harm in that. Would that be acceptable, Cabell?"

Cabell looked relieved. "That would be delightful."

Elizabeth looked daggers at her, but Nell merely smiled and took Cabell's arm. It was late in life to discover the thrill of rebellion, but Nell enjoyed it anyway.

They walked along the overgrown paths of the garden behind the house. Cabell kept Nell's arm when she subtly tried to withdraw it.

"Elizabeth certainly has changed since the days we were all young together."

"We've all changed," Nell said.

"Yes." His smile had a bitter twist to it. "Time and circumstances have a way of doing in youthful optimism, don't they?"

She tilted her head. "Is that what happens?"

"Or maybe we do ourselves in."

Nell hadn't the patience for wordplay. Their relationship had surely progressed beyond that. "Cabell, why are you here?"

"Trust Miss Nell Blanchard to get right to the point." Cabell cleared his throat, then stopped and gently spun her around to face him, holding her by the upper arms. "I'm here to tell you . . . I thought you would want to know. . . ." He sighed and took a deep breath. "Nell, I've found Rachel and Peter."

Her heart fell. "How?"

"I distributed a ream of posters all over the West. Just this morning I got a letter from a fellow who said he's found them. He needs funds to arrange for Peter's travel."

"Posters? Like wanted posters?"

"Well, yes. I suppose."

"You'll have every bounty hunter in the West going after them! Do you know what sort of men those are?"

Cabell's brows furrowed with irritation. "As much money as I offered for Peter, I'm certain whoever found him is taking extremely good care of him."

"And what about Rachel? How are they going to treat her?"

"Well—"

"You didn't think of that, did you?"

"No one's going to hurt Rachel!"

"How do you know? Honestly, Cabell. You don't think! You are so single-minded that you see only what you want to see!"

"If you had told me where she was it might not have come to this! I notice that you didn't ask where I found her."

"I never lied. I never said that I didn't know where Rachel was."

He released her, turned, ran his hand through his hair, then turned back with a calmer mien. "I'm sorry. I shouldn't be cross with you, Nell. You are a person who takes the vows of friendship very seriously, and I respect that. I understand why you couldn't tell me. Truly, I never meant to put Rachel in danger with what I did. But what's done is done, and Peter has been found."

"I see."

"I'm going to Arizona Territory. I think it will be easier on Peter if he makes the trip back with me."

They resumed walking, not touching as they had been before. Nell clasped her hands behind her back and looked at the ground in front of her. "I don't suppose you would reconsider and leave them alone."

"I can't."

Nell sighed. "You mean you won't." She knew what she was about to do was stepping over the edge, and for some strange reason she didn't care. Things that had seemed terribly important to her a week ago were no longer important. Right and wrong, proper and improper, had blurred. "In that case, Cabell, I will go to Arizona Territory with you."

He stopped abruptly and caught her arm. "You'll what?"

"I'll go with you. If you're going to take Peter, then

Rachel will need me. Heaven knows, I'm of little enough use here living with David and Elizabeth. I might as well go where I'm needed."

"Nell, that's preposterous!"

"I'll admit it's a bit improper for us to travel together—"

"A *bit* improper?"

"But I don't care. Rachel will need someone to turn to for comfort. And someone needs to make sure you treat her properly."

"What do you think I'm going to do? Beat her senseless?"

Nell shot him a look that was merciless.

His eyes dropped. "I supposed that was an ill-advised question. I've got that devil inside me under control, Nell. I haven't taken a drink since we . . . since that night."

"I'm still going."

The day had been the longest one in Rachel's life, but night had finally come. The Apaches were still there. A huge bonfire lit the center of the wagon circle, where the raiders celebrated with great volumes of the whiskey that the train had been hauling to Mesilla. Their shouting had mostly died down, as had the arguments, the laughter, the war whoops.

The time had come, Rachel knew. For better or worse, the waiting had to end now. She opened the wagon box a crack and angled herself so that she could see the fire. The bodies that lay around it were not massacred whites but Apaches who had succumbed to liquor. Five or six warriors were still upright, maybe more that she couldn't see, but they were swaying on their feet.

"Follow me," she said to Peter. "And be very quiet."

Rachel opened the door inch by inch and slipped out, clutching J.C.'s pistol in her hand and telling herself that even death was preferable to staying in the wagon box one more minute. Her cramped muscles screamed. Her legs almost wouldn't hold her when she dropped to the ground.

Peter groaned as he emerged from their prison. Rachel shushed him and froze, watching the Indians. They showed no signs of having heard, so she lifted Peter down from the wagon. Breathing hard, they crouched in the shadow of the wheel. Faint as a breath of wind came another groan. Rachel glared at her son. He shook his head.

Then Rachel saw the body lying beneath the wagon. Instantly she knew who lay there. J.C. The faint light of the bonfire gleamed off blood that soaked his left side and right leg, but he'd made a sound. J.C. was alive.

Rachel cautioned Peter to stay put while she slithered beneath the wagon. "J.C.!"

At the soft hiss of her whisper his hand scraped through the dirt and closed over hers.

"Can you move?" She tugged on his arm, and he swore under his breath.

"You've got to move, J.C. The Apaches are drunk and blinded by that big fire. We can get away."

A soft "Shit!" was followed by words even more unsavory, but when Rachel pulled on his arm, J.C. crawled slowly forward. She could feel the stickiness of his blood, smell its copper scent.

"Rifle," J.C. panted when they were clear of the wagon. "Get the rifle."

She handed Peter the pistol and dove back beneath the wagon for the rifle. Then she took one of J.C.'s arms, Peter the other, and they crawled into the darkness where the firelight couldn't reach them. When they'd gone twenty yards, J.C. wanted to give up.

"Go on," he urged Rachel. "I'm dead anyway."

"Don't give me that!" Rachel objected. "Quitter. Coward!"

The whites of his eyes flashed as he glared.

"Milksop! Craven!" she added for good measure.

"Bitch!" he groaned.

"That's more like it. Come on, bounty hunter."

It seemed to take half the night for them to reach the rocks of the Santa Rita foothills, only a hundred or so yards east of the wagons. Slowly and painfully they all but dragged J.C. up the hillside to a rugged outcrop that could conceal them from the valley below. When they looked back, it seemed as if no time had passed. The fire still burned. The Indians left conscious were drinking Mr. Coates's endless supply of whiskey. Two of the Apaches seemed to be arguing over something.

Then the horror began all over again. One of the arguing Apaches left the fire for a moment and came back dragging a man whose pleas could be heard even from where Rachel watched.

"A prisoner," J.C. said in a hoarse voice.

"Oh, my God! There was someone else left alive."

"We couldn't have gotten to him."

The Apaches that remained awake had gathered around the man, who struggled as they stripped him and tied him to one of the huge rear wheels of a wagon.

"No," Rachel groaned, closing her eyes. "No."

The prisoner screamed in anticipation of what his tormentors would do to him.

"Give me the rifle," J.C. said.

"What are you going to do?" she asked. "You can't kill all of them."

"No. But I can kill that poor devil whose brains they're going to boil."

Rachel bit down hard on her lower lip and handed him the rifle. "It's too far. You can't possibly make that shot."

"Watch me."

The mule skinner was screaming, sounds that Rachel was sure would echo in her nightmares for years. J.C. propped the barrel of the rifle on a rock and wiped the back of his hand across his eyes. She heard the painful intake of his breath.

Peter squeezed her hand. "Won't the Indians know we're here then?"

"We'll hide," she assured him. "They're drunk. They'll never find us."

Rachel closed her eyes, praying for J.C. to fire, praying for the screams to end. Then the sharp report of the rifle cut across her prayers. The cries of the mule skinner fell silent, then were replaced by the indignant howls of the Indians themselves.

"Here they come," Peter said.

14

Their flight was hampered by both darkness and J.C.'s condition, but the Apaches were hampered as well, for even those who were steady enough to pursue them were nearly falling-down drunk. Warriors who usually moved through the desert as smoothly and silently as shadows stumbled over themselves and their comrades and argued volubly in their own language. As Rachel and Peter helped J.C. over the rough ground, the position of their pursuers was easy to discern, and never very close.

When they reached the mouth of one of the narrow canyons that cut the western slope of the Santa Ritas, they felt confident enough to pause for a rest. J.C. was nearly a dead weight dragging them down.

"Why don't you two just go on?" J.C. offered in a voice hoarse with pain. "Just leave me here."

"Stop trying to be noble!" Rachel snapped. "It's not in your nature."

"I'll stop trying to be noble when you stop trying to be a heroine," he shot back.

"Hey, look!" Peter pointed to a darker shadow in the

jumbled black and gray of the rocks farther up the canyon. "What's that?"

J.C. looked in the direction Peter pointed, but just shook his head wearily.

"If we're lucky, it might be a cave," Rachel said. "You two stay here. There's no sense in all of us climbing up there if it's nothing."

"Ma! I want to go. I saw it first."

"Peter! Do as I say. You stay here, keep down, and be quiet." Rachel hadn't the energy for patience right now. Every step felt as though it would be her last before she collapsed in a heap of exhaustion.

Ten minutes later she reached the rocks below the shadow Peter had seen. By the time she had climbed to the level of the shadow, she was so tired, her head swam. Strangely enough, giddy laughter bubbled up inside her. What would her fellow students at Miss Wordsworth's Seminary for Young Ladies think if they could see her now, hands and knees scraped, nails broken, hair flying wild, clothing covered with J.C.'s blood and stiff with her own dried sweat, and searching for a hiding place in the rocks like a hunted animal? She stifled the hysterical desire to laugh, and the giggles came out as sobs instead. She knelt in the dirt, covered her face with hands raw from scrambling over the rocks, and sobbed. If Peter and J.C. hadn't been waiting for her back at the mouth of the canyon, she would have lain down and simply waited for death to claim her.

But there were at least two people in this wretched world who needed her, so she went on, stumbling into the deeper blackness that Peter had spied in the side of the canyon. It was indeed a cave, though how big or how deep she couldn't tell in the darkness. Cautiously she tossed a rock inside. No grunt, growl, or fleeing animal indicated that the cave was presently inhabited. When she went in, she could stand full height without her head hitting the ceiling, and when she turned to look outward, the whole north end of the Santa Cruz Valley was a panorama in the milky moonlight.

"Well," she said to herself with a sigh, "if the devils find us, at least we'll be able to see them coming."

It took much of the rest of the night for Peter and Rachel to help J.C. to the cave, all the while still hearing sounds of their pursuers. This time, instead of climbing up the side of the canyon to the cave, Rachel found, or rather stumbled over, a game trail that zigzagged up the slope and made the going much easier. J.C.'s every breath was a ragged gasp of pain. When they stumbled together through the cave's mouth, he collapsed and lay in an unmoving heap.

"Is he dead?" Peter asked in a worried tone as Rachel rolled J.C. away from the entrance.

Rachel lowered her ear to the bounty hunter's broad chest. For a moment she couldn't hear his heart for the pounding of her own, and a flash of panic jolted her nerves, but then she discerned the rapid beat of his pulse. "He's alive." His chances of being alive in the morning she couldn't even guess at.

"Are the Apaches gonna find us?"

"I hope not."

They crouched in the entrance of the cave, listening to the sounds of the Apaches in the canyon below. Eventually the sounds grew more distant. Finally they faded away altogether. Only the faint sigh of wind in the junipers and bear grass disturbed the night. They could still see the Indians' bonfire and the wagons just below the first slopes of the foothills, just beyond the canyon mouth. Occasionally a tiny silhouette passed in front of the fire. Rachel assumed the searchers had returned to the site of their victory.

"Will they come back?" Peter asked.

"I don't know." In daylight the Indians would be able to see their tracks, especially if they'd sobered up by then. "I suppose I should go brush the path up here so that our footprints don't show." Even the threat of being found hardly made it worth the effort to get to her feet. But she did it anyway.

Too soon the secure darkness of night faded away and morning spread its warm, rosy light across the valley. Though their little side canyon was still in shadow, Rachel woke early. She'd slept little after returning from brushing the game trail free of their tracks. Though her body had hungered for sleep, and still did, her mind wouldn't rest.

She rose onto one elbow and looked around her. The dim light showed a dry and dusty cave, high enough for a tall man to stand comfortably, and big enough for the dim light to be swallowed toward the back, leaving the depths of the cave in mystery. The dirt floor upon which she'd slept was roughly level, littered with rocks and animal droppings. The ashes of a long-dead fire were a gray smudge on the floor, and a dead tree trunk lay beside the old fire where someone had dragged it inside to serve as a bench. Obviously the cave had served as refuge before for both people and animals.

She lay back down and closed her eyes, weary to the core. Her shoulder ached abominally, and sorely abused muscles protested their hard bed as well as the treatment they'd received the day before.

"Ma!" came a whisper from the cave entrance.

Rachel slitted open one eye to see her son bounce toward her. With the resilience of youth, Peter seemed to be suffering no ill effects from yesterday's grim adventure.

"Ma!" The whisper was louder this time as Peter

shook her shoulder. "Come look! The Apaches are gone!"

That good news inspired her to crawl over to the cave entrance and look outside. Tiny with distance, the freight wagons looked like broken and abandoned toys on the valley floor. Their attackers were nowhere in sight.

"Thank God!" Rachel murmured.

Her fervent prayer elicited a groan from J.C.

"He's still alive," Peter announced.

Just barely, from the look of him, Rachel noted. Seen in the light, J.C. looked appalling. The left side of his shirt from shoulder to waist was crusted with blood, and a bullet wound high up on his right thigh oozed scarlet. His skin was pale and waxy, and deep lines etched his brow and framed his mouth.

"You look awful!" was all that Rachel could think to say.

"Yeah." He made a wan attempt to smile.

"The Injuns are gone," Peter repeated for J.C.'s benefit.

"Good for them. Probably nursing the grandaddy of all hangovers and forgotten all about us."

"Why didn't you shoot 'em all?" Peter demanded with sudden vehemence. "You could've!"

J.C. merely grimaced. "The way those Apaches have got to feel this morning, I'm sure they'd thank me for shooting them."

"If I'd had that rifle down there, those Apaches woulda been vulture bait!" The boy spat onto the dirt floor of the cave to punctuate his statement.

"Peter!" Rachel chided. "Don't be vulgar. And leave J.C. alone. Come over here and help me."

Together they assisted J.C. to a sitting position with

his back against the cave wall. Peter still muttered about killing Indians.

"Boy," J.C. finally gritted out, "if you'd had that rifle down on those rocks, you wouldn't have had enough ammunition to kill all those Indians, and if you had, what good would it have done?"

"I woulda liked blowin' their heads off!"

J.C. took a few deep, weary breaths, then pointed a finger in Peter's direction. "Let me tell you something, Big Red. It's easy to kill when you're hating. The Apaches hate the white man and the Mexicans because they moved in on their land, and so they kill them. The white man and Mexicans hate Apaches because they stand in the way of what they think of as progress, so they kill the Apaches. But killing someone always takes something away from the person who does the killing, no matter how much you think someone needs killing."

"Yeah?" Peter asked pugnaciously. "How many men have you killed?"

J.C. sighed and dropped his head back against the rock wall. "Let's just say I speak from bad experience."

"You're quite a philosopher for a bounty hunter," Rachel noted.

He met her gaze with a wry smile. "And you're quite a scrapper for a Southern belle."

"I haven't been a Southern belle for some time."

"Yeah, well, I wouldn't have been a bounty hunter much longer if my luck had held, which it didn't." He looked down at himself, at the useless leg, the blood-covered clothing, and let out a breath that seemed to deflate his whole body.

He was giving up, Rachel realized. J.C. was staring death in the face and conceding defeat. She forced herself to take a close look at the damage done his body. "Maybe I can tear up my petticoat and make some bandages. You look as though you need some. Peter, help me move him over here where the light is better."

J.C. endured stoically as they dragged him nearer the cave entrance, where bright sunlight was just beginning to penetrate.

"You ever doctored any wounds?" J.C. asked when he'd caught his breath.

"I took care of a rattlesnake bite once, and also a fellow who got shot in a brawl in Gallegos's saloon." Gingerly she peeled his crusted shirt away from shoulder and ribs. The wounds there were ugly but shallow. The bleeding had stopped, and his recent move hadn't started it again. "These don't look too bad."

The leg looked infinitely worse, though Rachel didn't want to say anything. Some of the blood on his trousers was fresh, and the trouser seams were strained to the limit by the swelling of his thigh.

"Cut it off," J.C. told her.

"What?" The worst possible image crossed Rachel's mind.

"Cut off the trouser leg. Use the knife in my belt."

"Oh. Yes. Of course."

Rachel gritted her teeth as she carefully slit the pant leg from crotch to ankle and peeled it back from his angry flesh. She looked at the wound and bit her lip.

J.C. looked down at himself, his face expressionless. "The bullet's still in there."

"How do you know?"

"I know how it feels. Do you see a hole where it went out?"

Rachel hesitated to look that closely. Her stomach was beginning to rise.

"Do you?"

"No."

"Then it's still there. You think you have the guts to

take it out?" It was a challenge, plain and simple, but Rachel wasn't in the mood to be goaded.

"I think we should wait until a doctor can do it."

J.C. chuckled dryly. "All right. Why don't you just run down the street and ask the doc to come?"

Rachel bit her lip. "Can't it wait?"

"Sure. It can stay in there forever. You can bury me with it in a day or two."

"I've never taken out a bullet!"

"Well, if you don't take it out, you might as well just take the pistol and shoot me."

She gave him a tortured look. His tone softened. "Believe me, Rachel, it'll be harder on me than on you. Just consider it revenge."

"Why don't we just hit him over the head with a rock so he won't feel anything?" Peter suggested.

"That ought to finish the job the Apaches started," J.C. said.

"Oh, damn," Rachel muttered. She was going to have to do it whether she wanted to or not.

"You might want to wipe some of the dirt off that knife before you begin."

Rachel didn't appreciate his weak attempt at teasing. "Behave yourself," she warned, "or I'll let Peter do it his way. And Peter, I want you to climb down to the canyon floor and see if you can find us some water. If there isn't any close by, then dig in the sand. And if you see or hear anything that might be an Indian, get back here fast."

Peter's chest swelled with the importance of his mission.

"Wait, Peter." J.C. motioned the boy to him. "Before you go, help your mother drag that tree trunk over here. Then find something to tie my hands to it. I wouldn't want to start flailing around and knock your mother over the head while she's cutting on me."

"Can't you be brave and not move?" Peter asked.

"I'm not that brave, kid."

Rachel and Peter between them moved the log to a spot where the light was the brightest, and helped J.C. prop himself against it. Then Rachel turned her back toward them and removed a petticoat. Most of it she cut into wide swaths to use as bandages. The rest she twisted into ropes that they used to securely bind J.C.'s hands to the log. Rachel tried not to think about what she was about to do.

"You two ought to be getting real good at this," J.C. observed as they tied him. "You've had enough practice."

"We're already good at it," Peter declared, tightening the last knot.

"I can tell you're enjoying the job."

Peter grinned.

"Peter, go on now," Rachel said. "And be very, very careful."

"I'll be sneakier 'n Cochise himself!" the boy boasted.

With a worried frown Rachel watched him bound out the cave.

"He'll be all right," said J.C. "There's no need for him to see this, and those Apaches are a long way from here by now. Probably bragging to their buddies about all the loot they stole from the train."

Rachel's fingers turned white on the hilt of the knife. "Are you sure we have to do this?"

"Yes," he said with cold determination.

Rachel followed J.C.'s glance downward at his exposed thigh. As men's legs went, this one was a classic, knotted with hard muscle, sculpted by sinew. But the picture was desecrated by the damage done by the lead ball. The hole was high up on the thigh and almost hidden by discolored, swollen flesh. Red streaks shot outward from the initial wound.

"I suppose I could try to dig it out myself," he offered.

"That's ridiculous."

He raised a brow at her and smiled. At least, she noted, the glitter in his eyes showed a determination to live. She looked at the knife in her hand and wiped the blade with one of the cleaner strips of petticoat. "I suppose we might as well get to it."

She focused on his thigh, on the hard muscle and sinew mangled into a bloody and swollen mess. Her squeamishness left her. As had happened other times during the last three years when she'd been forced to do something she thought was impossible, a calm fell over her. Suddenly she could think and act outside the distractions of emotion.

As gently as possible she probed the swollen area with her fingers, trying to locate the slug. "Hold still," she said as he flinched.

"Yes, ma'am."

She could feel it, or so she thought. It was deep into the muscle, and was going to be devilish hard to get out.

"It's down there."

"I could have told you that," he gritted out.

"Remember when you saved me from that Apache back in Tubac and then spent the next week changing my bandages and playing nursemaid?" She wiped the blood from her hand and once again carefully wiped the blade of the knife.

"Yeah. I remember."

"I think this makes us even. Actually, all things considered, I think I'm coming out of this being owed."

"Whatever you say."

"I'll remind you that you said that." She took a steadying breath. "You ready for this?"

He nodded, then grunted and clenched his jaw as Rachel made a cautious incision into the swollen wound. She wiped away the pus and blood that flowed out over his thigh and groin.

"Careful what you're cutting there." His attempt at a smile came out as a grimace.

"Maybe I should move the knife over a bit and spare womankind the burden of your attention."

"You wouldn't want to—" The words garbled into a groan as she cut again.

"Hold still." The opening was big enough now for her to insert a finger. She clenched her teeth as she searched for the slug. Every muscle in J.C.'s body tensed furiously against the pain.

"I'm sorry," she hissed through clenched teeth. "I'm sorry."

His agony wrenched the apology from her, but she managed to stay focused on her task. Finally she found it. It moved slightly at the touch of her finger. J.C.'s breath came in short spurts. Rachel could feel the beat of his racing heart.

She had to cut deeper. This time she found the slug with her knife. Her hands were slippery with J.C.'s blood, and the sweat dripping from her brow stung her eyes and blurred her vision. Again and again she tried to lift the lead ball from his flesh, and each time it slipped away.

"I'm sorry," she whispered hoarsely. "I'm so sorry."

J.C.'s eyes were closed. Every cord in his neck stood out; his arms and shoulders bulged as he strained against the bonds that held him to the log. Somehow he found the strength to hold his leg still.

It wasn't until he passed out and the muscles that had

worked against her relaxed that Rachel was able to pry the lead ball out of J.C.'s leg. When it was done, she wiped her hands and the knife on her already soiled skirts, untied and cleaned J.C. the best she could, then stepped beyond the cave entrance and threw up. Her stomach was empty of everything but bile, but she threw up anyway.

J.C. still lay unconscious, and there was nothing more Rachel could do for him, so she set out in search of Peter. She found him in the sandy bottom of the canyon at a spot where sand gave way to a rocky streambed shaded by mountain mahogany and juniper. A trickle of water ran down the streambed, pooling in potholes in the rock. Peter sat on a boulder twirling a bare toe in one little pool.

"Is he still alive?" Peter asked when he saw Rachel.

"Yes."

"Did the slug come out?"

"Yes."

Rachel knelt by one of the little pools and took a deep drink. The water was gritty and warm, but fine wine couldn't have tasted as good. "We need to find some way to carry water back to the cave."

"Yeah. I guess." Peter pulled his toe from the water and brushed a sweaty strand of fiery hair off his brow. "You know, Ma, now that the Injuns are gone, we could walk back to Tubac, you and me."

Rachel sighed, sat back, and rested her elbows on her knees. "And leave J.C.?"

Peter's mouth twisted this way and that. He looked down at the sand and sighed.

"You don't want to leave J.C. to die, Peter, no matter what he's done to us. You're not that kind of person."

He poked a finger into the sand and circled it in spirals and curlicues. "I guess not."

"J.C. saved our lives by hiding us in the wagon. You know that, don't you?"

"Yeah. I guess."

"So we have to be decent to him." Rachel grinned. "At least until he's well."

"But how're we gonna get home?"

"We'll watch for travelers in the valley and try to get help if anyone comes. Until then we'd better stay hidden in that nice cave you found."

"What're we going to eat?"

"Do you think you could get us a rabbit or a squirrel?"

His eyes brightened. "Can I use the gun?"

"No. If there's Apaches about, they might hear. Can you throw a stone or something?"

Peter rolled his eyes and gave his mother a long-suffering look.

"We can always just eat juniper berries," she suggested.

"I'll think of a way to get a rabbit," Peter said with a disgusted sigh.

Rachel cursed her lack of woods lore as she looked around the banks of the streambed for something that would hold water. The ground was littered with leaves, bark, stones, sticks, blue juniper berries, but absolutely nothing she could make into a water carrier. Finally she tore more strips from her one remaining petticoat, muttering that she was going to be naked before this adventure was done, soaked the strips in water, and carried them up to the cave. She cleaned J.C.'s wound as best she could, then dripped water from another of the strips into his mouth. His eyes slitted open and his tongue passed hungrily over his lips.

"I'm still alive?" he croaked.

"Does this look like the Pearly Gates?"

He closed his eyes and breathed deeply for a moment, as if the mere effort of talking had winded him. His face was flushed, and when Rachel ran one of the wet strips over it, the skin was hot to her touch. Before she could take her hand away, he caught it in his own and settled it on his chest.

"Rachel, thank you."

Rachel did not want the softening she felt in her heart. "I would have done the same for a dog, J.C."

He smiled faintly. "Lucky dog."

Peter returned shortly, proudly carrying a hare he'd managed to kill with a thrown stone. Rachel cooked the rabbit over a fire she started with the matches that J.C. had in one pocket. She discovered that a fire built on the ashy gray smudge of the floor vented upward into some unseen airway that carried the smoke away. Nevertheless immediately after the rabbit was done, she kicked dirt over the flames, fearing that the orange glow would attract hostile eyes. The Apaches who had attacked them might have ridden off to nurse their hangovers, but other bands might be in the vicinity.

The hare and a handful of juniper berries was the first meal they'd had in two days. J.C. didn't eat, though he thirstily drank every drop of water that Rachel could manage to transport from the spring. By dark he was consumed by fever, alternately sweating and shivering in the still, cool air of the cave. With the cold, hard stone as a bed and no blankets to warm him, he shivered more than he sweated, so Rachel and Peter tried to warm him with their bodies, Peter huddled against one side and Rachel huddled against the other. J.C. grew quiet for a while. Rachel lay for a few minutes listening to Peter's high-pitched little-boy snores echoing in the cave, and then fell asleep herself. Only an instant later, it seemed, J.C.'s ravings brought her awake. He'd been shivering when she fell asleep, but now he burned with a fire beneath his skin, and apparently in his soul as well, for his words were wild and garbled.

Rachel bathed his face and neck with a rag still damp from the spring. "Quiet, J.C. Quiet. Lie still."

"What's he saying?" Peter asked.

"It's just the fever, Peter. He's talking crazy."

J.C. started to rise, then fell back to the floor. One thrashing arm almost hit her in the face.

"Let's tie him up again," Peter suggested.

"No, Peter. Get me another wet rag from over there."

Rachel bathed his face again, then opened his shirt and ran the damp rag over his sweaty, heaving chest. His tossing and turning had opened the shallow wound along his ribs. Blood trickled down his side.

"Oh, J.C.!" Wearily Rachel leaned forward until her brow rested against his. It seemed monstrous, somehow, that something as small as a tiny ball of lead could bring down such a magnificent physical machine as this man. All the muscle and sinew, the strength and grace, and yes, intelligence, wit, and heart as well—all destroyed in a pointless savage raid by a stupid ball of lead the size of a pea.

Suddenly calm, J.C. breathed out a sigh. "Rachel?"

"Yes, J.C. I'm here."

"Rachel!"

It wasn't her that he called, Rachel realized then, but a Rachel who passed through his fevered dreams.

"Jesus! Rachel! Do it again. You've got the goddamned prettiest . . ."

Rachel's face burned as she listened to an enumeration of her charms that was a far cry from sweet nothings. Peter's eyes grew wide.

"You just march yourself over there, young man!" Rachel pointed her son toward the far end of the cave.

"And close your big ears. You're too young to be listening to what goes through a grown man's mind when he's out of his head."

J.C. sweated and carried on in great detail—sometimes in a whisper, sometimes a mighty shout—just what he would find entertaining to do to her if ever he got her alone in bed. Rachel cooled both his temperature and his ardor as best she could with the grimy damp strips of petticoat she'd carried up from the spring. Below his waistband, evidence that he was enjoying himself rose in proportion to his fevered, lustful imaginings. Rachel averted her eyes and covered the area with the fullness of her skirt. After all, Peter was probably watching, and there were some things a boy wouldn't understand at the tender age of nine.

"J.C.," she whispered to her patient. "You'd damned well better live. I need you alive and kicking so that I can get back at you for all of this."

15

Was this death? J.C. wondered. This chilly, gray, featureless plain? If so, death was a damned disappointment. He'd expected hell to be more colorful, certainly hotter, and filled with pain of a more spiritual kind than the sort he was experiencing right then. He felt as if he'd been worked over with a sledgehammer inside and out. Furtive voices skittered at the margins of his hearing. Probably imps plotting some devilish torture.

He tried to move, and succeeded at the price of a lightning bolt of pain that sizzled from his right thigh to his left shoulder, searing everything in between. The jolt made his senses swim, then dropped them back into focus. Suddenly he remembered where he was. The featureless gray plain that filled his vision was the ceiling of the cave where they'd taken refuge from the Apaches. The chill in the air told him it was morning, and the pain in his leg let him know that he was very much alive.

J.C. had only to turn his head to discover the source of the furtive voices. Rachel and Peter crouched on hands and knees at the mouth of the cave, looking out toward the valley and whispering in low, excited tones.

Rachel's backside was displayed to great advantage, J.C. noted. Even his present incapacity couldn't keep him from appreciating a sight like that.

"What's up?" he croaked.

His voice brought the two whirling around to look at him. A momentary softness glowed in Rachel's eyes, but she quickly banished it. "Welcome back," she said in a carefully neutral voice.

"We figured you would be dead by this morning!" Peter told him.

"I've been carved by worse than your mother and survived," he told her.

Rachel knelt beside him and laid a cool hand on his brow. "The fever's gone. Now I know what 'too ornery to die' means."

"I feel like hell."

"Well, your leg looks better. It's not as swollen as it was. I'll change the bandage. I expect it will hurt."

He flashed her a grin. "Don't sound so happy about it."

A smile tugged at her mouth, in spite of an obvious attempt to remain solemn. "You're mighty cocky for a man flat on his back and full of holes."

Once Rachel started to peel the crusted bandage away, J.C. endured in silence, concentrating on the fall of brilliant hair that spilled over her shoulders. He tried to lose himself in the color, to hide from pain by imagining the softness. Beautiful women were supposed to be blond, or at least brunettes with the sheen of silk in their hair, but J.C. had decided that men who didn't appreciate red hair and freckles had missed a lot.

"Your leg really is a lot better," she said. "I'm amazed."

"Luck of the devil, I guess."

"How does it feel?"

"About as bad as it looks." He raised a brow at the ruffled strip of material she wound around his thigh.

"Petticoats," she explained. "When I run out of petticoats, you're out of luck."

"Huh! Ruffled bandages! What's the world coming to?"

Peter brought over a heap of sodden cotton strips piled like noodles upon a slab of bark.

"What's that?" J.C. asked dubiously.

"Water," Rachel informed him. "Squeeze it into your mouth." At his incredulous look she bristled. "It was the only way I could think of to carry water up here from the spring. We don't exactly have a set of buckets here."

The water was rank, but it was wet. "We've got to come up with a better system than this," J.C. choked.

"If we catch the horse," Peter suggested, "someone could ride for help."

"What horse?" asked J.C.

"The one in the canyon," Peter said. "We were watchin' 'im. He's been here since the sun came up."

"Is there an Indian on him?" J.C. asked.

"No!" Peter rolled his eyes in youthful disgust.

Rachel sighed. "The horse is just wandering near the spring. We were trying to think of a way to catch it." She sounded none too happy with the prospect.

"A horse," J.C. said with a grin. "One of us must have a guardian angel on duty after all. Let's take a look at this beast."

They helped him to the mouth of the cave. The horse was right where it had been before, as though it were waiting for them. J.C. squinted at the bright daylight for a moment, then took a long, amazed look.

"Damned if it isn't O'Malley. I thought that was him beneath one of those Apaches, but I couldn't be sure. It's him all right."

"What's he doing here?" Rachel asked.

"Maybe he tossed the warrior who was riding him and stomped him into the dust!" Peter speculated.

"Not likely," J.C. said. "O'Malley's gentle as a lamb. More likely some drunken Apache fell off him when the Indians were riding away. He must have wandered into the canyon looking for water."

"No male animal is gentle as a lamb," Rachel declared. "And I don't see how we're going to catch that one."

"If I can get close enough, he'll come to me," J.C. said confidently. "That's my best friend out there."

Rachel and Peter helped J.C. stumble down the game path that led from the cave toward the spring. Standing upright made him want to puke, and every muscle in his body felt like rubber. He scarcely had enough strength to swear, but he did anyway. They stopped close enough to O'Malley for the stallion to hear them, but far enough away not to spook him. J.C. whistled. O'Malley stopped grazing, raised his magnificent head, and gave them a long look.

"Come on, big fella," J.C. urged. He whistled again. "It's me. Remember? All the apples I've given you? The sweet feed and clean hay I've been known to spend my last cent on?"

O'Malley snorted, turned away, and resumed grazing on the sparse grass that grew near the spring.

"Some best friend," Rachel said sourly.

"Contrary animal!" J.C. agreed. "That's gratitude for you. We'll have to catch him."

"With what?" Rachel asked.

"You see all this sotol growing around here?" He pointed to the numerous plants that sprang up from the desert soil in thick sprays of long, slender, fibrous leaves. "You and Peter take the knife and cut a bunch of those."

Rachel sighed and took out the knife.

An hour later J.C. watched Peter and Rachel move cautiously toward the spring and O'Malley. In Rachel's hand was looped the twenty-foot length of sotol rope J.C. had woven from the leaves they had cut. She hadn't hesitated to go after the horse, but he knew what it cost her. She had been afraid of O'Malley when he was saddled, bridled, and safely in control within the confines of the livery corral. Now the stallion was loose and in an uncertain temper. If J.C. could have moved more than two steps without collapsing to rest, he wouldn't have hesitated to walk right up to the stallion, but for Rachel it was an act of courage.

The woman had grit. J.C. had to grant her that. Over the past three days she had saved their lives by getting them away from the Apaches. She'd dug a lead ball out of his leg without fainting or killing him in the process. Now she stalked a creature that in her mind was as fearsome as a grizzly bear.

He wondered how that fool husband of hers had failed to appreciate the value of such a woman, and for the first time since he'd first heard Rachel accuse Dorset of being a violent drunkard, he allowed himself to explore the doubts that her words had sown. Just what form had the man's violence taken? Had he hit Peter? Had he beaten Rachel? The thought of any man raising his hand to the redheaded, freckle-cheeked, sharp-tongued, steel-spirited, brave-hearted woman who marched down the wash to meet O'Malley started a slow burn of anger deep inside J.C. He could allow himself to feel the anger now, and to acknowledge it, because he knew that there was no power in heaven or on earth that could make him take Peter away from her—if they lived through this.

If they lived through this. That was a big if, but getting O'Malley would dramatically improve their chances.

Rachel stopped about thirty feet from O'Malley while Peter circled to the other side of the streambed to get behind the horse. The boy's elaborate stealth was wasted, because O'Malley followed his every move with a knowing eye, but Peter looked as though he was having fun just the same.

"Here, O'Malley," Rachel crooned. "Here boy." She held out a handful of grass. "Wouldn't you like some of this? Green juicy grass, right here. Come and get it."

J.C. smiled at the show. If Rachel ever told him to come and get it in such a seductive voice, she wouldn't have to ask a second time. But O'Malley wasn't impressed. He pricked his beautifully shaped ears toward her and snorted in what sounded like amusement.

Distance muffled Rachel's reaction, but J.C. thought he heard some comment about males in general and horses in particular. "Here, O'Malley, you stubborn piece of equine wolf bait," she continued in the same alluring voice. "Come on, you big stupid lummox."

O'Malley shook his shapely head, then started forward. Rachel froze—probably out of terror, J.C. mused. The stallion trotted to within an inch of her hand, then wheeled and danced away tauntingly. He stopped just out of reach and gave Rachel a look of triumph.

"That son of a bitch," J.C. said to himself, trying to subdue the grin that pulled at his mouth. "Playing games like a month-old colt."

Twice more the stallion came almost within Rachel's reach, then danced away before she could slip the rope over his head. If horses could laugh, J.C. knew O'Malley would have been laughing.

Now Peter got into the act. He moved at the stallion from the opposite side of the narrow canyon floor, hooting and dancing, waving his arms like an idiot, and generally acting like a fool in order to drive O'Malley toward his mother. The horse watched Peter with a marked lack of alarm, then rolled his eye toward Rachel, who was still trying to cozen him in a sweet tone that had nothing to do with the words coming out of her mouth. Finally he shook his big head, walked calmly over to Rachel, and presented his nose to be petted. Looking as though she expected to be bitten, kicked, or trampled at any moment, Rachel carefully slipped the sotol rope over O'Malley's head.

Wasn't that the way it always was? J.C. reflected philosophically. In the end males were always suckers for a pretty woman and sweet promises.

Peter danced up to Rachel, obviously elated. O'Malley snorted and sidestepped, and Rachel clung to the rope like it was her only lifeline in a turbulent sea. She kept a suspicious eye on the stallion as she slowly turned and led him toward the rocks where J.C. waited. He got dizzily to his feet as the horse whickered a greeting.

"Oh, now you recognize me, you pea-brained idiot!"

O'Malley stood perfectly still while J.C. leaned on the horse's shoulder to keep himself upright while looking for signs of mistreatment. Horses that fell into Apache hands were as likely to end up in the stewpot as in some warrior's string of warhorses, and even the much-valued war ponies were sometimes treated roughly.

"Is he all right?" Rachel asked.

"He looks fine." He gave the stallion an affectionate thump on the neck. "Don't'cha, you old horse you. Am I ever glad to see you!"

"Now that we have him, what do we do with him?" She was breathing hard enough to have run a mile.

"You and Peter can climb aboard and ride him back to Tubac. It's closer than Tucson. He can carry both of you easily."

"What?"

"Just keep to the foothills so you'll be able to hide if you see any Apaches. The road by the river's too open to be safe."

"What about you?"

"He can't carry three of us, Rachel, and even if he could, right now I couldn't even get up on him, much less stay on. Get word up to Camp Lowell in Tucson. They'll send a troop out to bring me in."

"And in the meantime what do you do? You can't walk without help. You can't get to water with that leg of yours, much less bring down anything to eat."

"I'll manage," he insisted.

She looked at Peter, who was stroking O'Malley, and then at J.C. "I don't know how to ride. Neither does Peter."

"Oh, for Christ's sake! All you have to do is straddle his backbone! Is that so hard?"

"He'd toss us both off in the middle of nowhere. We'd probably break both our necks."

Her mouth was a stubborn line, her chin tilted pugnaciously. J.C. knew Rachel well enough by now to be certain that if she wanted to get on O'Malley and ride out with her son, a bit of squeamishness about the horse was not going to stop her.

"What were you saying to me about trying to be a hero?" he asked.

She crossed her arms and gave him a narrow look. "There's certainly nothing heroic about being afraid of a horse. It's too bad, but we'll just have to wait until you're strong enough to ride. Then we can all get out of here."

J.C. closed his eyes, but he didn't say what he was thinking. He figured that Peter's young ears had heard enough cussing for one day.

Rachel sat in the shade just inside the mouth of the cave, plucking the wild turkey that she had managed to bring down with a stone. She was becoming a regular Daniel Boone, she mused. The things one could do when one's survival depended upon it were absolutely amazing. J.C. sat ten feet away, his back propped against the stone wall, watching her with an unreadable dark gaze. In the back of cave Peter hand-fed O'Malley clumps of grass he had gathered by the spring.

"We need to talk," J.C. said. His voice was stronger, but Rachel could tell the morning's activities had taken a toll. Even in the dim light of the cave she could see that his face was flushed. By nightfall he would likely have a raging fever again.

"What is there to talk about?"

"How we're going to survive, to begin with."

He flashed her a careless smile that made her heart jump. Hearts were strange things. They ignored logic and reality and reacted to something like J.C.'s smile without a shred of sense.

"We're doing all right," she said, dragging her concentration back to the limp turkey.

"We're in the middle of Apacheland with limited ammunition, only the food we can scrounge, and a trickle of water that's a hundred-foot climb down."

"Really? I hadn't noticed."

He ignored her sarcasm. "I wish you would take O'Malley and get the hell out of here. And don't give me that garbage about not being able to stay on top of a horse."

She laughed softly, shaking her head. "J. C. Tyler, I wish I could decide if you're a villain or a hero."

"Neither," he said.

She smiled. "Or maybe both. Don't worry. I've thought of a solution to a couple of those problems— water and food, at least. I'm going down to the freight wagons and pilfer whatever the Apaches left. Don't know why I didn't think of it before. The Apaches destroyed most of the train, but I'm sure there's something I can find—food, water, blankets. I ought to be able to bring back enough on O'Malley to do us awhile. Then, when you're able to travel, we'll load you on your horse and go back to Tubac."

The look he gave her was stark and grim. "Rachel, it's not a good idea for you to prowl around those wagons. You won't like what you find down there."

"Do you think I don't know that?"

He sighed morosely.

"Do you have any other suggestions?" she prompted.

"I'll get what we need from the train. You just help me get down there."

Rachel laughed. "I'd end up rescuing you from the vultures." She could see the frustration in his eyes. He was a man not accustomed to being helpless, nor depending on someone else, especially when that someone else was a woman who barely came up to his chin. "It's all right, J.C. I'm a big girl, and I've seen plenty of unpleasantness in my life."

At least she thought that she had. But Rachel had never seen the kind of unpleasantness that greeted her at the broken and burned-out wagons that afternoon. The smell was enough to knock her off her feet, but the sights were worse. Empty whiskey bottles littered the circle. Blood had soaked the ground in places, turning it an ugly black. Vultures and other carrion eaters had been at work. Two mule skinners were still tied to wagon wheels, head down, their hair and scalps charred, their mouths frozen in their last despairing screams. Rachel threw up three times before she finished searching the first wagon. She hoped J.C. hadn't seen her reaction from where he sat with Peter behind the nearest rocks, his rifle trained on the wagon circle in case trouble appeared. She didn't want him to stumble down here just because he thought she wasn't tough enough to take the horrors in this place of grisly death, even though it was the truth.

It took her only a quarter hour to find three intact water casks, two cooking pots, several sacks of beans, rice, flour, a wrapped slab of salt pork that looked as if it might still be edible, and one case of liquor that the Apaches had missed. Fighting nausea, she stripped the saddle from the very dead mare that had been tethered to the back of their wagon and put the saddle on O'Malley, who was thoroughly spooked by the smell of death and didn't want to stand still. She was firm with him and got the job done, no longer fearful of his great hooves and strong teeth. She'd discovered things more worthy of fear than a horse.

On the long trek back to the cave with Peter leading the laden horse and Rachel helping J.C., Rachel felt as though she were made of fragile china that might shatter at any moment. The men with the freight wagons hadn't been her friends, yet the horrible nature of their deaths and the ghastly desecration of their bodies—by both the Apaches and the predators that had moved in when the Apaches had left—made a grim impression on her spirit. The world had grown harsher, crueler, more senseless. Instead of seeing life in every patch of bear grass, every tree, every flower that managed to survive the harsh sun, she saw death. She had always looked at cacti and admired the blossoms; now all she could see were the thorns. The birds in the juniper trees sang dirges. Death clung to her like a sticky spiderweb, and she wanted to tear it away, to shudder and scream her horror at what she had seen. She'd known what was there. She had been there when most of it happened. But walking among those burnt-out, looted wagons and those tortured bodies drove the horrible images deep into her soul. They would cling to her forever, she feared.

Now Rachel learned the advantage of having a mask such as the one that so often made J.C. as readable as a monolith. Out of necessity she found one of her own. If she wept, screamed, or so much as grimaced, Rachel feared she would never be able to stop. She would whimper and cry until she was wrung dry of tears, until only a dry husk of her remained and madness came to claim her.

She said nothing on the trek back to the cave, and J.C. didn't ask. Even Peter was silent. Dusk was gathering by the time they got back to their refuge. She went about the business of preparing the first real meal they'd had since the night before the attack, setting beans to boil in water from one of the casks, mixing flour and water for a fair imitation of biscuits, and stripping the last of the turkey carcass. While Peter and J.C. ate, she replaced the water she'd used by hauling water from the spring in one of the pots from the wagons. She was afraid to stop moving. To sit would be to let the waking nightmares command all her attention.

"Aren't you going to eat?" J.C. asked.

"I'm not hungry. I should change your bandage. Come closer to the fire so that I can see."

"It can wait until morning," J.C. protested.

"No, it can't." She ignored the opportunity to taunt him about his squeamishness. Teasing had lost its flavor.

"I thought you'd be raging with fever again tonight," she said as she unwound the cloth strips from his thigh. "Obviously you're not. This looks much better than I'd hoped."

"Only the good die young," he reminded her with a wry grin.

She didn't rise to the bait he offered. "Peter, bring me a bottle of whiskey from that case," she said.

J.C. eyed her suspiciously. "Somehow I think you're not going to offer me a drink."

Rachel managed a tight smile. "You're right. Whiskey is one of the best things I know to help clean up a dirty mess like this."

"I was afraid that was the plan. Yow!" He jerked in pain as she poured half a bottle over his leg. "What a waste!"

"Better on your leg than down your throat. If it weren't such a good disinfectant, I would have left it with the wagons." It was true, yet for the first time in her life, Rachel understood the need to seek solace in the oblivion of drink. Today she had discovered that some nightmares did not flee the daylight, could not be conquered by a stiff upper lip and determination. She wondered if getting stinking drunk, as Cabell had so often done, might banish the images gnawing at her mind.

She felt the probing of J.C.'s gaze as she rewrapped his leg, but he said nothing.

That night they had blankets to lie upon and to wrap themselves in, but Rachel couldn't sleep. She didn't dare sleep. If death, blood, and agony haunted her while she was awake, they would surely capture her soul if she slept. She took her blanket and moved to the mouth of the cave. Stars shone with a cold, adamantine light, heedless and uncaring of the struggles that transpired below them. The sky was empty of comfort; the land, bathed in chilly starlight, was unsoftened by the night.

She was still sitting there, staring bleakly into the darkness, when J.C. joined her.

"Can't sleep, I see." He sat down beside her, grunting in pain as he stretched out his leg.

She was silent.

"Rachel, I know what was down there. I saw it happen. I know what it looks like after it's sat in the sun a couple of days. I know what it does to a person to see it, get close to it. Take my word for it: Thinking on such things doesn't make them any better."

"I can't help but think on it," Rachel said, her throat aching with misery.

J.C. sighed, a weary sound—not the weariness of the body but of the soul. He took her hand, weaving her slender fingers through his blunt, callused ones, and she didn't pull away. His touch felt good. It brought comfort, and she was desperate enough for comfort that she didn't question the source.

"I fought in the War," he told her. "Saw enough battlefields to turn a stomach inside out. Believe me, gruesome as the Apaches can be, they aren't any worse than white men when it comes to drowning their hatred in other men's blood. I've spilled enough blood myself to know that it never gets prettier, never gets easier."

A dark silence followed. Rachel didn't know how to

put her feelings into words. But she didn't want J.C. to go back into the cave and leave her alone with her own thoughts. She didn't want to think about herself, or the remains of a massacre. She wanted to think about him.

"Why are you a bounty hunter, J.C.?"

"A man's got to make a living."

"No," she said. "That's not enough. You're not like Williams. You pretend that you're hard as iron, but inside you've got heart. There must have been something else you could have chosen to do."

He cultivated a long silence before he answered, as if dusting off memories that hadn't been looked at in a while. "My father was a dirt farmer in Kansas," he finally said. "A rock-solid sort of man. Ma was a schoolteacher before she married him. Smartest, funniest, sweetest lady in the world. Not that I appreciated them much when they were alive. Kids never do." His hand tightened on hers, as if the memories were painful. "One day when I was seventeen, I drove the buggy into town to run some errands. When I came back, I found both my parents and my kid brother killed by saddle bums. My pa and brother died clean, at least. Ma didn't. They'd had their fun with her before they killed her."

"Oh, God!" Rachel whispered. "J.C. . . ."

"I went after the bastards. Killed one. Brought the other one back to hang. Turned out I was good at that sort of thing. To a seventeen-year-old who thought he was tough, it seemed like a good way to live."

Rachel returned the pressure of his hand. For a while they sat together at the mouth of the cave, looking at the cold, uncaring stars, joined for that small space of time against the cruelty of the world. After a while he struggled to his feet, still holding her hand, drawing her with him. She went willingly with him to the spot near the smoldering fire where his blanket lay and settled there with him, their backs propped against the log that was the cave's one piece of furniture, both of them wrapped in a blanket that kept the chilly night air at bay. She didn't want to think about the right or wrong of accepting comfort from a man she had every reason to hate. At that moment she couldn't hate him. There were too many other things in the world more worthy of her hatred than J. C. Tyler. His arms around her made her feel more alive. The steady beat of his heart beneath her cheek made her own heart beat stronger.

"Does it ever go away?" she asked.

"No."

She sighed dispiritedly. That wasn't the answer she wanted to hear.

"It fades, though."

"How do you make it fade?"

"Concentrate on the good things. Try to look past the bad. Deal with it, then look past it."

She breathed in his scent. After what they'd been through, his scent wasn't any better than hers, but it was comforting just the same. "The good things . . . ," she murmured.

"Yeah. Like Peter, for instance, or that Peter's mother is one of the strongest, bravest, more determined ladies I've ever had the pleasure to know."

"Really?"

"Really. And as far as I'm concerned, that husband of yours—"

"Ex-husband."

"—that ex-husband of yours can go whistle. He won't get Peter from me. In fact if . . . when we get out of here, you tell me where you want to go, I'll get you there—once this leg you butchered heals enough for me to ride." She could scarcely see his smile in the dull red glow of the fire's dying coals, but she could feel it in his touch when he brushed her cheek with one finger. "I owe you at least that, Rachel. I owe you more than that."

Rachel looked at Peter, who slept on the other side of the fire, cocooned so completely in his blankets that she couldn't see his face. There were good things in life, and good people.

"Have you ever thought of quitting bounty hunting? Doing something else?"

He laughed softly. "That was what the four thousand dollars was going to do. James Cochran in Glorieta—that's just north of Santa Fe—is selling me the prettiest piece of land you ever saw. I have one more payment to make, and stock to buy. Then I'm going to make my money off horses." He glanced toward where O'Malley stood near the back of the cave. "Like you say, there are other fugitives with prices on their heads. I'll get there. It'll just take a little longer."

Other fugitives, Rachel thought sadly. Bandits, bank robbers, killers—most of them more than willing to kill to escape the law. Would J.C. find his money, and his dream, before his luck ran out and a bullet found him?

"I don't know what to say," she told him.

"Just go to sleep," he advised. "It will all be here tomorrow to think about."

His hand smoothed over her hair—warm, solid, gentle. She closed her eyes and let the steady drum of his heartbeat lull her into slumber.

J.C. closed his own eyes as he felt Rachel's breathing even out into the shallow rhythm of sleep, but a sound from across the fire brought them open again. Peter unwound himself from his blanket and quietly came to kneel next to his mother and look into her sleeping face.

"Is my ma all right?" the boy asked, his face creased in worry.

"She'll be okay," J.C. assured him quietly. Rachel didn't stir. "She had nightmares. That's all."

Peter sat back on his heels, his mouth working as he pondered. "I been thinking," he announced in a low voice. "Are we gonna die here?"

"No," J.C. said.

"Not even you?"

"No. We're all going to be fine."

"I saw a fellow in Tubac once who'd been shot up less than you. He died. His arm puffed up and turned black, and he smelled like rotten meat, you know?"

"Thanks for that news," J.C. said wryly.

"Well, even if you're not gonna die, I figure I better get something off my chest. You know, like a man. I don't want you to die thinkin' that I really hate you. I tried. But I don't really. I wanted to thank you for showing me how to skin a rabbit, and how to whittle. And thanks for tryin' to teach me to ride O'Malley. That's the best."

"You're welcome, Big Red."

"I heard what you said to Ma—about not taking me back. I knew you wouldn't, even before you said it."

J.C. nodded. Kids were scary sometimes in what they figured out.

Peter started back to his own blanket. "Ma likes you, too, you know. Most fellows she won't even let hold her hand."

Long after Peter was asleep, J.C. was kept awake by his thoughts. He wished he could call back the letter he'd sent to Cabell Dorset. If nothing else, the message would tell the man where to start looking for Rachel. Someone would find her, no matter where she went. J.C. knew the persistence of bloodhounds like himself once they caught the scent of easy money. J. C. Tyler might not take Peter back to his father, but somebody else would.

Not that those problems were much of a concern, because the chances of them getting out of the desert alive were slim.

 16

Two days passed while J.C.'s leg continued to mend and he regained some measure of strength. Rachel tried to let the daily routine of surviving dull the memory of the circle of horrors she had visited. On the third day they started for Tubac. J.C. and Peter rode double on O'Malley, along with one of the water casks from the wagons. Rachel walked. Peter offered to let her take his place on the horse, but she quickly turned him down. O'Malley was a decent sort, for a horse, but she was more comfortable traveling on her own two feet than putting her fate in the hands—or on the hooves—of a twelve-hundred-pound beast with a quirkish sense of humor.

Instead of going back to the road, where the traveling would be smoother, they stayed well in the foothills. The terrain was rough, everything either up or down, sharp rock or soft sand, with very little in between. But the arroyos and rocky outcrops offered numerous hiding places and natural fortresses in case they were spotted by hostiles. Rachel imagined an Apache behind every tree, bush, and cactus. She jumped at every noise, though J.C. assured her that if the Apaches were stalking them, they would never hear the Indians until they attacked. His assurance didn't make her feel any more secure.

Peter frequently walked to give O'Malley a rest. The boy seemed both tireless and fearless, running here and there to explore this and that, and chattering like a squirrel until Rachel reminded him that they were trying to be inconspicuous in their passage. He wound down as the morning rolled on and the sun climbed high, however, and resorted more and more often to riding. Long before noon O'Malley was dark with sweat. The tall, slender stalks of the yucca plants that grew on the hillsides seemed to shimmer in the heat, and Rachel felt every bit as wavery as they looked.

They made only a few miles that day. Midafternoon a fierce thunderstorm drove them to seek shelter beneath a rocky overhang, which, while not as secure as their cave, offered some shelter, concealment, and protection from the elements. They had exhausted their reserves of endurance for the day. J.C. all but toppled from O'Malley when Rachel helped him down. Unable to hold him, she fell back against the horse, who craned his head around to give her a bemused look, but otherwise stood like a rock. J.C. leaned heavily against her, his body pressing the entire length of hers.

"Sorry," he said, but the quick grin he gave her bore witness that he wasn't sorry at all. Tired as she was, Rachel felt a pulse of life rush through her veins as she looked up at him. For a short space of time she forgot where they were, the rain that beat the ground beyond the rocky overhang, her wet clothes, sore feet, dripping hair, and aching muscles. She didn't move. He didn't move. Finally O'Malley did move. Rachel would have landed on her backside if J.C. hadn't grabbed her.

"Are you two all right?" Peter cocked his head and wrinkled his brow as if struggling to understand adults.

"We're fine," J.C. answered. "Why don't you unsaddle O'Malley and rub him down with one of the blankets. Ooops!" He caught Rachel as she attempted to disentangle herself from him and lost her balance.

Rachel closed her eyes in embarrassment, gave up, and let her head drop so that her forehead rested against his chest. "I'm so sore and stiff that nothing moves the way it should."

J.C. chuckled. The sound vibrated all the way through her. "We're quite a crew. The only one of us with any spring left in him is Peter."

"I'll take care of you," Peter said condescendingly. "I feel great."

Rachel sighed.

The rain ended and the sun came out again, making them hot as well as soggy. The desert steamed. Rachel was glad that J.C. didn't suggest they push on; she thought they were lucky to have discovered the rocky shelter for the night.

"I'll go get us a rabbit for dinner," Peter offered.

"No, you don't, young man. I don't want you wandering around alone. This isn't as concealed as the canyon."

"But Ma!"

"We have beans for dinner. You wouldn't want O'Malley to have carried that sack of beans and the pot for nothing, would you?"

"I won't go far," he pleaded.

"No," she said.

J.C. intervened. "What you should hunt, Big Red, is some dry firewood. We can cook the beans and put the fire out before dark, so it's not a beacon telling the Indians to come get us. After we've eaten, I'll show you how to make a rabbit snare."

Instantly enthralled, Peter grinned. "Okay. How much wood do you want?"

"Just enough for an hour or so."

"Okay!"

"Don't go where I can't see you!" Rachel shouted after him. She sighed wearily and let herself slide down the smooth rock wall until she was sitting on the dirt. "I can't believe we rode this whole day without seeing one Indian."

J.C. leaned against the rock wall and looked out over the silent, steaming valley. "I don't care much if we see Indians," he commented. "Just so they don't see us."

The next day was harder. Rachel's shoes were not made for hiking, and her feet were blistered and raw. Her face was so sunburned that it no longer mattered that she had freckles, and every muscle, bone, and joint in her body complained. J.C. looked worse. Peter's seemingly endless energy was beginning to flag. He no longer darted here and there to discover what lay beneath a rock or behind a yucca plant. Where Rachel once had to caution him from his lively chatter, now she had to admonish him for whining. Even O'Malley was unhappy, snorting at the wind, spooking at the clank of the cooking pot slung over the saddle horn, fidgeting beneath his heavy load of two people, a water cask, and two burlap bags of blankets and food.

The going was as slow as the day before. The sky had opened up again during the night, drenching the land with rain. The soil underfoot was muddy, and in places slippery. Rachel's shoes were wet, her skirts sodden from dragging through the wet grass and bushes. As the day before, all was quiet. If Indians were in the area, they didn't show themselves, and no traffic braved the road that ran along the Santa Cruz River, which paralleled their path in the distance to the west.

It was about noon when disaster struck. Rachel's mind was in an overheated haze. She trudged behind O'Malley, putting one foot in front of the other without thinking, one after the other, over rocks, through the beds of dry streams, down the steep banks of arroyos and up the other side. Just to the east a rugged canyon cut the slopes of the Santa Ritas. Its extension into the foothills where they walked was a deep and treacherous wash with high banks of loose sand and gravel over hard, sunbaked soil. O'Malley, being in a flighty mood, danced around the crest of the bank and snorted objections to going down. J.C. told Peter to swing down, then insisted the stallion go on. Rachel and Peter followed, stepping in the horse's footprints.

Rachel was the one who started things rolling. Loose gravel slid beneath her shoe, and she landed on her backside, out of balance and tumbling with the minor cascade of rocks and gravel she'd dislodged. Just in front of her, O'Malley used her fall and the minor rockslide as an excuse to crowhop and generally raise hell. J.C. had just gotten the horse under control when an out-of-control Rachel slammed into O'Malley's rear feet. She shrieked. O'Malley lurched. Unprepared, J.C. flew off, hit the gravel, slid, and kept on sliding. The frightened stallion wheeled around, lost his balance, and went down with the rest of them. Peter stood staring until they all reached the bottom, then followed carefully, the only one of them still upright.

Scraped and coated with dirt, Rachel sat up and groaned. J.C. did the same, except that his groan came out in language more colorful than hers, disparaging O'Malley, the gravel, the heat, his leg, his own intelligence, and Arizona in general. Still cussing, he picked himself off the ground and limped over to Rachel. "Are you all right?"

"I guess so." She scraped the hair away from her eyes and looked at him anxiously. "You?"

"Oh, I'm great. Just great."

She allowed him to help her to her feet. "It was my fault. I'm sorry."

"No. I should've found a better place to go down. Goddammit all. Look at O'Malley."

The stallion stood ten feet away, looking chagrined and standing on three legs. His right front leg was held gingerly off the ground.

"He's hurt," Peter said.

J.C. limped toward the stallion, who stood patiently while he examined the injured leg. "Stupid horse," J.C. muttered while he ran a gentle hand from O'Malley's muscle-bound shoulder to the slender fetlock. "Brainless piece of horse meat. Useless nag." The fondness and concern in his voice took the bite out of the insults. As if he understood, O'Malley dipped his head and nuzzled J.C.'s back as he bent over, examining the leg.

"Apologizing, are you?" he asked. "Fat lot of good it does to say you're sorry."

"Do we have to shoot him?" Peter asked tremulously.

"Not unless we do it just because he's a jackass. The leg's not broken, no thanks to him. But he's strained a tendon."

"Poor O'Malley." Rachel gave the stallion a cautious pat on his velvety nose. "I'm sorry I scared you."

"Well." J.C. straightened with a sigh. "He's not going to be carrying any weight for a few days."

"None?" Rachel asked.

"Not over this terrain. We need to find a place to hole up for a little while."

"Let's go up the canyon," Peter urged. "Maybe there's another cave."

J.C. looked toward the shadowed ruggedness of the canyon. "Sounds like a good idea to me. At least it means we don't have to climb up the other side of this damned wash."

If there was a cave somewhere along the canyon walls, they didn't find it. Peter found something better. He darted ahead of J.C. and Rachel as they rounded a bend in the streambed. Rachel called him sharply back.

"No!" he shouted. "I see something!"

The something was an old miner's shack that clung to the hillside just below the dark entrance to an adit that tunneled back into the rock. Chunks of silver ore littered the slope in front of the tunnel. J.C. picked one up.

"Looks like someone hit paydirt here some time back. Probably left because of Indians."

Left because of Indians or lost his hair to them. Rachel was glad that J.C. didn't mention the other possibility.

"Can we stay here?" Peter asked eagerly. The prospect of not having to walk for a few days had revived his spirits.

"Looks like home to me," J.C. said.

"Can I set out some rabbit snares like you showed me?"

J.C. cocked a questioning brow in Rachel's direction, and she nodded.

"Just don't go far," she warned. "And be careful."

"Oh, Ma!"

"You heard me!" She bit her lip as he scampered away. "If he gets into trouble, I swear I'll wring his neck."

"Yeah." J.C. chuckled and sat down stiffly on a rock. "We're the only ones allowed to get into trouble."

Rachel started to reply, but thought better of it when she saw J.C.'s face. "You look awful."

"Thanks."

"No, really." She felt his brow, and he took her hand before she could remove it.

"I'll be all right. I'm going to take O'Malley up to the adit, where he'll be safe and sheltered. Then I'll rest while you cook me up a good dinner of beans."

"No." She pulled him to his feet and toward the shack, which, if nothing else, at least provided shade. "You'll stay here and rest, and I'll take O'Malley."

He questioned her with a lift of one brow.

"Really. I'll take him. He and I will be fine."

That J.C. took her up on her offer was a measure of how bad he felt. He hobbled to the shack, leaving the horse and supplies to Rachel's care. Keeping one eye on Peter, who was searching out likely-looking rabbit lairs, and the other eye on O'Malley, she unloaded the water cask, blankets, cooking pot, and food supplies, then slipped the saddle from the stallion's sweaty back. Rachel and O'Malley regarded each other with mutual reservations as she led him toward the mouth of the adit, but Rachel reassured herself by noting that the horse was in no condition to wreak havoc. He looked as stiff, sore, and lame as she felt.

That night as Rachel lay in her blankets listening to Peter's boyish snores and J.C.'s restless breathing, she thought back to her life in Georgia. She'd been gone only three years, yet it seemed a lifetime. Surely it was a different person who had regarded a picnic outing to the river as a major expedition, who thought having a bad day meant staining one of her gowns or having the cook burn the dessert pudding. The hardest struggle she had endured was a fight with her corset strings, and her worst frustration had been trying to pin her hair into the latest style. She'd never had a way with hair.

Ironically she'd been driven from that secure, placid, dull world not by courage or curiosity but by fear. She remembered sitting in her father's library, looking at the map of the western territories and quaking at the prospect of seeking refuge there. If someone had told her then what she would become, what she would endure, she would have declared, "Never!" then fainted dead away.

Never was a word she should forget, Rachel decided. Whenever she said "never," fate seemed to take special pains to prove her wrong. When she'd left Georgia, betrayed by both husband and father, she had vowed never to trust another man. Never to depend upon a man. Never to give her heart to another man. And here she was, foolish woman, lying in the dark listening to a man's breathing as if it were her own heartbeat, feeling his eyes search her out in the darkness and loving the half-fearful, half-ecstatic tingle that traveled down her spine from knowing that his eyes, his mind, and perhaps part of his heart were riveted upon her. A bounty hunter, of all things! A man who had already lied to her, already betrayed her. And here she lay, exhausted but sleepless because she was thinking about J. C. Tyler like a debutante dreaming of her latest beau. If anything was going to keep her awake, it should be the myriad obstacles standing in the way of surviving the next week or so.

On the other hand, with life so precarious, why was she concerned about what she ought to be doing and ought to be thinking? With that in mind, Rachel got up, wrapped her blanket around her, and limped over to where J.C. lay. "I know you're not asleep," she whispered, not wanting to disturb Peter.

"You're right."

"If we're going to lie awake, we might as well not be lonely while we're doing it."

J.C. opened the cocoon of his blankets, and she crawled inside, settling herself in the crook of his arm and pillowing her head on his right shoulder—one of the few places on his body that was not shot up, scraped, or bruised. He radiated heat, and Rachel knew with a sinking heart that his fever was returning.

She also knew at that moment that J.C. was not going to die. Someone so stubborn, determined, courageous, and intensely alive simply could not be destined to die a useless death in an uncaring wilderness. He wouldn't die, and neither would she and Peter.

Suddenly she felt very secure and drowsy. His arm, strong and comforting, closed around her as she drifted off to sleep.

Next morning, first thing, J.C. insisted on hobbling up to the adit to check on O'Malley. Peter, eager to be out and about, went with him. While they were gone, Rachel cleaned the shack as best she could. A mouse-eaten, nearly useless broom lay among the other rubble that littered the place, that other rubble being a rusted coffeepot and soup pan, a tattered red union suit, a filthy mattress that had, from the looks of it, served as a rodent hotel, a broken-handled shovel, and a yellowed and torn issue of the *Weekly Arizonian*, dated August 1861. Curious, Rachel read the faded and barely decipherable newsprint, in which the newspaper announced that from 1857 to 1861, one hundred eleven Americans and fifty-seven Mexicans had been slaughtered by violence in Tubac, which had been virtually abandoned by all citizens since early in the month.

Poor, bloodstained Tubac, Rachel mused. Its citizens had come back a few years later when the army had sent troops to protect them from the Indians, and now that the troops had been once more withdrawn, the town was being deserted again, left to the Apaches and border bandits.

Rachel swept the pile of litter outside—all except for a grimy kerosene lantern, half a can of kerosene, a box half full of matches, and a bottle slightly less than half full of—from the smell of it—Rachel guessed cheap whiskey.

Peter and J.C. returned an hour after they had left. J.C., rather gray in the face, sat down wearily on the pile of blankets Rachel had put in one corner. Peter bounced around the cabin with boyish ebullience announcing the morning's discoveries.

"There's a spring in the rocks up there!" he declared proudly, as if he had created the water rather than simply found it. "The water tastes good, and it's cold."

"Wonderful," Rachel said. "Maybe if there's enough water, we can all take baths."

Peter blinked. "Oh, there's not enough for that!"

Rachel and J.C. both smiled as Peter hastened to change the subject. "We staked O'Malley out so he could eat. J.C. says his leg doesn't look too bad, but we're going to have to stay here a whole week at least."

"Wonderful," Rachel repeated, not nearly as happy about this news.

"And my snares were all empty," he concluded with a grimace. "But it don't matter."

" 'It *doesn't* matter,' " Rachel corrected.

"Right. It don't matter, 'cause J.C. found us somethin' else for supper. Better'n beans." Peter's blue eyes flashed with a devilish twinkle. "It's outside."

"What is it?"

J.C. started to say something, but a pleading look from Peter stopped him.

"Go look," Peter invited.

Cautiously Rachel stuck her head out the door of the shack, and gasped. Peter crowed with laughter when she whipped around, glaring. Even J.C. gave her a grin glittering with mischief.

"It's a snake!" she exclaimed.

"Yeah!" Peter agreed enthusiastically. "A rattler! Isn't it somethin'?"

"Why . . . why on earth did you bring a snake back here? Where did you find it? Did it . . . did it . . . ?"

"J.C. killed it!" Peter announced. "You shoulda seen him! He grabbed that big snake by the tail and whacked its head against a rock faster than that ol' snake could rattle Dixie!"

"Peter!"

"Well! It's true! He said it'd be good to eat!"

"J.C.?" she demanded.

He shrugged. "It is good eating."

"A rattlesnake? What if it had struck one of you?"

"It didn't!" Peter was clearly disappointed by her lack of enthusiasm. "J.C. was too fast. He says it's easy. He says he's never gotten bit. He says he'll teach me someday."

"Not until you're thirty, he won't!" She glared at J.C. "Setting rabbit snares is one thing. Whacking rattlesnakes is something else entirely. Lord, that snake is as big around as my arm. I will not, absolutely will not, eat a snake! Never!"

There she went saying "never." An hour later Rachel ate her words as well as a snake. Once J.C. had cleaned and skinned the reptile, fileted the white, delicate meat, and cooked it over the small fire they built in the stone fire ring outside the shack, she had to admit that rattlesnake was more appetizing than she could have believed. It was a good thing, because a week in the shack was going to stretch their supply of beans to the very limit.

"Do you think the Indians know about this cabin and the spring?" Rachel asked while Peter went to the spring to refill the water cask. She sat with J.C. outside the shack, where the afternoon sun gave her good light to tend his leg.

"The Apaches know every rock, tree, and twig in these mountains," J.C. replied with grim certainty. "If we're lucky, they won't stop by to refill their water-skins."

"Do you think they will?"

"No telling. If they do, we could probably hold off a small army of them from that tunnel over there. The entrance is narrow enough so that one man with a rifle could make them think twice about sticking around to fight. In any case we don't have much choice but to stay here until either O'Malley's fit to carry me or I can walk on my own. I'm sorry, Rachel."

She slipped his knife underneath his bandages, sliding it along his bare flesh, and sliced through the soiled rags that wrapped his thigh. "What are you sorry for, J.C.?"

"I'm sorry about anything you want me to be sorry about as long as you have that blade in your hands."

She laughed and handed him back the knife. "There. Now answer my question. What are you sorry about? That you got shot up and can't walk? That you took Peter and me with those freight wagons? Or that you came after us in the first place?"

He pinched the bridge of his nose and sighed. "All three, I guess."

Rachel carefully peeled the bandages back from his leg and shook her head. "You're a pretty sorry fellow, J.C. What were you thinking of, letting the Apaches get the best of you?"

He laughed sheepishly. "That's been happening a lot lately. Bandits, Apaches, women, kids—I can't seem to hold my own with anyone anymore."

The teasing left her voice. "You've been doing all right as far as I'm concerned. You saved Peter's and my lives by stuffing us into that wagon box. And in Tubac you came after me when Aldona was killed. And now . . . if you had died back there in that wagon circle, Peter and I wouldn't have the first idea how to hold our own out here. We would have just folded up and died."

"Rachel, you would never just fold up and die. I don't think Cochise and Ezkiminzin, together with all their warriors, would take you on if they knew how fierce you really are."

She laughed wryly, then looked down at the ground, unable to meet his eyes. "I've got to tell you something, J.C."

"Yes?" His voice was suspicious.

"I wouldn't say this if it weren't . . . if we weren't . . ." She took a deep breath. "What I mean to say is . . . realistically, a day from now, or a few days from now, we might be . . . I might not be able to say this. And I want you to know."

J.C. was silent. He regarded her with an intensity that was unnerving—and exciting. Rachel didn't quite know how to say what she wanted to say without sounding as though she were a sentimental, idiotic female. But perhaps that was what she was, after all. And perhaps at this point in her life it didn't really matter.

"When I left Georgia," she said hesitantly, "I was very scared, and very bitter. I vowed I would never trust another man, that I would never let myself depend on anyone but myself for what I needed in life. I just wanted you to know that . . . well . . . I changed my mind. You changed my mind—in spite of everything. It may not seem momentous to you, but to me it's quite a change. You're a good man, J.C. You don't have anything to apologize for. And"—she grimaced—"and I'm sorry about all those names I called you in the past."

The words were not as strong as the feelings that were growing inside of her, but for Rachel the admission was a big first step. She kept her eyes glued on her hands, not wanting to look up. But he took gentle hold of her chin and turned her face upward.

"What names?"

"Oh, you know. Names. 'Skunk,' 'weasel,' 'worm,' and a few worse things."

"My ears are burning."

"You shouldn't make fun!" she said irritably. "I'm trying to apologize. It isn't easy."

"I'm not really making fun, Rachel. Truth is, I deserve every one of those names you called me. And a lot more."

"No, you—"

He shushed her. "Rachel, we're going to get back to civilization someday soon, and then we're going to talk more about this. I want to hear you say again that I'm a good man, and I want to show you that I can be."

She bit her lower lip, wanting to say more, but knowing this was neither the time nor the place. "Your leg looks better," she said lamely, glancing down at his wound.

"I've always been a fast healer. That's a good thing to be in my profession."

"Yes, I guess so. It's a miracle you didn't succumb to infection." She got up and ducked into the cabin. "Wait there!" she yelled out the door. A moment later she appeared with the ancient bottle of whiskey she'd found while cleaning.

His eyes narrowed. "Are you going to do with that whiskey what you did before?"

"Certainly. I'd almost forgotten it was in there. This stuff fights suppuration, you know," she told him with the hint of a twinkle in her eye.

"I think it would do more good going down my throat."

"Not so," she huffed, and carefully poured a bit of the alcoholic liquid over the puffy and mangled flesh.

He jerked and bit back a curse. "Lord, woman! I think you enjoy that!"

"Not a bit," she denied.

"At least you saved a little." He held out his hand for the bottle. She regarded the whiskey dubiously.

"Rachel, I'm not going to get drunk."

She raised a brow.

"Rachel! There's not enough whiskey in that bottle to get a flea drunk, much less a full-grown man."

Mouth tight with disapproval, she relented and handed him the bottle. He raised it to his lips while she bound his leg with the last remnants of her petticoat. Rachel didn't watch him drink the stuff. She concentrated on not hearing the sound of whiskey slipping down his throat—until the silence between them became heavy and dark.

"Do you drink a lot, J.C.?" she asked softly.

He sighed. "I've been known to tie one on a time or two."

She was silent.

"Okay. More than a time or two. I don't get invited to many tea parties, Rachel. In a lot of towns out here the saloon is the only place a man can put up his feet and relax."

"I didn't say anything."

"You were thinking it. Rachel, you said your husband was a violent drunkard. Did he beat you?"

Rachel hesitated. That part of her past was a shameful thing that was difficult to admit, but the intensity of J.C.'s dark gaze made it impossible to lie. "Yes," she said in a small voice. "When he got drunk, he beat me."

He continued relentlessly. "Did he beat on Peter?"

"No." Rachel chewed on her lower lip. "He came close a time or two, and right before I ran away, he shoved him. I was afraid . . . afraid he was going to start in on Peter as well."

J.C. dragged his fingers through his hair and sighed. "I'd like to have a word or two with Cabell Dorset."

"Cabell is his own punishment, I think," Rachel said softly. "I just want to stay away from him."

"Yeah," J.C. agreed with a sigh. He took her hand and enfolded it in his own. "Rachel, I'm not a mean drunk. You've seen me as mean as I ever get."

"That's pretty mean, all right." She smiled in spite of herself, reluctantly reclaiming her hand.

He was silent as she finished the bandaging. His leg was cooler, the flesh less angry looking. She ran her fingers beneath the upper edge of the makeshift bandage to ensure she hadn't tied the rags too tight. Out of the corner of her eye she saw J.C. drag in a pained breath and cast his eyes at the sky as if seeking divine help.

"Does that hurt?" she asked, surprised that such a gentle touch drew almost as much reaction from him as the sting of the whiskey.

"Not exactly."

Then she noticed what her repeated touch on his thigh had done. How could she not notice, with his trouser leg split open nearly to the crotch? She turned her face away, cheeks burning.

"Just pour what's left of that whiskey over that hole in my leg again," he suggested with a strained laugh. "That ought to take care of it."

Her face burned even hotter. "Stop it!"

He caught her by the wrist before she could flee. "Rachel, look at me."

Fascinated beyond her embarrassment, she obeyed, and once her eyes met his, she couldn't look away. Sharp as polished blue steel, his eyes drilled into her as if he would bore his words into her mind.

"Rachel, you don't ever have to be afraid of me. Never."

There was that word again. *Never.* But she believed him. "I know, J.C."

"Good. Keep that in mind, Rachel, because I'm going to be honest in admitting that you light a hell of a fire in my blood. I guess a lady doesn't like to hear that, but I'm telling you anyway. It seems to me a woman would want to know that a man feels that way."

"I haven't been a real lady for a long time."

"You are a lady. You are one hell of a lady." His fingers slipped from her wrist to fold around her hand.

Rachel had a wild urge to kiss him, to press her mouth to those firm lips and feel his strong arms enclose her with the passion she saw in his eyes. A host of forbidden images rose into her mind—bodies entwined, hands touching, mouths roaming hungrily over heated flesh. Shocking. Even a formerly married woman shouldn't have such pictures in her imagination.

"I have to go!" With a panicked jerk, she pulled her hand away from his and made a dash for the shack. At the door she paused and looked over her shoulder. "Thank you for telling me, J.C. I . . . I'm glad you told me."

He blinked as she disappeared, then laughed—at

himself, not at her. "Thank you for telling me? No 'I like you too'? No passionate falling into my waiting arms?" He chuckled. "Damn, J.C. You are such a stupid ass."

 **17**

The next week had a quality of dreamlike unreality to Rachel. The three of them settled into a routine that might have passed for the daily activities of any normal frontier family—as if they weren't stranded in the heart of Apacheland, surrounded by hostiles, heat, and wilderness; as if looted, burned-out wagons and the tortured bodies of the wagon masters were not just a few miles up the valley; as if miles of the most dangerous country in the West didn't lie between them and safety.

Rachel cooked the meals, nursed J.C.'s leg, kept the rickety cabin swept, and collected edible wild plants and tubers to vary their limited diet. Peter proudly became the mighty hunter, checking his snares daily and usually bringing back a rabbit or two for dinner. Rachel was heartily tired of rabbit stew, spitted rabbit, cold rabbit and beans, or any other way that rabbit could be eaten. J.C. teased the boy about decimating the local rabbit population.

"The coyotes will starve," he told Peter.

"Better them than us," Peter replied with a grin.

Rattlesnake was also on the menu for the week, for

the area around the mine shack was thick with them. The novelty quickly paled, and even Peter, who at first regarded eating snake as an adventure, started to complain after a few days of a steady snake diet.

Every day J.C. limped up to the mine adit to wrap O'Malley's injured leg. Peter was his willing assistant. Unsteady on his feet at first, J.C. let Peter do most of the work—under watchful supervision. By the time his leg improved and his strength began to return, J.C. suspected he'd been usurped in the stallion's heart. O'Malley seemed willing to do just about anything for the boy, and Peter glowed with happiness while he tended the stallion's needs.

"He's got a knack with horses," J.C. told Rachel one evening as they sat on a log outside the shack and she redressed the wound on his thigh. "He communicates with them. O'Malley minds him as well as he minds me. Better, sometimes."

"Then O'Malley is a more cooperative patient than his master," she scolded. "You've been on this leg too much. How do you expect it to heal if you won't rest it?"

"It's fine," he insisted. "Look, it's not even swollen anymore. Must be all that whiskey you poured on it."

She gave him a stern look.

"Stop being such a mother hen," he said with a boyish grin. "It's fine."

In truth his leg was much, much better. Either he was an extraordinarily fast healer, as he claimed, or Rachel was a darned good nurse. Either way, by the end of the week J.C. could walk a good distance and had regained much of his strength. The swelling and angry red streaks in his thigh had disappeared, and the wound was healing cleanly.

O'Malley was recovering as rapidly as his master, and J.C. announced on the sixth evening they spent in the cabin that he planned to leave for Tubac the next morning.

"If I ride at a steady pace, I can get there by midafternoon. By early next morning I'll have a wagon and escort ready to come back here. With any luck I'll be back the day after tomorrow with enough men to make sure you and Peter get back safely."

"Why can't we go with you?" Peter demanded.

"Because you're safer here, and O'Malley can't carry three of us. You don't want to leave your mother here alone, do you?"

Peter looked as if he would consider it.

"Do you?"

"I guess not," the boy admitted. "She can't shoot worth a darn, so I guess I'd better stay."

"Thank you, Peter," Rachel said dryly.

Next morning as dawn was beginning to paint the sky, J.C. was ready to leave. He looked disreputable indeed with a snakeskin band decorating his scruffy hat and his right trouser leg awkwardly sewn together by Rachel using a cactus spine and the tough fiber of a yucca plant.

"I'll be back before you know I'm gone," he told Rachel as she rolled two blankets together and gave them to him.

"No, you won't. I'll know you're gone."

He cupped her cheek with one hand and smiled. "I'll be back. You and I still need to have that talk we promised ourselves."

Rachel's cheeks grew warm. These days she was blushing like a schoolgirl at the mere drop of a word. The weakness was disconcerting. She was, after all, a grown woman—a divorced woman, for pity's sake! She should be immune to the glint in J.C.'s eyes and the lazy charm of his smile. But she wasn't.

"I shouldn't be needing these blankets," he said.

"Take them. Just in case."

Peter strutted down the path from the adit leading an eager O'Malley. The stallion tossed his head and snorted at the breeze, but Peter had him well in hand.

"You will be careful, won't you?" Rachel asked.

"Like a mouse in a barnful of owls."

She gave him a heated look. "That's not funny."

"I'll be careful," he promised. "Now, tell me good-bye."

Rachel was surprised when he reached for her, but she didn't draw back, despite the fact that Peter was looking at them with a grin stretching every freckle on his round face. J.C.'s kiss was affectionate rather than passionate, but Rachel could feel restrained desire tauten his body. His hands drifted down to her buttocks in a brief caress, then moved back to the more neutral territory of her waist.

"See what a careful, well-behaved fellow I am," he whispered against her lips.

They were so close that they breathed each other's air. Rachel could feel the jump of his pulse, could count the individual whiskers in the forest that had grown on his face during the last week. She desperately wanted to kiss him again, but now was not the time to abandon the control that she'd built up these past three years.

"Please be careful" was all she could think of to say—at least, it was the only safe thing to say with Peter looking on and her own emotions dangerously close to the surface.

Peter rolled his eyes toward the stallion. "Pretty sappy, huh, O'Malley."

Rachel flashed her son an annoyed look. "Peter, mind your—"

Her warning was cut off when O'Malley suddenly shied violently and pulled sharply back. Jerked off his feet, Peter held on to the reins. The snake that had startled the stallion slithered calmly away, but Peter alarmed the stallion even more by dragging at the reins and flailing to get up. The horse reared, and sharp hooves pawed the air above Peter's body.

Rachel cried out and threw herself forward, but J.C. pushed her aside and dove for Peter. Before Rachel could catch her breath, he had tackled the boy and rolled them both out of the way of the frightened stallion's hooves. With the reins dangling loose, O'Malley bolted.

Rachel flew to the spot where they lay in the dust. "Are you hurt? Omigod! You're hurt! Peter? J.C.?"

Peter was too shaken to object to her maternal hovering. He sat and brushed some of the dirt from his arms and chest. "I'm okay—I think."

J.C. got stiffly to his feet. Rachel took his arms and helped him up. "Are you all right?"

He straightened and groaned. "This sort of thing used to be easier."

Rachel clung shamelessly to his arm, breathless with the thought of what had almost happened. "J.C., thank you. You . . . you . . ."

"It's okay, Rachel." He took her hand and squeezed it.

"I'll never be able to thank you enough."

His smile was wicked. "Yes, you will. I'll think of a way."

Before Rachel could react, J.C. pulled Peter to his feet. "You still have all your bones in one piece?"

"Yessir."

"Then let's go chase down that stupid horse."

Peter's freckles stood out against a face that had gone pale, but he was game. Rachel bit her lip against the protest that sprang to her lips. For three long years she had trusted no one but herself with Peter's welfare, but she trusted J.C., she realized.

O'Malley hadn't gone far. A stirrup of his saddle had caught firmly on a mesquite branch. Foam coated his lips and sweat soaked his coat from the struggle to free himself, but he was hopelessly ensnared. The stallion rolled his eyes as J.C. approached.

"Easy, old son," J.C. soothed. "You are just about the stupidest piece of horse meat God ever put on this earth." The tone was affectionate, even if the words weren't. "Hold still, you sweaty piece of crow bait."

Rachel exhaled a gust of relief when J.C. gathered up the loose reins and carefully disentangled the stirrup, but she flinched as J.C. led the stallion toward her, for the horse put weight on only three of his legs.

"The miserable son of a jackass went and reinjured that tendon."

"And you told me O'Malley was such a smart, calm, gentle animal," Rachel recalled tartly.

"Yeah. Well, he's never liked snakes."

"What do we do now? Wait another week while he heals again?"

"It'll be longer than a week this time," J.C. said grimly.

Rachel turned and marched back toward the shanty. Her composure had been hanging by a thread already, and this latest setback did it in. "This is just dandy!" she muttered sourly. "It's a good thing we have all the amenities here. Another week or ten days eating rattlesnake and waiting for the Apaches to find us are just what we all need!"

"It's not going to be another week or ten days," J.C. said, following her with a sheepish, limping O'Malley.

"You just said—"

"I'll walk out."

She halted and turned. "You'll what?"

"I'll walk out. With luck I can make it to Tubac in two days. Three at the most."

"With that leg?"

"It's fine. I've walked for miles on worse."

She stared at him for a moment, taking in the grim, determined line of his mouth, Peter's wide-eyed face swimming in the background. "Well, then, we might as well all walk out."

"No," J.C. said firmly. "I can travel faster alone."

Rachel opened her mouth to deny it, but he silenced her with a finger clamped gently across her lips.

"I can. And you and Peter are safer here. I'll come back."

"What if you don't?" Peter demanded, his frightened voice asking the question that Rachel feared to face. More than the prospect of being alone, she didn't want to lose J.C. She hadn't realized how empty her life was before he came into it.

"If I'm not back by the time O'Malley is sound, you and your mother can ride out double on his back." He smiled. "Peter, you'll have to give your mother riding lessons. We wouldn't want her falling off and landing in a patch of cactus."

"Yessir," Peter said solemnly.

"But I should be back long before then. Trust me."

Rachel trusted J.C. It was fate and the Apaches that she didn't trust.

J.C. decided to put off his departure until the next morning. Walking to Tubac was a prospect quite different from riding, and he wanted another day's rest for his leg before starting out. Rachel spent the day avoiding the subject of his leaving. He let her get away with it until after supper. When Peter had nodded off in his blankets, J.C. hefted the water cask over one shoulder, picked up the kerosene lantern, and motioned Rachel to follow him toward the spring.

"We should wait to fill the cask in the morning," Rachel said as she scrambled up the path behind him. "It'll be fresher for you to take with you."

He laughed low in his throat. "You think I'm going to carry this all the way to Tubac? Uh-uh."

"But you'll need water."

"I'm going to stick to the foothills. I can find enough water to keep me going."

"If you're not going to take the cask with you, why are we filling it?"

"We're filling it to take up to the adit."

Rachel huffed out a frustrated sigh and stopped, her fists balled on her hips. "Would you care to explain why?"

He smiled at her over his shoulder. "Sure. Just come with me."

While they filled the cask at the spring and trudged up to the tunnel opening, J.C. explained he wanted water stored there in case they had to use it as a refuge against Apaches.

"If the Apaches drop by, you could hold off a whole band of them from that tunnel mouth," he told her. "Even if you can't hit the side of a barn five feet in front of you. Just make a lot of noise. They'll go away. You and Peter don't have anything they want."

Except our lives, Rachel thought, but she didn't speak the obvious in words.

J.C. placed the full cask well back from the mouth of the adit and then took Rachel by the hand. "Let's see how far back this goes. There might be another entrance."

They walked for several minutes, carefully picking their way through the rock rubble that littered the floor.

Most of the walls were solid rock. Here and there the adit crossed areas—faults in the earth, Rachel surmised—that were pulverized and soft, and the miner had shored up the tunnel with timber.

"Looks like the vein disappears about here," J.C. noted. He swept the lantern from one wall to the other. Shadows danced eerily, and weird dark shapes seemed to leap at them.

"I don't like this place," Rachel whispered softly.

"We can leave," J.C. said. "I don't see any sign that the tunnel surfaces anywhere but at the cabin. Wait! What's this?"

One of the shadows wasn't a shadow at all, but the dark entrance of a branching adit. J.C. went in. Holding on to his hand, Rachel followed.

"Stay there," J.C. commanded.

"Why?"

"We haven't found another entrance, but we found the miner who used to work these digs."

By the time they got out of the tunnel, Rachel was more than ready for a breath of fresh air and the comforting serenity of the night. After all she had already seen, one more death—especially one that had occurred long ago—shouldn't have made her sad. But it did. The miner's fate was one more piece of testimony to the precariousness of life. She hadn't looked at the skeleton, but J.C. told her there was no evidence as to how the man had died. In Arizona Territory there were so many things that could kill a person—Indians, snakes, heat exhaustion, and so many other pitfalls.

"Are you all right?" J.C.'s eyes searched her face in the soft moonlight.

"I was thinking about that poor man. Doesn't anyone ever make it out of this country alive?"

"We will, Rachel. I want your promise you'll take Peter and hole up here if you see any sign of Indians. That skeleton back there can't hurt you, but the Apaches can."

Rachel shivered, despite the warmth of the night.

"Promise," J.C. insisted.

"All right. I promise. But right now I'm going back to the spring. I feel like I have the dust of that poor man's grave in every pore of my skin, and I'm going to wash it off."

The spring was a tiny oasis secreted away in an alcove in the canyon wall. Fresh, cool water issued from a zone of shattered rock that probably was the same fault they'd seen in the adit. The water trickled down several stair-steps of rock into a small, clear pool. A riot of water-loving vegetation crowded the pool's banks and carpeted its floor.

Over the past week they had all scrubbed themselves at the pool's edge—even Peter, whom Rachel had threatened with eviction from the shack unless he bathed away some of the grime. Rachel had washed their clothes as best she could, using a root that Aldona had once told her the Indians employed as soap. In the surreal state of mind that had settled upon her, the spring seemed to have a quality of magic. It was a touch of softness in an otherwise harsh land, a lush green garden lifted from some gentler place.

J.C. knelt beside Rachel as she bathed her face. "I'm almost going to miss this place," he said. "Up here it sometimes seems like we're the only people on earth."

"You're right." Rachel sat herself on a patch of soft grass and turned her face toward the sky. J.C. sat close beside her, his arm touching hers. The scent of him tickled her nostrils—dust and clean male sweat mixed in with the fresh scent of the soap root Rachel had used on his shirt. "Sometimes I wish it were true, that you and I and Peter were the only people on earth."

She closed her eyes and savored the sudden peace that came over her. A resolve crystallized in her mind, clear and shining as a jewel. Any other time, any other place, she might have been shocked at herself, but here and now she knew her decision was right. She reached for J.C.'s hand. "I'll miss you when you go."

"I'll be back."

"I know you will. And the world will come back with you."

He didn't ask what she meant, because he felt it, too, Rachel reflected. The last two weeks had tried their very souls, but the days had given them at least one good thing. Fleeing death and torture, surviving by their wits and teamwork, here in the desert they had been just J.C. and Rachel, a man and a woman, no bounty hunter, no fugitive mother, no pursuer, no pursued.

"J.C., I can't let you go without letting you know how I feel."

He turned toward her, the moonlight softening the weathered planes of his face and gleaming silver in his black hair. The way his smile reached into his eyes told her that she was not alone in her need. Hesitantly she brought his hand to her lips and placed a shy kiss on each finger.

"I'm not good at this." She smiled at the amazed expression on his face. "You'll have to help me."

"Rachel . . ." He cleared his throat and made a lame attempt to reclaim his hand. "Rachel, what are you doing?"

"Kissing your fingers."

"Rachel . . ." He closed his eyes and sighed as she turned his hand over and kissed the palm. "Much . . . much as I like that, I've got to warn you: My gentlemanly instincts are damned close to zero, and what you're doing is pretty near to making me go up like a stick of dynamite."

"I was counting on that."

He let out a slow breath between clenched teeth as she brought his hand to rest on her breast. Her heart raced, driving her pulse until her whole body seemed to flutter.

"Rachel . . ." he groaned. A muscle jumped rhythmically in his jaw.

"Am I going to have to do this all myself?"

"Christ! You would, wouldn't you?"

She could almost hear his control snap as he pulled her against his chest and kissed her, invading and demanding, thrusting and nipping. She met him with open mouth and willing lips. Slowly he bent her down until she lay on her back in the grass. One hand massaged her breasts while the other traveled up and down one thigh. Desire exploded inside her, unexpected and delicious in its intensity. She had never before experienced such a rush of passion. With Cabell, before their time together had turned sour, sex had been pleasant, if a little embarrassing in its intimacy. To be the object of her husband's intense enjoyment had been satisfying in itself. But this! This flood of pleasure, this heart-pounding, pulse-racing, galloping need, sweetened with anticipation! This was a whole new world.

J.C. was panting when he released her. The eyes that looked down at her were bright with craving. "Rachel, are you sure?"

"Oh, yes."

"Be very sure, because if we continue, the only way you're going to get me to stop is to drag me over to that pool and hold my head under water till I drown."

"I am very, very sure," she said with a smile.

She could have given him a ten-minute speech on why she was sure, about her sudden awareness of life's fragility and the necessity to capture every moment of the time allotted them, but it would be ten minutes wasted, because she could convey everything she felt in the smile she gave him. "I want to show you with my body how I feel in my heart. Make love to me, J.C. Please make love to me."

The look he gave her scorched all the way through to her soul. With a tense muscle jumping alongside his jaw, he began to carefully unfasten the buttons of her bodice.

"Damned tiny things! I swear women put these on dresses just to frustrate men."

Rachel laughed and helped him, her small, nimble fingers working alongside his. When they were unfastened to her waist, she started to work her cotton chemise up over her head, but J.C. stopped her.

"Wait. One step at a time, sweetheart. One step at a time."

He was more patient than Rachel, first feasting his eyes on the way her breasts swelled against the thin white cotton, how her pebble-hard nipples jutted upward from the smooth mounds. She closed her eyes as his hands caressed, squeezed, teased. He pushed a breast upward into his mouth and sucked at the nipple through the cotton. First one, then the other. Her pulse pounded, her body ached.

"What are you trying to do to me?" she groaned.

"Make you crazy." He blew softly against the flushed, wet flesh above the chemise's neckline. "Take this thing off."

She hastened to obey, and when his eyes devoured her bare breasts, she felt none of the embarrassment she had experienced when Cabell had looked upon her.

J.C. brushed a nipple with his finger, and the breath left her body.

"You're so beautiful, Rachel."

She sighed with bliss as he caressed one full, aching globe.

"I often wondered how far down those freckles go. I like 'em."

"You!" She made as if to hit him, but he caught her and bent her back over his arm so that her breasts jutted upward to meet his mouth. She clawed his back as he nuzzled and tongued, desire making her wild with wanting. He released her just long enough to shed his shirt. She traced the hard slabs of muscle in his chest, stopping at the puckered flesh that marked the healing wounds on his left side.

"Oh, J.C.! How could I forget? This must still hurt."

"Beautiful Rachel, the only thing that's hurting me right now is this." He pressed his hardened groin against her, and she arched against him, eyes closed with the sheer rapture of feeling the heat of his arousal and knowing that she had put him in such a state.

J.C. laughed. "I always figured you had a lot of the siren in you. Now I know." He kissed her mouth, her eyelids, the tip of her nose. His chest hair tantalized her breasts as he rubbed himself across her.

"You make me feel so . . . so . . ."

"I know," he whispered against her lips. "How far down do those freckles go, anyway? This far down?"

She cried out and arched against him as his hand slid between her legs. Her breath came in gasps as he rubbed against that most sensitive, vulnerable area.

"You could . . . you could find out," she managed to suggest.

"I intend to." He pulled her dress down over her hips, down her legs, over her ankles, and threw it impatiently to one side. Her drawers joined the dress in short order. When Rachel lay entirely naked, spread out before him like a feast, he took a moment just to look, but she was impatient. She wanted his hands upon her, wanted his mouth to teach her lessons of passion that were only half completed. She reached for his hand and rubbed it against her naked thigh, not yet quite bold enough to place it on the spot that ached so badly for his touch.

"The freckles do go all the way down," he said with a chuckle. "Rachel, you are glorious."

She bit her lip as his hand moved up the inside of her thigh. Gently he spread her legs and touched her intimately, tenderly. She arched against his hand with a groan.

Kneeling between her knees, he spread her legs wider and slipped a finger inside her, then two. When his thumb found the center of her desire Rachel thought she would scream. She bit down on her lip instead.

Still caressing her, he leaned forward and kissed her abused mouth. "Don't do that," he whispered. "I like your lips just the way they are."

The movements of his hand became relentless and aggressive, and Rachel surrendered to the grip of passion. Her body strained, ached, panted as his hand sent her spiraling up to a precarious peak of desire, until every fiber of her being seemed to convulse at once in a paroxysm of release. The world faded out, and she comprehended only the thunder of her heart and the sweet, bright streamers of joy that lit this new and joyful universe.

Finally her breathing slowed. She opened her eyes. The stars still wheeled above her, and J.C. still knelt bare-chested between her upraised knees, regarding her with a heated and predatory anticipation.

"I didn't know," she breathed, not caring if she made any sense. "I never . . ."

He smiled knowingly. "It helps to be in love."

She was in love, and the need still ached within her to show him. She had no intention of accepting such a gift of pleasure without giving the ultimate pleasure in return. Slowly she got to her knees so that she faced him. Anticipation tightened his features and glittered in his eyes as she slid her cool fingers over the line of coarse hair that arrowed down his chest and disappeared inside the waistband of his pants. "We're not through, are we?"

His breathing grew quicker as she unfastened his belt and then, slowly, one by one, flipped loose the buttons of his fly. When she slid her hand inside and caressed him through the barrier of his drawers, he gasped.

"I don't know how to do this," she said softly.

"You're doing just fine," he choked out. "If you were doing any better, I'd go up in flames."

She peeled down his trousers and followed her instinct in treating him to sweet torment. He closed his eyes and threw back his head. His chest was slick with sweat, and she could feel his racing pulse as it jumped against her fingers. He grew and hardened until he seemed hot enough to brand her, hard enough to rival stone—but alive, so alive.

"Rachel . . ." he gasped. "Come here, sweet woman."

He dragged her down with him and pinioned her on the grass, spreading her legs wide. She was hot and aching for his touch, crying out when he rubbed the head of his erection against the cleft between her thighs.

"No!" she gasped.

"No?"

His voice was so desperate that she laughed, and the

laughter itself almost sent her over the edge. "You're going to undo all my patient nursing if you treat your leg that way."

"To hell with my leg!"

She pushed him off her and rolled with him, landing on top, straddling his hips. "Better this way."

When he saw her intent, he grasped her hips in big, callused hands and slowly, carefully helped her to impale herself. She gasped as he filled her, half in pain, half in joy. It had been so long that she was tight as a new drum, but she stretched to take all of him. The pain wasn't sharp enough to erode the intense pleasure. Experimenting, she lifted herself slowly, then sank onto him again.

"Again," he urged her in a hoarse voice.

She complied. He thrust upward, taking charge, grasping her hips and rocking her in time to his bold strokes. There was no more teasing, no more thinking. Only him. Only her. Joined, merged in a plane of passion and warmth that went beyond the realm of sex and invaded the realm of the soul. The convulsion that shattered her, when it came, when J.C. allowed it, towered over her other climax as a volcano might dwarf a firecracker, for just as the first shudder coursed through her body, she felt J.C. pulse deep inside her. They rode out the explosion together, and when it was over, Rachel collapsed limply onto his chest. He rolled them over so that they lay side by side, arms wrapped around each other as if they would never let go.

"I love you, J. C. Tyler."

He nuzzled her hair, and his arms tightened. "I love you, too, Rachel. May God have mercy on us both."

18

J.C.'s leg hurt like hell, and he had scarcely started his journey. He was only two hours away from where he'd left Rachel and Peter at the mine shack, and already his legs felt as though they were made of rubber. Hell, every part of his damned body was made of rubber! A man never appreciated his own strength until he lost it. The walk to Tubac was going to take more strength than he had, J.C. knew, but he would make it. He would make it if he had to crawl on hands and knees.

He tried to calculate how long it would take him to reach Tubac and get back to the mine with a wagon and armed men. Longer than he wanted to leave Rachel and Peter alone, that was for sure. The old Canoa Ranch was closer, and there might be someone there—then again, there might not. Tubac was the safer bet. He toyed with the idea of traveling the river road in the valley instead of staying in the foothills. The going would certainly be easier on his aching leg, but he would be a sitting duck for any passing Apaches who were in the mood for murder and mayhem—and Apaches generally were these days. He didn't entirely blame them, seeing that they were fighting not only for their way of life but for their very survival. All the same, he didn't fancy becoming another pathetic number in the Arizona death toll, and he'd be damned if he would let Rachel and Peter end up that way either.

He paused at a rocky streambed to drink. Tiny pools remained from the thunderstorms that had ripped through the valley in the early hours before dawn. He had lain awake as thunder had shaken their tiny shack and lightning had lit the single window with eerie flashes of blue-white. The rain had been short-lived, but for a while it pounded upon the shack as loudly as the thunder. The roof had leaked in at least a dozen places, none of them, fortunately, directly over where any of them slept.

Frightened by the storm, Peter had scampered to crawl in beside his mother. J.C. would have liked to do the same thing, but for an entirely different reason. He could make love to Rachel the whole night through and still want more, weakling though he was these days. That kind of strength didn't come from the body; it came from the heart and soul. Before Rachel had given herself to him, J.C. had always believed that a man making love to a woman was a strictly physical thing. Now he knew better. She taught him a whole new side of loving—gentle laughter, teasing, and a deep caring that added depth to the raw passion flowing between them. He could spend the rest of his life with Rachel and not grow tired of touching her, laughing with her, loving her. Even fighting with her contained an element of intimacy.

Just his luck, J.C. mused wryly, to find a woman like Rachel and have a snowball's chance in hell of living long enough to enjoy her.

He walked on. The day grew hotter, his leg more

painful, his breath shorter. To keep his mind from the heat and his own misery, J.C. passed the time thinking up ways he could propose to Rachel if he was ever given the opportunity. Was she the type of woman who wanted a man to get down on one knee? No, he decided. She would laugh at that, laugh with that musical trill of good humor that always made him smile. Maybe he could start out making a joke about them marrying, ease into the subject and find out how she felt about it before making a total fool of himself. That probably wouldn't work. A man was expected to make a fool of himself during a proposal. It was all part of the process. Besides, Rachel was likely to see through any ploy he used—see through it and make some tart comment to put him in his place. She didn't let a man get away with much. Not most times. And yet other times—he smiled when he thought of the night before—sometimes she let a man get away with anything and everything. That was his Rachel—beautiful, gentle, clever, don't-mess-with-her-or-she'd-knock-you-over-the-head-with-a-skillet Rachel.

His Rachel. J.C. chuckled, and the sound had a hollow, bitter ring in the still desert air. Rachel wasn't *his* Rachel, and probably never would be. Despite the miracle that had taken place the night before, he couldn't ask her to marry a man who had next to nothing. It was ironic that if he turned Peter over to Cabell, he'd have his ranch and a life he could ask a woman to be a part of. By giving Rachel the thing she wanted most, he put her beyond his reach. Without Cabell Dorset's four thousand dollars, God only knew how long it would take to complete the purchase of his land and buy good stock to be the foundation of his ranch. In the meantime he'd go back to a wandering, violent life that no woman could share.

So intent was J.C. on his unpleasant dose of reality that he almost stumbled unaware upon a small party of Apaches who sat their mounts like statues atop a rocky ledge and looked up valley toward the mouth of a shadowed canyon. Even out in the open the warriors seemed to blend into the landscape—still as rock itself, rugged as the mountains behind them. Only a harshly spoken word from one of the Indians called them to J.C.'s attention.

Brought abruptly to his senses, J.C. ducked behind a jutting outcrop of rock and crouched as still as death itself. This was why he had chosen to stay in the foothills instead of walking the easier road by the river. In the broken terrain, hiding places were always close at hand.

The Apaches' attention was elsewhere, fortunately. They sat boldly in the open, eyes riveted on the road that emerged from the mouth of the canyon into the valley. If they had been paying more mind to what was going on around them, J.C. reflected, he would be dead right now instead of hiding behind a rock.

One of the warriors—little more than a boy, from the looks of him—spoke to a gray-haired, craggy-faced fellow who spoiled his mien of solemn dignity by laughing. Wondering what the Apaches found so amusing, J.C. searched for what had drawn their notice. From his hiding place he could see the road that led out of the canyon. Just beyond the shadows of the canyon mouth, a wagon loaded with lumber and drawn by six mules bounced its way toward the Santa Cruz River.

J.C.'s gut tightened as he swore silently. Should he play hero and try to warn the wagon driver? Or pick off one or two of the Indians with his pistol and hope they would leave their prey and make a dash for the safety of the mountains? In either case his chances for living through the encounter were somewhere in the vicinity of zero. If he got himself killed, what would happen to Rachel and Peter? He would likely be trading their lives to give the wagon a chance to get away.

The decision was taken from his hands when the Apaches exploded into a wild gallop down the hillside. J.C. cursed as he choked on their dust. Instinctively he drew his pistol and started to follow, unable to sit there and do nothing. To his great surprise, however, the wagon didn't flee; it stopped. The warriors surrounded it, whooping and hooting with glee. The driver didn't try to defend himself, and neither did the Indians fire a rifle or draw a bowstring.

"What the hell?" J.C. muttered. He stood and watched as the gray-haired leader of the band conversed with the wagon driver. The heat must have gotten to him, J.C. thought, because he thought that the two of them were actually laughing together. He was so puzzled that he almost forgot to duck for cover when the Apaches turned and rode back up the hillside. After the Indians were safely away, J.C. stood and stared after the wagon, which continued on its way as if nothing had happened.

"I'll be damned!" Sore leg and all, he trotted toward the road. The Apaches might not want that wagon, but he certainly did.

O'Malley stood rock still in the coolness of the adit while Peter and Rachel wrapped wet rags around his swollen fetlock. Rachel had washed out some of the soiled bandages that had been on J.C.'s leg to use for the stallion. Peter had sworn that the wrap would help the tendons recover.

As Peter tied the bandages in place, Rachel ran her hand along O'Malley's sleek, muscular neck. "Sacrificing my petticoats for J.C. was one thing," she told the horse. "Having you wear them is just ridiculous. I hope you appreciate this, horse."

"Oh, Ma!" Peter rolled his eyes.

"Well," Rachel said with a smile, "I'm not sure he deserves to be wearing that nice cotton eyelet ruffle, even if it is secondhand from being used on J.C. and a bit bloodstained."

"It wasn't O'Malley's fault he was scared by a snake. See how good he's behaving?"

"He's behaving *well*, Peter. Not *good*. And he might be playing the gentleman now, but just yesterday morning his hooves were waving above your head like twin anvils."

"He wouldn't've hurt me," Peter insisted.

"Is that why you and J.C. were rolling in the dust and thornbushes trying to get out of the way?"

"Well . . ." Peter's face puckered thoughtfully as he tried to come up with an answer.

"All I'm saying is that you need to be careful around him. He's bigger and tougher than you are, and he doesn't have the brains of a squirrel."

O'Malley swung his big head around and gave her a look of offended dignity. "You're not fooling me, big boy," Rachel told him. "I can see right through that innocent act."

In truth Rachel had become almost fond of the big stallion. Tending him made her feel close to J.C.—wherever J.C. was. She glanced out the tunnel's mouth to see the sun starting its afternoon descent in the West. J.C. had left at dawn. By now he had walked eight or nine hours. Was he all right? she worried. Was his leg holding out? Was he finding water to ease his thirst? Had he been bitten by a snake? Stung by a scorpion? Scalped by an Apache warrior?

"Ma?" Peter interrupted her grim speculations. "I'm going to go check my snares. Okay?"

"Be careful," she warned. "And keep your eyes open."

"Yes, ma'am."

Peter left, and O'Malley and Rachel regarded each other with mutual suspicion. "You're not so tough," she told the stallion. "In fact you and your master have a lot in common. You're both cocky male animals with a mischievous glint in your eyes, but you're both gentlemen in spite of that bulk of muscle and rip-snorting facade. Though neither one of you would admit it."

She thought of J.C.'s efforts at being restrained and gentlemanly the night before. She'd surprised him with her invitation, Rachel knew, but he was trying so hard not to take advantage of her that nothing would ever have happened between them had she not taken the initiative. Bless him. She closed her eyes, thinking of their loving. The joy of intimacy with a man she truly loved had come as a delightful surprise to her. Now she knew how sweet lovemaking could truly be between a man and a woman—the intense sharing, the unrestrained, unembarrassed intimacy, the merging of hearts as well as bodies. She loved J. C. Tyler, and she didn't care if he was a bounty hunter, farmer, rancher, tax collector, cowboy, or lion tamer. He was deep in her heart, and likely he would stay there until that heart stopped beating.

Peter came back and dumped an armful of grass on the floor beside O'Malley.

"Why don't we just stake him out by the spring?" Rachel asked.

" 'Cause J.C. said I should leave O'Malley where he is."

And of course whatever J.C. said was the law, Rachel

noted with amusement. Peter had passed through his anger and contempt for the bounty hunter and landed squarely on adoration. Rachel didn't mind. It was going to make things easier. If they got out of this alive, she wondered if J.C. would propose or if she would have to take the initiative once again. Either way she wasn't going to let the man go.

"I found a rabbit in my snares," Peter announced proudly. "Those things are sure a lot better idea than tryin' to hit 'em with a rock."

"You're getting to be quite the provider," Rachel told him. "I guess I'd better go clean and skin your catch for supper.

"I can do it!" Peter offered. "J.C. taught me how. Can I have the knife?"

"Be careful."

"Yes, ma'am."

"And don't run with that knife!" she called after him as he dashed down the path.

Rabbit again. Rachel sighed. If she never saw another rabbit, it would be too soon.

By the time she reached the shack, Peter had the rabbit spitted over a small fire. Rachel cringed every time they built a cookfire, even though J.C. had taught them both how to make a fire that was nearly smokeless. Apaches had sharp eyes and noses, and even a little smoke might draw them to the shack to investigate.

"It'll be done in a bit," Peter told her.

"Thank you for making supper," Rachel said, "not to mention catching it."

"It was nothing," Peter claimed, eyes shining.

What a difference a little pride made, Rachel reflected. J.C. had made as much difference in Peter's life as in hers.

Suddenly she was aware of something not right. She

looked around. Nothing had changed that she could see. Everything was peaceful, quiet. Too quiet, Rachel realized suddenly. The usual background flutter and chatter of the birds was gone. There were no scurryings or scamperings in the grass by the population of ground squirrels or the rabbits that had so far outwitted Peter's snares. The whole canyon seemed to hold its breath.

"Peter, put out the fire and go to the tunnel. I think someone's coming."

For once Peter didn't question her directions. He quickly threw dirt on the flames. "Indians?" he asked, wide-eyed.

"I don't know. Go! I'll get the rifle."

Rachel was right behind Peter as he climbed the path to the adit. She continually looked over her shoulder, but could see no one. After a brief whicker of greeting when they reached the mine, O'Malley's attention was riveted somewhere in the distance, his ears pricked, his neck arched.

"Someone *is* coming," Rachel concluded. "Get back from the opening, Peter." She crouched at the mouth of the tunnel, rifle cocked and ready, praying silently that whatever had set the canyon on alert was not a band of marauding Apaches. J.C.'s image filled her mind—his smile, the twinkle in his eyes when he teased her, the hard, masculine feel of his body when he made love to her. Never in Rachel's life had she been so glad of anything as she was glad that she had made love to John Charles Tyler before he left.

As Crazy Jake Sumner's wagon clattered up the overgrown path to the mine shack, J.C. jumped off and limped up to the door.

"Rachel!"

The shack was empty. Outside, a single wisp of smoke curled up from a hastily buried fire.

"Rachel!" J.C. called. There was no answer, and for a moment his heart jumped in panic. Visions of Apaches carrying them off leaped into his mind, but they scattered when two familiar voices called his name. Then he saw them running down the path from the tunnel.

"J.C.! J.C.!" Peter waved a half-cooked spitted rabbit in the air as if it were a pennant.

"J.C.!" Rachel flew into his arms and hugged him hard. He inhaled the sweet scent of woman—his woman—and forgot pain and weariness. Rachel Dorset was better than whiskey or any medicine a doctor could give him for reviving his energy and making him feel like a whole man once again. "J.C.!" She pushed away to arm's length but still kept her hands firmly on his shoulders. "What are you doing here?"

He grinned. "You want me to leave?"

"No! Of course not!" Suddenly she blushed, making the freckles stand out on her tanned face. Self-consciously she let her hands drop as Crazy Jake climbed down from the wagon.

"Rachel," J.C. said, "this is Jake Sumner. He's got a lumber camp in the mountains a bit south of here. I ran into him in the foothills."

"Hello, Mr. Sumner."

Jake swept his sweat-stained, battered hat from his head and bowed elaborately. "Charmed, ma'am. Just call me Crazy Jake. Ever'body does. A lady like yerself is shore a sight fer sore eyes."

"And this is Peter," J.C. told Jake.

Peter looked with awe at Crazy Jake's long white beard. "Hi. See my rabbit?"

"Howdy, young man. Did you get that rabbit all on your own?"

"Yessir." Peter turned to J.C., his face alight. "I skinned it and cleaned it myself! Ma said she'd do it, but I told her I could, and I did, just like you showed me. And O'Malley's leg is lots better already. He let me sit on his back in the tunnel, and—"

"Peter!" Rachel scolded. "When did you get up on that horse?"

"This morning while you was off at the spring sittin' and starin' into space."

Rachel flushed again, and J.C. couldn't stifle his laugh, because he knew exactly why Rachel had been mooning around the spring after he left.

"And Ma thought you was Indians comin' up the canyon, so we went up to the tunnel to hold you off, and—"

"Peter, that's enough now," Rachel warned.

Both men laughed. "This is quite a family you have here, Tyler. I always say a man who's got family ain't never poor. That's what I always say."

Rachel opened her mouth to correct Jake's mistaken assumption, but J.C.'s proud grin stopped her. "Yeah," he agreed with Jake. "They're quite a family all right. They are at that."

His eyes caught Rachel's and twinkled at her, and she had to smile.

The rest of the afternoon was spent resting. Rachel rewrapped J.C.'s thigh and clucked over the swelling. Crazy Jake entertained them all with tales of his years in Arizona; he'd been in the territory since 1855, shortly after the southern part of the territory had been purchased from Mexico. In 1860 he'd saved the daughter of an Apache chieftain from being raped and sold into slavery by Mexican bandits, and the girl's father had made Jake a blood brother.

" 'Twouldn't do me any good up north with the Tonto Apaches," Jake said. "But all the Pinals know me, and most of Cochise's bunch—in other words most of the troublemakers around these parts. They don't bother me, so I've got the advantage on everybody else who's trying to make a living around here. I been doin' good business hauling lumber to Tucson, 'cause those people down there are always building somethin'. There's a coupla other sawmill operations around in these mountains, but the Injuns give 'em a heap a trouble. Back in 'sixty-one some young fella had a lumber camp not too far from here and took his new wife with him up to the mountain, along with a little girl who was a friend of theirs. Danged if the Apaches didn't run off with that woman and little girl. That was the Tonto band—don't know what they were doin' down this way, but it was them all right. Made their way north up the ridges till they finally speared and clubbed the wife and left 'er for dead. Quite a woman, her! Larcena Page was 'er name. She crawled for nine days on hands and knees back to that lumber camp, eatin' plants and bugs, gettin' there more dead than alive. Goldarned if she didn't live. Still lives down in Tucson. Good woman. Gutsy."

"What happened to the little girl?" Peter asked, his eyes bright with fascination.

"A bit later some friendly Apaches bought the little girl from the Tontos and got her back home. She was all right. Most times the Apaches treat the children they capture pretty good. They raise 'em like one o' theirs. 'Specially the boys." Jake's eyes twinkled teasingly. "How'd you like to be an Apache brave, son?"

Peter grimaced. "No thanks!"

They all laughed. Peter basked in the attention of the older men. Jake had a real bow and arrow in the wagon, and Peter's attention was rapt when the older man explained how the weapon was made. As the sun sank lower in the west, J.C. and Jake taught Peter to play poker, somewhat to Rachel's distress.

"You're going to turn him into a cardsharp," she complained.

"Nah," Jake said. "He'd need lots more practice before he'd be that good."

After supper Jake and J.C. engaged in a tall-tale contest, each trying to outdo the other in spinning yarns with every possible embellishment and little attention to the truth. Peter listened, breathlessly enthralled. The men were obviously in their element. Her son's spellbound bliss made Rachel feel happy and sad at the same time—happy that Peter liked J.C. so much, sad because she was uncertain what their future held.

Feeling a need to be alone with her thoughts, Rachel used the excuse of taking O'Malley to the spring for a drink to get off by herself. The stallion's limp had improved in only a day, Rachel noted. She took off the wrappings and bathed the fetlock in the cool water of the spring.

"I imagine you'll be happy to get back to a nice barn and good hay instead of living in a mine adit," she commented to the horse. "We're headed for Tucson tomorrow. It's farther away than Tubac, but Crazy Jake says there's a lot of Apaches between here and Tubac right now."

O'Malley seemed to take in every word as if he understood what she said.

"Tucson's scarcely what I would call a metropolis," Rachel told him. "But it's big enough the Apaches don't attack it. They'll never get you there, big fella. You'll like it."

The question was would she and Peter like it? Strangely enough, Rachel found herself reluctant to leave this place. The scene she had left back in the shack was so much like a happy family evening that it made her heart ache. Her heart ached for Peter, who was so needful of a man in his life. Her heart ached for J.C., who was trapped in a violent life he didn't want, and for herself, who was also needful of a man in her life—one specific man: John Charles Tyler.

But an end was coming. Their adventure together was nearly over. With luck and Crazy Jake's help, they would make it to Tucson with their scalps still firmly on their heads. Then what? Did J.C. want her with him? Did he love her? How lasting were words spoken in the heat of the moment, when they'd both thought they were facing death? Last night the future had been an uncertainty, a distant prospect that in all likelihood they would never see. Now, it seemed, the future was almost upon them. Facing that future, Rachel found she was more afraid of endless loneliness than she was afraid of Apaches.

"What do you think, O'Malley? You know anything useful?"

The stallion raised his dripping muzzle from the pond and gave her a bored look.

"I'm talking to a horse," Rachel groaned. "My wits are gone."

"I wouldn't say that," said J.C.'s voice from behind her. "I talk to O'Malley all the time."

Heat flooded Rachel's face as she whirled to face the object of her fretting. She instinctively raised her hands to her cheeks to hide her reaction, then let them drop when she realized how useless the gesture was. "I thought you were back at the shack."

He shrugged. "Peter and Jake are swapping yarns, and I thought maybe you could use some company."

"Jake and Peter are swapping yarns?"

J.C. grinned. "Peter learns fast."

Rachel couldn't help but smile back at him. "First poker. Now spinning tall tales. What else is he going to learn from you?"

He was silent, and as his eyes caught hers, Rachel knew he wasn't thinking of Peter. She looked away, unable to meet his intense gaze.

"Do you think we'll make it to Tucson?" she asked.

"Yeah. I think we will."

Then what? she wanted to ask. But she held her silence. She had struggled so long to be an independent woman, to rely on herself and her own resources. It wouldn't be right to stick to J.C. like some burr in his blankets.

"I'm glad we're headed for Tucson instead of Tubac," she said. "There's stage lines that go both east and west from there. I'll have to decide where I can go that Cabell won't find me."

J.C. took her chin in his hand and turned her face so that she had to look at him. "Rachel, I told you that I'd help you get settled someplace. You aren't afraid that I'll change my mind, are you? I'm not going to turn you over to Cabell."

"I know. I trust you, J.C. But what about the money you need?"

"There's always a pile of wanted posters in Tucson. I'll get the money. It will just take a little more time."

The hooded look of his eyes had returned, telling Rachel that he held something back. Something was yet unsaid, but she knew better than try to pry it out of him. When he got that look on his face, he was like a clam. The harder one pried, the tighter he closed himself.

"I hope you get your ranch, J.C."

"I will. I'm going to work like hell to get every single thing I want. Don't you doubt it."

"I don't. I wish I were as certain of where I was going."

He sighed, and the growing tightness of his face made him look weary. They sat down on the grassy bank of the pond and both held their silence for what seemed like long minutes. The only sound was O'Malley's loud munching as he grazed on the little spring's offering of green.

Finally J.C. broke the silence. "You can't run forever, Rachel. I've tracked down a lot of people who thought they could, and I tell you true that you can't."

She rested her chin in her hand and sighed. "I don't need to run forever. Only until Peter is old enough to take care of himself with Cabell. Eight or nine years."

When she said it, it sounded like an impossibly long time. Impossibly long.

"Rachel . . ."

"I'll make it," she said with false brightness. Her instinct was to soften, to launch herself into J.C.'s arms, cry on his shoulder, and beg him to stay with her, help her, love her. But this wasn't J.C.'s problem, she reminded herself sternly. "Don't worry about us, J.C. We'll make it, Peter and I." Rachel wished she believed her own reassurances. She hoped J.C. believed them.

"I can't help but worry about you," he said firmly.

He put his arm around her, and she couldn't resist the temptation to lay her head on his broad shoulder. For J.C. that wasn't enough, however. He cradled her head in his hand and kissed her, at first gently, then hard. His strength, his passion, his need invaded her as his tongue thrust deeply and sensuously. When he finally released her, she was breathless with the need for one more gift of love, one more indulgence of desire and longing before the future consigned them to separate fates.

As if someone had thrown a torch on the dry desert

brush, a fire ignited between them in a searing explosion. J.C. pressed her back onto the same grass that had cradled them the night before. He took her mouth in a scorching possession while he worked at the buttons of her bodice.

"Rachel," he breathed against her lips, "if you want me to stop . . ."

"Oh, no! Don't stop!"

He freed her breasts and paid them homage with his mouth, sending fire shooting through her with every stroke of his tongue and gentle nip of his strong teeth. Rachel was not in a mood to tarry. She ached for completion, half out of wildness to have him inside her, half out of fear that Jake or Peter would come strolling up from the cabin to find them.

"Hurry, J.C. Please hurry. I need you inside me. Please."

He pushed her skirts up to her waist and plunged his hand between her legs, massaging her moist cleft through the cotton of her drawers, drinking in her eagerness as she arched into his hand. He drew down her drawers and lifted her up to his mouth. His tongue stroked her into a state where she could no longer think, only feel. Her body poised on the brink of explosion, but he wouldn't let it happen, ruthlessly driving her to frenzy and then letting her slide backward to mere desperation.

"J.C., please!"

He was near the breaking point as well, for he rose to his knees above her and worked frantically at the buttons of his trousers. "Rachel, you can drive a man to heaven and hell at the same time," he said in a hoarse voice. "Someday I'm going to get you in a room all to myself, in a nice soft bed, without grass tickling your backside, without some damned horse looking on, and without an old man and nosy little boy likely to pop in on us at any minute, and then I'm going to take all the damned night to enjoy this like it should be enjoyed."

She breathed deeply in anticipation as he poised above her. "I don't know about you," she told him with a half smile. "But I'm enjoying myself right now."

"Oh, I'm enjoying myself," he said in a husky voice, then thrust inside her, eyes closed, head thrown back in exultation. She arched to meet him, taking him deeper with each stroke, her legs wrapped around his hips, her hands gripping the bulging muscles of his arms as he propped himself above her.

Their ascent to a scalding climax was fast and merciless. He drove her upward, and she soared. She felt every mighty pulse of his shaft as he exploded deep inside her, and her body contracted around the fire within, every fiber of her convulsing with joy. Drained of everything but contentedness, she waited for the earth to stop spinning, minutely aware of every sensation of her body, of the feel of his flesh still inside her, the tickle of his chest hair brushing against her breasts, the warmth of his breath on her cheek, the possessive grip of his hands on her hips. She closed her eyes, savoring it all, knowing she might never have him again and not wanting to think about it.

Now was not the time to remind herself that she shouldn't need this man; she shouldn't need any man.

19

Any Georgia planter would have considered Tucson a mere wart on the backside of the wilderness. Arizona Territory's capital city in this summer of 1870 was a dusty village of drab adobe buildings sitting in the valley of the Santa Cruz River. The rugged Santa Catalina Mountains rose above the settlement, making it look even more insignificant. Cultivated fields softened the landscape to the west, made green by water brought from the river in the local irrigation ditch, or *acequia*.

To the three bedraggled travelers who rode into Tucson on Crazy Jake Sumner's lumber wagon on a hot August morning, the territorial capital, unprepossessing as it was, looked like a mecca of civilization. The village was busy. Mexican and Papago Indian women strolled to and from the village spring balancing earthen water jars on their heads. Wagons and buggies of all descriptions clattered along unpaved streets that were so cut by ravines in places that the traffic had difficulty getting through. A chain gang of prisoners worked along Main Street, sweeping away the leavings of oxen, mules, and horses, disposing of the occasional dead chicken or dog that decorated the avenue, and trying to fill in some of the washed-out areas with dirt and gravel.

Jake's big wagon clattered along Main Street with the other traffic. At one point it was barely able to squeeze by a line of huge freight wagons lumbering toward the Tully and Ochoa transportation and freighting office. Rachel was surprised at how much the town had grown since she had passed through a year ago on her way to Tubac. On just a short section of Main Street they passed several dry goods stores, a fish company, the Tully and Ochoa freighting company, two saloons—one incongruously named the Ice Cream Saloon—and a restaurant. Some of the adobe store fronts were dressed up with plaster and paint to look like brick.

"You can find anything you want in this town," Jake told them, "long as you don't get too fancy in your taste. There's a good doc down the street a bit if'n you wanna get that leg looked at," he told J.C. "He pulls teeth, too, fer them that need it done. First I'll get you people set up—the Stevens House up here is as good lodging as anywhere else. Tell 'em you jest crawled in from an Apache attack an' they're likely to give you rooms fer free. Folks around here gener'ly turn purple in the face if you mention anything Apache. You might wanna let the sheriff know about what happened to those freight wagons you were with. They'll tell the army folks over there at Camp Lowell, and the army'll send out a troop to clean up the mess. The folks around here wouldn't want to miss a chance to complain about the local savages."

Stevens House had very little to distinguish it from the other adobe, mud-roofed residences around it except that it was slightly larger. It was a long, low structure dominating the corner of Main and Pennington Streets—Pennington Street, Jake told them as he pulled to a halt in front of the place, was named after the pioneer Pennington family, of which the brave Larcena Page that he'd told them about was a daughter. Not far in back of the lodging house was El Presidio Plaza, and across from it were several stores, a saloon, and a fairly nice-looking restaurant.

J.C., Rachel, and Peter were taken in with sympathy and open arms. A Señora Cotera showed them to their rooms, which were, despite the rustic appearance of the place, clean and reasonably well appointed. The proprietress was very vocal in her sympathy for their ordeal and adamant about the need to wipe every last Apache from the face of the earth, or at least from Arizona.

"Is that what you mean about whites and Mexicans and Indians hatin' each other?" Peter asked when the proprietress had left them alone. He had begged to room with J.C., and Rachel had relented.

"Yeah," J.C. answered. "That's what I meant. Everybody around here is real anxious to wipe everybody else off the face of the earth. The Indians aren't alone in feeling that way."

"They're just better at it," Peter said with certainty.

"They're pretty good at it, all right, but I'm not sure they're much better than the rest of us."

After a knock on their door the proprietress stuck her head in and gave them a sympathetic smile. "Señor, if you would like me to wash your clothes, my husband is about your size, and I have five sons as well. I could find you and the *niño* something to wear if you wish."

"Thanks, but I think we'll go out and get some things. Once we get into some clean clothes, I think you can burn these."

The woman laughed. "That is the same thing the red-haired señora said."

"You got money?" Peter asked when she had gone.

"I won some from Jake at poker two nights ago. Remember?"

"Sure! I helped you win. I was the one who told you to keep that nine."

"Yeah. You were. So I'm thinking we should take our winnings and get us into clean shirts and britches and buy your mother a new dress."

Peter thought about it. "Ma always sews her own clothes."

"Well, she can't very well do that here. I saw a nice frilly thing ready made in the store across the way."

"How do we know what size?"

"Well, she's . . ." J.C. held his hand even with the bottom of his nose to indicate height, then drew an hourglass figure in the air to outline her width. His mouth slanted into a crooked smile, and a slightly glazed look came into his eyes. Peter had seen that look in his eyes before when they talked about his mother. You'd think a grown-up would be able to keep his mind more in hand.

"Are we goin' out?" Peter asked impatiently.

J.C. sighed and dropped his hands. "Yeah. Let's go. I'll just ask your mother what size she takes. Women's dresses come in sizes, don't they?"

Peter shrugged. "I dunno. But you'd better not bother Ma about it right now." He nodded toward the wall that adjoined the next room, which was his mother's. "Listen to all that splashin'. She's takin' a bath, I bet, and she don't like bein' walked in on. I came into the room at the roadhouse once when she was sittin' in the old tin tub, and she threw a wet rag at me."

"Hmmm." J.C. nodded. "We could knock on the wall and ask her."

Peter shook his head. J.C. was a fine fellow, but he

sure didn't know anything about mothers. "Ma says yellin' through walls is rude."

"We wouldn't want to be rude," J.C. agreed.

"Maybe they only have one dress anyway. That'll make it easy."

J.C. grinned. "You're right, Big Red. Why didn't I think of that?"

Peter was feeling smarter by the minute. He was really glad his mother had said he could stay in the same room with J.C. J.C. was easier to talk to than most grown-ups. "Listen to all that splashin'!" he chortled, falling onto the bed and giving a few experimental bounces. "Ya know? If I made that much noise in a bath, Ma would whup me."

"Is that so?" J.C. asked with a smile. "How many times has your mother whupped you in the past few years?"

Peter thought back. Surely there must have been a time or two. She got mad enough to take a stick to him about once a day, but she'd never actually done it.

"That's what I thought," J.C. said when the silence drew out.

"Do we hafta take a bath too?" Peter asked.

"I suspect so." J.C. took a cautious sniff at the sleeve of his shirt and grimaced. "Women are peculiar about not stinking. They don't put up with it very well. Remember that if you ever want to stay in a lady's good graces."

"Why would I want to do that?"

"You'll figure that one out in a few years."

"Well, if it means I hafta take a lot of baths, I don't want to."

J.C. just smiled.

Peter was happy to get away from the lodging house—and the threat of a scrubbing—and follow J.C.

on his errands. As they walked down the street, he noticed the glances that came their way. Men gave J.C.
looks of caution. Women hastily lowered their eyes
when they passed, but not without glancing their way
with furtive interest. The looks might be because they
were white people, Peter decided. Most of the people
on the streets were Mexican or Indian. Or it might be
because J.C. was big, and the scraggly growth of beard
on his face gave him the appearance of some kind of
desperado.

Peter wanted to be as big and broad as J.C. when he
grew up. He might try growing a beard, too, but a red
beard might look silly instead of dangerous. In any case,
when he was a grown man, he wanted people to look at
him the same way they looked at J.C.

"Where we goin'?" Peter asked, bouncing along at
J.C.'s side.

"To mail a letter."

"What letter?"

"This one." J.C. showed him the envelope. "To your
father."

Instantly wary, Peter stopped bouncing. "Oh."

"When I first met you, I mailed a letter to your father
telling him where you were. Now I'm letting him know
that the boy I found wasn't you."

Confused, Peter screwed up his face. "I'm not me?"

"That's right."

"Why?"

"Because I don't want him to know where you and
your mother are."

J.C. slowed his pace so that Peter was able to catch up
with him. Nine-year-old legs just weren't long enough to
match J.C.'s pace, even when he was limping.

"You know, Red, I'm really sorry that I ever tried to
take you away from your mom. I should have seen right

when I met her that she was a lady who had a good reason for everything she did."

"Is Ma still mad at you for that?" Peter inquired.

A strange smile came to J.C.'s face. "No. I don't think so. Are you?"

When J.C. looked down at him, Peter could see that the question was a serious one. It mattered if Peter was still angry. Peter was important. What Peter thought was important. That in itself was enough to dispel any lingering shred of resentment the boy had. "I'm not mad," he said. "Not anymore." He was rewarded by a warmth that radiated from J.C.'s eyes in a fan of sunbaked crinkles. It shot right into Peter and made him feel like smiling inside, the same way J.C.'s eyes smiled. It also started him doing some serious thinking.

Peter was quiet while they dropped the letter off at the Southern Overland U. S. Mail and Express office to go out on the next stage. He listened without comment as J.C. grumbled to himself about the lack of a telegraph, and plodded along silently as they walked to the doctor's surgery. By the time the doc had Rachel's petticoat bandages unwrapped from J.C.'s leg, Peter had made his momentous decision.

"Am I ever going back to my father?" he asked J.C.

"Not any time soon," J.C. told him. "Not if your mother has anything to say about it."

Peter withdrew into thought again as the doctor peered and probed at J.C.'s leg.

"Not bad," the doc commented. "You're a lucky fellow, Mr. Tyler. That was a nasty wound, it looks like."

"Yeah, well, it felt nasty too."

"You're fortunate to be walking. Actually I'm surprised you have a leg left at all. But it's healing nicely now. In a week or two you should be able to walk without a limp. Until then try to take it easy."

"Sure, Doc."

"Now, let's have a look at those ribs and shoulder."

J.C. peeled off his shirt to reveal the furrows that marked his left side. Peter was impressed with the array of muscle. He hoped he looked like that when he grew up.

"Say, J.C.?"

"What is it, Red?"

"I been thinkin'."

"Is that why you've been sitting there so quiet?" he asked with a teasing grin.

Peter was serious, though. This was really important stuff he was thinking about. "Just listen, J.C. Ma isn't married anymore, you know. She told me so. And it's really dull livin' with just ladies, you know? If you're not gonna send me back to my father, why don't you become my father? You could teach me how to shoot, and ride really good. I could help you with O'Malley and help you get the money for your ranch. And," he added as an afterthought, "Ma likes you. I can tell. Her face gets all sappy when she looks at you."

"Ouch!" J.C. cried. "Watch what you're doing, Doc!"

"Sorry." The doctor gave Peter a curious look, then bent assiduously to his work.

"Peter, I'm . . . uh . . . flattered that you'd want me to be your father. But it's not that easy."

"Don't you like my mother?"

"I like your mother a lot. A whole lot."

"If you like her, then why can't you just marry her? Then I'd have a father again."

The doc chuckled knowingly and earned himself a glare from J.C. "You just stick to your bandages, Doc."

The doc lifted a brow, but the smile didn't leave his face. J.C. glanced at Peter, then looked at the ceiling, as if maybe something was written up there that he could read. When he looked down, he still looked unhappy. "Peter . . ." He grimaced, scowled, cleared his throat, and tried again. "Peter, I'd like to marry your mother and be your father . . ."

"Okay!"

"But you've got to understand, boy; a man doesn't marry himself a wife until he's got something to offer her. I don't have anything but a good horse, a couple of guns, and a piece of land that hasn't been paid for yet. And the way things are going, I don't know when it'll be paid for."

Peter didn't see the problem. "So you don't have anything much. Ma doesn't either. If she had you, she'd have more than she has now."

The doc laughed softly as he wrapped a clean bandage around J.C.'s leg. Undeterred by J.C.'s quelling look, he commented, "The boy has a point, you know."

Rachel reveled in cleanliness as she pulled on the clothes Señora Cotera had brought her—they belonged to her sister's daughter, the woman had told her.

"She was tiny like you, Señora. Last year she died in childbed—three days after her little one was born. It was very sad. She was always giving things to people poorer than her; she would like you to have the clothes. I am sure of it."

The señora's niece had apparently been just Rachel's size, for the embroidered cotton blouse and ankle-length gathered skirt fit very well. Against the bleached white of the blouse Rachel's skin looked as brown as any Mexican woman's. She had either lost her freckles or become one gigantic freckle. If not for the flaming red of her hair, she could fit right in with the stately women traveling to and from the town spring with their jars balanced upon their head. Berry-brown skin in combination with her green eyes and glaring hair must make her quite a sight, she mused.

Almost glad she didn't have a mirror, Rachel sat cross-legged on the bed and took a borrowed brush to her wet hair. The desert sun and dusty wind had dried it and split the ends. She was tempted to swear when the brush snagged on a tangle, then laughed at herself.

"Barely escape with my life after days in the wilderness and here I am mad because the sun dried out my hair."

She could laugh about it, but the thought of how narrow their escape had been could still take away her breath, and would, she suspected, for years to come. Yet she would almost gladly be back in that mine shack or dirty cave if it would mean having J.C. to herself again. Just John Charles Tyler and Rachel Manchester, together without the world intruding—except for Peter of course. Peter had to be there. He had brought them together and in a perverse way had been the connecting link that kept them together. Peter was a part of whatever she and J.C. had between them.

She yanked at her hair, suddenly impatient with the whole coil—not only of her hair but of her life. Just what was it that she and J.C. had between them? She would dearly like to know. Was it love? In the desert Rachel had convinced herself she loved J.C., but what was love? She had learned the hard way that romance was an illusion, fairy tales didn't come true, and Prince Charming didn't exist. Yet she didn't think J.C. was Prince Charming. He was a bounty hunter: a man who lived by his gun, rough, ruthless, dangerous. He'd lied to her, betrayed her trust, had been ready to tear her life to shreds for the sum of four thousand dollars.

Yet despite everything, he could be kind. He had his own code of honor and stuck by it. He could laugh at

himself as well as others—a wonderful laugh that came
from the heart. He had the patience to listen when her
son talked, and to teach him to whittle. He could be
gentle, and loving, and even noble, on occasion.

Rachel sighed. J. C. Tyler wasn't Prince Charming by
a long shot, but he was a strong, courageous, good-
hearted man. He lit a fire in her—not only of passion
but of life. He changed her days from something to be
endured into something to be enjoyed.

Foolish, foolish Rachel, she chided herself. *You do love
him.*

And perhaps he loved her, too, at least a little. He'd
said so, but such words came naturally in the aftermath
of desire. And, to be honest with herself, Rachel had to
admit that at the time he must have doubted that either
one of them had a future in front of them. She couldn't
set much store by a declaration of love given at the
precipice of death.

She finally untangled the last knot in her hair,
brushed the flaming mass back, and caught it at her
nape. She started to wind it into a tight, neat bun, but
stopped and shook it loose. She didn't want to look like
a staid matron. What message would that send? She
could braid it, but that was much too girlish. She was far
from being an innocent girl; no one knew that better
than J.C. She could try to pin it on top of her head like
some fashion plate out of a ladies' magazine. No. The
man would fall down laughing if she tried to primp like
some society belle.

"I don't believe this!" she complained to herself.
"What does it matter what J.C. thinks? It doesn't! It
doesn't matter!"

They had no future together. They'd had a few moments of passion at a time when she had been the only
woman and he the only man on earth. That was all. How

could there be anything more? A fine couple they would make: a wandering bounty hunter and a divorced, disgraced woman running from her ex-husband and a Georgia state court order. A fine couple indeed!

"You need to find your own future," she lectured herself firmly. "Don't force him to pry you off of him like a thistleburr stuck in his stockings. Grow up, you ninny."

With pride fueling her determination, Rachel confronted Señora Cotera in the tiny lobby of the lodging house.

"Have you heard any news from Tubac?" she asked the woman. In Tubac at least she had the roadhouse. It might be a failing business in a dying town, but it might hold them until she could decide on somewhere better to go.

The señora shook her head. "Things are very bad down there. Two days ago the post rider got turned back to Tucson before making it halfway. Word is that there are a lot of Indians between here and there. Will Oury thinks it's the Pinal band and Eskiminzin causing the trouble, and some others think it's Cochise and the Chiracahua. If you ask me, one Apache's as bad as another. These days you can't get a half mile from town without being afraid for your scalp."

Well, Rachel thought, that settled that. She hadn't really thought they could go back to Tubac, but she'd had to ask.

Just then Peter and J.C. walked into the lobby.

"My goodness!" Rachel exclaimed. "Look at you!"

They certainly didn't look like the two who had ridden into town on the back of Jake's lumber wagon.

"Yeah," J.C. said with a grin. "Isn't it something what a bath and shave can do?"

"I got a shave too!" Peter crowed, rubbing his downy little chin. "With shaving foam an' everything!"

"Well, you certainly needed one," Rachel said as J.C. winked at her. "And you both got your hair cut as well! I'm very impressed with how gentlemanly you look."

Would the bounty hunter have been so quick to shed his scruffiness if he hadn't been trying to impress her? Rachel mused. In spite of her recent practical resolve, her heart warmed. Something else inside her warmed as well; she had known J.C. was handsome, but not quite so handsome. He certainly cleaned up well.

"We saw Jake at the barbershop!" Peter announced. "He's going to go to supper with us at the Shoo-Fly Restaurant!"

Rachel's brows shot up. "The . . . Shoo-Fly?"

"It's the truth," J.C. confided. "Buck up, Rachel. After the last couple of weeks you should be used to sharing your food with flies. Besides"—he held up a paper-and-string wrapped package—"wait till you see what your son bought you to wear."

The dress was a green that matched her eyes and was trimmed with ruffled white muslin. Señora Cotera brought a full-length oval mirror to Rachel's room. It was the only mirror in the house, and heavy enough that the señora needed J.C.'s help to move it.

"You must see how beautiful you will look," the proprietress insisted when Rachel objected to the trouble. Then she shooed out J.C. and Peter and helped Rachel undo all the tiny pearl buttons and try the dress on.

When they finally had the last button fastened and the last frill in place, the woman that stared back at Rachel from the glass was full of vivid color, red and green like a Christmas tree, she thought to herself. In Savannah she would have been laughed right out of her Ladies' Improvement Circle if she'd appeared in such a getup. In Tubac, Aldona would have chuckled heartily at the boned bodice, tight sleeves, and pinched-in waist that made movement a taxing effort. But J.C. had bought it for her—bless his heart. She didn't believe for one moment the dodge about Peter getting it. J.C. had given it to her, so it was special, and she would smile while wearing it.

Señora Cotera nodded politely. "A great improvement from the clothes I burned."

Rachel laughed. That at least was true.

The Shoo-Fly Restaurant was fortunately cleaner than the name implied. Rachel got more than one curious look from the other diners when they sat down. There were a few other white women in Tucson, but not many, and apparently for a woman to appear in a public restaurant was unusual—especially a woman who looked like a Christmas tree, Rachel mused with a private smile. A few of the eating places in Tucson banned women altogether, Jake told her.

"That's positively medieval!" Rachel insisted.

"Yes'm," Jake agreed. "Whatever that means. When a woman takes that tone, I always agree. Don't you, son?" he asked J.C.

J.C.'s eyes twinkled. "You think that's bad, Jake? You should see her when she really gets mad." He rubbed the back of his head while Rachel glared.

Rachel was not the only victim of teasing. As their meal progressed, Jake joked with Peter about his "shave" and his store-bought britches, J.C. rubbed Jake's nose in the fact that the store-bought britches had been bought with coin J.C. had won from Jake at poker, and even Peter got into the act by telling how the barber had threatened to cut off Jake's long, ragged beard—the pride of his life—along with trimming his hair. Rachel felt as though she were in a dream and about to wake, for this illusion of familylike togetherness and camaraderie could not last. Much as she didn't want to face it, she had to decide where she and Peter would go, and make plans to get there.

Eventually the conversation got around to horses—inevitable with both J.C. and Peter seated at the same table. Jake commented on what a fine piece of horse-flesh O'Malley was. What fine foals the stallion would produce, he enthused. Rachel could see both J.C. and Peter swell with possessive pride. J.C.'s plans for his ranch were then dragged out for discussion. A ranch that he could have had with a reward of four thousand dollars. J.C. didn't bring that up, of course, but it was in Rachel's mind. She felt even more keenly the chasm of their separate futures. She had to make reality clear to Peter before his dreams and affections got even more engaged with J. C. Tyler.

"There's a horse auction goin' on tonight, I've heard. Over on the east end of town by Camp Lowell." Jake's face wrinkled into an impish smile. "You want to go with me, young man?" he asked Peter. "I could use some company."

Peter looked hopefully at Rachel, his heart in his eyes. "Please, Ma!"

Rachel looked at Jake, then darted a glance at J.C. His slight nod made her feel more confident. She trusted Jake, but knowing J.C. trusted him made her feel that much easier in her mind. "You can go if you promise to do everything Mr. Sumner tells you to do."

"I will! I will! When can we go?"

"Well," Jake said. "Right about now would be a real good time." He sent J.C. a canny smile. "Want to come, J.C.?"

"I think I'll just stay with Rachel for a while."

"Suit yourself," the old man replied, his eyes twinkling.

Rachel shook her head as she watched her son

bounce along beside Crazy Jake as they left the dining room. "Peter and horses!" she lamented.

"Yeah. The boy's got good taste." J.C. pushed back his chair. "Want to go for a walk?"

The evening was warm, but the searing heat of the day had faded now that the sun was down. Windows of residences along the street glowed with the light of candles and oil lamps. Dogs barked. Music and conversation leaked from the doors of busy saloons.

For a few moments Rachel and J.C. walked in silence. Rachel felt a growing awkwardness as if there were a barrier in the air between them, transparent yet impermeable to words and feelings, forcing them into themselves until they could scarcely even meet each other's eyes in the darkness.

Rachel told herself that she should get it over with, let J.C. know that she didn't expect anything from him other than the freedom he had already promised.

"J.C.?"

"Rachel?"

They spoke at the same time. "Ladies first," J.C. conceded with a wry smile.

"Oh . . . well . . . it's just this, J.C. I've been thinking about . . . about where Peter and I should go now that Arizona has become such a dangerous place. I thought maybe California. I was noticing that the Tucson, Arizona City, and San Diego Stage Company goes from here directly to the West Coast. I think they leave once a week, though I'm not sure. It would take a while for me to earn the fare, of course, but I think I could find work with Señora Cotera. She needs another housekeeper, and—"

"Rachel, wait." J.C. stopped in midstride and swung her around to face him. "Maybe I should have talked first." He lifted his battered hat and ran his fingers

through his hair. If Rachel hadn't seen him face down
Apaches, Chester Williams, rattlesnakes, and not least
of all herself, she would have thought he was afraid.

"I'm sorry," she said. "I was running on at the mouth,
wasn't I? The truth is, I just wanted you to know that I
. . . that I don't expect you to . . . that I'm not assum-
ing . . . oh, damn!"

He laughed. She glared. "Don't get mad," he cautioned, playfully fending her off with a hand. "Don't say
anything else, Rachel. Just hear me out." He took her
arm. "Come on. I talk better when I'm moving."

His hand slipped down her arm and squeezed her
hand. "I had a long conversation with Peter today. It
made me realize that kids sometimes see things more
clearly than adults. They cut through all the unimpor-
tant stuff and get right to the meat of a matter."

"What did you talk about?" Rachel enjoyed the feel
of his hand curled around hers. She enjoyed the sound
of his voice, the occasional brush of his muscular arm
against hers.

"Well . . . what we talked about was . . . Peter
thinks that . . . oh, hell!"

Where he had laughed at her frustration, she merely
smiled at his. "Oh, hell, what?" she asked.

"Well . . . Jake offered me a job at his lumber camp
today. It's not a whole lot of money, but he'll give me a
cut of the profits, and that could amount to something if
business stays good. It'll take a while, but I'll get that
money I need for my ranch."

"That's wonderful, J.C."

"Yeah. But the point of it is . . . well, dammit! Rachel, I want to marry you. God knows I don't have much
to offer, and you've had some occasions to think I'm the
world's biggest jackass, but I love you. I love you so
much, I can taste it. I can't breathe without thinking

about how good you smell. I can't sleep without dreaming about how beautiful you are. But you're more than beautiful. You're good, and you're brave, and you try like hell to be tough, but you've got the softest, sweetest heart of any woman I've ever met."

The words tumbled out of him in a flood, and when they were out, he looked drained. Rachel was stunned. After all her agonizing about not being a burr in his blanket, he wanted to marry her. He did love her. He wanted to make a life with her. "What does your conversation with Peter have to do with all this?" was all she could think of to say.

"Peter wants a father," J.C. blurted out.

Rachel laughed. "That's the reason you want to marry me?"

J.C. pulled her into the deeper darkness of a nearby alley. His hesitation had disappeared. "No. That's not why I want to marry you. This is why I want to marry you."

He kissed her with a thoroughness that left her breathless. Backed up against a rough adobe wall, she reveled in the joy of his mouth taking hers, his hands traveling the curves of her body. When he pressed her against the hard ridge that swelled at his groin, her whole body started to pulse in time to his.

"I think we should go back to our lodgings," he murmured against her mouth.

"But Peter—"

"Is happily admiring horses with Crazy Jake. Come on."

Rachel allowed herself to be guided hastily down the dark street the short distance to Stevens House. J.C.'s urgency was a warm tension that seemed to pulse in the air around them. For her own part Rachel wavered from excitement to amusement to embarrassment and back again. Such brazen behavior might find an excuse in the desert when they were threatened by death and mayhem, but in a town, surrounded by people, it was another thing entirely.

None of that mattered, though, when they reached her room and J.C. picked her up and carried her to the bed. Everything but excitement faded before the blossoming of passion. Without bothering to douse the lamp, J.C. made short work of their clothing. Breathing hard, his eyes traveled her naked body in hot appreciation.

"I've never seen you in full light," he said softly. "You look every bit as beautiful as you feel in my hands."

An all-over blush heated her skin. J.C. was quite a sight himself, bronzed and brawny, hard muscle and aroused masculinity. He gathered her to him, and every place he touched caught fire.

"I promised I would make love to you on a soft bed someday," J.C. reminded her.

Rachel couldn't answer, because his hand was between her legs and her breath was caught in her throat.

In the end it wasn't the soft bed that mattered for Rachel. What mattered was J.C. moving upon her, inside her, filling her with his magic, capturing her with his tenderness. Her universe narrowed to just him—his mouth, his hands, and the hot, hard flesh that drove them both to the limits of rapture. When it was over, they both lay exhausted in each other's arms, waiting for the earth to settle once again on its axis.

"So," he asked in a voice still husky with the aftermath of passion. "Will you marry me, Rachel Manchester Dorset?"

She fought off sleep just long enough to smile up at him, at the handsome, rugged face that had grown so dear to her, the sky-blue eyes that no longer hid any of his feelings, at the sensuous, masculine mouth that had just spoken the words that linked her future with his.

"John Charles Tyler, didn't I just say that I would?"

 20

When Rachel woke the next morning, sunlight was
streaming into the room. J.C. was gone, and the bed
beside her was cold, but that didn't chill the glow in her
heart. J.C. loved her. They were going to marry. Peter
would have a father, and she would have someone to
love for the rest of her life.

Rachel hugged herself, enjoying the warmth of those
thoughts. Problems abounded, but she chose not to
think of those right then. They would deal with the
dearth of money, lack of a home, and the very real danger from Cabell. In time she and J.C. would deal with it
all, but just then she wanted to bask in the glow of being
loved.

She didn't have long to bask before the door to her
room banged open and Peter burst in.

"Ma! You're still in bed!" He rocked back and forth
with blistering impatience. "Get up, Ma! J.C. said I
should take you to breakfast!"

Rachel drew the covers up to her chin. "Where is
J.C.?"

"I can't tell! He's got a surprise for you." Peter

smirked. "He said to tell you he has someone he wants you to meet."

Rachel's face puckered in puzzlement.

"Come on, Ma! Get dressed. Miz Cotera has coffee and rolls ready. J.C. said there'll be big doin's when he gets back!"

"If you want me to get dressed, then leave," Rachel said, shooing him out with a wave of one hand. "And shut the door behind you!" She chuckled as he zipped out.

They took the rolls and coffee—milk for Peter, though he insisted he should have coffee also—back to Rachel's room, where Peter prowled before the window to watch for J.C.'s return.

"Are you certain you don't want to tell me where J.C. is?" Rachel cajoled.

"Nope!"

Rachel decided that now was as good a time as any to tell her son the news. "Peter, I have something important to talk to you about."

Peter darted her a cautious glance. "What'd I do now?"

"Nothing." She smiled. "At least nothing that I know about yet. I want to talk to you about J.C. He asked me to marry him last night, and I told him I would. Do you mind?"

Peter puffed out his bony chest. "I already told J.C. he could marry you. Yesterday afternoon. He's always getting sappy-eyed when he looks at you. I figured if you were married, he'd get back to normal."

Rachel couldn't stifle a laugh. "Thank you, Peter."

"Well, a son hasta look after his ma." The cockiness vanished and he gave her a look that reminded her of the lonely little boy he'd been before J.C. had come into their lives. "I like him, Ma."

"I like him, too, Peter. I like him a lot. Let's go down to the porch and watch for him."

Señora Cotera snagged Rachel as they passed through the small lobby. "You were asking yesterday about Tubac," the woman reminded her.

"Yes?" Rachel put a hand on Peter's shoulder to restrain his impatient bouncing. "Go ahead, Peter. I'll be right out."

Peter shot out the door, and the señora smiled. "Such a fine boy you have."

"Thank you. You were saying about Tubac?"

"Ah, sí. Why anyone would want to go there I don't know, but there's a man from Back East who's headed that way. He came in last night. The señor seems very important, and he has hired many outriders to guard him and his lady. If you are very determined to go there, Señora Manchester, you might be able to go with them."

No longer interested in going to Tubac, but curious just the same, Rachel asked, "Who is it?"

"I will look up the señor's name in my register, but I saw him just a few minutes ago." The proprietress took a step onto the rough wooden planks that fronted the house and looked up and down the street. Rachel followed her. "Ah! There he is, señora."

Rachel looked in the direction Señora Cotera pointed, toward a man emerging from the A. & L. Zechendorf Store two hundred feet down Main Street. He was tall, good-looking, and carried himself with the unmistakable air of the rich and privileged. Rachel's heart plummeted into her stomach as she recognized Cabell Dorset.

Trying to stay calm, Rachel went to where Peter sat at the edge of the boardwalk scuffing his feet in the dust of the street. She laid a hand on his shoulder. "Let's go inside," she said in a shaky voice.

"But Ma!"

"Peter, this instant!"

Both Peter and Señora Cotera looked at her strangely.

"I'm sorry," she apologized. "Suddenly I'm not feeling well. Peter, come on, please."

Peter complained all the way back to their room, but once the door closed behind them, Rachel silenced him with a look. "That man coming out of the store was your father," she told him.

His mouth fell open.

Panic made Rachel short of breath. Her heart pounded, her stomach knotted, while confusion, doubt, and dismay made a tangle of her mind. Had J.C. betrayed them after all? Was Cabell the someone J.C. wanted her to meet? Had J.C.'s lovemaking and attention merely been ploys to keep her trusting and pliant until Cabell arrived?

Her heart told her no. J.C. would not do that to them. He would not do that to her. Her brain reminded her that she had trusted before and been betrayed—Cabell, her own father, and yes, even J.C. himself. Her heart had been mistaken too many times.

"Let's pack," she said tersely. "We have to go."

"But Ma! What about J.C.? You're going to marry him! He's going to be my pa! We have to wait for J.C.!"

Rachel's panic left no room for patience. "Peter, don't argue with me just this once! We have to go before your father realizes that we're here."

"Why can't we just tell him I want to live with you and J.C.?"

She couldn't give voice to her horrible suspicions

about J.C. It was bad enough her own heart was breaking. Must she break Peter's as well?

"Just do as I say. J.C. will find us." It was true. For good or ill, J.C. would most likely track them down. Rachel wanted to burst into tears. Only Peter's presence kept her from it.

"He won't find us!" Peter all but shouted. "He'll think we don't want him! He'll think you changed your mind and we're still mad at him!"

Rachel's panic was contagious. Peter was wide-eyed, his alarm feeding off his mother's. "I'm going to find J.C.!" he cried wildly. "He'll help us!"

"Peter!"

He flung the door open and bolted from the room before Rachel could stop him. Now her dread soared to a frenzy, for if Cabell was still where he could see the boy, he would probably recognize him. Obeying only her terror, Rachel ran after her son. She paused at the door of the lodging house and flung desperate looks up and down Main Street.

"Did you see my son?" she asked a bewildered Señora Cotera.

The proprietress pointed. "He went that way."

"Thank you!"

Rachel ran in the same direction, giving no heed to dignity or decorum. A flash of red hair darting left onto Ochoa Street spurred her to greater speed. Finally, breathless and panting, she caught up to Peter just as he dashed into a livery barn beside a huge corral. She stumbled through the barn door and immediately collided with the solid wall of J.C.'s chest.

"You told her, you little snitch!" J.C. caught Rachel with one hand and sent a mock scowl toward Peter.

Peter gasped for breath. "She's gonna take me away!" he panted. "I don't wanna go! J.C., do something!"

While Peter shouted into one of J.C.'s ears, Rachel was crying into the other and struggling to get loose from his grip. "You Judas! Traitor! Double-crossing, two-timing snake! I don't believe I fell into the trap again! I trusted you. Dammit! I loved you!"

Jake peered around the divider of a horse stall. "What's goin' on here?"

J.C. refused to release Rachel, and he managed to get himself heard by the sheer volume of his command. "Quiet!"

Peter's face crumpled into tears. Rachel huffed into a furious silence.

"Jake asked a good question. What is going on here?"

"Cabell is here," Rachel informed him. "In Tucson. I just saw him."

The immediate flush of guilt on J.C.'s face confirmed all her doubts—and broke her heart. "You did arrange this!" she cried. "I'm a fool! Lord, when am I going to learn?"

J.C. gripped her shoulders hard, and refused to let her turn away from him. "Jake, take Peter out back and let him help you fix that wagon wheel of yours. If anyone you don't know comes within sight of you, bring him back in."

Jake shrugged, bewildered but willing. "Okeydokey."

J.C. gave Rachel a gentle shake as Jake took Peter out. "Rachel, I did not arrange this! You still don't trust me? Goddammit, woman! I asked you to marry me! You think I'd do that if I was plotting to turn Peter over to Cabell?"

"Cabell's here!" Rachel snapped. "How do you explain that?"

Again he looked guilty. Rachel tried to twist away from him, but he refused to let her go. "Listen to me!"

he insisted, giving her another gentle shake. "When I first met you and Peter, I sent Cabell a letter to tell him I'd located you. I asked him to send money to pay for safe passage back to Georgia. I sent him another letter—yesterday—claiming I was mistaken in identifying you." He grimaced. "Obviously I locked the barn door after the whole damned stable escaped. Cabell thinks Peter is in Tubac, and he's probably on his way there now."

Rachel closed her eyes as her heart clamored for her to believe him. Slowly her panic ebbed, and she realized J.C.'s story was very plausible. "I'm sorry," she whispered in a miserable voice. "Peter said you had someone you wanted me to meet. My mind just leaped to the worst possible conclusion. How could I have thought—?"

He cut short her apology by kissing her. It was a quick, hard kiss that told her better than words that she was forgiven. "The one I wanted you to meet is over there. Her name is Bess."

Rachel looked where he pointed and saw a dainty gray mare regarding her from the corner stall. Her eyes were soft and mellow, her neck arched in friendly curiosity. "A horse?" Rachel asked incredulously. "You wanted me to meet a horse?"

"Yeah. The fellow who owns this place traded her to me in exchange for a foal of hers sired by O'Malley. I figured she could be your horse. She's very gentle."

Rachel had a hysterical urge to laugh, but her situation was far from funny. She leaned forward into J.C.'s arms. "J.C., I don't know what to do besides run again. If Cabell finds Peter here, I'll lose him, and I can't bear to lose my son. I love you so, and I want to marry you, but I have to get Peter away from here. I don't know what else to do."

J.C. wiped a tear from her cheek. "You can't run for the rest of your life."

"I only need to run until Peter can face Cabell on his own. We've discussed this before," she reminded him.

"Rachel, it's going to get harder. In fact it's going to get nearly impossible. With four thousand dollars on Peter's head, every down-on-his-luck bounty hunter between here and Canada is going to be on your tail."

"Like you?" she asked, the hint of an edge to her voice.

"Yeah. Like me. Only don't count on all of them to fall in love with you and change their minds."

She let her head fall forward against his chest. "I'm sorry. I shouldn't have said that."

J.C. kissed the top of her head. "You didn't say anything that wasn't true. Let me take care of Cabell for you, Rachel. I can't lose you because of this. I won't lose you."

She frowned up at him. "How would you take care of him?"

"I could tell him that both of you were killed in the attack on the wagons."

Rachel sighed and let J.C. gather her close. His heartbeat calmed her. The strength of his arms made her feel safe. Once again she could think rationally. No matter what Cabell had done to her, she couldn't deceive him in a way that would cause him such grief. He might not grieve for her, but he would certainly grieve for Peter. For all Cabell's faults, disregard for his son was not one of them.

"We can't do that," she told J.C. "It might work, but it would be too cruel."

"All right. Then I'll tell him it was another red-headed, green-eyed temptress I found." He smiled down at her. "And that the boy wasn't Peter at all. You both keep out of sight until Cabell leaves town, and he'll be none the wiser."

"Then what? What of all those other bounty hunters? That four-thousand-dollar reward will still be out there."

"None of them will get past me. I promise you that."

"It's too much for me to ask of you, J.C. I want to be with you so much that I'm tempted to say yes. But it's not fair to you. This isn't your problem."

"I'm making it my problem. I love you, Rachel. And I love Peter. Let me protect you."

When she hesitated, he kissed her, hard. She willingly let herself be folded into his possessive embrace, knowing that his urgent domination stemmed from worry over her, not a need to subdue her. She took the comfort of his strength and let herself hope that she was doing the right thing.

"All right," she whispered to the demand of his eyes and lips. "I trust you, J.C. We'll do as you say."

An hour later, though, penned with Peter in her room at the lodging house, she worried that she was making a mistake. She paced up and down before the window, trying to shake the feeling that she had come full circle. During her entire childhood and youth her father had been the one to shield her. Then she had turned her life over to Cabell. Her self-reliance over the past three years had been hard won. Every step had been painful. Every trial had been a battle. But she had learned. She had grown. And pride had blossomed along with her ability to fend for herself.

Now, once again, she was depending upon a man to stand up for her. J.C. wouldn't betray her. Now that she was thinking straight again, she had no fear of that. She also had little fear that he wouldn't succeed in his mission. She and Peter would hide. Cabell would leave.

And she and J.C. and Peter could live in peace—until the next bounty hunter got an eyeful of red hair and freckles and matched up her and Peter with Cabell's wanted poster.

Peter sat on the bed, legs crossed Indian style, elbows resting on his bony knees, and mouth pulled down into a frown. "Did J.C. go to find my father?"

"Yes, he did."

"Is he gonna tell him I don't wanna go back?"

Rachel sighed. "He's going to tell him you aren't here."

"Oh." The boy pondered for a few minutes. "He's gonna lie?"

"Yes." Her voice was sharper than she intended, but Peter's ingenuous honesty brought the unpleasant notion into the open. J.C. was going to lie. They were going to live a lie, and every time the truth caught up to them, they would need to run. At that moment she felt more a coward than she'd ever felt in her entire life.

Unhappy with both herself and the situation, she went to the window and stared out at the bright, hot day. She was not a person of natural courage, Rachel admitted to herself. Some people charged into trouble, trying to find solutions and fighting until they found one. But she had made a habit of running from trouble. She was a compromiser, not a confronter. She didn't take big risks unless something very dear to her was at stake, unless she didn't have a choice.

The more she thought upon it, the clearer she realized that something very dear was at risk on this very day—her life with J.C. How could they possibly settle in one place and build a life together if Cabell was still searching for her? She couldn't ask J.C. to give up his dream of a horse ranch and flee with her every time someone compared her and Peter to the description on a wanted poster. Their love would never survive.

The time had come to make a stand, Rachel realized. She had run when forced to save herself and Peter; now she must stop running to save something equally precious. Ironically, for all she had grown in these past three years, she was no less afraid of this threshold than she had been of the first one.

"Peter, you're right!"

"I am?" Peter gave her a bewildered frown.

"J.C. should not have to lie for us. Telling the truth is always the best way."

"Did I say that?"

"Yes, you did. And I'm proud of you. I'm going to find your father and talk to him. I want you to stay in this room until J.C. or I get back."

"You're not going to let him take me, are you?"

"No."

"What are you gonna say to him?"

Rachel sighed. "I don't know yet."

She tried to hang on to her courage as she marched down the hallway to the lobby. "Señora Cotera, I left Peter—" She gasped, for standing with the señora was someone she hadn't seen in a very long time. "Nell!" she choked out incredulously. "Nell! I don't believe it! What are you doing in Tucson?"

Nell seemed equally surprised. "Rachel!"

The two women stared at each other in shock, then, at the same moment, plunged forward into an embrace.

"Nell! Oh, Nell! You look absolutely beautiful! What have you done to yourself?"

"Rachel! Look at you! You look like a red-haired Indian girl!"

They both babbled at the same time, then laughed and took turns.

"You look positively radiant," Rachel told her friend.

Nell smiled impishly. "I do, don't I? And you look—my goodness! You're so brown!" She gave the green dress a dubious once-over but was too polite to comment.

"It's very bright, isn't it? I didn't pick it out."

"I should hope not!" Nell said with a laugh.

"What on earth are you doing here?"

"I came looking for you! Come to my room, Rachel. We need to talk."

"Your room? You're staying here at Stevens House?"

"Yes."

"We'll have that talk," Rachel promised. "A long talk. I've missed you so much! But right now I have to go. It's a long story, and I'll tell you all of it later, but I have to find . . ." Rachel realized suddenly that two people from her former life being in Tucson at the same time could not be a coincidence. ". . . I have to find Cabell," she finished lamely. "My God! You're here with Cabell!"

Nell took her by the arm and guided her down the hallway. "Rachel. We really have to talk."

Totally disconcerted, Rachel allowed herself to be led to Nell's room. "Now, Rachel," Nell began as she closed the door. "I know you're going to be shocked, but I want you to keep your mind open. Cabell is not the same man you left in Savannah."

"What do you mean?"

"He's stopped drinking. He's trying to pull himself together, and . . . and pull his life together as well."

Rachel raised a dubious brow.

"It's a long story, really, but the bare bones of it are that I made him take me with him when he was so determined to go galloping off to the wilderness in search of you and Peter. He got this letter, you see—"

"I know all about the letter," Rachel told her grimly.

"Well, he decided to come after you himself. I thought you would need my help, and that perhaps I could intercede on your behalf. Cabell and I already had a . . . an entanglement, so to speak. Somewhere around San Antonio he came to his senses and married me."

Rachel was horrified. "You *married* Cabell? Oh, Nell . . ."

"Don't look like I just invited you to my funeral! I know how he was with you. But Cabell is not a monster. He has a monster living inside him, and liquor is the elixir that lets the monster out of its cage. But Cabell no longer drinks. He's dealing with the past by facing it. I love him, Rachel. And he loves me. We're working out the problems. Be happy for us."

Rachel bit back the words that came to her lips, but the feeling of dread in her heart must have shown on her face, because Nell shook her finger in admonishment.

"Ah-ah! Before you launch into that lecture that's gathering in your mind, tell me your story. Cabell thinks you and Peter are in Tubac. So did I. What happened?"

Rachel told her an abbreviated version of what had happened since she had received Nell's letter. Her friend's eyes got wider as she related the story of the Apache raid on Tubac, of J.C.'s betrayal, the disaster on the freight wagons, and their fight to survive. When Rachel was through, she sat down on the bed and puffed out a breath of amazement.

"And to think I came all this way thinking poor little quivering Rachel was going to need my help to get through this confrontation with Cabell." Nell smiled. "Cabell is not the only one who has changed since you left Savannah."

"I hope for your sake that Cabell has changed, Nell. And for Cabell's sake too. It took a stronger woman than me to help him."

Nell shook her head. "You always had strength inside you, and you've grown ten times stronger over the last three years. Mercy! Even thinking about what you've been through makes me shudder."

"It wasn't strength that got me through. It was necessity. I'm still not above huddling in corners while others do my fighting for me. Right now J.C. is out looking for Cabell to tell him that the woman he wrote about in that letter wasn't me at all. But I realized that I can't let him do that. I was on my way to find Cabell myself and confront him with the truth."

Nell took Rachel's hand and squeezed it. "You have grown up, my dear friend."

For a moment Rachel clasped Nell's hand, remembering all the things they had shared in the past. She didn't even want to think about the irony of the two of them marrying the same man. "Nell, I'm not going to let Cabell have Peter. I don't care how much he's changed. And I don't care what some judge in Georgia said about me being an unfit mother. I'm going to marry a wonderful man, and we're going to make a good life together."

Nell raised a brow. "The bounty hunter?"

"I love him. Peter loves him. Maybe now that you and Cabell are married, and, as you say," she conceded with a hint of doubt, "Cabell has changed, then Peter can visit. I don't really want to deprive him of his father."

"You'll have to convince Cabell," Nell told her with a faintly worried frown. "I said he'd stopped drinking. I didn't say he'd stopped being bullheaded and angry. We're still working on that."

"I don't intend to give him a choice," Rachel said with grim determination.

Nell smiled and patted her hand. "And I thought you needed me to defend you! I see you can defend yourself very well. You can find Cabell at the bank. He's arranging for some money to be transferred out here from his accounts in Savannah."

"Then I'll go to the bank."

"Just leave enough pieces of the poor man for me to put him back together," Nell said as she gave Rachel a quick, hard hug.

Cabell tried to keep his face impassive as he looked across the bank meeting-room table at the man who had announced himself as J. C. Tyler. He was a formidable-looking fellow, this bounty hunter. Enough so that the bank president and head clerk, who sat at the table with Cabell, appeared distinctly uneasy in his presence. They were understandably nervous of a man who wore a pistol on his hip with such easy familiarity and showed total disdain of their bureaucratic orderliness. The man had walked in on their meeting, a half-dozen protesting and dithering clerks in his wake, and announced to Cabell that he would want to hear what he had to say before conducting his business.

Such forthrightness appealed to Cabell, so he had heard the man out while the banker fidgeted and waited. Now he struggled to keep the sharp disappointment from his face, for a man who too easily revealed emotions also revealed a weakness, and instinct told him that showing weakness to Tyler might be the same as baring a soft, vulnerable throat to a jaguar. He didn't much care for the way the man looked at him.

"How did you know I was in Tucson?" Cabell asked.

"Señora Cotera at Stevens House told me. It wasn't hard to find out where you were this morning. Not many men in Tucson walk around in such fine clothes. I'm sorry about the inconvenience, Mr. Dorset, but I never asked you to make the trip out here. I sent you another letter explaining the mistake. It should be waiting for you when you get home."

Tyler was most likely telling the truth, Cabell decided. What did he possibly have to gain by admitting such a mistake? Besides which, Cabell didn't fancy calling the man a liar to his face. The bounty hunter had an air of deadly competence that made Cabell very glad that he wasn't the man's prey. Poor Rachel! She wouldn't stand a chance against Tyler or his ilk. He almost regretted setting such a man on her trail. Just the frost in the bounty hunter's eyes would wilt her like a hothouse blossom.

"Well, Mr. Tyler," he said with a sigh, "this is a disappointment. But I can't lay all the blame at your feet, can I? I was the one who decided to come out here myself and settle matters. I suppose—"

The door flung open with a bang. Again the flock of hand-wringing clerks milled in confusion in the wake of an intruder, who sailed into the room like a one-woman cavalry charge. The bank president was fed up.

"Madam! We are having—!"

Cabell didn't give the man time to finish. "Sit down, Mr. Scott!"

The bank president obeyed almost before he knew what he was doing, his legs cut out from under him by the ice in Cabell's voice. Cabell stood, scarcely daring to believe she was there. Not only was she there, but she looked more vibrant, more alive, and more determined than he'd ever seen her in an acquaintance that stretched back to their childhoods. Out of the corner of his eyes Cabell saw the bounty hunter grin.

"Well, now, Mr. Dorset," J.C. said. "It's plain as the

nose on your face that I'm a bald-faced liar and you shouldn't be listening to a thing I say."

"Yes," Cabell said slowly. "It does look that way."

"Hello, Cabell," Rachel said.

"Hello, Rachel." Cabell spoke softly, almost fearing that she was an apparition who would disappear at a harsh word. "It's been a long time."

"Yes, it has."

Cabell looked down his nose at the bankers. "Would you gentlemen grant us the privacy of this excellent meeting room for a few moments?"

The president and clerk scrambled out of their chairs and made haste to leave, driving the fretting clerks out of the room ahead of them. When they were gone, Cabell looked coldly at the bounty hunter.

"He should stay," Rachel said firmly. "This involves him."

"Does it indeed?" Cabell kept his expression neutral. The bounty hunter had taken a chair and stretched his legs out in front of him, looking as though he was enjoying himself. Cabell was beginning to find the man a bit annoying.

"J.C. and I are going to be married," Rachel announced. "Peter is going to stay with us."

"The devil you say!" Cabell certainly hadn't expected that. His annoyance climbed several notches. "So that was why your bounty hunter friend was willing to lie for you."

"Peter loves J.C., and he wants to stay with us."

"Peter is not a competent judge of what is best for him. I am his father, and the Georgia state judicial system says he comes home with me."

"No one in Arizona Territory gives a damn what the Georgia state judicial system says, and neither do I!" Rachel declared.

The tone of her outburst took Cabell by surprise. Where was his little hothouse blossom, his meek little mouse?

"What's more, Cabell, I am through running."

The mouse had become a lioness, Cabell decided, noting the glitter in the green eyes that once had been so soft and compliant. His curiosity about the new creature that had blossomed from the wife he'd thought he knew almost overshadowed his anger.

"Rachel," he urged, "try to see reason."

"I am seeing reason, and it's about time," she replied. "If you try to take Peter away from me, I will go to Georgia and bring suit against you."

He smiled confidently. "You would never win!"

Cabell was reminded once again of a lioness—one with a cub—as Rachel's eyes narrowed dangerously. "I might not win. The law looks the other way when a man beats his wife. But society doesn't, Cabell. I would make sure that everyone in the state knew exactly how you behaved and what kind of man you are."

Cabell's ire stumbled over an instant of shame at the haunted look on Rachel's face. How he had behaved. What kind of man he was. What kind of man had he been with Rachel? Half the things that had passed between them when he was drinking he didn't remember.

"I kept a journal, Cabell. That journal was a best friend other than Nell, and it was the only friend I confided in completely. It has details that newspapers would love to print. If you take Peter from me, I promise you I will destroy your reputation in a way that makes Sherman's march through Georgia look like a nature walk in the park—the same way you destroyed mine when I was too cowardly to stand up for myself."

"Rachel . . ." Cabell couldn't finish the statement, because he didn't know what to say. Up until this moment he'd always considered himself the wounded party in his failed marriage—hiding the truth behind anger, perhaps not even recognizing the truth. Certainly he hadn't realized how deeply he had wounded Rachel—not until he stood face-to-face with her and saw the truth in her eyes. How much of the truth had liquor erased from his brain? he wondered. How much of his own guilt had his stubborn mind refused to acknowledge?

But to give up his son—could any father willingly do such a thing? "You would do that?" he asked softly.

Rachel looked surprised at his change of tone, but the iron determination on her face didn't falter. Cabell had to admit a grudging admiration.

"I would."

"I've known you all my life, Rachel, and I never realized you had such a core of steel."

For a moment she seemed nonplussed by his compliment—and he had meant it as a compliment. Then an uncertain smile tugged at her mouth. "I've grown up, Cabell. I've learned that sometimes you have to stand and fight rather than cut and run."

Cabell caught the exchange of glances between Rachel and J. C. Tyler. He had lost, he knew. But as if to remind him that he'd gained as well as lost, Nell chose that moment to come in the door.

"Cabell, my love, I've been standing outside the door very rudely eavesdropping. I heard every threat that Rachel made, and as much as I love you—or perhaps because I love you—I want you to know that I'll help her every step of the way."

The damned bounty hunter grinned like a jackass. "Might as well take the easy way out, Dorset. Otherwise I'd be doing you a mercy if I just up and shot you. These

Southern women can take a man and turn him inside out when they get riled. Take my word on it."

"Christ!" Cabell blasphemed under his breath.

Nell continued in a sweetly reasonable tone. "What's more, Cabell, I think it's only fair that you give that reward to Mr. Tyler. After all, he did deliver Rachel and Peter straight into your hands."

Cabell looked at his bride incredulously. Then he had to laugh. If he hadn't laughed, he would have exploded, and laughing, he discovered, did him much more good. "I suppose he did at that." He looked at his wife and his ex-wife and shook his head in dazed surrender. "Mr. Tyler, heed my warning. If you value your sanity, never marry."

The bounty hunter wasn't listening, Cabell noticed. His eyes were locked on Rachel, whose cheeks were wet with tears and whose expression had melted from grim determination to the soft glow of joy. Tyler went to her side and, as if they were the only two people in the room, kissed her.

With Rachel weeping into his shoulder, he looked at Cabell and smiled. "I'll take my chances."

Epilogue

On a ranch north of Santa Fe,
June 1873

Rachel watched the wagon from the time she first saw the plume of dust on the distant road. From where she stood on the porch of their log cabin, she could see the wagon crawl slowly south along the high prairie that rose into the foothills. Eventually it disappeared into the pines, traceable only by a trail of dust.

J.C. came up behind her and circled her waist with his arms. "Are you sure you want to do this?"

"No," she replied. "I don't want to do it at all. But I think it's right . . . and necessary. The final decision is Peter's, not mine."

Her husband rested his chin on the top of her head, and Rachel snuggled back against him. She never tired of getting close to him. She never tired of waking up beside him, breakfasting with him before dawn, working side by side with him, and then, after a day of hard work, making sweet love with him in the warm intimacy of their bed.

"How's Bess?"

"I don't think she'll foal until tomorrow, but I'll sit

with her tonight. She's big, and I think I can feel two inside her. Maybe she'll have twins."

Rachel laughed. "Better her than me."

"Oh, I don't know! Twins wouldn't be so bad." He nuzzled her neck. "We could work on it."

"Mind your manners, you brute. They'll be coming up the road any minute now."

He settled for a nip on her ear that was a promise for the night to come, company or not.

"Ma! Ma!" With a high-pitched shriek, an auburn-haired, green-eyed toddler tottered from the door of the log cabin onto the porch. "Peter pulled my hair! Make him stop!"

"I did not!" Peter chased the little girl and grabbed her by the bow-tied sash of her pinafore. "I was just braiding it!"

"I don' wan' it braided!"

"You look like a ragamuffin!"

"I don' care!"

"Elizabeth!" J.C. thundered. "Let your brother braid your hair."

Accustomed to the volume of her father's commands, Elizabeth merely giggled. She broke free of Peter and raced past J.C., who scooped her up and sat her atop his broad shoulders.

"And you accuse me of spoiling her!" Rachel berated him with a fond smile.

J.C. merely grinned. Peter folded his arms across a still-boyishly narrow chest and glared at his little sister. "You can't hide up there forever!"

She wrinkled her nose at him.

That was how Cabell and Nell found them when they drove up in their buckboard. Cabell pulled the team to a halt, and for a moment the two families just looked at one another. Then Nell jumped down from the wagon and Rachel stepped down from the porch.

"Nell!"

"Rachel! Mercy, it's good to see you!"

"How do you like Denver?"

"It's wonderful! A bit rougher than what I'm used to, but if you can be a frontier wife, then so can I!"

While the ladies embraced, J.C. and Cabell eyed each other uneasily, as did Elizabeth, who still rode her father's shoulders, and the two-year-old gamin-faced little boy who sat on the wagon box with Cabell. Peter gripped the porch post as if he had to physically keep himself from running back into the cabin.

"Nice place you've got here," Cabell finally said.

"Thanks."

"Saw some fine-looking horses in that pasture that runs beside the road."

"Those are the yearlings," J.C. said.

"Yearlings? They're well grown, every one of them."

"I've got a damned fine stud horse. Climb down from the wagon and I'll let you see him."

While Nell and Rachel took the children into the house, J.C. and Peter took Cabell to meet O'Malley. Peter was stiffly polite to his father and returned to the cabin when the men started talking bloodlines, endurance, and speed. Ordinarily he would have been contributing more than his share to that conversation, but not today.

Cabell watched Peter go. "Is he happy?" he asked J.C.

"No kid that age is happy. He loves the ranch and his sister and mother, and sometimes he admits it. He was pretty definite about wanting to accept your invitation for a summer in Denver, but I think he's nervous about it just the same."

Cabell met J.C.'s eyes directly. "Is she happy?"

"You'll have to ask Rachel if she's happy." J.C.'s tone was solemn, but he smiled. "Why wouldn't she be? She's got me wrapped around her little finger."

Much later Cabell got his chance to ask Rachel herself. Elizabeth and Joshua were fast asleep in bed, Peter was teaching Nell how to play poker, and J.C. had gone to sit with Bess in the big horse barn just south of the cabin. Rachel stepped onto the front porch and saw Cabell leaning against the top rail of the corral, staring at the moon. She joined him.

"You're looking up at that moon as if there were something up there to see."

"Just thinking," Cabell said.

"Nights out here are good for deep thoughts."

Cabell looked at her, his eyes searching her face in the moonlight. "I was thinking about new beginnings. Mine. Yours. Nell's."

"It looks as though yours has been a good new beginning, Cabell. Do you know, I think you look younger than you did six years ago."

"I feel younger. You look as though you're doing all right yourself." He smiled wryly. "That bounty hunter I sent after you seems like a good man."

"He is a good man. The best." Rachel chewed her lower lip, hesitating, then tentatively put her hand on Cabell's arm. "You're a good man, too, Cabell."

Cabell smiled down at her. He offered his arm. She hesitated a moment, then took it. Together they walked toward the cabin.